I0656861

James H. Graff, Angus Bethune Reach

Clement Lorimer

The Book with the Iron Clasps

James H. Graff, Angus Bethune Reach

Clement Lorimer
The Book with the Iron Clasps

ISBN/EAN: 9783337348915

Printed in Europe, USA, Canada, Australia, Japan

Cover: Foto ©Andreas Hilbeck / pixelio.de

More available books at **www.hansebooks.com**

CLEMENT LORIMER

OR

THE BOOK WITH THE IRON CLASPS

A ROMANCE

By ANGUS B. REACH

——————— --

LONDON

GEORGE ROUTLEDGE AND SONS

THE BROADWAY, LUDGATE

NEW YORK: 416 BROOME STREET

LONDON :

SAVILL, EDWARDS AND CO., PRINTERS, CHANDOS STREET,

COVENT GARDEN.

TO

SHIRLEY BROOKS,

THE AUTHOR'S DEAREST FRIEND,

THE FOLLOWING ROMANCE

Is Inscribed.

CONTENTS.

CONTENTS.

CLEMENT LORIMER;

OR,

THE BOOK WITH THE IRON CLASPS.

THE FIRST CHAPTER OF THE PROLOGUE

THE TWO LIGHTS.

On the night between the 30th of April and the 1st of May, 1610, the moon shone brightly on the town of Antwerp. It lighted up the wide panorama of fertile level land which stretches round that ancient city; it gleamed upon the broad Scheldt and the white sails which here and there glided upon its waters; it lit up the Gothic spires and chiselled architraves of many churches; and it brought into relief against the clear sky the thousand high quaint gavels, with their lofty peaks and rickety-looking projections of carved stone and wood, and little Gothic turrets and pinnacles, which are such striking features in all the old Flemish towns. Our story leads us to the large open place in which the cathedral of Antwerp stands. Few people were about, for the deep tones of the bell, swinging far up in that most marvellously beautiful of spires, had sounded eleven, and the scattered lights, gleaming from high windows, were disappearing one by one, so that when the chimes from the steeple proclaimed that the night had waned another quarter of an hour, but two were left, and they shone from houses which faced each other.

Into the room in which burnt one of these lights the course of our story conducts us. It was a small, low-browed apartment, wainscoted with old and polished oak, and decorated with coarsely carved mullions and cornices. Mighty beams of the same species of wood, but black and polished as ebony, stretched across the ceiling, giving the whole place an aspect of clumsy, antique strength and ponderous solidity. This apartment was partially lighted by a taper placed in a massive silver candelabrum, which stood upon the broad window-sill, and which threw an uncertain glare into the gloomy shadows which it could not entirely dispel. The principal feature of the sombre apartment was an antique and massive bed, whereof the head rose in the fashion of a canopy almost to the ceiling, terminating in pinnacles of quaintly-carved wood, from whence depended masses of heavy and gloomy-looking drapery. On the floor lay a large open box, heavily clamped, and secured with iron bolts. This box was lined with metal, and divided into three compartments. In one of them was arranged a drawer, full of small crystal and silver phials, all of them carefully stoppered and sealed with red wax. The centre compartment of the box was empty; but upon a small table, drawn close to the bed, lay a book, which, from its size and shape, appeared destined to fill it. This volume was a thick quarto, bound in coarse, rough vellum, without lettering or gilding of any sort, except on the back, whereon were printed the two Italian words "La Vendetta." In the third compartment of the chest was arranged a large compact bundle of papers, tightly tied and labelled in a neat Italian hand and in the Italian language.

A chair or two, of ancient and ponderous construction, flung at random about, completed the furniture of the apartment. It was occupied by two individuals. One of them, an old man, lay upon the bed, propped up by a pile of cushions. His companion, who was a youth, stood gazing upon him in an attitude of the deepest reverence.

For awhile there was deep silence in the room, and the old man appeared to doze upon his pillow. The youth took the taper and flung the light full upon the face of the sleeper. It was an old meagre face, dark and swarthy. A few long grey hairs straggled from beneath a close skull-cap of black velvet, and the chin was clothed with a scanty and grizzled beard. The old man's features were worn and wasted, but the type of the Italian countenance was very visible in the high aquiline nose, and strongly-marked and arched eyebrows. The skin of the forehead and cheeks was seamed with innumerable small lines, such as may be seen in the old portraits of Voltaire; and the whole physiognomy of the man was instinct with an expression of the most exquisitely delicate nervous organisation, and of that subtle, intellectual power which was stamped in the countenance of Machiavelli.

The old Italian was dressed in a loose robe of velvet, the folds of which his long horny fingers clutched and twitched at. Suddenly he pressed both his hands to his forehead and withdrew them, wet with cold perspiration. Then his lips moved, and his companion heard him muttering. He bent his head and listened. The old man spoke in a *patois* of Italian used by the inhabitants of the mountain districts in Corsica.

" The Mistral," he murmured,—" the keen wind of the sunny south — the wind of home — I feel it on my cheek — waving my hair — oh, how different from the dank gusts of these northern fens! Ah, it shakes the olive-grove and the trellised vines upon the trees, and tosses the bright Mediterranean waves, till they gleam and sparkle on the white sea-sand. Oh! I am back — I am home — Paolo, Benedetto, your hands—'tis done — Ha! you see the red stain! — yes! vengeance is ours — it hath tracked its quarry through many lands—and, at last, it hath swooped upon its prey! Look — look — my arm is red to the elbow — 'tis the heart's blood of the Teuton."

" He is raving," said the watcher; " he will pass away, and leave me but half instructed." Then, bending over the old man, he said, in Genoese Italian, " My father!"

" Who calls?" answered the dying man.

" Michael Benosa."

The Italian opened his eyes, they were fierce and black, and burning with hot fever. He glared wildly about for a moment, and then clasped his fingers and compressed his lips, as though he were striving by a physical effort to recall his scattered senses. Then the unnatural glare of the fever passed away from his eyes, and he sat for a moment motionless and musing. At length he spoke,—

" If I grope and stumble, boy, it is because there hangs over my spirit the darkness of the Valley of the Shadow of

Death. Therein no man sees clearly how to walk." He paused; then resumed, "I know I have somewhat to say to you — give me the clue."

"The family of the Vandersteins," said the son.

"Ah! La vendetta! la vendetta!" exclaimed the Corsican, his hands clenching and his eyes gleaming. "Yes, I have yet to give you charges touching that great task — charges which, if they be not in your lifetime fulfilled to the uttermost, you will, in your turn, bequeath to your son, even as I now bequeath them to you."

"I listen, father," said Michael Benosa.

"Stand close to me and hold the lamp to your face, that I may truly see whether you be my son or no."

Michael complied, and his father gazed long upon him. He was a slight, but well-made youth, dressed in a sober doublet and cloak. His face bore the same stamp of Italian lineage as did that of his father. Its expression was severe and grave, the eyes lustrous and black, and the skin of the temples already began to exhibit those fine lines, or wrinkles, which appeared to be a distinguishing family feature.

"Yes," said the old man, "Monna Doro was honest; there is none of the northern swamp-blood in your veins."

"I am," answered the young man, proudly, — "I am of the race which three times ruled the world, — by Arms, by Arts, and by Faith."

"And, therefore, a sure avenger of blood. Look into the night."

Michael appeared to understand what he was to look at, for he stepped to the lattice, and glanced in the direction of the second light, which, as we have said, shone from a window opposite to the Italian's house.

"It still burns," he said.

Just at this moment the clock of the cathedral tolled twelve.

"His life has entered on its last hour," murmured the Corsican.

"Some one trims the lamp, — it flickers," said Michael Benosa, looking earnestly through the window.

"They trim it for the last time," said the father; "Erpa is a sure nurse, and she has sure drugs; when she extinguishes that lamp, Stephen Vanderstein will be dead; and she will extinguish it within the hour. Then comes my turn. When you extinguish the lamp upon that table, I shall be dead; and you will extinguish it within the hour."

There was a short pause.

"Michael!" exclaimed the old man, "did not the clerk say that the grave triumphed over vengeance?"

"He did, my father."

"Then he lied; I shall rot, but my vengeance shall ride onward to its uttermost goal. Fetch me the book upon the table."

Michael obeyed.

"The Supreme Vendetta has been declared betwixt the families of Raphael Benosa and Stephen Vanderstein. The Fleming knows nought of it — of our customs. No matter; the black wings of Azrael are above his house, and they may not close while there is life beneath the roof-tree, or fire upon the hearth. Michael, the Fleming wrought our family unutterable wrong; what that wrong was, being done in secret, may not, by the laws of the Vendetta, be disclosed until that Vendetta be accomplished. The cause of the feud I have written in this book. If you witness the extermination of the Vanderstein family, you will read it; if not, you must pass the volume unread to your successor, for only to him who consummates the vengeance must the cause of that vengeance be known."

The youth bowed low and reverently.

The old man resumed: "We are not now in our own land, where men think little of the gleam of the poniard or the stroke of the stiletto. These boors of Flanders are slow of hand and chary of blood, except that which the law spills. Let the Vendetta, then, be wrought stealthily and in secret. If the heart be bitter, let the face be smooth. Italian wile to match Flemish bluntness. Cast the net and spread the snare, and watch warily, as the fowler, until the bird flutters in the toils. Use cold steel but as a last means. The art of the chemist is more deadly than that of the armourer who forges the blades of Ferrara or gives their temper to the rapiers of Toledo. Drugs, like disease, kill, and no blow struck. See those phials" — pointing to the chest — "they were filled by one to whom was handed down the deadly lore of Pope Alexander VI. and his terrible daughter, — ay, by one who practised as well as studied his art; and amongst these papers are instructions for the wielder of the drugs, written in the chemist's hand, and signed with his name — René, of Florence. But, hark! words, written or spoken — ay, thoughts — can kill as well as poison or steel; and poison or steel kills but the body. Let our vengeance be more terrible. Compass to smite the spirit as well as the flesh. Strive that as each Vanderstein leaves the world, he may leave it with a heart broken by woe or a soul hardened in guilt. To me it has been granted but to begin the task. I have struck down Stephen Vanderstein. He leaves three sons and three daughters. Be close on their track. If any of them survive you, your descendants must follow up the work; and so must it be from father to son, until this, the most terrible Vendetta ever planned by Corsican brain, be accomplished. You see this book. In its pages you—and after you, your children—must enter, each what he has done; what members of the Vanderstein family he has cut off, until the last of the detested race be purged from the earth. All this you understand, and all this you will do?"

"All this," said Michael Benosa, kneeling, — "all this I understand, and all this will I do."

The old Italian placed both his hands on his son's head, and his lips moved silently. Then suddenly adopting a more familiar and conversational tone than he had used in instructing Michael in his terrible mission, the Italian said,—

"Give me pen and ink."

The youth dipped a pen into ink, and placed it in his father's hand. The old man opened the iron-clasped book at the first vacant page, and held the pen ready to write.

"Watch the lamp, Michael. Erpa will soon give the signal."

The chimes in the steeple rang half-past twelve. For about five minutes there was silence; then Michael exclaimed,—

"It is over — the light is out!"

Without manifesting any emotion, the Italian wrote in the book the following words:—

"The first of May, in the year one thousand six hundred and ten, in the first hour of the day, expired Stephen Vanderstein, the first victim of the VENDETTA. He died in the vigour of manhood, and the hour of his death was fixed at a crisis in his fortunes when his loss will most probably impoverish the family. He was killed through the agency of Raphael Benosa, the first executant of the VENDETTA."

The old man then shut up the book, clasped it, and in obedience to his instructions Michael deposited it in the iron-bound chest, which he secured by shooting the bolts of a series of ponderous locks; and then placing the key in his bosom, stood gazing on his father.

The old Italian had resumed his recumbent posture; convulsive twitches passed over his face, and his breath came in gasps.

"Michael—forget not—and—when I—am dead—ex-..nguish the lamp—and watch beside me—in—the—darkness——"

The young Italian bowed, and felt with his hand his father's extremities. They were already cold. Then the features of the old man became pinched and blue, and the rattle sounded in his chest.

As the son gazed upon the dying father, the chimes proclaimed a quarter to one.

"He said it should be within the hour," the youth murmured. Then Michael looked, with dry, hot eyes, upon the dying. "I cannot weep," he said; "my destiny and my mission are too great for weakness of body or soul. I must be something more or less than human."

At this moment, a change passed over the old man's face which caused Michael to take up the extinguisher of the lamp; and just ere the clock tolled one, the Flemish sentinel before the Stadthouse, who had been idly gazing upon the light in the house of Raphael Benosa, the Italian money-changer, saw it go out.

"The withered old atomy is gone to sleep," he muttered. So he had—for ever.

THE SECOND CHAPTER OF THE PROLOGUE

THE SHIP-OWNER AND THE SHIP-CAPTAIN.

A CENTURY has elapsed since the death of Raphael Benosa. A century to a month, for the breeze which sweeps across the meadows which line the Rhine below Rotterdam, and makes the weathercocks and vanes upon the trim farm-houses point to the south-east, and rustles along the lines of priggish pollards, and heaves round the sails of lagging windmills, and toys and wantons with, and swells into rustling waves, the white canvass of the loosened foretopsail of the substantial American trader the St. Nicholas, — this breeze, we say, is the pleasant breath of the early May. Furthermore, the St. Nicholas is riding with her anchor apeak a couple of miles below the Boomjees. The wind favours her ; she is but waiting that Captain Schlossejib may receive on board one lady passenger, and also take the last instructions of his owners ; after which events the gallant captain anticipates, that, with such a breeze, three hours or so will see the St. Nicholas beyond the Brill, and speeding merrily over the tilting seas of the German Ocean.

" Here's the boat at last, Captain Schlossejib," said Jin Karl, the first mate of the St. Nicholas, a good-humoured, open-faced, Dutch-built Dutchman, with flaxen hair and light eyes.

" Ay, ay, I see," replied the captain, stopping his impatient walk along the quarter-deck. " Get the accommodation-ladder rigged out, and see to the side ropes. The owner is bringing our lady-passenger on board himself. Well, he's a polite man, Meinheer Benosa."

" And a liberal," said the mate. " Not a shipowwner from the Seine to the Elbe is more beloved of officers and men. He's a prince to sail under. The best pay — the best provisions — the best treatment. Long life and prosperity to the house of Benosa ! "

" Of which here comes the head," observed Captain Schlossejib, as a fast-pulling boat, impelled by the labours of six sturdy rowers, shot alongside of the St. Nicholas. In the stern-sheets of this boat were two ladies, both closely hooded and veiled, and a portly man, dressed like a substantial citizen of Holland. The latter, with very elaborate politeness, assisted the females to mount to the deck of the St. Nicholas, and, following them himself, and taking the hand of one of them (the younger), said,—

" This lady, Captain Schlossejib, is your passenger to New York. You will be particular in paying to Mademoiselle Vanderstein the utmost attention so long as she remains on board the ship St. Nicholas, commanded by you."

The captain, hat in hand, bowed low to his owner, and nearly as low to the two ladies, who returned the greeting, and then, attended by Jin Karl, proceeded to the cabin, which had been fitted up with a due regard to the requirements of her who for some weeks was to be its inhabitant.

The door of the state-room bolted behind them, the two women rushed, as with one accord, into each other's arms.

" Sister, sister," exclaimed the elder of the two, " we shall never meet again!" and, tearing aside the head-dress of her companion, she smothered her with kisses.

" Hush, my silly Treuchden!" the other said, repaying her sister's embrace fondly, but with calmness ; " hush ! the Atlantic is broad, but it is not a Styx, that we should not return across it, nor a Lethe, that its waters should wash away the remembrance of each other."

" No, no, Louise, we shall never forget each other, but I shall never hold you in my arms again!—my heart tells me so. I have hoped against hope; but since our brother's death—his death upon the eve of his marriage, upon the very night of that joyous supper at the Lust-Haus of the good Benosa—I have believed that there is a black doom hanging above our family."

" Misfortunes are the lot of all, Treuchden, and they come in troops. What have we done that they should be specially billeted upon the Vandersteins ?"

" Do not laugh, Louise! Remember our family history : not a Vanderstein has prospered since the death of our ancestor Stephen, who died so suddenly in Antwerp a century ago."

" Then let us hope," said Louise, " that the curse will

lose its strength by lapse of time. If it survive the hundred years, I shall pronounce it a malediction of the most robust constitution and the most hopeless longevity."

"Has one of our family," said Treuchden, still pursuing the argument, "died in the ordinary course of nature and at a ripe old age? Has not misery in its every shape been heaped upon us? Have we not wrestled with poverty, and calumny, and contempt? Have we not either died young— died in the bloom and the blush of our hopes—or dragged on a dreary life until we met some fearful or some mysterious end? Tell me not, Louise, we are a fated race;—we are doomed to unhappiness ourselves, and we drag into the gulf all who are connected with us."

"But, at least," answered the younger sister, catching some portion of the serious mood of her relative,—"at least these misfortunes have only happened when we lived all toge- ther in Flanders. Now, when we are to be separated— now, when the only three survivors of our race—you, my dear sister, Margaritta, and myself—will shortly be known but by our husbands' names, and live with them apart—you in London, Margaritta in Paris, and I in America—surely, if there has been a fatality upon our united house, it will not pursue the scattered remnants of a broken race."

Treuchden shook her head sorrowfully, but, after a mo- ment's pause, added,—

"I will bear up, my dear sister; I will hope for the best; I will trust that happier days may see us re-united. At any rate, I will strive not to darken your departure from Europe by what may be, after all, but idle fancies and superstitious forebodings, although springing from (Heaven knows) a series of unheard-of calamities."

And the two sisters, after another close embrace, busied themselves in making their little arrangements in the cabin.

Meantime the owner of the St. Nicholas, Meinheer Be- nosa, attended by the captain and Jin Karl, made a tour of inspection round the ship. The prosperous and kind-looking merchant had a good-natured word for every body on board.

"Ha, old Schuytz! before the mast still? We must see whether we cannot give you a push up the stairs of the

quarterdeck after this voyage.   Well, Hans, as stout as
ever! It is an everlasting marvel to me how you can go
aloft in so many pairs of breeches! Hey-day, Peterkin!
leaving your young wife to go across the blue water?—but
sailors have wives in every port.—Nay, never interrupt, man!
I tell no tales.   Captain Schlossejib, I hope — duty being
duly done—that you do not stint the poor fellows in the
articles of tobacco or schnapps.   I would not have a seaman
who treads a plank over which flies the private signal of the
House of Benosa who could complain of clear pipes or empty
goblets."

The captain bowed, and the score or so of seamen around
raised a hoarse cheer,—

"Long live the Benosas, the noblest merchants of the
Netherlands!"

The shipowner raised his cocked beaver hat, acknowledged the greeting, and then, taking the captain by the arm,
led him to the private cabin of the latter, and carefully
secured the door.

"I have something to say to you, Captain Schlossejib,"
said Benosa.

The sea-captain bowed and listened.

"You have sailed south of the line, captain," began the
merchant, in a low, even tone, and fixing his black, keen
eyes intently upon the browned and battered visage before
him,—"you have sailed under many flags?"

"Yes," replied the captain, in the same confidential tone
of voice—"yes, English, Spanish, Dutch, French, and ——"
And here the speaker hesitated.

"Go on, man!" replied the merchant;—"and another
which the men of no nation own, but the men of all nations
fear."

The ancient pirate fixed a puzzled look upon the merchant.

"Well, well," continued Benosa, "young blood will be
hot, and youth will have its swing."

"Meinheer Benosa," said the captain, "I wish I knew
in what intent and with what purpose you speak."

"But the laws of nations," resumed Benosa, as if talking
to himself, "make but little allowance for such frolics. Dear,
dear, the proceeding s summary! Reeve the rope, load the

gun, and up goes a choking man to the end of the fore-arm
in a wreath of white smoke."

Schlossejib made no immediate reply, but his breath came
in thick gasps, and the large beads of perspiration stood upon
his forehead.

"Meinheer," he said, speaking with difficulty, and in a
hoarse, broken voice, "I have served you well!"

"I am aware of it," replied the other; "but you don't
know me well.   You see, however, the ignorance is not
mutual."

Again the captain cast a long, inquisitive glance at his
owner; but in the calm and handsome features before him,
in the depth of the lustrous black eyes, and the quiet smile
which curved the lips of Benosa, and which might mean
much or nothing, he found little to guide him.

"Is the St. Nicholas a good ship?" abruptly inquired the
merchant.

"As stout as ever swam!" was the reply.

"Fit to go a cruise to the Spanish main, or round the
Horn, to look out for a galleon deep with the ingots of the
Spaniard?"

"Why," exclaimed Captain Schlossejib, in inexpressible
astonishment,—"why, *you* don't wish to go a-roving?"

"Not I!" replied the merchant; "but perhaps you do?"

"Meinheer Benosa," said the captain, "speak to a plain
seaman in plain words, and he will give you a plain answer."

"A man is sometimes lost overboard on a long voyage;
is he not?"

"Surely," replied the captain; "life is uncertain upon
the land, but more uncertain upon the sea."

"And if men drop overboard, women are liable to the
same fate?"

The sea-captain drew a long breath, and his coarse face
assumed an aspect of intelligence.

"What would you do in the event of a loss—some such
unhappy loss—on board the St. Nicholas?"

"I would," replied Schlossejib,—"I would make an
entry of it in the log-book — that is all I could do."

"Ah! in this style:—'June 1st.   Lat. so and so.
Long. so and so.   Steering W.S.W., under all plain sail.
Squalls with head sea   Lost overboard.'—what shall we

say? ah! for example,—'lost overboard Mademoiselle
Louise Vanderstein, cabin passenger, who, in a sudden lee
lurch of the ship, fell accidentally from the quarter-gallery
into the sea?' You would enter the occurrence in some
such words as these?"

" As near as may be."

" Then don't forget the form—nor the example I have
given you."

" Meinheer Benosa," said Schlossejib, "are you in
earnest?"

" It would be a very dull joke if I were not."

" I did not know you—I—I never should have imagined
—nobody would have imagined ——"

" Stop," said Benosa; "how many men in Holland, do
you think, know you—know the secrets of your soul?"

" Not one, I hope," replied the worthy addressed, " excepting, perhaps, yourself."

" And how many in Holland do you think know me?"

" Not one, I believe—excepting, perhaps, myself."

" Hum!—your knowledge goes a very little way."

" I know more than I did half-an-hour ago."

" That may be, and now you shall know more still—you
shall know your own fate. You will, winds and seas permitting, make your voyage to North America, and thence
back to Rotterdam. Off the Brill I shall board you—shall
come down to this cabin, and shall ask to see your log-book;
if there be no entry in it such as I have sketched, you shall
be denounced as a pirate and a cut-throat, and by your death
society will be avenged and the world so far purified. If,
however, there be such an entry in the pages of your log—
not a sham one, observe, and there are ways of knowing,—
you shall, after you have discharged your cargo, be formally
put in possession of this stout ship the St. Nicholas, and shall
use her, if it suits you, as a peaceful merchantman, or shall
hoist the old flag from her mast-head in the Spanish main or
in the track of the Mexican galleons. And now, Captain
Schlossejib, you know still more than you did half-an-hour
ago."

There was a long pause, and both the interlocutors eyed
each other keenly, the face of Benosa wearing the same

placid smile as before, that of Schlossejib quivering with emotion and wet with perspiration.

"I fear," said Benosa, "you would dread the possibility of such an accident in a ship commanded by you."

"Accidents," said the worthy captain, "are not of our making; do all we can, they will happen."

"Then I may possibly find an interesting entry in the log on your return?"

"You will find it."

"Good! then we shall go and look after the ladies; they must think us quite ungallant, I declare."

So saying, Benosa rose and left the cabin. Schlossejib lingered a moment to swallow a large glass of schnapps, and then followed his patron.

In the main cabin was prepared a collation, of which Benosa and the two ladies partook.

"When shall we take our next meal together, Louise?" said Treuchden.

"Pooh, mademoiselle," said Benosa, "you dread the sea. With a stout ship under you—and Captain Schlossejib will tell you that the St. Nicholas is as stout a ship as ever swam—you need care no more for the waves of the Atlantic than for the ripples of a horse-pond. Come! a glass of champagne all round, to carouse to the pleasant passage and the safe arrival of Mademoiselle Louise Vanderstein; and may she find—as I doubt not she will—her betrothed, my trusty and honoured friend, Heinrich Strumfel, ready to fold her in his arms ere the anchor of the St. Nicholas has sunk into the sands of the New World. Come! is every glass brimming? Fair winds for the sails of the St. Nicholas, and good fortune for the hearts which beat beneath them!"

Every glass was emptied to the toast except that of Captain Schlossejib, who watched the merchant with a strangely puzzled air.

"How! the captain refuse the pledge? Off with your wine, man!—off with it to the last drop, or our fair passenger will think you mean her evil."

The captain mechanically swallowed the contents of his glass.

At this moment Jin Karl appeared at the cabin-door

" The anchor is at the bows," he said, "and we are moving seaward." So the party went on deck.

" Meinheer," whispered Schlossejib to his patron, " has your purpose changed ?"

" Captain," was the reply, in the same tone, " has your mainmast fallen ?"

Schlossejib took the speaking-trumpet, which the mate handed to him, in silence, looking round as though he were in a dream. The sisters twined their arms round each other for the last embrace, and Treuchden was lowered weeping into the boat. The merchant prepared to follow her, but paused on the gangway. His eye sought Schlossejib's, and exchanged with him a long, meaning look. Then raising his hat, he said, with a loud voice, using the phraseology of the old bills of lading, " And so God keep the good ship on her destined voyage."

Three hours thereafter the St. Nicholas had crossed the Brill, and was standing to the westward.

THE THIRD CHAPTER OF THE PROLOGUE.

THE LAST DROP OF THE LAST PHIAL.

This history must make a second flying leap. The scene of this chapter is in the vicinity of London, and the time the month of May 1810, just a century since the St. Nicholas left the Maas, and two centuries since Raphael Benosa died in his house at Antwerp.

London of late years has been well explored and described, not by mere topographers or parish antiquaries, but by those writers whose fictions present, as in a glass, of more or less distorting power, the features of society in our own days. There is one district, however, which has escaped the literary scrutiny, and yet it is not one of the least remarkable. It lies on the eastern and northern outskirts of our city, stretching away beyond Spitalfields. It is neither quite a suburb nor quite the country. It is cut up principally into small strips of garden ground, and in each of these gardens there is a dwelling-house. The humbler class of these mansions are built entirely of the wood of old, broken-up ships. They look like those deck-cabins which we see in vessels from the Baltic ports, lifted from between the masts, and set down amid cabbages and gooseberry-bushes. You can trace the stains of coarse ship-paint and tar upon these brown, warped, shrivelled planks. Iron cramps and ring-bolts, once supports for the rigging which towered above them, still stand rustily out from the decaying, splintering wood; and, half overgrown by rank vegetation, lie around such naval mementoes as broken gun-carriages, rusty cabin-stoves, or staved and splintered water-barrels. Over each of these mansions there generally rises a mast, with cross-trees, and stays, and a vane; and upon high days and holydays the proprietor hoists a union-jack to the summit, and eyes it with great complacency, as he drinks his grog and smokes his pipe in the little arbour, whereof the planks have tossed many a stormy night and day upon the ocean. The sea-faring people by whom these amphibious mansions are reared are generally retired skippers and mates of coasting vessels, or small dealers in maritime stuffs, who instinctively keep as near as they can to the water-side and the docks. But houses of a different, though peculiar class, are not wanting. These are generally formal, old brick mansions, with small windows and heavy-browed doors, approached by flights of stone steps from the grass-plot which stretches in front. Most of these houses appear to date from the ugly and tasteless age of Anne. They are inhabited by old city families, who carry on an old-fashioned business in an old-fashioned way,—plodding, careful folk, who have no West-end visions, sigh for no opera-boxes, intrigue for no *entrée* to exclusive coteries, and dine before the western hemisphere has breakfasted.

Into a ground-floor parlour in a dwelling of this class our story leads us. The house stands apart, and a high brick wall surrounds both it and the gardens and shrubberies attaching to it. Thus the passenger can only command a view of the upper stories. At the outer gate, at the moment when we reunite the thread of the story, stands a quiet, and by no means dashing brougham. The first glance at its unobtrusive panels, and its steady, well-worked horse, would tell the initiated in the ways and things of town, that he was looking

at a doctor's carriage; and he would guess right. The
brougham is the property of Dr. Gumbey, and Dr. Gumbey
is at this moment in the ground-floor parlour, conversing
lowly and earnestly with the master of the house.

The room was dark and gloomy. Dr. Gumbey sat in the
lightest portion of it, and his companion in the darkest. The
doctor was a young man, plump and round-faced, with a
bald head. It is astonishing the number of doctors who
have bald heads; perhaps they pluck out the hair with
tweezers to make them look learned. The master of the
house, who sat opposite the doctor, we shall describe pre
sently.

"The case of Mrs. Werwold," said Dr. Gumbey, "is
absolutely the most unaccountable I ever came across."

"She got over her confinement well," remarked the
husband, in a low and slightly tremulous tone.

"Admirably — admirably; and the boy is positively the
finest boy I ever saw in my life. Nothing ails him. But from
the hour at which his poor mother ought to have got better,
she has got worse."

"But what do the peculiar symptoms denote?"

"Ay, the peculiar symptoms, — just so; there is the
puzzle. There are no peculiar symptoms — that is, none
other than a gradual wasting away of the vital energy, a
gradual absorption of the element of existence. Every individual organ appears healthy. We can discover no latent
disease. The effect is palpable to all; but human science —
so far, at least, as we can apply it — can point to no cause."

"There is a disease, a well-known disease, I believe,
called atrophy?"

"There is; but here is no atrophy. It is not the flesh
which wastes away, but the living principle which appears to
ebb from the flesh. Making the due allowance for her recent
condition, Mrs. Werwold looks as well as ever."

"Then," said Werwold, in a tone of deep despondency,
"there is no hope?"

"While there is life, there is hope," replied the doctor.
"Hope for the best — prepare for the worst. It is my sad
duty to tell you to do so, Mr. Werwold."

There was a long pause.

"Werwold," resumed the doctor, "if one could believe

in the trash one reads of the slow poisons of the mid ages — of their marvellous effects, of their blighting influ ence, of their power of killing, yet leaving, so to speak, no scar, — I say, if one could believe in the idle legends of the drugs in possession of the Borgias and the Medicis, — legends which modern science has utterly put to the rout, — if we could believe in such things, I would say that ——"

" What ?"

" That Mrs. Werwold had drunk the wine of Cyprus o the Roman, or worn the perfumed gloves of the Florentine."

" Or had her image fashioned in wax, and wasted before a slow fire by a New England witch," said the husband, with a sad smile.

" True — true," replied the doctor ; " fooleries — fooleries all, and I was in the wrong to talk of such nonsense. Well, I wish we were wiser."

" But," resumed the husband, " must all means be aban- doned ?"

" God forbid !" said Doctor Gumbey ; " but I talk to you candidly — drugs appear of no use whatever. We must trust more to regimen, and if possible to moral means — labour to keep the patient's spirits up, and promote a health- ful excitement, if we can, in body and mind. Meantime we must keep up strength by generous living and the moderate use of stimulants."

" The port wine, then, as before?" said Werwold.

" Precisely," replied the doctor, rising, and buttoning his coat. " I shall look in again in the evening. Meantime, I repeat, labour to keep the patient's spirits up, and for the rest, we can only hope that some turn, some crisis, may take place, and that this mysterious malady may depart as it came."

With these words the doctor took his leave. Werwold saw him into his brougham, and then, returning to the par- lour, passed through it into a little room beyond, fitted up as a study or small library, the door of which he locked behind him. In a corner of this apartment, bricked into the wall, was an iron safe of massive and ponderous dimensions. Wer- wold opened it by a key hung from his watch-guard. The various shelves were littered with papers, which he cleared away, flinging them carelessly behind him. Then touching a side-spring, there became visible the keyhole of a small inner safe, worked still deeper into the wall, and the door of which swung open between two of the shelves of the outward repository. From this crypt Werwold lugged forth a heavy box, opened it, and took out a small steel casket filled with phials secured by pieces of bladder round the corks, and which he examined one by one. With the exception of the last which he took up, they were all empty. In that one still lay a drop or two of glutinous, transparent fluid.

" The last drop of the last phial," he murmured. " The work is nearly done, and I shall know the grand secret."

So saying, he placed the phial in his waistcoat-pocket, shut the casket, replaced it in the box, replaced that in its crypt, restored the papers to the shelves of the outward safe, locked it, and passing out through the parlour, as-cended the broad flight of stairs which led to the bedrooms of the house.

On his way he encountered a withered old female, dressed in the prim style of the matrons of old Dutch pictures.

" Erpa," he said, " the doctor insists upon absolute quiet. I am going to your mistress for awhile. Do not come up or let any one of the other servants intrude until I call ;" and he passed on. After pausing for a moment at a door, he entered a chamber. It was the darkened room of an invalid. A portion only of one of the upper shutters was open, and a narrow gleam of sunlight fell upon a table littered with glasses, phials, and the usual appurtenances of a sick-room, and played upon the sombre drapery of the bed. One of the curtains was suspended in massive folds, so as to allow the interior of the bed to be seen. It was occupied by a lady, the patient of Dr. Gumbey, whose case we have just heard stated, and which puzzled the worthy doctor so com-pletely.

As Werwold entered, his wife turned her eyes upon him, but did not speak, and he stood a few moments looking at her in silence. Mrs. Werwold, as we have heard, betrayed none of the usual appearances of an invalid rapidly sinking to the grave. She was a mild, meek-expressioned woman, with blue eyes, a delicately white skin, and rich tresses of fair hair. Her features were of the ancient Flemish type, somewhat large and heavy, but with a full, soft, womanly expression. In her eyes alone the sign of the malady was apparent. They were lustrous, but suffused with a pearly-hued fluid, which glazed them, so that the pupils shone with a dimmed glare, as a red-flamed lamp would shine through a thin sheet of falling water. The slightest motion made by the patient shewed her extreme languor. Indeed, she hardly appeared to have strength to stir her hands, which were plump, yet wore a ghastly hue of yellowish white.

"Treuchden," said her husband, "the doctor wishes you to continue the wine."

A slight movement of the eyes indicated that she heard and was ready to obey. A cobwebbed bottle, with two long-stalked glasses, lay upon the table, which was drawn to the head of the bed, so as to be concealed by the curtain from the view of the invalid.

Werwold filled a glass nearly to the brim with richly-coloured wine, and then, pausing, looked keenly all round. The silence of death was in the room. The sick woman lay with her eyes partially closed—she appeared dozing. Holding the glass tremulously in his hand, Werwold cast upon the sick woman a glance of the bitterest agony.

"Oh!" he murmured, "accursed be the race of which I come, and the sentiments in which I have been nursed, which drag me on to fulfil this awful vengeance, even as madness hurries its victim over some ghastly precipice! But no! I may not pause!—there is a fate—a doom in it. If I dream of burning these horrible papers—that horrible book, it seems as though the phantoms of my dead fathers rose round me, and gibed and gibbered at the first man who, with Corsican blood in his veins, turned from the behests of a vendetta. No!—no!—I may go mad, but I must do the bidding of those voices from the grave!"

Then pausing, he glanced towards the bed. The invalid had not changed her attitude. He looked steadily at the glass of wine, and then, holding it to the light, permitted the last drop of the last phial to trickle into it. As the two liquids mingled, the rich glow of the generous port seemed for a moment to pale and thin in intensity, and then the deep colour reappeared, only a shade darker, and making the liquor appear more turbid and opaque than before.

With every muscle in his face strained and swollen, yet

rigid and fixed as iron bars, Werwold approached the bed, and drew back the curtain with one hand, while he held the wine in the other. His hands were clammy and damp, but not a nerve quivered in face or finger.

" Treuchden, your port."

He raised his wife up, and held the glass to her mouth, while she slowly drank the contents; then wiping her lips with a handkerchief which lay upon the bed, he replaced her head upon the pillows. Then he drew aside the curtain, and partially raised the window-blind. The light of the pleasant summer day streamed into the gloomy room, and Werwold placed himself by the foot of the bed, in its broadest glare.

" Treuchden," he said, " you are still very ill?"

A sad smile was the reply.

" You feel this unconquerable lethargy gaining on you?"

She gave the same sad smile again.

" Your strength waning, your mind weakening, the very spirit oozing from your body?"

The patient fixed an anxious and inquiring look upon her husband. The tone in which he spoke was very low, but singularly distinct, and though fraught equally with sternness and melancholy, it was neither harsh on the one hand, nor tremulous on the other.

" Treuchden," he resumed, " I love you, and I am killing you."

She started up. " You!—my husband!—you Michael Werwold!—killing me?" she gasped.

" My name is not Michael Werwold," was the reply,— " my name is Michael Benosa!"

The sick woman fell back on the pillows, and pressed her eyes with her hands.

" Oh! oh!" she murmured, " it is the delirium come back!"

" It is not the delirium come back," said the man; " when death is at hand the brain clears—it works ever the truer just ere it rests for ever."

" Then—then," sobbed the woman, " death is at hand?"

" In the chamber—by your bed!"

" Oh!" groaned the patient, " the heavy curse of the Vandersteins is on me!"

" It is!"

"And you—you—my love—my husband—my sworn protector—the father of my boy—you—what are you?"

"Your destroyer, my Treuchden."

She glared incredulously at him.

"Look at me!" he said.

She did. In his face were the features of old Raphael reproduced. The same swarthy, intellectual beauty, the same deeply-set, gleaming eyes, the same fine skin lines, threading, as it were, forehead and cheeks. The complexion was deadly pale, and the expression one of awful determination, toned down by placid, deep-fixed sorrow.

"I am not Michael Werwold, the Anglo-Saxon,—I am Michael Benosa, the Italian. I come of a fated race, I am predestined to a fatal end. Ties you can never understand bind me to my awful career. Would—oh, would that I were dead!—but while I live I must do that which I abhor! From that terrible task before me I must never quail—never turn!"

Treuchden lay and listened in a species of wandering bewilderment. The words of her husband rang continuously on her ear, and she strained her weakened faculties to catch their immediate purport, as one by one they were spoken, while the connected sense of his discourse seemed to escape and elude her.

"Treuchden," continued the Corsican, "I ask you not to think ill or well of me. I am but the hammer which, held by the strong man, breaks the precious vase, and spills the goodly wine. Listen! You are on your death-bed—the sins of the fathers are visited upon their children. You must die, and I must kill you. There is a fate above all; I bend to mine, which makes me a murderer. Shrink not from yours, which makes you but a victim. You die and I live, and your lot is happier than mine!"

The dying woman spoke not, but clasped her hands in the attitude of prayer.

"Yes, yes," continued Benosa, "pray, pray to our common God! You would not believe me, but I too can pray. The evil that I do is done that it may be as it is written. For two hundred long years the long vengeance has been working—for two hundred long years that vengeance has been ministered by those of my house upon those of yours.

It was decreed that the Benosas must exterminate the Vandersteins. No living man knows the cause of this hereditary enmity. It is written in a book which I possess, but I may not read it until the blood of the Vandersteins is purged from the earth. Now you know why you die — you know my fearful mission, handed down to me by my father, as it was to him by his. To compass that mission I became the husband of the last of the Vandersteins—to fulfil that mission it is by my hand you must die. Treuchden, my heart is as the heart of other men, and I could cherish you, wear you in my bosom, worship at your feet, but I am the tool of a destiny which discerns not until it has run its course. Poor, pale, guiltless victim of a wrath above the wrath of men, make your peace with God, and render up your spirit!"

Treuchden lay for a moment still, her eyes shut, and the nerves of her face twitching and quivering. Then she started up, and stretched her arms out to her husband.

"My child! — my boy!" she ejaculated.

"You would ask whether the fatality will pursue him?"

She nodded eagerly.

"The fatality clings to all in whose veins runs the blood of the Vandersteins, and in your boy's veins runs the blood of the Vandersteins."

"And of the Benosas, too," she exclaimed.

"Even so," was the answer.

"Monster! you would slay the unconscious infant!"

Benosa's face grew dark with suppressed emotion.

"Would I could!" he muttered, and then groaned aloud. "He must live to taste how sweet is life, that he may know how bitter is death!"

"Then — then," exclaimed the dying woman, raising herself in bed, the glazed pupils of her eyes dilating, and the beads of cold perspiration which had gathered on her forehead streaming, by the motion, down her face, on which a pale bluish tint began to be visible—"then you, the father, the protector, will be the demon to lure him, your son — your flesh and blood — to ruin, to destruction?"

Benosa's face became absolutely awful, as he raised himself to his full height, and, stretching his clenched hand upwards, said in low, deep tones, "It is so written!"

Uttering a low, wailing cry, Treuchden fell back upon the pillows.

The bluish tint spread over her face, and became especially visible underneath her shut eyes.

Benosa stood with unchanged countenance beholding her. The lips moved — Benosa bent over her — she was praying.

He paused for a few moments, and then muttered, "She is speechless! emotion has aided the effect of the drug. In ten minutes she will be motionless." And, in effect, the movement of the lips began to slacken, and the facial muscles to lose their power, when, stepping to the bell-pull, Benosa rang a loud peal.

Erpa speedily answered the summons.

"The change is at hand," he said, in a low tone to the attendant.

The woman replied by a mute gesture of sorrow and resignation, and they both bent over the dying.

For some moments Treuchden appeared to live only in her eyes; the light of existence shone in them still. Minute by minute it paled and dimmed, until nothing of them gleamed but the cold, glazed surface of the eyeballs.

Then Erpa placed a filament of down upon the lips; it remained there until the jaws dropped, and the feather, after floating a moment in the air, settled into the open mouth.

That night Benosa locked himself in his study, and, opening the repository in the safe, took from it an ancient, quarto-shaped book, bound in coarse rough vellum, on the back of which was inscribed, in faded gilding, "La Vendetta." The pages were nearly all written on ; and it was remarkable that the writing was in many hands, and traced in ink of different colours. The hue of the characters on the earlier pages was jet black, that of those on the latter leaves was a rusty brown. Every body agrees in thinking that they made better ink long ago than in more recent times. In this book Benosa wrote nearly two pages. As he shut it up and clasped it, he murmured, "The last entry but one!"

THE HISTORY.

CHAPTER I.

WHY MADEMOISELLE CHATEAUROUX DID NOT DANCE AT THE OPERA.

MADAME WERWOLD, or BENOSA, died in the year 1810, leaving a male infant. Our story commences twenty-three years after that date, and the scene shifts from the east to the west end of London.

We are in a room, then, looking over the green vistas of Hyde Park. It is furnished with luxurious magnificence, but with careless absence of harmony and taste. Elizabethan furniture jostles with the gaudy decorations, the meretricious gilding, and allegorical carvings, of the age of Louis Quinze. Vast mirrors gleam upon the walls, extending from the rich cornices to the lusciously soft carpet. Cabinet paintings of great cost are interspersed with vulgar prints of favourite danseuses, coloured portraits of fast-trotting mares, as they appeared performing celebrated matches against time, and ugly representations of ugly bull-dogs and snapping terriers, the property of various gentlemen known and esteemed in the most exclusive circles of the " Fancy." Sofas, couches, causeuses, chairs, armed and unarmed, of every dimension and every pattern, are jumbled together without order or regularity. Costly ornaments, some of them recently broken, Sèvres vases, and rich specimens of Bohemian-coloured glass, are strewed on marqueterie tables. Half-a-dozen time-pieces, pointing to half-a-dozen hours, stand about. Valuable classic books are jumbled on shelves with racing calendars, works on the noble art of self-defence, Little Warblers, French novels, and masses of the periodicals of the day. Every where there is the same chaos of things good and bad — things intellectual and trivial — things refined and vulgar; vases of flowers are

c

placed on open cigar-boxes; a hunting-whip is flung across a painter's easel; an open portfolio of memoranda and sketches is soaked through by the contents of a spilt bottle of wine; foils, pencils, musical instruments, single-sticks, lorgnettes, meerschaums, unfinished sketches, watches, piles of caricatures, pencil-cases, snuff-boxes, cameos, spurs; all this conglomeration of objects of taste, sport, ingenuity, and triviality, lies scattered on tables, chairs, on sofas and the floor; whilst in the centre of the apartment—this, part museum, part drawing-room, part study—on a magnificent couch, lined with Utrecht velvet, is stretched supinely out at full length a young man, the proprietor of the room and the house, Clement Lorimer.

He wears a morning dress, consisting of a loose, soft, velvet shooting-coat, and his feet are thrust luxuriously into crimson slippers. His features are well cut, frank, and open; but his cheeks are deadly pale, and there is an air of languid *insouciance* and lazy indifference apparent in all his motions. By the couch stands, in a respectful attitude, a second individual, an undistinguished-looking personage, decently dressed in black, with large shoes, and a very loosely-tied and ill-washed white neckerchief. His features are strong, harsh, and heavy, the skin coarse and yellow; but he possesses two small, clear grey eyes, as clammily cold as those of a fish, but as sharp and piercing as those of a cat.

"Blane," said Clement Lorimer, "I want money; I feel an extravagant fit coming on."

"Mr. Lorimer," replied the steward, in the sleek voice of a flattering dependant—"Mr. Lorimer need not balk his inclinations. God forbid! He is in possession of a splendid income."

"Derived no one knows whence," murmured the young man.

"But as punctually paid as quarter-day comes punctually round," continued the steward.

"Ay, therein lies the point," said the master. "Satan may send the money,—'tis all one to me, so long as the sovereigns do not turn into gooseberry-leaves."

"At least before they are spent," insinuated the steward.

"Blane," replied Lorimer, "there is a strict immorality about you which is absolutely refreshing. You never bore

me with good advice—you never annoy me with hints or
predictions that the unknown source of my income may some
day dry up—you never try to curb folly or check extravagance. Blane, you are a cold-blooded old rascal, and—and,
therefore, I like you."

The man to whom this contradictory eulogium was addressed made a movement, which might have been taken
either for a bow or shrug. He was accustomed to his master's particular moods, and appeared either not to understand
or to be perfectly indifferent to the tone of suppressed but
bitter sarcasm in which the words he had just heard were
spoken.

"I sometimes think, Blane," continued the young man,
"that you know more about me than I do myself."

The steward gave an almost imperceptible start.

"You have been near me since I can remember. You
brought me my pocket-money at Eton—you paid my bills
at Oxford—you manage my establishment here —— What
are you, Blane, and what am I ?"

"I beg your pardon, Mr. Lorimer, for reminding you
that you are already perfectly acquainted with the circumstances which led to my occupying the humble position I do
in your household."

"Yes," replied Lorimer, "I remember your version of
them. You answered an advertisement, you saw the adver-
tiser, he prescribed your duties, as regarded me, and you
never saw him since."

"Never !" answered the steward.

Lorimer looked long and keenly into the face of his
servitor. He neither quailed nor flinched before the gaze,
but fixed his cold grey eyes coldly and clearly upon his
master.

Lorimer, who had raised himself upon his elbow, flung
his form luxuriously back upon the yielding cushions. He
felt himself baffled by the unmoved, phlegmatic being before
him.

"Then let me have money, Blane; do you hear? I give
you a forced confidence. If I come down, you follow ; meantime let us enjoy. I dine from home to-day. See that the
horses are ready ; and, by the way, has that note been conveyed to Mademoiselle Chateauroux ?"

Blane bowed. It had been delivered an hour after it was written.

"Good! I am at home to nobody but her. Give orders accordingly."

Blane bowed again.

"And — ah, yes — there is person from Rundell and Bridge's below; is there not?

"Yes."

"Then send him up at once."

And the steward retired.

"He's as deep as a well, and as cold as a toad in it," said Lorimer to himself, when he was left alone. "I think he is cheating me — I am sure of it. Pshaw! never mind, he does it neatly! All the world's a cheat: those who think themselves honest mostly cheat themselves; and those who don't, at all events contrive to cheat the gallows."

As the man about town gave murmured utterance to this profoundly ethic remark, the jeweller's emissary entered the apartment. He brought a small morocco case under his arm, which, being opened, exposed a mass of diamonds and jewelled decorations of almost priceless value.

Lorimer took the box, and turning himself listlessly round on the sofa, played with his white soft fingers amongst the glittering stones. Presently he selected a gorgeous diamond necklace, and holding it up where a ray of sun-light shot into the room, watched the precious stones gleam and sparkle in the brightness.

"Ah," he said, "here is a necklace worthy of a queen!"

"It was the necklace of a queen, sir," said the jeweller.

"Ah?"

"Marie Antoinette wore it, sir, at her marriage with the Dauphin," replied the dealer, in the sing-song tone of a showman exhibiting his wares.

"So — *vanitas vanitatum!* — if the diamonds had not pressed her neck, the steel would not have cut it. Moral — don't wear diamonds — eh?"

The jeweller shuffled with his feet, smiled, bowed, unbuttoned a waistcoat button, and then fastened it again. It was a very good piece of pantomime reply, signifying, "I don't understand a word you say."

" Well," continued Lorimer,—" well, how much for this glittering vanity of Marie Antoinette ?"

The jeweller named a very large sum.

" Tolerably fair for crystallised charcoal. But you lapidaries ought to take care of the chemists."

The emissary of Rundell and Bridge went through his pantomime performance again. His notion of a chemist was made up of three green bottles in the windows, black draught, and a shop half open on Sundays. He did not see what that had to do with jewellers.

" Take care; the chemists will find out how to make diamonds from charcoal."

" Have they turned charcoal into diamonds, sir ?" asked the jeweller.

" Not exactly. But they have done a thing nearly as clever. They have turned diamonds into charcoal."

" Ah !" murmured the jeweller, in a tone which shewed that the cleverness of the feat did not strike him at all.

" And now," continued Lorimer, " leave me these pieces of crystallised carbon, and see my steward. He will conclude the transaction."

The man bowed, packed up his trinkets, and retired. Lorimer flung an embroidered handkerchief carelessly over the diamond necklace, and opened a morning paper which lay damp from the press upon the table.

" Ah !" he murmured, looking at the sheet, " to-night will be performed Rossini's Grand Opera Seria of ' Semiramide.' After which, for the tenth time, the new ballet d'action, called ' La Reine des Feu Follets.' The character of ' La Reine,' by Mademoiselle Fanny Chateauroux. Ah, good," he continued, " that remains to be seen. I think the Favoritta loves me sufficiently not to mind getting into a little hot water for my sake. At all events I must dress,—she will be here in a few minutes."

And accordingly, while Anatole, Lorimer's valet, was arranging the tie of his master's cravat, a dark brougham stopped at the door, and a lady, its occupant, skipped gaily upstairs. She was a little, slightly-formed woman, wearing a high, tight-fitting dress, disposed in perpendicular folds from the neck to the waist, where it was lost in the drapery of a splendid cashmere shawl, which, swathed lightly round the person above the girdle, hung in massive folds over the lower part of the wearer's figure. The face of the visitor was essentially French in contour and complexion. Its form was oval, its colour a sallow olive; the roughened skin of the cheek told its tale of cosmetics, and the dark circles traced beneath the eyes spoke of late hours and a life of feverish excitement. *Au reste,* the forehead was low, the lips and nose commonplace, and the eyes deep-set, coal-black, and lending, by their quick burning glances, an expression of acute, passionate intellect to the whole face.

The visitor flung herself on the sofa, and when Lorimer appeared smiled, pouted, and held him out a finger.

"*Me voilà, Clément,*" she said.

"Our compact, Favoritta," replied the young man. "English in England."

The lady pouted her lip again. "But you speak French, *mon Dieu!* You speak French well enough."

This was said with a marked foreign accent, but with perfect fluency.

"It fatigues me, Favoritta, and I hate to be fatigued."

"*Dame!*—have your own way."

"Yes, it is so pleasant."

The Frenchwoman looked at him with a meaning smile. "You won't have it longer than I can help," she said in the bottom of her heart. And to get to the bottom of that heart you had to dive deep.

There was a pause, broken by the lady resuming,—

"You will be at the theatre to-night?"

"No."

"Not when I dance?"

"You don't dance."

"Ah, *parbleu!* (I like *moyen-age* oaths!) Look here," and she took up the newspaper. "See—'Grand Ballet d'Action. La Reine, by Mademoiselle Chateauroux.'"

"Yes; but one mustn't believe all one sees in print. You don't dance at the opera to-night; because after dining at Richmond it would be a bore."

"But I must dance!—*Ventre Saint Gris!*"

"Must! There are two classes of people in the world to whom 'must' has no meaning: the one class consists of despotic monarchs, and the other of *premières danseuses.*"

" But if I don't dance, there will be an uproar ? "

" Well, let there be an uproar."

" The people will tear up the benches."

" Well, let them tear up the benches."

" *Corbleu !* the manager will be ruined."

" Well, let the manager be ruined. What have uproars, or broken benches, or ruined managers, to do with it ? I say you dine with me. Is it not so ? "

The dancer looked fixedly at Lorimer. " No, Clement,' she said, " it is impossible."

" The fact is," continued the other, as though he had not heard the last remark,—" the fact is, I wished to see how this bauble would become you ;" and he snatched the handkerchief off the necklace. The diamonds and Mademoiselle Chateauroux's eyes sparkled together, as though trying to out-gleam each other. " Will you wear it at Richmond ? " asked Lorimer.

The opera-dancer looked in his face. Doubtless there was meaning in the look ; for Lorimer rose, rung a small silver bell, and said to the footman who answered the summons, " Step down to Mount Street. Give my compliments to Dr. Gumbey, and say I should be glad to see him."

" Who dines at Richmond ? " asked Mademoiselle Chateauroux. " Clever people, eh ? I hate fools."

" Oh ! only Sir Harrowby Trumps——"

" Trumps, —*ah bien !* Yes—he is clever—he lives on his wife's soprano. Ordinary people can't do these things. Yes, he is clever. Well ? "

" And Captain De Witz——"

" Oh, he lives on nothing at all. He is cleverer still. He spends five thousand a-year. He has nothing, and nobody ever saw him work, or beg, or steal. *Corbleu !* "

" No. I'll answer for the two former ; and as for the latter, why, charity covers a multitude of sins, Favoritta."

" Yes, but whose sins ? "

" Oh, in this case, those of Captain De Witz." There was a thundering knock at the door.

" Here is the *cher docteur*," said the dancer. " What shall I be ill with, Lorimer ? "

" Oh, *mon amie*, as if I would force your inclinations ! Anything you like, from cholera to chilblains."

Mademoiselle Chateauroux drew her foot upon the sofa, flung her shawl round her, and assumed a languishing, invalid air.

"I look like a patient, eh?" she asked.

"Hush! you are one."

The door opened, and Dr. Gumbey entered. We have seen the doctor twenty-three years ago. He lived in the east then, but since, he had, like other wise men, come to the west. He was only a doctor once, but now he was a doctor and a courtier, and the queens to whom he paid his homage were the deities of the *coulisse*. An accident—with which we have here nothing to do — introduced the doctor to this new circle of society and practice. He stumbled about in it clumsily enough at first; but gradually he found his way, and soon began to feel like a puppy after the ninth day. His eyes were opened, and he saw a pleasant land before him. Now Dr. Gumbey had conscience and tact. His Tact told him that if he struck into the path which lay open to him, he might as well fling Conscience out of the window; and Conscience suggested that if he chose this path, Tact would become but a rascally guide. The doctor hesitated some time, then chose — Tact; and so passed from the docks to the squares. The twenty-three years had flown lightly over Dr. Gumbey, only gracefully dyeing his whiskers, and padding his chest and his calves as they went by. He was the smoothest-faced doctor in town. He came into a room as softly as a ghost or a waiter, and his words flowed forth as unctuously as castoroil, and without the nasty flavour.

"Doctor," said Lorimer, "you see a patient."

Dr. Gumbey bowed gracefully to the *danseuse*, then cast a rapid glance from her face to Lorimer's. He saw in an instant how the land lay.

"What! — bless me! — laid up! Oh, dear, dear! this is a sad business;" and he approached the sofa.

"So sudden, too," said Lorimer, with a half-perceptible smile.

"And what is it?—what is wrong?—what ails us?—eh?"

"Oh, doctor," murmured the sick one, "I feel a — a——" and she hesitated.

"To be sure," said the man of medicine, — "to be sure; but we must not be discouraged. How is the pulse?"

" Fast and febrile, I should say," observed Lorimer.

" Very odd," said the doctor ; " but it is fast and febrile, now."

" Ah, not far from one hundred and twenty ? " inquired Lorimer, hardly able to keep grave.

" Not far," replied the complaisant Gumbey ; " one hundred and seventeen."

" That denotes fever ? " said Lorimer.

The patient caught her cue, tossed restlessly, and flung her arms about, as though seeking for coolness.

" And you see fever is there," remarked the doctor.

" Is my face flushed ? " murmured the invalid.

" Terribly," said Lorimer.

" Awfully," said Gumbey.

" Oh, dear ! oh, dear ! and I have to dance to-night."

" You must not, I am sure, my dear doctor, hear of such a thing as her dancing to-night ? " questioned Lorimer.

Dr. Gumbey looked steadily into the faces of both, and then said,—

" Decidedly not."

" Bravo !" exclaimed Lorimer.   " Get up, Favoritta, the farce is played."

" Farce, sir !" said Dr. Gumbey   " I do not understand you."

" Pshaw ! doctor — it's all very right, of course, with the public ; but betwixt us three ——"

" Well, sir," replied the doctor, staring point blank in Lorimer's face, and repeating his words, with long pauses between each, — " well, sir — betwixt — us — three ? "

" Why," stammered Lorimer, looking from the face of Mademoiselle Chateauroux to that of Dr. Gumbey, — " why, I thought that — this — this sort of thing would be —— But, pshaw ! manage it your own way.   Here, I'll look as grave as an owl."

" I see nothing to laugh at, for my own part," said Dr. Gumbey,—" nothing to laugh at in the medical adviser of a lady suffering from severe febrile symptoms interposing to prevent her from taking violent exercise."

For an instant Lorimer thought that Chateauroux was actually ill without either she or himself having been aware of it.   Then dismissing the idea as quickly as it had arisen, he stood wa.ching the placid face of the doctor, with its calm, unconscious expression and stereotyped smile. The features of the Sphynx were not more immovably tranquil.

"Come," said Lorimer to himself,—"come, who says we have no great actors?"

"But, doctor," lisped the dancer, "there must be a certificate, the management is — *diable!* — so suspicious."

The doctor bowed, took pen, ink, and paper, and wrote as follows :—

"London, the 21st of May, 1832.

"As the medical adviser of Mademoiselle Chateauroux, I hereby certify that she is labouring under a smart febrile attack, and wholly incapable of fulfilling the duties of her profession.

"JOHN GUMBEY, M.D. F.R.C.S."

"And the treatment?" inquired Lorimer.

"Rest," said the doctor.

"A little country air ——" began the invalid.

"In that case," replied the doctor, "care must be taken of cold. I should recommend a veil — a close veil," he added, with emphasis.

"Ah, yes, I understand," observed Lorimer, with a significant gesture.

"Sir!" said Dr. Gumbey, putting on the face of the Sphynx again.

"Good!" said Lorimer, "I forgot ;" adding aside, "Confound the fellow, how well he does it!"

"I shall do myself the pleasure of calling at the residence of mademoiselle to-morrow, when I hope to find her better, if not, indeed, quite well. Good morning." And Dr. Gumbey bowed himself out as noiselessly as he had entered.

As the door closed behind him, Mademoiselle Chateauroux sprung from the sofa, caught up her shawl, and wreathing it into a scarf, flung herself into the attitude in which she graced the print-shop windows, and in which so many of her admirers hoped to see her that night. Then gaily bounding round the room with a wild, quivering, leaping motion, which every moment deceived the eye, and made it expect to see the dancer fly one way when she sprung another, Lorimer recognised the marvellous *pas* in which the Queen of the

Jack-o'-lanterns led astray the Wandering Prince of the ballet.

"Very nice, indeed," he said; "but not so good as Dr. Gumbey." Then ringing the bell, Blane appeared.

"This letter to the opera at eight o'clock." And he handed the doctor's certificate, duly addressed. "And now, the cab to the door!"

"The cab!—*Ventre Saint Dieu!* you forget—the cold air."

"True; the doctor was right—the carriage."

Blane bowed, and in half an hour the carriage, containing Lorimer and La Favoritta, as he called her, rolled away. Meantime Blane walked eastwardly. He was charged with one letter to be delivered at the Opera; he handed in two.

The dinner at Richmond was a gay and a protracted one. The sun had set behind Windsor castle, and a thin grey mist had risen from the river, and floated like a gauze veil over the vast panorama of wood and field, copse and meadow, which diners at the Star and Garter love to look upon: the long dim twilight of the summer-time was deepening into calm night, and star after star was coming twinklingly forth, and still the party lingered joyously at the board. Sir Harrowby Trumps had retailed all the freshest scandal of town. Captain De Witz, who had more imagination, had invented a huge stock of strongly confirmatory and exceedingly piquant facts; and Mademoiselle Chateauroux, installed in an easy chair by the open window, had been as saucily witty as any of them. Lorimer leant luxuriously back, imbibed the aroma of the claret, listened, laughed, occasionally threw in a careless sentence of sarcastic inference, or playful yet biting commentary. He was in a mood which he loved. He was allowing himself to be amused. In his heart—or rather in his brain—he despised the people who made up his entertainment; but they were useful for the moment. They made him smile; they kept him from thinking how slowly the hours went by; they kept him from thinking at all.

"Ah!" said Sir Harrowby Trumps, "I wonder what they're doing at the Opera this moment?"

"Yawning," replied De Witz. "Semiramide is not over yet. Rossini's serious operas are fearful things."

" They may be opening their mouths with weariness before the curtain, but they're opening them with horror behind. No ballet. No Reine de Feu Follets!"

" *Apropos*, Favoritta, how goes the severe febrile attack?" inquired Lorimer.

Mademoiselle Chateauroux twitched a handful of exotic flowers from the china vase in the centre of the table, and flung herself luxuriously on the rich soft cushions of a sofa.

" An invalid is privileged," she laughed. " Has the fever made my eyes bright?"

" Very bright," responded Lorimer; "the fever or the champagne?"

" Libeller!" said the dancer, flinging a camelia at him. It fell on the carpet, and De Witz, bowing for permission, stuck it in his button-hole.

There was a moment's pause.

" We are getting flat," drawled Lorimer. " I wish something funny or something dreadful would happen."

At that moment a waiter flung the door open, and proclaimed,—

" Mr. Grogrum!"

Mr. Grogrum was the *impressario* to whom Dr. Gumbey's certificate had been despatched.

Every one started but Lorimer. The dancer made a motion as if to rise, cast a quick glance at the founder of the feast, then muttering some incoherent words in French, flung herself back on the cushions, beat a tattoo with her foot, and set to work, with downcast eyes, to pick the flowers she held to pieces.

Sir Harrowby Trumps laughed a loud horse-laugh, and De Witz muttered to Lorimer, " A traitor in the camp." The latter only waved his hand, and Mr. Grogrum bounced headlong into the room. He was a large man, with heavy, stolid features, purple-dyed whiskers, and a wig.

" And so, mademoiselle — so," he exclaimed, " this is the indisposition — the — the smart febrile attack! By the Lord! mademoiselle, you may think you'll play such pranks, but you're mistaken — you're ——"

" Mr. Grogrum," said Lorimer, with infinite calmness, " that lady is my guest; you will address her as my guests at my table ought to be addressed."

" Ay, ay, that's all very well, Mr. Lorimer; but I'm not going to be ruined, for all that! My theatre is not going to be ruined! As luck would have it, I got notice though."

" Ha!" said Lorimer.

" I got notice where mademoiselle was; there is time yet. I've a chaise and four at the door. Come along, mademoiselle. You dance to-night in spite of your false or forged certificate!" And the manager, frantic with anger and excitement, made towards the Favoritta.

Lorimer confronted him.

" Who dare detain you?" shouted Grogrum; " who dare come between me and my lawful rights?"

" *I* do!" said Lorimer, drawing himself up to his full height, his eye flashing, and his face instinct with haughty determination, — " *I* do."

There was a pause.

" Come — come," muttered Grogrum, at length, " every minute is worth gold. Let this finish — there's law in the country."

" Plenty of law," said De Witz, " but very little justice."

" Well, sir?" said Lorimer, addressing Grogrum.

" And mademoiselle knows her own engagement, and the fine for any breach of it. If mademoiselle refuse to dance to-night, she owes me two hundred pounds, and I'll have it to the last penny. So, once for all, does she come?"

Mademoiselle Chateauroux, who was visibly cowed by the catastrophe taking place, seemed about to rise, when Lorimer again spoke,—

" I invited this lady here; of course I pay the expenses of the evening."

The dancer started up in a flutter of surprise; Sir Harrowby Trumps shrugged his shoulders, and whistled to himself; De Witz pressed his host's foot beneath the table, and the manager stared in amazement on the group.

" Are you serious?" he gasped.

" I am not in the habit of allowing considerations of expense to come between me and my enjoyments," Lorimer said.

" Very good, sir," replied Grogrum. " In that case I suppose I am safe; but the public, sir—the audience will be dreadfully disappointed, I assure you."

" And are you called upon to bear the disappointment of the public, Mr. Grogrum ?" asked Lorimer, gravely.

The *impressario* shrugged his shoulders, shook his head, and smiled knowingly, while Mademoiselle Chateauroux, bounding from the sofa, flung herself into the attitude in which the heroines of the ballet are supposed to invoke blessings on their lovers, exclaiming,—

" *Ce cher Lorimer !—comme il est généreux !—dis-donc c'est superbe ! — C'est magnifique ! — c'est à la Louis Quatorze !*"

" Sit down, Favoritta," said Lorimer.

There was another uneasy pause. Lorimer had flung himself back in his chair, and was gazing earnestly at his companions. A bitter, scornful smile, which welled up from the bottom of his heart, had just begun to curl his lip, and the idea, " And are such beings necessary to my happiness ?" had just begun to suffuse his brain, when a sinister side-look from Sir Harrowby Trumps, and a furtive glance from the black eyes of Mademoiselle Chateauroux, both of them evidently interrogative as to whether his pre-occupation was caused by regret for what he had done, changed the bitter smile into a loud, reckless laugh.

" So—bah !" he exclaimed ; " to Satan with thought ! Waiters, more wine—clean glasses !—Grogrum, sit down ! Bumpers ! bumpers ! every one of you ! You must drink—I shall, and you must ! Now for a night of it ! Shade of Alcibiades ! shade of Richelieu, hover in the perfume of the wine ! Come hither, Favoritta. Your bright eyes cost bright gold. Bah ! don't pout — they're worth the price ! Come ! fill to the brim — to the brim — to the brim ! We four human Jack-o'-lanterns carouse to our empress—our goddess—la Reine des Feu Follets !"

CHAPTER II.

THE SPIDER IN THE WEB.

BLANE, the steward of Clement Lorimer, after he had delivered at the stage-door the letter he was charged with, and another besides, as we have seen in the last chapter, continued his walk down Whitehall towards Abingdon Street. In all wide London there is not a drearier district than that lying near the river's bank, to the westward of the Abbey. The ground was once a swamp, where the dull waters of the Thames soaked into the earth, and nourished rank crops of slimy bulrushes and creeping aquatic plants. And still the place seems to retain an unwholesome savour of the original marsh. The paving-stones are damp when other streets are dry, and at high tides water-drops come oozing through the grimy walls of frowsy underground cellars. The aspect of the quarter is one of shabby, smouldering decay; it does not appear dead, but palsy-stricken. The houses are irregular in structure, heavy, ghastly, and grim. Some of them have been brave in their day, for they shew antique porches and massive, carved lintels. But mean dwellings stand side by side with these faded mansions: shabby cookshops, where unwholesome-looking meat simmers and soddens all day in the steaming windows; and low, gloomy public-houses; and rank-smelling chandler-shops, illuminated at night by feebly-burning yellow tallow candles. The streets are narrow, dark, ill-paved, neglected. Mud encrusts the lower part of the walls. The windows are small, and dusty, and dirt-stained. There is neither stir, nor show, nor comfort, about the place. It looks cursed. If we wished for a house where we should be likely to hear dim, rumbling noises in the dead of the night, and echoing taps against the mouldy wainscoting, and spectral footsteps creaking in dark, nailed-up rooms, and the nibbling and scampering of rats in cellars and choked-up drains, and the beating of death-watches in damp, crumbling walls,—we should, we say, if we wished for such a dwelling, go and look for it in Abingdon Street, Westminster; and after looking, we should probably fix upon the very house before which Blane paused, and into which, by the aid of a latch-key, he proceeded.

As the steward pushed open the mudded door with its heavy rusted knocker, the waning light of the summer evening shone faintly into a dark, fusty-smelling lobby, carpetted with half-rotten matting, and furnished with one or two rickety chairs, and when he closed the portal behind him, he remained in almost total darkness. With the readi-

ness of one accustomed to the locality, Blane groped his
way towards the stairs, but he had not ascended many of
them when a low, half-choked sound of sobbing, caused him
to pause suddenly. Then there came the creak of footsteps,
as of a heavy man pacing furiously up and down a room.

"He's in one of his moods," Blane muttered; "I dare
not cross him till the hour be past."

He sat down upon the stairs, and listened intently. Presently the voice of a man, a loud, but hoarse and exhausted
voice, was heard, raised in furious exclamation.

"There!—there!" it shouted; "back! touch me not!
—am I not doing your will?—I must do it—you know that
well! You drive me on with that withered, fleshless, merci-
less arm, that stretches down through two centuries!"

"He's mad," murmured Blane; "I often thought it,
now I'm sure of it."

"Father and son," repeated the voice,—"father and
son, have we not been obedient for centuries? In the Netherlands, in Holland, in England, have we ever spared, ever
flinched, from the work set before us to do? Be merciful!
spare Him! He is the last!—our blood is in his veins!
—our blood!—the blood of the Benosas! Spare!—spare!
—spare!" And the voice was lost in an agony of sobs.

"There's some deep secret in all this," thought Blane;
"if he's mad, it is what is on his mind that has made him so.
He's an awful man!"

There was a pause. The mood of the maniac, for such
he seemed, appeared to have undergone a change, and he
suddenly uttered a loud, discordant burst of laughter.

"Ha! ha!" he screamed, "am I turned chicken-
hearted?—do I shrink from the Vendetta—I—the art of the
Benosas? Never fear! I'll do it! SHE is gone, and HE
will follow! Ha!—oh, 'tis a wild tale! but I am worthy of
you, fathers! I'll track him down—hunt him down—crush
him! Look ye, I see you all, and do I blench? I can see
your faces gleaming in the darkness! I see you, old Raphael Benosa, as you looked two centuries ago in the old
house at Antwerp, when one of the two lights went out. I
see you, Mark Benosa, as you looked when, on the gangway
of the St. Nicholas, you wished Louise Vanderstein a goodly
passage, a hundred years ago. I see—I see you all!—and

do I shrink?—do I fear? No! I will do it, I tell you, and, when it is done, the Vendetta will be over and our family will be gone, and our blood dried up, and we will haunt this earth no more; but we shall cease from troubling, and at last—at last—we shall be at rest!"

A loud outbreak of mingled laughter and weeping wound up this extraordinary rhapsody, and then came a heavy fall, as of a man upon a bed or sofa.

Blane sat shuddering upon the stairs, the blood curdling in his veins.

" The paroxysm is over for the present," he said, "but he must have time to recover a little. He'll die in Bedlam, that's sure; but till then he's a good paymaster, and I'm his faithful—spy."

Then, after allowing about five minutes to elapse, he felt his way up the stairs, and stopping at the door of a room on the first floor, knocked. There was soon heard a stir within as of a man rising from a lying posture, and the same voice as he had already heard, but speaking in weak and exhausted tones, bade him enter.

The room, which was almost dark, was scantily and meanly furnished. A very old-fashioned _secrétoire_, littered with papers, stood opposite the curtained window. Near it was a worn arm-chair, and behind that a very large black sofa, reclining on the pillows of which lay a man.

" I have been ill, Blane," he said; "my head is not what it ought to be;" and he wiped his forehead with a handkerchief, and then squeezed it with both hands. " These nervous attacks grow on me — I must have advice — I — I — my brain is wandering yet—it seems as if I had just waked up out of a nightmare."

Blane muttered a few commonplace words of condolence.

" Light the lamp!" said the other abruptly.

Blane bestirred himself, and by the help of a box of chemical matches lighted a small lamp. Then, standing in an attitude of respectful attention, he gazed upon the being before him. Our readers have doubtless recognised Michael Benosa. Twenty-three years have elapsed since we saw him, and they have done the work of forty. When his wife died, Benosa was not above twenty-three. His appearance now was that of a man considerably over sixty; he was miserably

D

wasted in person; his hair was thin and long, and perfectly white; his cheeks hollow and sunk, the bones of the face and forehead standing prominently out beneath the clammy yellow skin, which was deeply seamed with those myriads of minute lines which appeared to be stamped as a distinctive mark upon his family, and which became more numerous and more distinct as each member of it advanced in years. The eyes of Benosa alone retained somewhat of their former brilliancy; but now they gleamed and glared with a fierce, baleful, and unnatural light. Those who are accustomed to the appearance of the eye in cases of mania would at once pronounce that Benosa was suffering from chronic disease of the brain—probably induced by continuous mental emotion, which had so far exaggerated an enthusiasm in the discharge of a particular agonising task, as to convert it into a species of monomania, which occasionally, however, as in the paroxysm we have seen, suffered a partial and temporary revulsion from its own very intensity, and became for a moment directed in favour of the object the destruction of which it was generally bent upon effecting.

" Now to business !" said Benosa, slowly; and, sitting down to the desk, he opened a manuscript book, took up a pen, and jotted down Blane's replies to his inquiries.

" Clement Lorimer is deeply in debt ? "

" He is—over head and ears."

" All claims against him have been purchased by me ? "

" They have. You can crush him by shutting your hand."

" Where is he now ? "

" Dining at Richmond with Mademoiselle Chateauroux of the Opera, Sir Harrowby Trumps, and Captain De Witz."

" Yet Mademoiselle Chateauroux dances to-night ? "

" Mr. Lorimer persuaded her to break her engagement, partly by the gift of a diamond necklace, which cost him seven hundred pounds."

" Is the money paid ? "

" I paid it to Rundell and Bridge's—here is the receipt.'

" But Mademoiselle Chateauroux renders herself liable in a penalty to the management for breach of engagement ? "

" She does, to the amount of two hundred pounds a-night ? "

" What is her excuse ? "

" Indisposition. Dr. Gumbey signed the certificate."

" Dr. Gumbey is a clever man ; he attended a near friend of mine once, and knew perfectly of what she died ;—it was a curious case. Is the management aware of the scene of Mademoiselle Chateauroux's indisposition ? "

" It is — I gave the information. I have no doubt but that, ere this time, Mr. Grogrum is on his way to Richmond ; and I have as little doubt but that Mr. Lorimer will become responsible for the amount Mademoiselle Chateauroux is liable to pay to Mr. Grogrum."

" Good — good," said Benosa ; " the Star and Garter is not a cheap house, but to-day it gives an especially expensive dinner. Let us see : the diamond necklace, value seven hundred pounds ; the broken engagement, value two hundred pounds : total dinner-bill, nine hundred pounds, besides some little extras, which we need not set down."

Benosa paused, chuckled, flashed his eyes triumphantly about the room, and then resumed,—

" Lorimer is thoroughly dissipated, thoroughly extravagant, thoroughly selfish. What do you think he would do were he flung penniless on the world to-morrow ? "

" Shoot himself."

" Ah! you think so ? Good—we shall see. Does he love Mademoiselle Chateauroux ? "

" As a child loves a toy."

" Then we need not mind about her. He has a horse entered for the Derby ? "

" Yes, the Favourite ; the odds are two to one for Snapdragon against the field. Nothing is thought to have a chance with Snapdragon."

" Indeed — ah ! Take your money." He handed over a rouleau of gold. " Here, in this room, at this hour, this day week ! You will be punctual."

Blane bowed respectfully, pocketed the sovereigns, and withdrew. As the door closed, Benosa called him back :—

" The odds are two to one for the Favourite against the Field ? "

" Yes."

" Well, do you want to make your fortune ? "

" Yes."

" Back the Field against the Favourite."

CHAPTER III.

THE JOCKEY.

WE are again in the room overlooking Hyde Park, where Clement Lorimer is lounging, as is his wont before dressing, on a combination of easy chairs. Apparently his musings are of no agreeable sort, for his brow is clouded, and his lips bear the mark of having been bitten till the blood came.

" I'm a fool!" he muttered to himself—" a thrice-sodden fool, to live the life I do! What do they care for me, but for what they can get out of me?—Ay, what does *she* care? Bah! they're all alike, men and women. And my money—it may stop any day: there's no certainty—it may stop, and leave me, perhaps, some forty thousand worse than a beggar. *Mort de ma vie*, as Favoritta says. I'll pull up—I'll—I'll make a grand *coup* on this Derby—I'll bet as man never did before.—Snapdragon shall win as horse never did before, and then I'll have the yacht out and be off—off from Europe, and try to find some place where there is no civilisation to make people savages, and no religion to make them heathens."

A footman appeared at the door, and announced laconically,—

" Tim Flick."

" The man I wanted — up with him directly !" and straightway Tim Flick appeared.

He was a very little man, not five feet high, and a perfect marvel of thinness; he had an old, wrinkled, meagered face, with two sharp grey eyes, and the facial muscles worked under the dry, tawny skin, like sharply-tugged whipcords. His body seemed formed of nothing but skin, bone, and sinew; his arms were long and wiry; and his legs, which were very bandy, were of a uniform thickness, or rather thinness, from the thigh to the ankle. This odd-looking personage wore a white cravat fastened with a huge silver horse-shoe, a tight-fitting coat, the waist of which appeared rather below the hips, and which was garnished with a vast number of outside pocket-holes; and he had encased his flute-like legs in a pair of corduroys, which clung to him like a second skin, and were ornamented with half-a-dozen buttons above the ankles.

"Bravo, Flick!—you're come in the nick of time!"

"Yes," was the reply, in a harsh, dry, grating voice; "I got the office, an' I made the running."

"Well, sit down."

Mr. Flick deposited his grey hat upon the carpet, took a cotton handkerchief out of it, with which he appeared about to dust the chair; but, suddenly changing his purpose, he dusted the seat of his trousers instead, and then, perching himself on the extreme edge of the *fauteuil* which Lorimer pushed towards him, waited to be spoken to.

"Well, Flick, how does the horse train? All right down at Hawleyden, eh?"

Flick looked cautiously around: the door was closed, and the windows fastened. Then, leaning forward, he said in a low, hoarse whisper,—

"It's a safe thing—it is! I've a-ridden seventeen Derbies and won five, and I tell you so. Inwest, Mr. Lorimer; inwest!"

"He trains well, then? I'll go down to-morrow and see him gallop."

"I was pretty nigh, as I may say, born in a stable, and I never see such a pace as that 'ere 'oss can put out. I'm proud o' him—as proud o' him as if he wor mine—every ounce of horse-flesh o' him, Mr. Lorimer!"

"How about the other horses? I've heard no gossip—hav'n't been at the Corner for a week."

"Don't tell me, of other 'osses!" replied the jockey. "We're safe. I know 'em all—saw 'em all take their gallops. There ain't the stride of our Snap in any two of them. Barring accidents, Mr. Lorimer, I'll win by four lengths, and not a hair turned. I've a-ridden seventeen Derbies, Mr. Lorimer. and won five; and this I'll say, there ain't a 'oss going as 'll touch Snapdragon—unless, mayhap, the ghost of Flying Childers come on the Downs, with the devil for a jock——"

"Look here, Flick," said Lorimer; "I believe you to be an honest fellow!"

"Thank ye, sir—thank ye! I'm no better than I ought to be in many things, but I never sold a race. I've a-ridden seventeen——"

"Yes, yes," interrupted Lorimer, "I know. Well, Flick, this race must be won!"

"It shall, sir. Gents may laugh at a jockey's word——"

"I laugh at the word of no man who I believe pledges it sincerely."

"No, sir, no; but we're the dog as has an ill name, and there's a good many on us as deserves it—there's no denying that. However, sir, as I said, I never sold a race; I may have done a many things wrong, but I never sold a race to any one, and it's not likely I'd do it to you, who has been kind to me and mine, and who——"

"Well, well, you fully believe that Snapdragon can win?"

"I've laid out every penny I have in the world on it, and I'd a done so if it wor twice as much."

"Snapdragon can win, and you ride Snapdragon; therefore Snapdragon will win."

"Sir," said the jockey, "the stakes is as good as in your pocket!"

Lorimer mused.

"You should ha' felt that horse rise under you, sir! His muscles is like ropes o' steel, and his wind is as good arter a sweating gallop as though he was standing idle in the stall."

"Of course, Flick, I need not tell you to keep a good look-out in the stable."

"Lord bless ye, sir, I sleep in it! And there's Thor and Odin, your two Saint Bernards, chained on each side of the stall. He'll be a clever fellow, sir, that'll play tricks with Snapdragon!"

"Bravo, Flick! I'll be at Hawleyden to-morrow, and in the meantime my mind's at ease—I trust you, my man —I trust you."

"If it wouldn't be asking over-much?" said the jockey, holding out his brown, horny hand.

Lorimer shook it heartily.

"Win this Derby, Tim Flick, and you're a made man!"

"Mr. Lorimer, I've a-ridden seventeen——"

"Good—never mind that now. Have something—wine? —a thimble-full of brandy?"

"No, Mr. Lorimer, with your leave, not a drop."

" Why, man, it will do you good — with your hard exercise and sweatings."

" After Snapdragon is placed, Mr. Lorimer, but not before. You mind the Mazeppa Derby!"

" Certainly — five years ago — you rode the second horse, Firefly. It was a close thing — Mazeppa won by a neck."

" Mazeppa won by a tumbler of champagne!" said the jockey—" a tumbler of champagne I drank in the paddock."

" Ah?" inquired Lorimer, " tell me how it was."

" It needs a clear head, Mr. Lorimer, to ride a Derby. There ain't no excitement in the world equal to it. I hadn't had much breakfast that day; I couldn't look at anything to eat, and I felt faint when I was on my 'oss — I suppose my backers see it, for one of them says, says he, ' Take a drop of champagne, Tim,' says he; so I emptied the glass, and sure enough I felt the better for it. Well, we came to the scratch, I felt the wine in my head — but it was quite comfortable and pleasant like—and I thought, ' I'll win, I'm sure on it.' Well, ' Go!' says the starter; and go we did. Sir, a good 'oss under one is always exciting, but a racer at the pace is enough to madden one. It did me. What with the fury of the gallop, and the rush of the air, and the roar of the people, I felt as if neither heaven nor hell could hold me. I headed 'em all in the first hundred strides — I dug the spurs into the 'oss — it answered me, sir — I felt how it rose — every time I punished it. Then I looked over my shoulder, there was green turf between me and the second 'oss. I got sure of my race — we came up the rise like a whirlwind — and round the corner; and the broad course, sir, and the swarming crowd, and the carriages, and the stands, all flashed on me like a dream. It was just then I felt Fairfly flag in his stride — I welted him with the whip, and dug his flanks with the spur. He swerved, but he didn't answer as before. Then my head began to swim, sir — I wasn't cool from the first, but then I lost all presence of mind. I pressed the 'oss—checked him—punished him, but I couldn't work him with hands and knees as I felt I ought. Then I hear the second 'oss close on his haunches — I had given Firefly too much to do at first, and he couldn't keep it up — I rode him as bold as ever man did — but with no judgment, sir. Mazeppa come abreast of me — I could see his rider was cool and comfortable. We glared in each other's eyes as we went stride for stride together, until, just fifty yards from the post, he lifted his 'oss—lifted it, sir, past me—and won by a neck. I had the best 'oss, but my 'oss hadn't the best rider; no one blamed me, but I made an oath then —and I kissed my mother's Bible on it—that never, s'help me God! from that day, would I touch drink for a month before the Derby day."

"And I won't press you," rejoined Lorimer. "How 's your son? Does he like his place in the City?"

"He does, sir, he does; and he blesses you as got it for him. He's a good boy, sir, is Dicky, and fond of his old father. I hope I'll get him kep off the turf, though—sir——"

Lorimer smiled.

"Ay, sir, I've had my share of luck in it, too. I've a-ridden seventeen Derbies, and won five; but it ain't a good trade, and I hope Dicky 'll stick to his pen, and never go a calculating the odds, nor a backing either Field or Favourite."

"What! not even Snapdragon?"

The jockey winced—smiled—blew his nose, and fidgeted uneasily. His audience was over, and presently, with a profusion of bows, he took his leave. On the stairs he met Blane, but resolutely declined that worthy's invitation to have a snack in the steward's pantry.

"But—I say," he whispered, "you're a true blue sort o' chap, and you belong to us. Back the Favourite. Snap is to win: it's on the books. Inwest, and no mistake."

Blane marched slowly into his own room, sat down, and meditated.

"I wish," pondered Blane, "that nobody could tell lies but myself, what a world it would be then to be sure! Now, here's an honest jockey; that's at once a fool and a phenome-non; but he is honest, and he believes master's horse is going to win. Again, there's the old hunks in Abingdon Street, he's not honest, but he's deep—deep, and he believes master's horse is going to lose; what shall I do? Ah! I'll do what I've done all my life—I'll try to butter my bread on both sides—I'll hedge."

CHAPTER IV

THE SNAKE AND THE BIRD.

In a dim court off Fenchurch Street is the counting-house of Messrs. Shiner and Maggs. The establishment occupies the ground-floor; and if you have business there you enter a large low-roofed room lighted on dark days by gas, and behold a dozen or so of clerks scribbling busily, or handing huge ledgers about from one to the other over the brass rails of the desks. From this room two doors, of frosted glass, lead to the private business apartments of the two members of the firm. On one of these portals is painted ' Mr. Shiner's room," on the other " Mr. Maggs' room;" and if you were suddenly to push open the first, you would probably find Mr. Shiner drinking soda-water and sherry, and reading a sporting paper; while, if you were to swing open the other, you would, in all likelihood, discover Mr. Maggs drinking nothing at all, but deeply absorbed in the report of the mission to Quashybungo,—a pleasant tropical coast, where the good missionaries have got possession of some twenty square miles of land and two converts, who are continually striking for more wages. People wonder what could have brought Messrs. Shiner and Maggs together, but together they are, and carrying on, principally under the management of their head clerk, a very thriving business.

It is, however, with the clerks, not with the merchants, that we have now to do. Nine o'clock is striking from a neighbouring church tower, and the former-named gentlemen are dropping hurriedly in. Each, as he arrives, signs his name in a book, and a porter stands ready, after the five minutes of grace have expired, to draw a line below the last signature, and thus expose the misdeeds of the lazy and the lagging. The five minutes are nearly up when the two junior clerks arrive together. The names they inscribe are Richard Flick and Owen Dombler, and having hurriedly scribbled these appellations, they proceed to their desks, in

.he darkest corner of the office; and as they check off the
entries of the books under their care, manage to carry on a
whispered and interrupted conversation.

Flick is an open-featured, freckled, country-reared-look-
ing lad, the expression of his face simple, ingenuous, and
confiding; Dombler is a pale London boy, with long, sharp
features; ugly, pinched, and bilious-looking.

"Dick," he said to his companion, "you're quite
browned by the sun since Saturday."

"Yes; I've been to Hawleyden to see the old boy at the
stables. Oh, ain't he a good old fellow—just! He says he'll
get us both into the grand stand at the Derby; and the horse
he's to ride — Mr. Lorimer's horse, Snapdragon — you know,
is sure to win."

"Ay, but will they let us off? old Maggs hates races."

"Yes, but Shiner don't; and the governor is to ask Mr.
Lorimer to ask Mr. Shiner to give us a holiday."

"I'd like to go. I hav'n't had a bit of fun since Spiffler
left our lodgings."

"Who was Spiffler?"

"Oh, don't you know? he was an odd sort of chap —
literary they said—connected with newspapers, and theatres,
and all that. He stayed in bed all day, and was out all
night, and paid for his lodgings in orders for the play —
little, dirty pieces of paper, with 'Admit two,' and 'Before
seven o'clock,' written on them. I never get an order
now."

"Oh, I'll manage that for you, if you care about it.
can get as many as I like."

"You!"

"Yes—orders or almost any thing. Hush.—in your ear
—I never told you of my new friend."

"No, who?"

"I don't know his name, I call him — the man at the
eating-house. It's an old gentleman who has taken such a
fancy to me—oh, such a nice old chap, he goes every day to
the eating-house at the same time that I do. We sit in the
same box, so he got to speak to me, and he tells me such
lots of things, and gives me treats, and I like him so —
only I don't know, sometimes I'm afraid of him—he's so
solemn and grave, and has such staring black eyes, that

when he looks at you you somehow feel as if he was burning you."

"What is he like? I never saw him at Boffle's."

"No; you don't dine till after me, and by that time he's gone."

"Well, but what is he like?"

"Oh, an old man with black sunk eyes that glare so, and grey hair, and a thin pale face, and long skinny hands, and funny marks, like threads all along his cheeks and forehead."

"And will you see him to-day?"

"Oh, I suppose so; he's got such a manner, and talks so to one. I've told him every bit about myself, and what I am here—yes, and about you too, and ——"

"Take care, Dick; perhaps he's a cheat, and wants to get information about the house."

This supposition staggered Richard Flick for a moment, but he speedily recovered himself, and treated the suggestion with disdain.

"A cheat—he's more like a bishop—he's as good a man as any in the world—he's as good as my father;" and then, in a lower tone, "But even—even if he were a scamp, do you think he'd get anything out of me? Oh, you may call me countrified, but I tell you, Owey, I'm down—down as a hammer."

Dombler gave a grin and a shrug, and at that moment the head clerk called out,—

"Now then, you two, you're chattering a deal too much for work. Take care there's not an error in your books—that's all."

And so the tasks were plied in silence until two o'clock, when Richard Flick, after interchanging meaning looks with his comrade, went out to dinner.

Now, not only that day, but for several days thereafter, it was a mighty puzzle with the *habitués* of Boffle's, who the old gentleman might be who seemed, in the vernacular of the speculators, so "thick" with young Flick of Shiner and Maggs. His dinner—generally a plate of beef and greens—bolted down, the boy would lend a devouring ear to the whispered discourse of the old man, the pair being generally ensconced together in the furthest corner of the most deserted box; and those who stole furtive glances at the couple, and watched the eager, upturned face of the boy, and the cold, clammy, glistening eyes which were fixed upon it, and caught the low-murmured, but deeply-musical tone of the voice, which the boy appeared to drink up with his very soul,—the people who saw and heard all this thought of the stories they had read of fascination, and how tropical birds flutter, screaming from the branches, into the very jaws of the serpent beneath.

To be sure, it was a vulgar place for charms and enchantments that cheap city eating-house, with its steaming atmosphere, redolent of over-cooked meat and simmering watery vegetables, and crowded all day long with hungry clerks munching large and small plates of boiled and roast, and ceaselessly demanding more " breads," and additional " half-pints," and inquiring whether the potatoes were " nobby mealy 'uns," and whether the waiter could, upon his credit as a gentleman, affirm that the pork was " in prime cut." It was a vulgar, shabby, uncomfortable, hot, steaming, greasy place; but there, nevertheless, day after day, the young clerk remained up to the very last moment he could devote to dinner, in earnest converse with his unknown friend.

And in the meantime Richard's general manner became gradually silent and pre-occupied. The chief clerk of Shiner and Maggs had no longer any necessity for checking his chattering propensities. Dombler questioned him, quizzed him, threatened to quarrel with him, but could obtain nothing save the very driest answers. The lad's character seemed suddenly changed. He gave Dombler the orders he had promised him, but without any further explanations as to the old gentleman at the eating-house. In fact the conversation which we have just narrated was all that passed between them upon the subject. Dombler bored perseveringly for further information,—

" What had happened ?" " Happened ! Nothing had happened. What made him ask ?" " What was the matter ?" " Nothing was the matter. Why should he think that anything was the matter ?" " Had Shiner and Maggs been saying anything ?" " No, of course ; what could they have to say ?"

So Dombler shook his head, gave it up, and waited for the mood to change, concluding either that his friend was labouring under a tremendous fit of the sulks, or that something unpleasant, which he did not care to communicate, had occurred at home.

So stood matters, when, on the Monday before the Derby, Flick repaired at his dinner hour to Boffle's. The old gentleman was there as usual; Dick ate little or nothing, which his companion observing, and attributing his want of appetite to illness, caused some hot spirits and water to be prepared, and pressed the boy to drink. We have now to let the reader into the secret of this apparently odd companionship.

"Richard," said Michael Benosa — we presume he has been recognised,—"you say you love your father?"

"Dearly; you know I do."

"And to make him comfortable in his old age would be the joy of your youth and the pride of your manhood?"

"Yes—yes—a thousand times yes!"

"You know that old bones cannot bestride racers, and that the men who own racers are proverbially selfish and indifferent to the welfare of those—men or brutes—who have won for them their cups or their stakes, when the strength and the speed, or the skill which gained those trophies, have passed away?"

Richard nodded acquiescence.

"Well, your father cannot ride many more Derbies. He is past fifty."

"How do you know that?"

"No matter, I do know; and you have seen, Richard, that I know many things besides."

The boy half sighed.

"Well, have you considered what I said yesterday?"

"I cannot do it."

"Reflect, Richard. Have I not your good, and your father's good, at heart? A month ago I was a stranger to you. I came accidentally to dine at this place, I was struck with your face—your air. I liked both. I am an odd, eccentric old man, I have whims, and take caprices and sudden tastes. I liked you—we soon got acquainted; we got to be friends—good friends I hope; and so you told me about yourself, and about what you are, and what you did, what you liked, and what you hoped for. I encouraged you, sympathised with you, and wished well to you, and you liked the old man's talk and the old man's stories. Is it not so?"

"Yes, until—until that day——" and Richard hesitated.

"Good—go on. You would say until the day when, becoming thoroughly acquainted with your particular position, and your particular opportunities of acquiring certain knowledge by which vast amounts of money can be gained, I laid before you a simple, harmless plan, by means of which in a week from this time you may be the possessor of a fortune."

"Yes, but the means; it would be to do evil that good may come of it."

"And why not? Listen, Richard. Near us is the cathedral of St. Paul's. You have seen the paintings on the cupola; they were executed by Sir William Thornhill. One day, forgetful of the dizzy height whereon he stood, the artist walked backward, step by step, to watch the effect of a group he had just painted. He neared the edge of the planking— still, step by step, he unwittingly approached it. A stranger was on the scaffolding, he saw the artist's peril, he saw that another backward pace and he would be a mangled mass on the marble pavement below. To call to him would be but to hasten his fall, so he seized a brush and flung a daubed smirch over the dainty flesh tones and the pencilled draperies; the artist rushed forward to save his work; the painting was indeed injured, but the painter was preserved. Evil had been done that good might come of it. And was not the doer of the little evil the author of the great good?"

Poor Richard was no match for the subtle casuistry of his antagonist. He could only murmur some argument at once unintelligible and inaudible.

"But in this case," resumed the tempter, "there is not even a little evil to be done. It is only the semblance of evil. The law has rightly said, that he who shall imitate another's signature, with the intention or in the hope of obtaining another's goods, commits a crime. But the law does not say that he who imitates another's signature, without any such intention, is guilty of offence. Suppose you wished to imitate the signature of Charles the First; to imitate it without intent to deceive any body, could that be called a crime? It would only be a feat of penmanship, like drawing a swan of flourishes. One would be just as harmless as the other."

"But Shiner and Maggs are not dead and gone two hundred years ago, like Charles the First."

"No; but the imitation will no more hurt them—can no more hurt them, than it would or could hurt Charles the First. Crime consists in intent to injure, not in the act of injuring."

"Still what you want me to do is forgery."

"No—it is only imitation. Suppose you go to your room, and draw a check for a thousand pounds, and sign it with the name of Rothschild, and then tear it up or burn it,—you perform an act of imitation. But if, instead of destroying the paper, you present it at the counter of a bank as genuine, then you commit an act of forgery."

"But in this case I am not to destroy the paper without presenting it."

"No—but I am. You doubt me? Fie, fie, Richard! Why should I present it? I would then be the forger, because the presentation makes the uttering, and the uttering constitutes the crime. I should thus be punished, not you."

"But why do you not commit the for—— I mean, make the imitation yourself?"

"Because I am not at all acquainted with the signatures to be imitated, and because, even if I were, I am old, and my hands shake."

He held forth his long, skinny fingers—they trembled with a palsied motion.

"You say that the reason why you wish for the imitation cheque of Shiner and Maggs is just to shew it, to flash it about among people who are not intimately acquainted with the signatures of City firms——?"

"Precisely: so as to get credit, and by means of credit to get riches."

"Is credit necessary in betting?"

"Credit is necessary whenever money transactions are concerned. Do you think a man would bet five thousand with a person who might not have the means of paying if he lost——"

"And do you mean to bet five thousand?"

"Five thousand—ten—twenty, if I can; the more I bet the more we win."

" But if we should lose ?"

" Lose! What did your father tell you, last Sunday when you were at Hawleyden?"

" That Snapdragon will run fourteen inches for every foot that any other horse in England can cover."

" Good, he can win. The question then is, Will he be ridden to win?"

" Sir," exclaimed the boy, with a glowing face, " my father never sold a race."

" I know it; the race, so far as human calculation can go, is then already won."

" But human calculations are not infallible."

" Granted; but we must act on the best calculations we can make. We may die to-night, but we do not the less provide for to-morrow. See, if I have the cheque, I get the credit; if I get the credit, I make the bet; if I make the bet I win the money."

There was a pause.

" I—am—afraid," murmured the boy.

Benosa, unseen by his companion, made a gesture of violent anger, and then resumed the conversation in his softest and most musical tones.

" Wednesday come and gone," he said, as if speaking to himself, " and fortune will have come with it,—fortune destined for high and holy ends,—that the poor may be enriched, and the aged pass their evening days in peace."

Richard's face flushed, then grew deadly pale. The tempter eyed him keenly. Then the boy set his teeth, and clenched his hands, and said, " I will do it."

" A bold boy and a good son," said Benosa; and then in a whisper, " Have you the cheque?"

" Yes."

" I knew it," said the old man to himself. " He kept his hand in his pocket, and I knew the precious paper was grasped there."

Richard stole a quick glance round,—no one was looking, and he rapidly passed an envelope to his companion. Benosa opened it leisurely.

" Take care!—take care, for Heaven's sake!" whispered the clerk, in an agony of apprehension.

" There is no fear, Richard,—no fear whatever," replied

his companion.   He glanced at the contents of the packet.
It was a cheque on Messrs. Smith, Payne, and Smith,
in Richard's writing, and purported to be for the amount
of five thousand pounds.   The signature was an approxi-
mation to that of Shiner and Maggs.   As Benosa read
it, Richard made a half snatch, as though he would recover
possession of the fatal document.   Benosa observed the
motion.

" My dear boy," he said, " if you repent what you have
done, you may undo it.   Here is the cheque ;" and he held it
out to Richard, who took it, and gazed for a moment on the
face of his companion.   It was calm and smiling, and the
eyes had their usual glassy, lustrous stare.

" No," he muttered.   " No—I was a fool—there, take
t ;" and he returned the cheque.

" Would you like it to be destroyed by me or by yourself ?"

" By myself," said Richard, in a choking voice, and
wiping the perspiration from his forehead.

" Good—by the time the horses start it will be on its
way to you.   Shall I address to Shiner and Maggs ?"

" No, no—to my lodgings."

" Then, on Wednesday evening, by the six o'clock deli-
very, it will be there."

" Oh, indeed — indeed, I have done this innocently.   I
have done this for my father—my poor, old, good father ! On
you be the shame, if there be shame, — and on you the guilt,
if there be guilt !"

Having uttered this burst of passion, the boy flung his
arms on the table, and rested his head on them.

When he raised it the old gentleman was gone.

CHAPTER V.

THE FIELD AGAINST THE FAVOURITE.

It is the night before the Derby, and the whole of sporting London — and for that matter, a great part of London to

E

wh:ct the term cannot in strictness be applied — is in a state
of nervous restlessness, anticipating the chances of the morrow. The thousands who have risked money upon the race
are on the *qui vive* for any stray information which may
enable them, even at the last hour, to improve their prospects
of success. Reports and rumours fly hither and thither from
mouth to mouth. The last editions of the evening papers
are ransacked for hints from sporting correspondents, and the
latest shade of variation in the betting at the Corner. The
sporting taverns are crowded with those who are knowing on
the turf and those who desire to be thought so. Mysterious
intimations — half-spoken, half-retracted hints of one horse,
which is to be made "safe," of another which, at the eleventh
hour, will be "scratched," of one stable which has "declared
to win," of another which boasts a wonderful "dark horse;"
secret information touching one steed which, it is whispered,
has mysteriously fallen lame; dark doubts flung out as to a
flaw in the pedigree of another, and certain news of the
style in which a third had that morning taken its sweating
gallop — all this chaos of hints, nods, winks, morsels of exclusive intelligence, and scraps of secret information, is discussed, amplified, canvassed, disputed, amid the fumes of
tobacco and spirits, until the young gentleman who has
started a "book," and dropped into the sporting public-house
in quest of information for his hedging projects, drops out
again, utterly bewildered by the mass of contradictory intelligence and diverging advice which a dozen of high au-
thorities, each in possession of authentic and exclusive
particulars, have favoured him with.

And the excitement is not confined to the more vulgar
haunts of gentlemen who speculate on the turf. Wherever
you go the words, "Snapdragon," "Odds," "Field," "Favourite," "Safe to win," strike your ear. You catch them in
the whispered converse of the opera-box; you distinguish
them in the noisy hum of the theatre when the act-drop has
fallen; even ladies catch the universal epidemic, and lay
reckless wagers of gloves and flasks of eau-de-Cologne; the
clubs echo with the chances of to-morrow; and the debate in
the House of Commons must be exciting indeed, if groups of
members, under the galleries and in the galleries, be not
clustered together, eagerly discussing the merits of the line

of horses which will be to-morrow drawn up before the
starter on Epsom Downs.

Snugly ensconced in his well-littered stall, in the training
stables of Hawleyden, stands one of the unconscious objects
of all this excitement, all this anxiety. Snapdragon, as he
arches his neck, tosses his head, and neighs and snorts in the
flush of his rampant energies, has little idea of the noise his
name is making in the world. The animal itself, muffled in
warm cloths, and the padded sides of his stall, shew the care
of the comfort and the health of the racer.

The hour of ten can be faintly heard tolled by Epsom
clock, when the door of Snapdragon's stable opens, and three
gentlemen, attended by Flick the jockey, and one or two of
taken his subordinates, emerge into the yard.

" Bring the horses out, and we'll ride over to the Spread
Eagle at once," said one of the group; " I think, Flick, we
may sleep sound upon the chances of to-morrow."

" Yourself saw the 'oss, Mr. Lorimer; he couldn't be in
better condition for running," replied the jockey.

" Mind you keep him so, my old Trojan," said another of
the party, in the hoarse voice of Sir Harrowby Trumps.

" For if you don't," continued the third, " my address, in
twenty-four hours from this blessed moment, will be the Hôtel
de Suède, Brussels, — a good house that, Trumps; and if
Snap's heels should not be the speedier, I would recommend
you to patronise it. The air of Belgium is always my specific
for complaints of the money-making organs."

So saying, the party mounted their horses.

" I shall be over to-morrow morning by six, Flick —
meantime don't leave the horse — I know your people here
are honest, but they may be tampered with; and this is just
the nervous night."

" Never fear, Mr. Lorimer; I slep over the stable for a
month, and I shan't go for to be caught napping the last
night: whoever touches Snapdragon, sir, must put me out of
the way first."

" Good, I have all trust in you. Come, gentlemen,
supper waits at the Spread Eagle." And the party rode
briskly away without noticing the figure of a man, who
crouched behind a cart in a dark corner of the stable-yard.

Flick watched his patron and his friends until the ring of

their horses' hoofs died away in the distance. He then turned into the stable. It was a small building, containing four stalls, of which Snapdragon and another racer occupied the two centre ones, while, in each of the others, was chained an immensely powerful dog of the Saint Bernard breed. Both of these animals lay with their grim muzzles resting upon their outstretched forepaws, and their deep dark eyes twinkled suspiciously around, as Flick moved about the stable. The place was dimly lighted by a large dusty lamp suspended from the roof; and at one end a ladder, rising upwards through a trap-door in the ceiling, led to the garret apartment above, which, as Flick had intimated, had lately been occupied by himself.

The jockey carefully locked and bolted the stable-door, and, after casting a hasty glance at the horse, took from a large chest, which stood in the far corner of the stable, a light racing-saddle, and commenced an examination of the girths and leathers — so minute that it seemed as if every particular thread in their stitching underwent an individual scrutiny.

"All right," he murmured, as he laid the article down he then cautiously proceeded into the stall with Snapdragon, and, stooping down, appeared to occupy himself in feeling and chafing with his hands the joints and legs of the noble animal.

"Not a bit of stiffness or swelling," he muttered, as he rose and patted the neck of the racehorse. "You'll do your work to-morrow; won't you, old Snap?" he continued, speaking in a caressing voice to the horse. "You'll shew 'em the blood you come of — ay, and how Tim Flick can ride you — won't you? eh! old Snap?"

The racer, as if he understood the questions put to him, tossed his delicately-moulded head upwards, and answered by a loud shrill neigh. It had hardly subsided into silence when a low growl rose from the next stall.

"Hey! Odin!" said Flick, "what makes you angry, old dog?"

He left the racer's stall and entered that of the Saint Bernard mastiff. The dog was on its legs, straining upon the strong chain which bound him to the manger; his outstretched muzzle sniffing anxiously in the direction of the stable-window, and his muscular tail lashing his sides with long measured sweeps.

" The dog scents something," said the jockey; and just at that moment, Thor, the mastiff, in the other and further stall, took up the growling concert.

" Can there be any body lurking about the stable?" thought Flick. He went to the window and glanced out. Every thing was dark and silent. He then cautiously undid the fastenings of the door, slipped out, examined narrowly all round, but saw or heard nothing to alarm him. Then, after lingering for a moment upon the threshold, he re-entered the stable and closed the door as before. As he did so, a man cautiously slipped down from the lower branches of a huge elm which overshadowed the stable, and took up his position behind its trunk.

The night waned slowly. One by one all the lights in the buildings of Hawleyden were extinguished, except that which gleamed from the window of the stable in which stood the Favourite. Eleven had long ago struck upon the distant Epsom clock. The night breeze made a moaning music over the bare Downs, and in the creaking branches of the old elm. The stars appeared and disappeared as sailing clouds passed between them and the earth. Now and then a swallow, accidentally awakened, would twitter in the eaves. Now and then, with a loud buzzing hum, a flying beetle would shoot past upon the damp night air; and now and then the rusty weathercock which surmounted the stables would creak and rattle as a gust, fresher than ordinary, caught and twisted its painted vane. With the exception of such night noises, there was the silence of midnight over Hawleyden.

It might be one hour towards the morning when the man who descended from the elm advanced cautiously to the stable-door, and looked through the keyhole. The light still burned. He stood a moment, as if undecided. Then there was heard a recommencement of the former growling. Neither Thor nor Odin had gone to sleep. This seemed to decide the lurker, for he immediately rapped, not loudly, but distinctly, at the door. The dogs replied with a volley of hoarse baying, in the midst of which Flick's voice, demanding, in startled tones, who the knocker was, could be barely distinguished.

" Are you alone?" was the answer of the applicant.

"What's that to you? What do you want?" returned the jockey. "Be off! or I'll loose the dogs on you!"

"I am armed," replied the stranger; "and if you do I must shoot them, which I should be sorry for. I dare say they are fine animals."

There was a pause.

"I must speak with you!" continued the stranger.

"About the race?" inquired the jockey.

"About that in the second place — there is a more important matter for the first."

"But you said you was armed. How do I know you're not come here to do some mischief to the 'oss or to me?"

"Will this prove to you that my purpose is inoffensive? — see, here are my pistols." He produced the weapons he spoke of and shoved them beneath the stable-door. "Now I am defenceless," he said.

Apparently the jockey was satisfied with this demonstration of confidence, for he undid the fastenings, and, partially opening the door, held up the lamp, which he had lowered from the ceiling, to the stranger's face. It was one he had never seen before — the face of an elderly man, with keen black eyes, an aquiline nose, and thin grey hair.

"What do you want with me, and at this hour of the night?"

"Admit me, shut the door, and I will tell you," said the jockey's visitor.

"No, d—— me, tell your business first!"

"It is about your son."

"My son!" exclaimed Flick, starting backwards, and evidently alarmed. The stranger took advantage of this movement to make good his entrance.

"I trust in God, sir," said the jockey, "that there's nothin' wrong!—nothin' turned up agin the lad! Richard is a good boy, sir! It would break my heart if there was any thing wrong ——"

"I know that," said the stranger; "that is the reason I am here. Shut the door and silence those dogs." Thor and Odin were still growling at the intruder. The jockey hastily did as he was directed, and, then turning to his visitor, saw him seated upon the corn-chest, over which Flick had spread a small mattrass, and upon which he had been dozing when disturbed as we have seen.

"Now, sir, if you please," said the jockey, with considerable nervous anxiety—"now, sir, if you please, about my son—about Richard ——"

"So that is Snapdragon—that is the Favourite!" said the unknown.

Flick's suspicions as to his mission revived at the keen glance the stranger cast upon the horse, and he flung himself between his visitor and the racer.

"You need not be afraid, Mr. Flick," observed the intruder, "I shall not do any thing to the horse without your full permission."

"You had better not try," muttered the jockey.

"Nor will I —— To business."

"Ah, to business—the sooner the better."

"Good! You have a son in the firm of Shiner and Maggs —— ?"

"General agents and commission-brokers, Curney's Alley, Fenchurch Street, City," continued the jockey, with volubility.

"A fine lad—I see him often," replied the stranger. "Shiner and Maggs bank with us—with Smith, Payne, and Smith, I mean—I am a cashier in that house."

The jockey rubbed his hands nervously. He could not divine what was coming, but he feared that all was not right.

"I do a little in the sporting way, however," continued the cashier. "One must have some other amusement than counting sovereigns all day long which don't belong to us—eh, Mr. Flick?"

The jockey assented. "But what's all this here got to do with Richard?" he inquired.

"Oh, every thing in its proper time," replied the cashier. "We are very methodical, we bankers."

Flick stamped with impatience, and cast his eye towards the dogs, who from time to time shewed their teeth and snarled.

"I have invested largely this Derby, Mr. Flick," pursued the cashier, "and I've backed the Field against the Favourite."

"Then, as sure as Snapdragon stands in that stall you'll lose!"

"As sure as Snapdragon stands in that stall I'll win!"

The jockey started back.

"No tricks!" he exclaimed. "Hands off!—no tricks! —I'm awake!—I am! Oh, the d—— fool I have been to let you in! But lay a finger on that 'oss, or stir a step towards him, and by the God above both of us I'll blow your brains out with your own pistols!"

And so saying, Flick presented one of the weapons at the head of the cashier. The eyes of the latter flashed, and his nostrils dilated, but he neither shrank nor quailed, but looked steadfastly into the muzzle of the pistol, which was not two feet from his forehead.

"To return to your son," he said, with the most perfect coolness; "one of two things will happen—either Snapdragon will lose, or your son will be hanged!"

The jockey's face grew ghastly pale, and the pistol dropped upon the ground.

"What's that you mean?" he stammered, pressing his hand forcibly upon his heart, as if to control its throbbings.

"Nothing can be clearer," returned the cashier. "Look at this;" and he produced from a closely-clasped pocket-book a cheque.

"Do you know the hand in which this cheque is drawn?" said the cashier.

"Oh, God!—yes, it is Richard's!" gasped the father.

"Do you know the hand in which this cheque is signed —'Shiner and Maggs?'" continued his questioner.

"Yes—yes—it is the same as the other—it is Richard's!"

"So the hanging I spoke of, Mr. Flick, is not quite such an improbable business as you seemed to think."

The poor jockey staggered against the wall, hid his face in both of his hands, and sobbed convulsively.

Benosa—he must have been recognised—looked at him, his big black eyes flashing with excitement. Yet the expression of that terrible face was not a vindictive one; on the contrary, there was an undefinable look of pity in the gaze.

"Oh!" groaned the jockey—"oh, I thank God that his mother didn't live to see this day!"

"Your son, Mr. Flick," continued Benosa, in his former

unmoved tones, and putting the cheque carefully away in his pocket—" your son, Mr. Flick, presented the document I have shewn you, this afternoon. Fortunately for him, he presented it to me. I saw the forgery at once; and I could have guessed it from the boy's manner if I did not hold the proof in my hand. But there it was—in black and white. Now, Mr. Flick, I do not pretend to be better than my neighbours, and a notion came across me as I looked at that forged cheque. I told your son that the hour for paying money was past, but that he had better leave the cheque and call the first thing in the morning. He was afraid to object; so here I am, now, to await your decision."

" My decision on what, sir ?" faltered the jockey.

"On your son's life," said the pretended cashier.

"It is in the hands of the law," murmured Flick, wringing his hands. "O Richard — Richard! that it should have come to this! You I always thought the best — the best of boys. O my God, but this is hard to bear ! "

" Your decision!" said Benosa, sharply.

Flick looked vacantly up.

"Listen. I have told you I backed the Field against the Favourite. If the Favourite wins, your son hangs ! You understand that ?"

" Snapdragon must win," murmured the jockey. " He could do it in a canter."

" Not if he had half-a-dozen drops from this bottle down his throat," said Benosa, drawing from his breast a phial filled with a dark-coloured fluid.

" It is pison !" exclaimed Flick. " You would pison the 'oss."

Benosa uncorked the phial, and allowed a drop or two of the liquid to trickle into his own mouth.

" What is poison for horses is poison for men, Mr. Flick; except for throwing him off his speed for four-and-twenty hours or so, the mixture is as harmless as mother's milk."

" No, by G—! no! I won't do it, nor suffer you to do it. There stands the swiftest horse in Europe, and he sha'n't be doctored. Keep off, I say — keep off!" and the jockey, snatching up the pistol, stood between Benosa and the stall.

" Did you ever see a hanging?" muttered Benosa.

The jockey shrunk backwards as though bitten by a reptile.

"Hinder me from giving this dose to the horse, and you'll see one that will interest you. Permit me, and by the time the news reaches London that the Favourite has disappointed her backers, the cheque will be in your son's hands; and I presume he will not again try the experiment of cashing it in a hurry."

The jockey groaned in bitterness of spirit. Benosa's keen eye saw the inward struggle which was going on.

"A gambler's interests," he said, "or a son's blood — choose!"

But the jockey remained dumb.

"O, Mary — Mary!" he murmured at length, "that your boy — that our boy should have done this thing!"

Benosa saw the direction of his thoughts, and skilfully availed himself of them.

"Richard is like his mother, is he not?" he inquired.

Flick writhed in mute agony at the question.

"It's hard — very hard," muttered the false cashier,—"a favourite son, and an only son, and one that reminds the father of a dear one gone."

The jockey uttered a loud inarticulate cry of agony, and then fell on his knees.

"Spare him! — spare him! — spare Richard! Spare my son!"

"Then you consent?"

Flick bent his head in answer. His hands were stretched before his face.

"Turn the horse in his stall," said Benosa, in as cool a tone as though he were giving an ordinary stable order.

The jockey quietly complied, undid Snapdragon's halter, and the docile animal, obeying his voice and the pressure of his hands, wheeled himself round, with his tail to the manger.

"Now fetch the lantern."

Benosa spoke in the composed but decided tone of a man to whom command was habitual.

Again Flick mechanically obeyed, placing himself between the racer and his visitor.

Benosa uncorked the phial. "Stand aside," he said.

Poor Flick flung his arms round Snapdragon's neck, and

then, shrinking from the piercing gaze of Benosa's eyes, staggered to the corn-chest, instinctively supporting himself upon it, while he held the lantern so as to light his companion.

"You swear it will do no lasting harm to the 'oss?" he exclaimed.

"You may enter him for the St. Leger, and win it too," replied Benosa. "Only you will be in the ruck to-morrow."

The jockey groaned aloud.

"How am I to face Mr. Lorimer?" he gasped.

"Are you responsible for the horse's health or the horse's humours?" answered Benosa. "It is enough for you, that having watched all night in the stable, you know that he has not had foul play."

During this brief conversation Snapdragon began to snort and move restively, as though his instinct told him that all was not right. Benosa stood upon the near side, soothing him with word and touch; all at once, with his left hand he grasped the nose and jaws of the horse. The animal snorted, flung aloft his head, but the long thin fingers of Benosa grasped its flesh like firmly-screwed iron bars.

"Open — brute! So — there!" he exclaimed, violently wrenching the upper jaw, and at the moment that the teeth parted, dashing between them the phial, which was rimmed with brass. The noble animal reared upwards, Benosa clinging to it, and still holding the phial between its open jaws.

The jockey stared wildly at the struggle. For a moment it was a terrific one,—the horse plunging and snorting in its terror,—and Benosa, with his long arms twined round its neck, and his bright black eyes flashing into those of the racer's, dashed upwards and downwards, as the animal wildly flung about his head, and struck out alternately with his fore and hind legs. But the strife only lasted a moment. All at once Snapdragon dropped down upon all fours — his ears, which were laid back, assumed their natural position. He breathed hard and quickly, and then became motionless in the stall.

In a moment Benosa slipped from its side, recorking the phial.

"The sedative does its work at once," he said.

He took Flick's hand, it was trembling and moist with perspiration.

"I have lost the honesty," murmured the poor jockey,
—"I have lost the honesty I was proud on for them twenty
years—I have sold a race!"

"You have saved your son," said Benosa, "and you
have read him a lesson. Henceforth let him count as enemies all who have not proved themselves friends."

The jockey looked at the false cashier wonderingly.

"Richard will explain the rest. He is not so guilty as
you think him. You may be a happy father yet—a happier
father than I am. Farewell. God forgive you and me, and
all of us."

Turning to the door, Benosa rapidly undid its fastening
and glided out. Flick followed in haste, but his mysterious
visitor was gone.

"God help us," said the jockey, turning back to the
stable. "It seems like a dream of the night."

CHAPTER VI.

THE DERBY.

THE great yearly festival of London is the Derby day.
Christmas-tide brings its associations and its joys. Easter
inaugurates the Spring, and Whitsun-tide crowns Summer on
her throne. All these are festive times—times of holyday-
making and epochs in the story of the year, but the especial
day on which London rouses itself, and pours itself forth
beyond its bricken barriers, is undoubtedly the 25th of May,
when the great race of England—of the world—is run on
Epsom Downs. Describe the English, if you will, as a
shopkeeping nation, as a peerage-worshipping nation, as a
roast-beef-eating nation, or as a bell-ringing nation, their
proper definition is a horse-racing nation. England alone
worships with unbounded devotion at the shrine of the
Turf. In some countries racing is a passion—in others
it has become a *mode*—but in England it is at once a rage,
a fashion, a science, an art, a trade. Men give up their lives
to it. Men study it as they would study an abstruse branch
of philosophy. Men make and lose fortunes by it. The
turf furnishes at once a matter of business and a game of

chance. We devote our commercial energies to it. We lavish our gambling propensities on it. We have erected it into a profession, a science, a mystery. It has its technicalities, and its outer and inner secrets. It is represented in every place and degree of our social system It has its partisans in parliament — its representatives and its advocates in every department of public and domestic life. Developed by certain mental features in our national character, it has created new ones. It has its calendars, its journals, its hand-books, its guides. It has fostered schools of literature and art exclusively its own. Nay, more; at a period of political disorganisation it gave a party in the legislature a leader, ready cut and dry; and in the most matter-of-fact times the world has ever seen — times of stubborn facts and rigid figures — has not the turf furnished us with the only race of vaticinators who have ever found not only honour, but profit, in their own country—with those far-sighted soothsayers who, mounted on the tripods of Journalism, prophesy the fate of sweepstakes, and announce the hidden destiny of horse-flesh !

This, then, is the Derby day, and Snapdragon is still the favourite ! Every bridge leading from Middlesex to Surrey is a highway of that grand procession which marches annually from London to Epsom Downs. That long jolting, rattling, glancing, glittering train of equipages, which could be poured forth by no city of the earth, save our own Island Capital,— that interminable cataract of toiling, panting, perspiring pedestrians, rushing forth in endless march—pushing, hustling, swarming — blackening the broad highways of the suburbs—blackening the winding roads of the open country—straying and straggling away from the main line, across fields, and in search of soft turf and yielding grass, fresh and grateful to hot and blistered feet—that wonderful annual Pilgrimage—that great British Caravan on its annual journey to the Mecca of the Grand Stand -- is in full, roaring march. We need not here stay to describe the minutiæ of the procession; we need not dwell upon the upsets — the collisions — the crushed panels — the slaughtered horses — the battles round the turnpikes — the general engagement before the Cock at Sutton — the shoutings and yellings of rural charioteers — the plungings and lashings of frightened and infuriated steeds — the gibes, and jokes, and flying " chaff," bandied from pedestrian to equestrian, launched from britska and landau, and caught up by van and donkey-cart — all this has been done, and well done, again and again — is annually done, in fact — in the pages or the sheets of magazines and journals, which every year find a feature in the great racing festival of England. It will be enough to say that, on the present occasion, the throng, the crush, and the excitement, were as great as ever — that the usual array of dashing equipages smoked along the dusty road — that the usual number of slangy four-in-hands were "tooled" down by knowing whips — that the usual number of creaking, lumbering vans went jolting by — that the heterogeneous mass of wheeled things, carts, gigs, phaetons, buggies, cabs, and masses of vehicles to which any name, or no name at all, can be properly applied, filled up, as usual, every interstice in the procession — and that the whole moving mass of men, women, horses, carriages, equestrians, and pedestrians, rolled on together,— one long column of dust, noise, smother, and excitement!

On the road to the Derby, or on the Downs, might be found, with one exception or two, all the personages introduced in this history. Mr. Maggs, of the firm of Shiner and Maggs, had, indeed, chosen to manifest his contempt for the great racing anniversary by presiding on that day over the first annual meeting of the Society for Inducing the Ashantees to wear Nankeen Breeches; but his partner, Mr. Shiner, was rattling along the road in a snug, open phaeton, drawn by a couple of nettlesome bays, and occupied, besides himself, by one of the most dashing and agreeable wits of the Stock Exchange — a gentleman who had invented more lies, in the way of getting the fluctuations of the funds to suit his own particular purposes, than had been ever perpetrated by the combined efforts of the diplomacy and the press of Europe,—and a couple of young ladies, presumed to be connected with the ballet department of one of the theatres, of very gay and flaming exterior, and such childlike simplicity that they never blushed or fidgeted at the most self-evident *double entendre*. Mr. Shiner had likewise given a holyday to several of the clerks — Richard Flick and Owen Dombler amongst the rest; but, to the intense astonishment of Owen, his friend had hung back from accompanying him. Dombler was there, however, in full fig, perched upon the top of a four-horse coach, beside his friend Spiffler, who, having made a decided rise in his profession of penny-a-line literature, had come out very strong in a second-rate weekly sporting paper as a Derby Prophet, and who, grounding the prediction on the information which he had received from Richard Flick through Owen, had finished his prophetic poem, published the Saturday before, as follows :—

> " On none — though, like *Lavinia*, they have friends —
> On none of these the laurelled crown descends,
> For, pure in blood, symmetrical in bone,
> The 'FAVOURITE' claims the DERBY as his own :
> Yet, unless every sign and omen fail,
> JIM CROW, placed second, sees SNAPDRAGON'S tail ! "

Not far behind the flying chariot of the Derby Prophet rolled a low, open landau, whisked along by four thorough-bred greys, bestrode by the smartest of post-boys in the smartest of jackets and caps. It was occupied by three persons — Mdlle. Chateauroux, Mr. Grogrum, and Dr. Gumbey — who were proceeding in great and confidential amity together. For these three worthies could only afford to quarrel in the make-believe style — not that they did not distrust each other up to the very limits, and perhaps beyond the limits, of a good, wholesome, mutual hatred, but so long as their interests pulled in the same way, the three strands of a cable could not be more amicably unanimous.

" They say, if he loses this race, he's a gone 'coon," said the manager ; " regular up the tree, and no mistake."

" Let us hope that these are but the malicious rumours of the enemies of our good friend Mr. Lorimer," replied the doctor, in his castor-oiliest of tones.

" Well, I don't care, I don't hold his paper," rejoined Mr. Grogrum. " He has had his day, like any other dog ; there's people been cheating him long enough. When he's sucked dry, let him turn to and suck some one else ; that's the way the thing is done : d— it ! I ought to know."

(And, to do him justice, so he ought.)

" Nay, nay, Mr. Grogrum, hush now ; remember our dear friend here ;— you are positively quite unfeeling."

" Let him alone, *mon cher docteur*, let him alone," said Mdlle. Chateauroux, in her foreign accent ; " he's a great, coarse man, who has no feelings and no *délicatesse*. Lorimer will win the race, I feel it here ;" and she indicated her heart. " I know it, he must win ; or, if he loses, and what you say be true, why then ——" And she stopped and touched her eyes with a handkerchief, which appeared one bundle of lace.

" Well, mademoiselle," said the manager, winking at the doctor, and affecting a voice broken by sympathy, " you were saying—' why then?' "

" Why then," exclaimed the lady, briskly twitching the nandkerchief from her face,—" why, then — *Ventre St. Gris!* — as your English proverb says, ' There is as good fish in the sea as ever came out of it!' "

And the sympathising three burst into a loud laugh.

The landau had hardly assumed its position on the Downs when Clement Lorimer appeared by its side. He was deadly pale, but his manner was as quiet and composed as usual. His appearance was of course the signal for a volley of greeting.

" *Ce vieux chéri Lorimer,*" murmured the *danseuse,* leaning over the side of the vehicle, and whispering in her sweetest tones,—" We shall win—*ne c'est pas?* It is what you call 'safe?' Oh, I am in such a state of terrible anxiety ! *Corbleu !* I did not sleep a wink these three nights."

" It's all right, Lorimer, my boy?" said the manager. " Gad, we'd be broken-hearted if there was a miss: but all the knowing ones say the thing is safe."

" I hope the knowing ones may be right," said Lorimer quietly. " Much hangs to-day upon a horse's sinews;" and he began to compliment Mdlle. Chateauroux on the fashion of her parasol.

" He's d—d down in the mouth, Gumbey," whispered Grogrum. " There's a screw loose, depend upon it."

" I hope and trust our friend Snapdragon is in full feather this morning?" said the doctor.

" I hope so, too. I see nothing wrong with the horse. But it does strike me that his eyes looked dimmer, and his motions were not quite so fiery this morning as usual."

Gumbey and Grogrum exchanged glances.

" Tell me, Lorimer," whispered Mdlle. Chateauroux, " there is nothing wrong?"

" Absolutely nothing. But one has all sorts of whims and fancies when one is jaded and excited. I took it into my head, for example, this morning that Flick, the jockey who is to ride Snapdragon, looked flurried and confused. I can hardly tell what made me think so, but I did."

"Pshaw! You are tormenting yourself. *Sacré bleu!* Is he still as confident as ever?"

"In words: but the tone seems altered."

"Pooh! You are nervous. There, go drink a glass of sparkling Moselle. That wicked *docteur* has stolen one out of the hamper already, on purpose to pledge to Snapdragon."

But here the saddling bell rang, and Lorimer hastily left them to be present at that important ceremony in the paddock. In a short time the competing horses appeared one by one before the Grand Stand. The crowd pushed and hustled in their eagerness to see and criticise. Opinions and hopes were loudly bandied about. Books were reopened to enter final bets. Profound amateurs of horse-flesh discussed action, blood, and bone. Mounted jockeys received final hints and instructions from their backers, and the limbs of the competing horses were chafed, and their nostrils sponged for the last time. A loud shout proclaimed the appearance of the Favourite; and the noble animal, with its arched, glancing neck, its thin, finely-chiselled head, its widely-dilated nostrils, and sinewy, stag-like legs, paced proudly out upon the turf, becoming an immediate centre of interest and admiration. Flick was already in his saddle, bearing himself as though he were part of the animal he bestrode.

"Here, Flick," said Lorimer, "let me feel your hand."

"It's steadier than most upon the Downs, sir," replied the jockey, putting his hand within that of his employer. It did not tremble certainly, but it was clay-cold.

"You look very pale, Flick," said Lorimer.

"Watching, sir. I haven't had over-much sleep lately, and I was werry nervous last night."

The owner of the Favourite looked long and anxiously at his horse, felt its joints, and then, patting its neck, said,—

"Do your best — man and horse."

In half-an-hour after this the start was momentarily expected. There was the dead hush of expectation, gradually wrought up to its highest pitch, over all that vast assemblage; the course, like a bright, broad, green riband, stretched down between two masses of breathless human beings. Not a face but was either preternaturally pale or preternaturally flushed. People grasped each other's hands and strained their eyes till their heads grew dizzy. Every body was on tiptoe —

F

every body pressing forward—every body looking towards the same point, the famous Tattenham Corner. All at once a throb, like a flash of moral electricity, passed through the crowd.

"THEY'RE OFF!"

There was a movement—a wave, so to speak, rolled through that human ocean—those behind were pressing on to the front. Then came a moment of noisy turmoil. "Keep steady!"—"Down in front!"—"Hats off!"—"Hurrah!" —"Hush!" and the murmur subsided.

A cluster of horsemen were seen at a full gallop dashing over the ridge of the eminence to the right.

"Here they are!"—"They're coming! they're coming!"—"Hurrah!" and one of those indefinable, indescribable noises, which none but an excited crowd can produce, rose with a mighty murmur into the summer air.

At that moment, the point where the broad green course forms a portion of the horizon near the corner, became, as if by magic, dotted with the hurrying figures of the racers. The next moment they were careering down the course, as it seemed, in a cluster.

Then the low, universal murmur, rose and swelled into a loud hoarse roar, and voices, frantic with excitement, shouted and screamed their hopes and fears.

"White and Pink! White and Pink! Where's the Favourite?"—"Red is leading! Hurrah! Red! Red! Tom Tit for ever! Where's Snap? Where's White and Pink?"—"Hurrah, Red!"—"No, Blue! give it 'em, Blue! Go it, Jim Crow!"—"My G—! the Favourite's in the ruck! Red! Red! Red! Hurrah!"—"Blue does it! Blue does the trick!"—"Red! White and Pink! Blue! Here they are! Hurrah! hurrah! hurrah!"

And amid one loud, universal, roaring shout, and speeding, fleeting, impalpable as a vision of the night, there shot past hundreds of thousands of dazzled eyes a dozen of careering horses, flying at a speed which made the eye dazzle and the brain whirl, and beating the turf with their hoofs like a loud, fast roll of drums!

It was over in a moment:—the Derby was lost and won!

Instantly the spectators on either side burst the barriers of rope, and the course was obliterated by a rushing, shouting, jostling throng.

" Tom Tit had won !"—" Jim Crow had won !"—" Bubbly Jock had won !" So announced a discordant babble of voices.

" Hush ! there's the figures !"

Jim Crow was placed first, Tom Tit second, the Favourite — nowhere !

CHAPTER VII.

THE LOSERS.

As soon as Clement Lorimer was aware that Snapdragon had lost the Derby, he retired alone into a private room attached to the betting accommodations of the Grand Stand, and locked the door. As he moved towards the table, his eye caught the reflection of his own features in a mirror hanging on the wall ; he paused, and gazed upon the glass, then, flinging himself into a chair, muttered,—

" The first time I have seen in a mirror the face of a ruined man."

Then pressing his clenched hands against his forehead, he leant back and mused.

All around him rose the loud murmurs of the crowded race-course ; the tramp of hurrying feet shook the structure in which he sat. He heard his own name loudly demanded, and from time to time the door was rudely knocked by applicants for admission ; but he never stirred or gave token of his presence. A mean spirit might have guessed that the waking dream of the ruined turfite turned on pistols and deadly drugs, but the firm mind of Lorimer gave way to no such morbid fancies. The rudeness of the shock only proved the strength of the sinewy springs of his intellect. It was his first misfortune ; for a moment he staggered under it, then he grappled, he wrestled with it, and many minutes had not flown ere the big spirit of the man rose the conqueror from the strife.

A first misfortune is often the turning point of life. If there be nothing in you, down you go—crushed ; but if there be the dormant stuff which hereafter will make a good, great, brave man, then be thankful for the shock ; and as you rise

to the battle, as you feel every mental muscle, every bit of
sinew in your mind, swell, and stiffen, and strengthen for the
fight, why, thank God for the rough stimulant—jump bravely
to your feet; reflect that you must put down your misfortune,
or it will put you down; and then, having conquered in your
own brain—and if you feel what we have sketched, conquer
you will,—why climb proudly to the very summit of the op-
posing woe, trample it down beneath you, and feel that you,
a Man—erect upon the ruins of a hostile Circumstance—stand,
conquering and to conquer, a God upon a prostrate Titan!

If Clement Lorimer did not speak these words, he felt
dimly, yet intensely, the thought which these words convey;
and as that thought illumined his soul with a flood of
burning, purifying light, he felt, for the first time in his life,
he full innate dignity of Mind.   An instant more, and he
ras almost grateful that he had lost the Derby.

"Strange!" he murmured, "but since last night a presentiment that my life is entering on a stage of storms has
taken hold of me.   It is not fancy,—I am cool, perfectly cool,
and can look steadily in upon my soul.   It is the warning
shadow of coming events which darkens it.   Up to this time
my hopes have not known a disappointment, my schemes
have not known a cross.   The tide has turned, and I must
pull against it.   Aye, and I am glad of it.   I have lived long
enough in gilded sloth, careless of all but the excitement or the
pleasure of the hour.   Now for a plunge into the icy current
of a struggling life, now to try if its waters will not brace
me to dare—to do,—aye, and to suffer!"

In a few moments Lorimer had settled his plans.   He
would go to sea for one week in his yacht, in order to enjoy
perfect solitude, and to refresh and re-invigorate his physical
powers.   Then he proposed to return to town, manfully face
his disasters, examine into his affairs, and find, if possible, the
clue to the secret of his birth.   As soon as he had settled
this in his mind, he rose, glanced at the glass, and then
proudly murmured to himself,—

"No, I have seen many, but I never saw the face of a
ruined man so calm before."

As he continued almost instinctively to gaze upon the
glass, he saw that it reproduced another face besides his own.
Framed, as it were, in the window opposite to the mirror, was

the head and upper part of the figure of a man. The features were distorted with a wild expression of demoniac triumph, and the black eyes glared and sparkled beneath the bushy grey eyebrows.

"A winner by the race," thought Lorimer. "Luck seems to have turned his brain." Then he saw that the man was gazing through the window at the reflection of his (Clement's) own features in the mirror; and it struck him that the mad expression of gratified hate, which glared from the face of the stranger, appeared to fade away as he contemplated the calm features revealed to him by the glass, until at length all indication of strong passion—passion perhaps occasionally uncurbed by the bond of reason—had passed away, leaving the bright eyes illumined only by the light of intellect, and the features noble in their calm placidity. For a moment Lorimer, as though fascinated, continued to gaze upon the two faces reflected in the mirror: his own, pale and young; the stranger's, pale and old. Both pale, and both —ha! what a thought flew through the startled soul of the gazer!—both similar in feature and in expression—the one the young version of the other,—as it were the faces of father and son. The vision lasted but for a moment. Lorimer felt again that foreboding of coming events, that undefinable stir within him, as though his soul, forewarned from without, was girding up its loins for great deeds or great suffering. Then making a desperate effort he wrenched himself round towards the window—the man was gone. He rushed to the casement, flung it open, and looked out, but hundreds of figures were moving restlessly backwards and forwards. Many faces were there, but the strange old double of his young features was nowhere to be seen; so with flesh, which in spite of himself crept and shuddered, he shut down the window.

As he did so Raphael Benosa turned the corner of the Grand Stand, and as he pushed his way amid the crowd muttered to himself,—

"So—a calm voice and a strong soul. With the brave the first blow is *not* half the battle. Be it so. I hate to fight —sapling to steel. Now it will be blade to blade, and hilt to hilt. Yet I have the advantage. I have the knowledge! Ha! I have the sun!"

As the old man pronounced these words he flung aloft his arms with a passionate gesture. Immediately a voice sounded in his ears,—

"Now, then, old Shandrydan! are you going mad for grief because you've lost a glass of brandy-and-water on the Derby?"

"There's only one specific," remarked another voice, in a tone of drunken gravity,—"there's only one specific against sorrow occasioned by the loss of bets, and that is, to hug yourself in the consciousness that you can't pay them: I'm embraced in that species of hug myself."

The question and the advice came from the box-seat of a four-in-hand coach, and on that box-seat were stationed Owen Dombler and his friend Mr. Spiffler. The former not having lost sufficiently to take away his appetite was eating; the other, being about as much ruined as a gentleman not possessed of either landed or personal property could be, was drinking. The natural consequence was that the clerk was sober and the prophet drunk. As may be supposed, however, the object of their remarks paid little attention to them, and the next moment they were "chaffing" somebody else.

Meantime Lorimer stood motionless by the window in his solitary room. A rapping at the door caused him to unlock it, and De Witz entered. The captain's face was partly flushed, partly pale, and his hand trembled very much. He sank down into a chair, and looked at Lorimer with a fixed stare. At length he spoke.

"I'm off! By —! is not it a smash? U P, and no mistake!" And the captain uttered a long, loud whistle, which gradually subsided into a species of whine, the which dying away in its turn, the performer finished off with a discordant burst of song, the words keeping some sort of hobbling time to the good old tune of Malbrook, in this wise,—

> "'He won it in a canter,
> And so, to end all banter.
> I turned a gay Levanter,
> And walked myself away!'

"That's the time of day—eh, Clem? Brussels—Brussels

.—the sanctuary—the free city of our modern days—I salute thee! Any commands for the *Montagne de la Cour?*"

It was quite easy to see that Captain De Witz had sought for consolation under his misfortune at the same source to which the ingenious Spiffler had applied.

"Here, Lorimer," he continued, pouring out half a tumbler of wine from a decanter on the table, "drink, man! sorrow is as dry as a lime-kiln in the Great Desert."

Lorimer took up the wine and looked at it.

"How do I know," ne thought, "but that the devil which is besetting me may not now lurk in that crystal?" Then he threw the glass with its contents into the fire-place, and poured out and drank a tumbler full of clear water. "There is nothing so cowardly," he said, "as Dutch courage."

At that moment there was heard a clamour of voices in the passage, then a scuffling of feet, and in an instant the door was burst violently open, and from the midst of a shouting, struggling group, Sir Harrowby Trumps dragged Flick forward upon the floor. The coarse, pimply features of the baronet were purple and swollen with passion; the foam he had churned lay in flakes on his thick, worm-like lips; his dress was soiled and disarranged; and his brown, brawny hands, glistening with rings, were twisted in the neckcloth of the poor jockey, who, with his white-and-pink jacket almost torn from his back, had evidently been dragged violently along by the maddened turfite.

"Shame! shame! Let go the man! Shame!" shouted the crowd who mustered about the door. "Shame!—Where's the police? Where's the stewards? Is a man to be throttled for losing a race?"

"Back, ye curs! Back, d— you!" roared Sir Harrowby. "He's sold the race—he did!"

"For shame, Trumps!" said Lorimer. "Unloose your grasp!"

The baronet stared at him.

"I tell you he sold the race!" he said between his grinding teeth.

"Hands off, I say, or —— "

"Well, then," thundered Trumps, "there!" and h. pushed poor Flick violently away, and glared at him as he stood pale, and panting, and rolling his eyes wildly about the room.

"Trumps, are you a man — a gentleman ? Be cool — be cool, sir ! If money has been lost, honour is still at stake."

"Oh !" roared the excited gambler, still glaring at the jockey. "Oh, if this country was like Russia, and you were one of my serfs, oh, by the Lord ! wouldn't Europe ring with what I'd do to you !"

" Sir Harrowby Trumps," interposed Lorimer, " you are in my room. You talk to a person in my service, not in yours. Be silent — or leave us !"

There was a hum of approval from the spectators. Trumps, perceiving that he had no supporters, grumbled out some inarticulate oaths, and flung himself heavily into a chair, wiping the perspiration from his hot, flushed face.

"Well, Flick," began the calm, rich voice of Lorimer, "we made ourselves too sure, you see. Snapdragon was a good horse, but not so good as we thought him."

The jockey made a mighty effort to speak, but there was a big swelling in his throat; and he moved his lips and gesticulated, but no voice came from his chest.

"I trusted you, Flick," continued Lorimer. "I trusted you yesterday, and I trust you to-day. I know it was not your fault."

The jockey wrung his hands and shook his head.

"Ah," said Lorimer, "not yours ! Well, and whose was it ?"

Just at this moment the jockey uttered a loud exclamation. Lorimer, we may mention, was standing with his back to the mirror, looking towards the window, and the jockey fronted him. Consequently, when the stranger, whose appearance had already filled Lorimer with such strange emotions, passed again, as he at that moment did before the casement, the owner of Snapdragon saw the reality of that vision in the glass, on which the eyes of the jockey were fixed at the moment he uttered the involuntary cry which proceeded from his lips. Again Lorimer sprang to the window — again he looked vainly for his extraordinary visitant. When he turned into the room, the jockey appeared to have recovered and partially manned himself. He was closely questioned, first, as to the cause of his exclamation, but he gave no satisfactory reply. "He did not know what had made him behave so — it was involuntary — it was nervousness. Sir Harrowby had used him so roughly. He had seen nothing in particular — nobody in particular. He did not know why they asked him." As to the race and the horse, Flick's answers, though perfectly respectful, and given with every evidence of deep feeling, appeared to Lorimer unsatisfactory. "He was disappointed — of course he was: so were many other people. These things did happen sometimes. He could not help it — could not account for it: the race was lost, and there was an end of it. He hoped and trusted for better luck next time." It was evident nothing more could be made of him, and so for the time he was dismissed.

Lorimer then sat down and wrote a hurried note to Blane with respect to arrangements to be made for settling-day. As he wrote, Trumps and De Witz, who still remained, observed that at almost every second word he cast a keen, quick glance at the window. When he had sealed his despatch, Lorimer stood up and passed his hands across his forehead.

"Like an ancient knight," he murmured, "I must go forth to the task alone. Trumps, De Witz, good-by!"

"Good-by!" said the baronet: "and for how long?"

"I know not," replied Lorimer; "perhaps for ever!" and passing out he left them staring at each other.

CHAPTER VIII.

THE FLY-BY-NIGHT.

HEAVING and rolling with a long, sickly motion upon the successive ridges of a tumbling ground-swell, her timbers creaking and cracking as she wallowed in the deep trough of the sea,—her canvass flapping in loud-sounding surges against the rigging which restrained it,—there lay upon the restless ocean a small, jauntily-rigged cutter vessel, with sharp, wedge-like bows, and a long, low, graceful quarter. It is black night when we introduce our readers to her deck; a lowering and gloomy night to a landsman's eye, a threatening

one to a sailor's.   The fitful breeze, which has blown in puffs
all day, has taken off, and, with the exception of the slight
movements and currents of air, partly, if not wholly, produced
by the heaving of the waters, there is not a breath to stir the
heavy, torpid atmosphere which broods over the sea.   Overhead all is pitchy dark, except occasionally when the haze
partially opens, and shews a planet twinkling with the dim,
uncertain lustre of a star of the third magnitude.   Only on
the south-eastern horizon of the ocean is there a wide, palpable break in the dusky masses of cloud; there, a broad
straight streak of dim, ruddy light stretches across the line
of vision, in the midst of which, partially veiled by blur-
ring masses of shifting and spreading vapour, the moon is
surrounded by successive rings of murky halo, each getting
paler and paler, until the outward circle fades into the dim
glare of the horizontally lying belt of light, which rests, as it
were, upon the saw-like horizon of the distant waves.   All
on board the cutter is hushed.   The tiller is lashed amid-
ships, and the steersman, whose post is a sinecure in the calm,
is sitting on the low taffrail, swaying his body to keep time, as
it were, with the motion of the vessel, and occasionally looking
anxiously out in the direction of the boding streak of light in
the south-eastern sky.   Presently a man ascends the little
companion; two steps bring him to the binnacle; and the
steersman rises and leans upon the jerking tiller,—

"Her head is west and by south now, sir," said the latter;
"but she has been boxing round and round for the last
hour."

The new-comer looked abroad on all sides.   Standing
with his face to the westward, he saw before him a bright,
steady light; a little to the right was a ruddier and more
distant speck of fire, which was now and then obscured;
about eight points of the compass to the left might be seen,
but only occasionally (when the cutter rose on the sea), a
small constellation of three lights, in the shape of a triangle,
with a very broad base.   These appeared to be displayed on
board a ship.   Behind the observer, placed in the position
which we have indicated, but still rather to the left, burned,
at a comparatively great elevation, two bright lights, one
above the other; and right behind him could be indistinctly
seen a dim, ruddy point of fire, lying low, but fixed and im-

movable. From these lights the mariner accustomed to the
pilotage of the English Channel could at once fix the position
of his vessel. The one high, bright light burned in the
market-place of Calais; the intermittent, ruddy glow crowned
Cape Grinez; the constellation of three was displayed from
the light-ship which marks the southern extremity of the
Goodwin Sands; the two lights placed one above the other
denote the bold promontory called the South Foreland; and
the low, ruddy speck is the harbour light of Dover.

Clement Lorimer's cutter-yacht, the Fly-by-Night, is
therefore lying, tossed by the billows, in the Straits of Dover,
about seven miles off the English coast, and Clement Lorimer
himself is standing by the steersman.

" Go forward," our hero said to his companion, "and ask
Captain Blockey to step this way.

" I suspect we shall have it presently," murmured Lorimer.
" Well, no matter; the Fly-by-Night shall not turn tail to a
Channel blow, like a fresh-water craft from the cruising-
ground at Cowes."

He was interrupted by the approach of Captain Blockey,
the acting commander of the yacht, a Dutch-built old sailor,
with a face browned and tanned by the suns and seas of
every latitude from the Line to the Antarctic Circle. For
Captain Blockey had led a tolerably roving life. He had
harpooned whales amid the icebergs, and shipped negroes from
the Bight of Benin; he had groped his way through the
Straits of Magellan, and smuggled opium in China. The
man had passed a long life, which was nothing but a series of
escapes from death. But Captain Blockey was tough. The
yellow fever could not kill him in Cuba, and he had weathered through the plague in the Levant; he had once had
a wonderful escape from being roasted on the white beach of
a beauteous coral island in the South Seas, and had been al'.
but snapped up by a shark in the middle of the surf at
Madras. Of course, Captain Blockey had served many
masters. When he was a man-of-war's man on the coast of
Africa, he had chased slavers, and when he sailed as mate on
board a slaver he had evaded men-of-war. Many colours had
flown over the grizzled head of this sailor of fortune. He
had knocked about in the Baltic under the glaring flag of the
Hanse Towns; he had hoisted the tricolor on board of the

Brest lugger *Le Coq Chantant,* unfavourably known to many
English revenue cruisers ; he had served the Spaniard west
of the Horn, and the Dutchman amid the spicy islands of the
Indian Archipelago.   Captain Blockey had battled with
Nor-westers on the banks of Newfoundland, in a clipper
Yankee schooner, and seen white squalls amid the Isles of
Greece in a trim Maltese speronare.   There was no rig he
did not understand, no language of which he had not a smat-
tering of the naval terms, no Cape which he had not doubled,
no roadstead in which he had not anchored.   But Captain
Blockey had not been so prudent as he had been adventu-
rous ; he had made money like a horse and spent it like an
ass ; and so old age had surprised him, unable to continue
his longer and more perilous voyages, and fain to direct the
coasting operations of a pleasure-yacht.   Such was the gallant
tar whose opinion Lorimer now asked upon that all-important
topic at sea — the weather.

Captain Blockey pronounced decidedly in the matter.

" In an hour, these swells will begin to comb white hair,
and we shall be taking in a reef; an hour after, we shall be
plunging bows under, with three reefs in the mainsail and a
storm-jib ; and by daybreak, why, we'll either be lying to
under a trysail, or scudding under next to nothing at all, as if
the devil were kicking us behind ! "

" So be it," said Lorimer ; " it may be the last time I
shall sail the cutter.   We sha'n't put up the helm till the Fly-
by-Night can't shew her nose to it."

" D— it ! " said the captain, in great delight, " you
ought to have been a sailor, Mr. Lorimer ; you've got the
savour of the brine in you.   You don't think the sea is the
sea till it begins to dance, and till the froth is flying like barm
out of the lee scuppers."

So saying, and rubbing his hands with delight at what he
considered the pluck of his patron, Captain Blockey walked
forward to see all put in readiness for the gale which he expected.   It was not long in coming.   Lorimer, as he gazed
anxiously out upon the dim, leaden sea, saw the bright belt
on the horizon suddenly become clearer and wider, and then
white streaks glanced out upon the dull, dusky expanse of
water.   The wind was coming fast.   A low, hoarse roar —
the mingled sound of the moving current of air and of the

combing and breaking crests of the waves—made itself heard amid the plunging of the cutter and the wild flapping of the heavy canvass.

" Stand fast! Here it comes!" shouted Blockey, grasping the tiller ropes; and he had hardly spoken when a damp column of cold air swept by the cutter, bellying out the canvass with a jerk, and wrenching the yielding mass, until it bowed heavily over before the shock. Recovering from the first impulse, the cutter struck her sharp bows into a rolling sea, driving the green water over her weather bulwarks, from the bowsprit almost to the mast; and then, rising gaily from the encounter, and pouring, by a heavy lurch, the fluid from her decks, the yacht moved rapidly on, —her head kept towards the French coast, and as near the wind as she would lie.

The captain's prognostications as to the probably increasing strength of the gale were amply verified. An hour had not elapsed ere the Fly-by-Night was leaping from sea to sea, plunging her sharp bows into the tumbling masses of water with shocks which made her quiver to her keel, and urged forward in her mad career by a tearing and struggling mainsail, diminished almost to one-half its bulk by three reefs and a tiny jib, which was frequently driven bodily down into the water. It was a wild scene for a landsman's eye; but a sailor, confident of the qualities of his craft, and aware that he had unlimited sea-room, would see nothing to excite alarm in the situation of the yacht. Above, all was black and starless, but the light eliminated from the beds of sparkling foam, produced as each sea curled, combed, and burst, more than made up for the gloom caused by the density of the clouds. The gale itself blew with steadily increasing strength, the roaring wind, coming thick and heavy with the driving brine, caught up in pelting showers from the summits of the waves.

Captain Blockey, aided by the oldest sailor on board, was at the tiller, watching the run of the seas, and easing off the cutter's bow as each mass of tilting water swept foaming by her cutwater. Lorimer stood on the weather quarter, his arm twined round a cracking back-stay, strung to the tension of a harp-string, and his eye sparkling with excitement as the little craft beneath him tossed and leaped, and tore through

tne water. For he enjoyed the strife of the elements. The
unbridled storm without seemed an echo to the surging
agitation of his own soul. The presentiment that the stirring
epoch of his life was at hand had deepened and intensified
upon him; and as the wind howled aloud, and the wet
canvass struggled and surged against the resisting cordage,
and the labouring yacht staggered and wallowed with roaring
plunges deep into each successive ridge of foaming sea, his
working brain seemed to attune the mangled uproar into a
grand prelude to the unknown events beneath whose shadow
he was standing—into a fanciful and terrible overture to the
drama of a struggling manhood!

Hours passed thus. The yacht had of course made
several tacks so as to keep well away from either coast, and
the glimpses caught of the shore lights, when the haze
occasionally lifted from the water, shewed that, although an
extremely weatherly craft, she was barely holding her own
against the combined fury of the wind and sea.

Still Lorimer kept his position upon the weather-quarter,
his drenched hair flying back from his face, and his features
streaming with salt water.

" What a look-out you'd make," shouted Captain Blockey
in his ear ; "and to do it for the love of the thing too ! "

" A light on the lee bow ! " roared one of the men
forward.

" You see you had better not trust to me," replied
Lorimer.

" It's a steamboat's light, sir, I think," put in one of the
hands at the tiller, bending down to see under the boom.

And so it was. She was standing athwart the hawse of
the Fly-by-Night, at half a cable's length, and the sails of the
latter were accordingly shivered to allow the steamer a wide
berth. She was proceeding down Channel in the teeth of
the gale; battling her steady way, against wind and seas, as
though endowed with a fixed purpose which neither gale nor
waves could bend. There was something grand in the
onward passage of that dusky mass, urged forward by a self-
impelling power, her bows diverging neither to the right nor
the left, but keeping ever, as it were steadily fixed to one
unseen, unknown point. The gazers in the cutter could see
that a great portion of her paddle-boxes had been rent away.

and the huge revolving wheels flung the foaming water high into the air. Not a sign of human life was visible on board, but high above the roar of wind and water the shriek of the escaping steam rang up into the air, and a long bright streak flying to leeward from the aperture of the waste pipe shewed like a white pennant streaming forth upon the night. And so, plunging heavily on, tilting with sea after sea, and flinging the baffled waves loftily aside, the steam-driven ship passed on her way and was seen no more.

The gale was now near its height. It was not a storm of the first magnitude, but one of those stinging bursts of wild weather which occasionally break in upon the gentle summer-time, and leave their handwriting on the shores in the shape of stranded coasters and capsized and foundered boats. The little Fly-by-Night behaved nobly, tipping like a duck over the wild ridges of angry water, bending under her close-reefed mainsail and storm-jib, so as to immerse three or four of the leeward planks of her deck in the buzzing, foaming brine; and sometimes, but not often, when she plunged at a combing wave taking in a ton or two of clear green water over her bows. It might have been about an hour before day, —when the darkness is always most intense,—that Lorimer, who still kept his station on the weather-quarter of the yacht, thought, as the cutter rose upon the crest of a sea, that he caught a glimpse of a pile of white canvass standing out against the dark sky, and appearing to belong to a large square-rigged vessel, careering before the gale, and pursuing a course which, in all human probability, would bring her right upon the cutter's broadside. Uttering a half-stifled exclamation, he caught Captain Blockey's arm, and pointed eagerly to windward. At that moment they sank into the deep trough of the sea, and the foaming crown of the coming wave formed their only horizon. In an instant the yacht was of course again swung upwards, and then, apparently close upon them, roaring through the waves, and driving a huge double column of foam from her ample bows, appeared the dusky hull of a large ship, urged onward right before the wind by the ample spread of her courses and double-reefed topsails. She appeared to be barely twice her own length from the cutter. Lorimer saw the glitter of her copper as she rolled and her bows rose dripping from the sea. Another second, and it would appear as though the huge, careering mass would have thundered down upon the tiny cutter, crushing her as falling granite would crush an egg-shell.

Forming a trumpet with his hand, Blockey uttered a roar which spread around above the hoarse uproar of the elements,—

"Helm a starboard! hard a sta-a-arboard—ahoy!"

Lorimer grasped the stay with fingers as rigid as the rope they surrounded. The cutter fell again into the trough; but they could see the sails of the scudding ship broad upon the quarter.

"A shave—for our lives—it's touch and go; if we scrape clear, then I was not born to be drowned after all!"

The words had hardly passed the captain's lips, when lo! within a fathom of the cutter's boom, flinging herself, as it were, on the towering crest of a tremendous sea, there shot past them, amid the loud hissing roar of rapidly cloven water, the massive bulk of a huge ship, with her glancing copper and dusky bulwarks, and dimly-seen fabric of masts and spars, and tense rigging, and bellying, struggling canvass. Lorimer involuntarily held his breath and closed his eyes: when he opened them the ship was but a half-blurred mass far down to leeward.

"Thank God," he murmured, "we are still afloat!"

"I have had a good many close squeaks," replied Blockey, "but nothing ever closer than that. No thanks to the Yankee, though, that we are not at this moment inspecting the sea-weed some thirty fathoms under the keel."

"You think the ship was an American, then?"

"A New Yorker—most probably a liner. Did not you see the squareness of his yards? To give the devil his due, the star and stripes float over as ship-shape crafts as any on the ocean." And the captain of the yacht, giving his German tinder a smart rub over a dry spot of the bulwarks, set to work to light his cigar.

In half-an-hour the pale grey of the dawn began to shine upon the turbulent waters, and Captain Blockey gave it as his opinion that about sunrise the gale would favour them with a parting salvo, wilder than any thing they had yet experienced, and would then probably rapidly subside. The morning came, dim and grey; a pall of driving mist swept over the white crests of the seas, and reduced the visible circle of their horizon to a ring of about a mile in diameter. Of course no land was visible ; but the cutter, when the light came, was, according to Captain Blockey's estimate, not very far from the place she had occupied the previous evening, before the coming on of the gale. It was then that the parting blow, which the weatherwise captain had predicted, fell upon the struggling craft. There was a momentary lull, and the cutter rose on an even keel, while the wet mainsail flapped like thunder. Then suddenly the mist to windward was rent asunder, shewing an expanse of water, not furrowed into the usual ridges, but one white tumbling bed of foam. In another moment, the cutter, struck down as though by a powerful enemy, wallowed on her beam-ends, the sea pouring like a cataract over her weather bulwarks, and the tempest hurling through the air a loud hissing shriek, which rose over the deeper thunder of the waves.

"Up helm!—hard up! Get her before it, boys!" roared Blockey from his post in the weather rigging, as soon as the water would allow him to fetch breath. A less lively craft than the yacht would probably have gone bodily down as she lay ; but every man on board was confident in her splendid capabilities as a sea-boat. Nor did she disappoint them. Raising herself from the shock, and moving heavily onward, she felt and yielded to the impulse of the rudder. Then the bows fell off from the sea, and in a moment her crew felt the sharp pitching dig of a close-hauled vessel, changed for the buoyant, luxurious roll of a ship travelling with wind and sea.

"Ease off the main sheet!" ordered the captain. The heavy boom swung away broad on the beam, and the Fly-by-Night, bounding forward like a racer, flew on in the very heart of the squall, chasing and beating the foaming seas as though ship and waves were living things, gambolling and speeding on together.

"Up through the Downs, I suppose, Mr. Lorimer?" said the captain, pitching his wet cigar into the sea. "We'll be obliged to grope our way for an hour or so; but I think the worst is over, and the fog will lift before we're much past Deal. Here, you forward—rouse out a lead-line!" and the captain seriously addressed himself to the important business of

G

sounding. Twenty minutes had scarcely elapsed when he confidently pronounced that the cutter had doubled the South Foreland and was running into the Downs. The wind had gone considerably down, and the speed of the yacht had, of course, fallen with it; but the sea still combed and broke with great fury, and the mist still packed heavily upon the ocean. All at once a deep smothered explosion rolled over the water. Captain Blockey pricked up his ears, and stood motionless, with the lead-line twisted round his hand. In a moment it was heard again, coming from seaward, and in a direction rather ahead of the cutter.

"Boat ahead, sir!" sung out one of the men from the forecastle.

"Boat on the starboard bow, sir!" roared another.

"Aye, aye," said Blockey, "it's plain enough. Look, sir." Lorimer obeyed, and saw two lugger-rigged boats, each of them carrying a mere rag of canvass on their fore-masts, and a still smaller mizen-sail aft, rising over the white crests of the waves, and then disappearing, sails and all, in the troughs of the sea.

"There's a ship on the sands. That was her firing; and there's two Deal men going off to her."

"If it should be the American who so nearly ran us down last night," suggested Lorimer.

Blockey thought for a moment, made a mental memo-randum of the course which they were steering when the liner crossed their track at right angles, and then, lighting a fresh cigar, coolly said, he should not wonder. Just then a third gun was fired to seaward, but this time the report appeared to come over the cutter's quarter.

"We have passed her, whatever it is," observed the captain.

"Port the helm, sir!—hard a port!" was shouted from the forecastle. "There's floating wreck just ahead."

The direction was obeyed, and, as the cutter diverged to the right of her course, a cluster of broken spars with a mass of tangled rigging rose upon the crest of a wave, so close to the bows that it might have been touched with a boat hook from the forecastle. At the same moment the cutter rose high upon a sea, and Lorimer's keen eye caught the flapping of female drapery amid the coils of cordage and the splinters of broken wood. Springing on the low bulwark, and at the same instant winding the lead-line round his arm, Lorimer, heedless of the cry which burst from every man upon the cutter's decks, sprang with one vigorous bound into the foaming sea. The water closed over his head with a surging crash; then he rose to the surface—the wreck was close to him—three desperate strokes, and he had grasped a tangled mass of blocks and cordage and raised himself out of the water. He was right; a female figure lay in the midst of the wreck, clinging with a death-grip to a broken spar. An instant sufficed to unclasp her hold, to grasp her firmly in his arms, to cast round both of them half-a-dozen coils of the lead-line, and then to spring boldly back into the sea. The water surged and boiled around Lorimer as he half swam, was half dragged to the cutter's side, and the thunder of the chafing sea was mingling in his ears with the rousing cheer of the crew, as he found himself on the deck of the yacht kneeling by the insensible form of a young and lovely woman, who lay wan and motionless before him, her long hair streaming over her shoulders, and her face, cold, blood-less, placid, the blue-veined lids of her eyes closed, her lips white, and still quivering, as it seemed, with the motion of departing life.

"My poor one—so pretty and so young! Is she gone?" murmured Blockey, kneeling beside her, and speaking in as plaintive a tone as could be assumed by a voice which for fifty years had been accustomed to shout in the teeth of hurricanes.

There was a pause.

"No!" exclaimed Lorimer, gently raising the head of the insensible woman—"no! By heaven she breathes!"

CHAPTER IX.

AN AUTHOR IN SEARCH OF A SUBJECT.

Mr. Ranson Spiffler—his Christian name was John, but he called himself "Ranson," because it looked better at the head of an article—returned from the Derby very tipsy, was assisted to bed by Owen Dombler, and woke next morning with a rousing headache, and an abominable swimming in his brain, which rendered a matter of some difficulty the perusal of a letter which arrived with the earliest post, and which contained his dismissal from the honourable post of Sporting Prophet in ordinary, to that famous weekly journal, " The Time o' Day." This accident affected Mr. Spiffler very little ; for being used to the chances and changes, the fortunes and misfortunes of war, which the Modern Literary Free Lance must put up with — as did his ancient prototype before him — he immediately addressed himself to search for another banner beneath which his services might be enlisted. Pending his success, however, — divers pressing claims having to be attended to, — Mr. Spiffler was obliged to undertake a rather severe course of magazining, corresponding with country papers, furnishing the literary and dramatic matter for minor weekly journals, and so forth ; so that, by the end of a week, nobody will be astonished to learn that Mr. Spiffler's ideas, though well spun out, were running somewhat short, and that occasionally, in place of writing, he found himself drawing a series of cartoons of doubtful genius upon his blotting-paper pad.

It happened, at length, towards the afternoon of the day following the night the events of which have been detailed in the last chapter, that the author found himself perfectly aground. He had still an imaginative article to write, and not the ghost of an idea would rise at his bidding. He fidgeted on his seat, tried a course of new pens, made an experiment with note instead of post paper, flung himself on his face on the sofa, sat in extraordinary positions on chairs, and finally poured cold water on the back of his head ; but all in vain ! For the time being, he was exhausted. The most desperate efforts could only evoke dreary platitudes, and little by little the ability to produce even those vanished, until, as Mr. Spiffler himself said, all his brain seemed melted down, and his skull was full of nothing but fog. Then, flinging down his pen, he caught up his hat. " I'll walk this off," he said to himself: " nothing like a stroll for making you think." And the next moment he was in the Strand. Mr. Spiffler stood a moment undetermined at the corner of the street which debouched upon the great thoroughfare, and then turned East.   He sauntered gloomily along, his eye ranging carelessly over the well-known objects of his walk—the familiar shops and the swarming street.   The air and the change of scene produced their usual stimulating effects.   An idea for a tale struck him.   His eye brightened and his step quickened, as the subject grew and expanded in his vivifying mind.   It was a complicated love story.   The mutual attachment of hero and heroine commenced in Fleet Street; a necessary cause of misunderstanding was found in St. Paul's Churchyard; and an unexpected incident thrilled upon the author's brain in Cornhill.   "Good—decidedly good!" said Spiffler to himself; and seeing an inviting tavern, he entered and regaled himself with a glass of stout, as a reward for his ingenuity.   Then he continued his ramble: the tale prospered all along Aldgate and High Street, Whitechapel, and he was not far from Mile-end gate when a most dramatic *dénouement* flashed upon him.   "Bravo!" he thought; "I'll have another glass of malt, and then be off home again." But, whether there was a screw really loose in the purposed wind-up of the plot, or whether the second glass of malt had rather a muddling than an inspiring quality, it so chanced that Mr. Spiffler found his brain rapidly becoming as hazy as before, and the strands of the tale, as it were, starting and untwisting beneath his hand.   Uttering a few inward expressions of more vigour than sanctity, the author pushed rapidly on, plunging from street to street, as though he were pursuing the fleeting ideas of his brain.   For nearly an hour he walked utterly at random—threading his way through labyrinths of mean streets, and occasionally crossing large thoroughfares, of an open and suburban character, with broad and partially unpaved *trottoirs*, and occasional rows of ancient elms, until at length, with an exclamation of disappointment at the non-success of his mental travail, he stopped short and looked about him.

He was in an unfrequented and shabby-looking street. Close to him stood an unpretending bricken church, o poverty-stricken Gothic; and stretching along the way lay the churchyard, in which a man was digging a grave. Spiffler was tired, so, entering by the open gate, he sat down on a tombstone, and began to curse the hero and heroine **of** his tale for their obstinacy in refusing to be worked into the plot which he had been constructing with so much useless toil. Then leaning upon an upright stone, he began mechanically to read the inscriptions about him. Amid the commonplace monuments around, one tombstone particularly excited the author's attention. It was a round block of pure white marble, without a stain or flaw, on which, upon the eastern side, was engraved, in deep, black letters, the single word,—

Treuchden.

Spiffler inspected the stone curiously, but it bore no other memento—not even a date or an initial. Then he sat down opposite to it, and began to muse.

"There's a story connected with that stone:" so ran his ponderings. "A single name—a female name—a foreign name. I may as well pick up a hint or two if I can. I'll go and ask that fellow digging the grave."

And so saying—or rather so thinking—Spiffler walked off to the labourer. He was a squat, commonplace-looking fellow, and as the author approached he stood breast-deep in the grave, leaning on his spade.

"Curious tombstone that," remarked Spiffler, indicating the marble block. "You don't happen to know who's buried there, eh?"

"No I don't," said the man, civilly; "it was there afore me or my pardner worked this ground. I reckon it's put on some one as 'ad a misfortune—a young lady, perhaps. You know"—and the man winked significantly: "the friends was close, likely, and didn't want no names spoken of."

"Ah, not a bad guess," said Spiffler. "I thought as much myself. Poor girl! died of a broken heart! Treuchden! what a funny name!—there's nothing rhymes to it! And so no one knows anything about her?"

"Yes, but there does," said the gravedigger quickly.

"Ah! who is that?"

"An old gent, the rummiest old cove you ever see, as comes here most days in the week. He has fits—he has—sometimes—and falls down among the graves, a-hollerring and whooping like mad."

"Tell me," said Spiffler, greatly interested,—"tell me all you know about the old man. Come, I'll make it worth your while."

"Yes; but I have told all as I knows on—except, perhaps, that if he'd any friends they'd a-been and locked him up long ago."

"I see," said Spiffler, tapping his forehead.

"That's about it, sir, and no mistake," replied the gravedigger.

"It's clear—it's quite clear," muttered the author, his thoughts running on bookmaking. "Treuchden—a Dutch or Flemish name. Ah!—yes!—of course—a young English student at—Leyden, perhaps—the Burgomaster's daughter—romantic attachment—elopement—arrival in England—desertion—death—remorse and ultimate madness of the seducer—with an epilogue about the tombstone! I see—it will do capitally!"

"Hush!" exclaimed the gravedigger. "Talk of the devil—here he is!"

And a tall old man came pacing amongst the tombs.

"By Heaven!" cried Spiffler, "I've seen that face—I've seen that face before! Where was it? where could it have been?" And he racked his brain to discover.

Meantime Benosa walked straight to the white marble tomb, and stood before it in an humble attitude, as a criminal might before a judgment-seat. Spiffler watched him closely. Sharp twitches passed over his grim features, and now and then he bowed his head, as though listening to an invisible speaker. Then he flung his arms wildly about, his lips moved fast as though he were muttering to himself, and his gaunt frame shook with emotion.

Presently the church clock struck three. The stranger started, turned quickly round, made what appeared to Spiffler to be an obeisance to the tomb, and then, with a rapid motion, buttoned to his chin his long surcoat, and walked away.

"There's a old lunatic—just," remarked the gravedigger.

The author sat on a stone plunged in thought.

Meantime Benosa walked out of the churchyard, and stopped upon the pavement opposite the central door of the church. Here, as the chimes struck the quarter past, he was joined by Blane.

"Mr. Lorimer will be at home to-night—he has written," said the latter.

"To-night he will be homeless," replied Benosa, in his usual calm, impassible manner.

"He is bringing some people to London he saved at sea."

"Let him find a roof to shelter them. The legal possession of the Park Lane house now rests in me?"

"It does; all that was easily arranged. I could have made Lorimer sign anything."

"Then, within an hour, my agents shall be in actual possession, and from them he shall learn that he is penniless. Is Sir Harrowby Trumps in London?"

"I believe so; but out of the way."

"Good! I have no more need of you at present. Go to Abingdon Street and sleep there."

The speaker waved his hand, and the twain parted without further words.

All turned out as Benosa had spoken. That night a post-chaise drew up at a house in Park Lane: admission was refused to the man who demanded it. There was a violent altercation. A crowd collected. It was dispersed by the police, and the post-chaise, with all its occupants, moved away. It stopped again at a West-end hotel, and from it there descended a thin elderly man, a stout elderly female, a young girl, exquisitely beautiful, but deadly pale, and a young man, who, instead of following the party who entered the hospitable portal, turned abruptly away and disappeared.

At that moment the thin man said, with a strong American accent,—

"Ne-ow, then, where is Mr. Lorimer?"

The stout lady echoed the inquiry; the beautiful girl looked it. But no one could give any information upon the subject.

Clement Lorimer was gone.

CHAPTER X.

A NIGHT IN THE STREETS.

WITH his hat pulled low upon his forehead, with knit brows and clenched teeth, Clement Lorimer strode away from the door of the hotel. What he conceived, in his short-sightedness, to be the crowning-blow, had fallen on him. The cloud had been gradually darkening; for days ruin had been in prospect, and he had dared to look it in the face; but now the actual crash rung around him. Lorimer had as brave, as tough, and sinewy a spirit, as falls to the lot of most men, but he was stunned, bewildered, by the last catastrophe. Literal beggary was what he had hardly contemplated; but here he was homeless, houseless—absolutely a pauper! He put his hand into his pocket. With the exception of some two or three shillings, he was destitute. For a moment he seemed inclined to laugh: there was something wildly ludicrous in the idea. He, Clement Lorimer, who had never in his life felt the want of a hundred pounds—he, the owner of a west-end palace, of carriages, of yachts, of racers—that he should find himself, in a single instant, a homeless, penniless man! The idea could hardly be realised. It overwhelmed, as it were, the brain; numbed and paralysed it, as an electric shock might the limbs, leaving behind merely a dull aching thrill—a sense of heavy, half-felt, half-frozen pain.

Presently, little by little, the mind began to rally from the blow. Lorimer thought of the transformations in the Arabian Nights—of princes and emperors changed by magic into dogs and owls—and began to wonder if their state of mind after the catastrophe could have been in any degree like his own. For, cavil as you will, the man who finds himself at one crash turned from a millionaire into a pauper, undergoes, if not in fact, at least in effort, very nearly as tremendous a revolution as befel any of our childhood's Eastern friends, when some potent enchanter sprinkled over them a few drops of clear water, upon which, instead of the merchant or the prince, there stood before the magician a bird or a beast.

Thus musing Lorimer began to recover his self-possession, and to turn his mind with calmness to the exigencies of his position, when another consideration burst like lightning upon him. His debts! how did they stand; —who were his creditors?—and, above all, his turf debts! the vast sums for which he had become liable by the defeat of Snapdragon on Epsom Downs! The thought was appalling. It scared his very soul. To be stripped of what he possessed was a blow; but he could bear it, he had manfully borne it. But the debt, an unknown, mighty load of debt, hanging like a rock of granite above his head! No mortal, neither flesh nor soul, could withstand its crushing fall. Then, for the first time, Lorimer felt his blood grow cold within him, and his stout heart shrink, and quail, and sicken.

" Madman!" he muttered to himself. "Infatuated! doomed! could I not have foreseen a fate different from other men? Has not my life been a black mystery even to myself? have I not been the toy of some tremendous hidden power—the toy long played with, long cherished—but now, at last, to be broken in the hollow of the hand? And I never sought to discover the secret of my birth—of my parents! I lived on in idleness, and folly, and debauch, thoughtless and careless, until, in a moment, from out the sunny air the levin bolt has struck me."

Uttering an inarticulate cry of agony, Lorimer rushed mechanically forwards, uncaring and unwitting whither he went. His heart beat thick and fast, his temples throbbed, and, when he pressed them with his hand, he felt how the heat of fever radiated from his brain. The long lines of lamps began to dance and flicker before his eyes; passengers and vehicles dashed past him like the dim half-seen images of a troubled dream. Then the whole outward scene around seemed strangely blended with the turmoil of thought within. He hardly knew whether he looked upon realities or upon phantasms. He heard voices in the air, which mingled with the roar of passing carriages; he saw mocking faces, which hovered about his own. In his madness he shouted aloud, struck random blows at the phantoms which beset him, and then, suddenly losing all consciousness, fell heavily upon the pavement.

When he opened his eyes, he found himself stretched upon a bench in the bar of a small and quiet public-house. The landlady, a buxom dame in satin, was bending over him, and untying his neckerchief; the landlord, a meek little man with an apron, was holding his wife's vinaigrette to his nose; two or three *habitués* of the place were smoking clay-pipes, and wondering whether the gentleman had got apoplexy or was simply intoxicated; and the policeman, who had raised Lorimer from the ground, was in the act of hurrying off for the divisional surgeon.

"We're never to lose time in them cases," said the latter functionary; "perhaps it's a stomach-pump business, you know."

"No, no! I've taken no poison!" said Lorimer, faintly.

"Ah, bless you! There! he'll soon come round—the colour is coming back to his cheeks already," murmured the landlady. "Make him a little port-wine negus—poor gentleman!"

"Well," grumbled her husband, "it's as well to be charitable; and, besides, he looks as if he could pay for it."

A mouthful of the hot mixture in some degree revived Lorimer, and he was lifted in a reclining position against the wall. He was still unable to stir his limbs, and he felt deadly faint as, with closed eyes, he lay listening mechanically to the conversation around him. The policeman, under pretence of looking after the gentleman in the fit, was being treated by the men with clay-pipes at the bar, and in return was regaling them with some choice morsels of police experience.

"Ah, he's a reg'lar bad un, is George," said one of the men.

"He's wanted now very pe'ticklar," replied the policeman. "For that job down by Ponder's End—a reg'lar out-and-out burglary that was, sure-ly! It 'ud be worth twenty pound in a poor man's pocket to meet him—it would!"

"Who are you talking of?" inquired the landlady, with some disdain.

"Of Georgy Simmons, ma'am!—old Simmons' son as kept the chandlery shop down King Street—him as broke the old man's heart.

"And that's true," struck in the landlord "He was bad from the beginnin'. I know'd him when he offer a bad shillin' at this bar for avannar cigars,—did that boy—before he was ten years old."

"He warn't more nor twelve when I had him in charge the first time as he was locked up," said the policeman. "My eye, warn't it a rum go, nyether!"

"What was that, polisman?" inquired the landlady, in a tone of dignified curiosity.

"Why, you see, 'um, there was an old lady as lodged in Simmons's—the three-pair back—and teuk the fever, and died on it. So in course they laid her out all regular, and, 'case the old lady was somethink of a lady, and had some tin, they put a couple of bright crown pieces, as she kep in a shamoy leather-bag round her neck, a-top of her eyes to keep 'em shut. Well, ma'am, who should see the body but Georgy Simmons, and thinks he, 'Them crowns 'ud be jolly useful to me, and penny-pieces would do just as well for the old gal.'"

"Ugh—the brute!" said the landlady.

The men laughed.

"Well, 'um, sure enough, that very night up he goes, with a shaded rushlight, into the room, and whips off the crowns. Blow'd if the old lady didn't open both her eyes, as though she wor in astonishment! 'Never mind, mum,' says Georgy, 'it's all right—it is, mum,' says he; and he claps on the coppers, and cuts down stairs like winkin', and off out with the money. The grandson of the old lady comes to our station next day, and gives information of the robbery, and that very evening I see the young un loitering about the Yorkshire Stingo. He got three months for it—he did!"

"And serve him right!" said the landlady, in great indignation; "and I hope he'll soon be among the kangaroos."

"Well, ma'am," said the officer, "I think that's pretty sure—that is ——"

The gossipers were interrupted by a movement of Lorimer, and turning round they saw that he had risen, and was supporting himself against the wall.

"I have to thank you all," he said, in a low, feeble voice; "you have been very—very kind! I—I am better now, and the fresh air will quite restore me!"

"Are you sure—quite sure, sir?" said the landlady.

"Quite," replied Lorimer. "It was only a fit—a sudden faintness—a giddiness! I have been excited and worried; but I am well now—quite well!"

All offer of remuneration being generously and firmly declined—by the landlady, because Lorimer was such a mild, sweet-spoken young gentleman—by the landlord, because his wife would not let him touch a farthing—and by the policeman, because he was afraid of taking money for the discharge of his duty before witnesses—Lorimer turned to go, when his eye fell upon a figure which rivetted him to the spot.

In a window recess, on the opposite side of the bar to that in which he had been deposited, sat, apparently in a state of tipsy torpor, his clothes torn and soiled, his face sunken and unshaved, and sodden with continued drunkenness, the once smart and trimly-attired Tim Flick. He looked up at Lorimer, but there was no recognition, no mind, in the glare of his fixed, blood-shot eyes.

"How long has that man been here? how long has he been in this state?"

The landlord shook his head.

"It's a humbling sight, sir! That there's Flick the jockey, who rode the Favourite at the Derby. I hear he's never been sober since: they say there was foul play, and the owner of the 'oss was ruined."

"Ah!" said Lorimer. "Who says so?"

"I don't know, sir," replied the man. "I only hear it talked about like."

"And has that man, Flick, said anything?"

"Nothin' sir!—nothin' that can be made out! He grumbles and mutters; but you see the state he's in yourself, sir! It will not be many more Derbies that he'll ride."

The jockey caught up the word.

"Derbies!" he muttered, in thick, almost unintelligible accents. "Derbies! I've a-ridden seventeen and won five, and I never sold —— "

He did not complete the sentence, but, with a sudden start, became silent, and seemed to shrink within himself. Of all those present Clement Lorimer alone knew how, in former days, the assertion would have been finished

All at once the drunkard started up,—

"Back!" he roared; "stand back—he's the swiftest 'oss in Europe, and no one shall doctor him. No one—back—back I say! Eh! what's that?—the check!—oh, mercy, mercy!"

And staggering forwards, he fell heavily upon the table, splintering the glass of spirits and water which stood before him.

The bystanders looked at each other.

"Delirium tremens!" said the policeman. "I often see men like that. Unless he's looked to soon, that's a gone man, that is!"

"Let all care be taken of him here," said Lorimer. "Get medical attendance—every thing requisite—I will be responsible."

The landlady would be only too happy: the landlord coincided, only he would be glad of the gentleman's address.

The word went like a red-hot wire through Lorimer's brain. The blood mantled up in his cheeks as he stammered out, in evasive reply, that he would return on the morrow, and that, in the meantime, his friend Dr. Gumbey would receive instructions to call upon the poor wretch before them.

In a moment afterwards Lorimer was in the street. He was faint and exhausted, but the cool night air revived him, and he walked slowly on, his limbs trembling and shivering beneath him. Again and again he tried to discipline his mind to a calm and steady consideration of his position. But the over-wrought brain refused to perform its functions of thought. It received the images conducted to it by the organs of sense, but it failed to arrange, or classify, or retain them. Often during his after-life Lorimer tried to recall distinctly the events of that night, but in vain. A dim haze hung over it. The fever-fog was abroad upon his mind, and only broken, disjointed recollections rose, like pinnacles, above it. He remembered standing under a pillared portico. Lights flashed about him—carriages, all glancing in the

glare, dashed by—groups of company flocked around—
women enveloped in cachemeres and ermined drapery—and
men in all the elegance of evening toilet;—while on every side
there rose up into the summer night the rich joyous sounds
of laughter and mirthful words.   Then it appeared to
Lorimer that he was one of the crew assembled in a night
musical tavern.   There were flaring gas-lights toned down by
rolling clouds of tobacco smoke, and long tables, lined down
all the vista with double rows of red, excited faces, and the
walls around rung to the roaring chorus of a drinking-song.
Anon the scene changed—the grey dawn was pale in the
almost deserted streets, and red streaks of light stretched
along the eastern sky behind the steeples.   A group of men
and women—the former principally muffled and great-
coated cabmen, the latter slatternly and painted outcasts—
stood round the barrow of an early-breakfast man, and with
drunken glee guzzled down the hot, unsavoury liquid, he set
before them.   Then gradually the summer's sun filled the
silent streets.   The air seemed as pure as ever was Parisian
sky.   The far-extending lines of roofs cut the blue heavens
clearly and sharply.   The hum of the returning day commenced to sound,—shops opened, and passengers began to
press along the pavement: the day had begun again.   Then,
as though utterly unable to retain the mere ordinary phenomena of common-place life, Lorimer's memory was obscured
by an utter blank.   He only remembered a sense of weariness—a sensation of dreary, purposeless wanderings—a
dreamy vision of houses, streets, hurrying crowds, and some
dim, indefinite power, which always hurried him on—on
—on!

At length a light and gentle touch was laid upon his arm,
and a sweet voice sounded in his ear,—

"Mr. Lorimer—my preserver!   Thank God we have
found you!   The General, and Mrs. Pomeroy, and myself,
have all been watching your return.   We have heard something of how it stands with you—nay, do not start!—and I
thought it likely, very likely, you would wander here."

Lorimer made a violent effort, turned his face from the
sweet countenance which gazed into his, and looked around
He stood opposite his late house in Park Lane.

With a faint exclamation, he would have broken free from the firm, yet gentle clasp, which detained him.

"No! you are ill—very ill!" exclaimed his companion, at the same time signing to a passing coachman.

It was just in time: Lorimer was lifted in a senseless condition into the vehicle.

"O God!" murmured the lady, "how inscrutable are Thy ways! Yesterday he saved me—to-day I have saved him!"

And then the carriage drove away; she who engaged it having given an address in Cecil Street, Strand.

CHAPTER XI.

AN EVENING AT THE OPERA.

WE are at the Italian Opera. The orchestra has just burst into the opening strains of the prelude to Norma. The pit is nearly full, and although many of the boxes—nearly all in the grand tier—are yet empty, there are signs by which the *habitué* can guess that the house will be a brilliant one. In the front of the pit, not far behind the conductor, occupying, indeed, the two places upon the foremost bench, next the avenue which runs up the centre of the *parterre*, stand two of our personages with whom the reader has already some acquaintance—Mr. Spiffler and Owen Dombler. The former is gazing round the house with that familiar air which betokens a man who is perfectly at home—the face of the latter wears that expression of eager, but awe-struck curiosity, which so particularly distinguishes those to whom a visit to the Opera is an era in their lives—a thing by which, for months afterwards, events are to be dated. From time to time Mr. Spiffler, with a patronising air, handed his companion his double-barrelled ivory lorgnette, and condescendingly pointed out the great folks around.

"I'm afraid the attendance will be thin," Mr. Dombler ventured to remark.

"My dear boy, don't shew your ignorance—a brilliant

night! But people can't be expected to hurry away from their dinner at eight o'clock, you know."

"Oh, of course not!" said the City clerk, humbled and rebuked.

Mr. Spiffler was busily sweeping the house with his lorgnette.

"Do you expect anybody in particular?" asked his companion.

"No—no—nobody: merely the Box-office Barometer!"

"The Box-office Barometer! who or what is that?"

"Ah!—I see!—so—in the pit—good!" murmured Mr. Spiffler to himself. Then addressing his companion, "You see a square-shouldered man with red hair, standing at the back of the pit?—he's the Box-office Barometer."

Dombler was still in the dark.

"Why, don't you see, he always has boxes somehow or other for nothing. It's a very useful art that of getting boxes for nothing—there's lots of fellows who live by it. Well, the red-haired gentleman is very clever at it. If there's a box unlet in the house he's sure to have it; so you can always tell the state of the box-list—particularly when it ain't a subscription night—by his position. If he's in the grand tier, put down the performance as a dead loss to the lessee; if in the second, there's a little. His apparition further up denotes a so-so state of things; but if he's only in the pit, you may be certain there's over a thousand pounds in the house."

And having delivered this luminous exposition of the state of things denoted by the red-haired man, Mr. Spiffler continued to scan the house with his glass, considerately informing his meek and wondering companion of the result of his observations.

"The Duke of Gravesend—in that box, three from the proscenium—and the Honourable Erith Marshe. Look at the duke! it always takes him twenty-five minutes to put on his left-hand glove, and half-an-hour to put on the right. Chalkstones on the joints, you know—terrible thing gout, by Jove! Ah, there's the countess and her daughters! Did you ever see a more beautiful arm? how it does come out against the crimson, eh! Ha!" with a wave of salutation to a gentleman who entered a box on the third tier,

II

came to the front, looked about the house with a rather disparaging air, and then sat down, resting his chin on his
hands, and gazing moodily into the pit. "That's Dorling,
the critic for the —— " (Name of the journal whispered.)
"He's so conscientious that we call him 'the only correct
card!' But, then, look in the omnibus-box. What, the
deuce! you don't think the omnibus-box is in the gallery?
So, you see that young fellow with the slight moustache?
He broke the bank one night, when I was present, at Aix-
la-Chapelle. De Mythe's his name. You'll see it to-
morrow among the men whom the fashionable-intelligence
reporters of the papers always observe at the Opera.
Ah!"—in a louder tone to an acquaintance at a little distance—"how do, Colonel Black?" Then, *sotto voce* as
before, "A most curious chap—nice, good-hearted, agreeable, gentlemanly little fellow—remarkable for being like a
bird, everywhere at once! You think he's only here at
present. Stuff and nonsense, I'd take ten to one he's talking
to one man at the French Plays, and another at the Adelphi,
at this very moment. You see the pale, thin man beside
him; he's a noted hand at play, that fellow! He never wins
hardly, but he's always making wonderful combinations of
figures, and thinking he has discovered the doctrine of
chances. Lord, what a swarm of Jew music-sellers as usual!
That's Moses, the sheriff's-officer. I know the scoundrel's
muzzle well—I was two days in his den in Cursitor Street—
the thick-lipped black fellow there, with the lot of rings, in
the box on the second tier, by the third lustre. Hillo!—
old Flethers!—that stupid-looking old man. He was
introduced to me once, at a mild party at Islington, as a
literary character, and the author of the celebrated conundrum, "When is a door not a door?'"

And in this manner did the multifariously informed
journalist run on, until his companion, in utter wonder at his
stores of information, exclaimed,—

"Ah, Spiffler! what jolly times you have of it—going
every night to the Opera, and getting up to all these things
—compared to us poor fellows in the City, who have to
drudge away until foreign-post hour! I wish I knew enough
of music to be a critic!"

"So you do," said Spiffler.

" But I don't know anything."

" That's enough ! "

" What ! and music so complicated a science ! "

" Music may be a science, but writing about music is a dodge, and one dodge is worth three sciences any day in the week — that is, of course, if you know how to work it ! "

" I don't understand — I —— "

" Hold your tongue, and I'll make you a musical critic in three words. Call all tunes 'movements' — never say anything is correctly played, but 'conscientiously interpreted;' whenever you hear a slow air, and then a quick one, lug in a sentence about a 'largo,' and a 'cabaletta' — write as much about 'diatonics,' 'major-fifths,' and 'chromatic intervals,' as you please, because nobody but fiddlers and pianoforte teachers know anything about them. If you want to do the severely classical, you can always talk about some old Dutchman of the name of 'Bach,' who wrote fugues — go into raptures about '*Iphigenia in Tauris*' — sneer at any one who writes lovely melodies as a quadrille composer — and say good-naturedly, that of course Auber and Bellini are very well in their way. Then, as to vocal music, take care you don't get confounding mezzo-tintos with mezzo-sopranos, for that is awkward; but be sure, when a *débutante* comes out, to be great upon the quality of the tones of the upper or lower 'register' — don't forget that word — nor 'flexibility' either — nor 'wiry' — nor 'timbrée.' Never call a voice a voice, but always an 'organ;' and above all, and here's half the secret of musical criticism in a word, make it a solemn rule never to conclude an article without complaining that the brass drowned the stringed instruments, and finding fault with the conductor for taking the time of the adagio 'too fast,' or, if the allegro, 'too slow.' "

Dombler was expressing his obligations for this piece of enlightenment when the curtain rose, and the grand marching chorus of the Druids burst over the house. Mr. Spiffler, who seemed to make it a rule to look as little at the stage as possible, was still hard at work bringing his lorgnette to bear on the various tiers of boxes, and it was not until, amid the most solemn silence, as the first notes of the opening recitative were chanted by the stern priestess from the altar, that he turned languidly round, muttered approvingly, —

" Ah, good! Grisi *is* in voice to-night !" and then, half
shutting his eyes, leaned back to enjoy the " Casta Diva."

In due time the opera was over, the curtain fell, half
the pit was in motion, and the corridors and staircases became
crowded with that mob of fashionable idlers who night after
night haunt, with such indefatigable perseverance, the brilliant avenues of the Opera. Amongst these was a sleek,
faultlessly dressed man, who walked as softly as a cat, and
seemed to know, and be known by, everybody. You
couldn't tell whether his whiskers or his coat were glossiest,
and his face was all one silent smile. He was accosted by
a showily-dressed man, wearing a profusion of rings and
chains.

" Ah, Gumbey ! how de do ? Grisi 's good to-night !"

" To-night only, Mr. Shiner ?" in a low, oily tone.
" But the treat is to come — Chateauroux's new *pas !*"

" *Apropos* of Chateauroux, does any body know what's
become of Lorimer ? That was a smash, by jingo ! warn't
it, doctor ? Good for us we weren't much in advance,
too !"

" Oh ! Lorimer has been distinguishing himself ! Haven't
you seen the evening papers ? "

" No ! what is it ? Hung himself, or cut his throat, eh ?"

" Fie, fie, Shiner ! You ought not to speak so — Lorimer
is a very dear friend of mine."

" Was, you mean !" said the dashing merchant.

" And a very, oh, a very gallant fellow to boot !" the
other went on, not heeding the interruption. " After the
Derby—oh, a sad affair ! dear, dear !—he went off to sea in
that yacht of his. Well, sir, it appears by the evening
papers, that there was bad weather the other day down in
the Channel, and that an American liner was, shocking to
say, totally lost on the Goodwin Sands. The yacht, the
Fly-by-Night he calls her, was near, and, gad, sir ! if Lorimer
didn't,—I don't know the story perfectly,—but, somehow, he
saved a lady who was clinging to some spars, and then was
instrumental in rescuing a lot of passengers from the wreck,
particularly some American general or other, and his wife :
and—and I believe the lady I told you of was their daughter,
or belonged to them somehow or other, but — in short it was
very gallant, and all that sort of thing, and—and — but in

fact you'll find it all much better than I can tell you in the newspaper!"

"So, so!" answered Mr. Shiner. "Well, I must say that was like Lorimer — keeping other people's heads above water when he can't keep his own!"

"Don't be too sure of that," said Dr. Gumbey, mysteriously.

"Why, it was an out-and-out smash; and those two fellows that were always with him, Trumps and De Witz, are both nowhere — never been heard of since the Derby day!"

"You have not heard the latest news, my dear fellow!" replied Gumbey, in the same silky tone of mystery. "Sir Harrowby Trumps was at the Corner this morning, and honourably paid every farthing he owed upon the late race."

"By the living jingo! did he though? No, d—n it! the man hasn't a rap! and they say he has mortgaged his wife's salary. The thing 's impossible, doctor!"

"The thing may be impossible, but the thing is true. I saw De Mythe this morning with a handful of bank-notes he had from Trumps. Why, man! he's in the house, you can ask him."

"In the house!—who? De Mythe or Trumps?"

"Both! De Mythe is in the omnibus. I saw Trumps in the stalls, staring round as if he were looking very sharp after somebody."

"There's a good many people looking devilish sharp after him. Well, by heavens! we're coming to the times of miracles again! I won't despair of seeing an honest Jew before I die!"

"Stop!" said Gumbey; "a miracle is an impossibility in fact; an honest Jew is a contradiction in terms. But, touching Trumps' resurrection, here he comes to answer for himself."

And the coarse, pimply-faced baronet, dressed in elaborate evening costume, swaggered up. He only stopped, however to grunt out a harsh, "How de do, Gumbey?" and an equally curt, "Ah, you here, Shiner!" and then passed hurriedly on, and they heard him roaring for the boxkeeper.

"Mr. Werwold's box — it's on this tier, isn't it?" he said, looking nervously at the numbers displayed upon the doors.

"This way, sir!" said the functionary addressed, and bustling down the corridor, he threw open the door of a box, and Sir Harrowby Trumps entered.

The curtain was drawn on the side furthest from the stage, so as to screen from general view the occupant of the box, and as the baronet entered, the former hitched his chair into the corner, and flung the drapery before him, so that Trumps could only see that he was a tall old man, with long straggling grey hair. The face of the unknown was the more effectually concealed, inasmuch as he held to his nostrils a large bouquet, over which gleamed a pair of piercing dark eyes.

Such seemed to be the appearance of the figure which motioned to Sir Harrowby Trumps to take a chair. The baronet obeyed, casting half-curious, half-sheepish glances, upon his mysterious host.

The prelude to the ballet had began before either of them spoke.

At length the old man, with a slight inclination of the body, said, in a cold, measured tone, —

"A nobody like me has reason to be proud of the punctual attendance of so *recherché* an individual as Sir Harrowby Trumps."

The word *recherché* sent a thrill through the baronet's veins. It had a complimentary meaning, and an unpleasant one. However, he stammered out, that the circumstances of the invitation were too strange for him readily to have forgotten it.

"Yes, the circumstances do appear strange at first sight! You last night received a visit from a stranger?"

"How he found me out, Satan only knows!" exclaimed Sir Harrowby.

"There is nothing more likely," resumed the other, in his glacial, impassible tone. "Satan only knows!"

Sir Harrowby stared at the speaker with his big blood-shot eyes. Were it not that he was in the centre of a gay, crowded theatre, he would have felt nervous. But, like many other people, the baronet was only afraid of the devil in the dark.

Meantime the man with the bouquet resumed,—

"The stranger brought you a letter, and delivered this message,—'If you think fit to comply with the recommendations contained in this letter, do so to-morrow morning, and to-morrow evening meet the writer at the Opera. Ask for Mr. Werwold's box, and bring with you the letter as a token of identity.' These were the words?"

"The very words."

"Give me the letter."

Sir Harrowby mechanically produced a paper from his breast coat pocket.

"I shall read it—I may, as I wrote it!"

The baronet bowed, and his companion read the following lines, in his usually cold and measured tones,—

"SIR HARROWBY.—The writer of this note may prove serviceable to you: you in turn can prove serviceable to him. You have little money, and need much: he has much money, and needs little. A contract mutually advantageous may be made. As an earnest, the writer encloses a cheque—it is for the amount of your present turf debts. Pay them, and appear in public. The bearer will add a verbal message, and bring back a verbal answer."

There was a short pause.

"The bearer brought me back word that you would comply with the contents of the note. You have done so!"

"Almost to the last farthing of the cheque, and here I am now. What do you—what can you want with me?"

"I want," said the old man, "I want a man who is covetous and unscrupulous—a man who is heartless and debauched—a man who has many acquaintances and no friends! I want a ruthless agent—a pitiless mercenary tool!"

Sir Harrowby leaped upwards from his chair.

"By all the gods ——!" he was beginning; when the clear, keen tones of Werwold, penetrated the hoarse sounds of his husky voice.

"Man, man!" exclaimed the latter; "cannot such as you hear the truth from such as me without starting up like a beardless boy at Oxford, or a greenhorn cornet of dragoons?"

Trumps muttered some unintelligible words, and grasped the chair in his brawny fists as though he intended to hurl it at his companion. The latter never moved a muscle, and his eyes gleamed over the bouquet, in the dark corner, like two glow-worms.

"Sit, man, sit!" said Werwold. "We must hear and speak many hard, cold truths, if we are to be useful to each other!"

The baronet mumbled something to himself, of which the words "old madman!" were alone audible. But Werwold took no heed of them. Then Trumps flung himself sulkily back into his chair.

"You are a friend and associate of Clement Lorimer?" began the old man.

"I must know what you are driving at before I answer that or any other question."

"You shall know in good time. I ask for no ordinary purpose—the events of last night may convince you that I am no ordinary man. Deal by me as I want, and I shall deal by you as you would wish. I have need of truth in this matter. I don't want to buy your soul—I only want to hire it: will you lend it out for gold?"

Trumps paused, and then said, "Go on—but I must make my bargain ere you go far."

"Good, and only reasonable! You are a friend and associate of Clement Lorimer?"

"I was — he's ruined now."

"Of course you helped to do it?"

"I wasn't the only one.

"Who else?"

At this moment, a loud round of applause welcomed the appearance of a favourite upon the stage, and the heroine of the ballet came bounding down the boards and bowed before the footlights — bowed, so low and so long, that the upper part of her figure appeared as it were to sink into and fade away amid the misty wreaths of her muslin drapery. She represented a bright aërial spirit, who once a year, upon the anniversary of a beatified saint, was permitted to appear upon the earth, to try and reward the purity of virtuous love.

"Who else?" repeated Werwold.

"Her," said Trumps, indicating with his elbow the pure aërial spirit.

"Humph! And Mademoiselle Chateauroux cares as much for the victim as you do?"

"Just as much."

"Notwithstanding, Lorimer may not prove so pitiable a victim, after all."

"Why he's plucked!" said Sir Harrowby; "plucked to the last feather! Perhaps you don't know his history. He never knew his parents; he never knew where his fortune came from; and now, all at once, the supplies are stopped."

"Perhaps," repeated the other, in a freezing tone of sarcasm, "perhaps I don't know his history—perhaps I do."

Trumps looked at the speaker keenly; but he only saw the two eyes glaring over the bouquet.

"He must have hundreds of creditors," continued the baronet, "and not a rap to stop the jaw of one of them."

"He has not hundreds of creditors. He has only one."

"One!—and who is he?" gasped Trumps, in amazement.

"You—if you like," answered his companion.

The baronet started almost off his seat, and stared at Werwold.

"Come, by G—!"—he at length exclaimed, with a horse-roar of laughter—"confess, old cock, that all this is a hoax."

"Was the cheque this morning a hoax?"

Sir Harrowby's mirth ceased, and he fidgeted uneasily on his chair.

The old man resumed.

"Lorimer owes tens of thousands. Suppose his debts were made over to you?"

"Yes—but who can make them over?"

"I can."

"And much good they'd do me. He might rot in prison; but what better should I be?"

Werwold's eyes twinkled, with an odd expression, as he answered,—

"Perhaps I don't know Lorimer's history—perhaps I do.'

"You must speak more plainly, then, if we are to work this game together: I'm not good at riddles. If you can make it worth my while to help you, tell me how it is to be done."

"Listen, then. I am a cautious man: therefore I will not say that I state facts. I will simply put a case. Suppose, in days long gone by, I had been wronged. Suppose also that I am of an unforgiving temperament. Suppose my enemy has a son—a son by ——; no matter, that we have nothing now to do with. His fortunes depend upon his keeping the birth—the existence of that son, a profound secret. Still he lavishly expends money upon the youth—loves him while he indulges him—suffers him to fall into the worst of company—into your company——"

Sir Harrowby stifled an oath in his throat. His companion went on.

"Until, on a sudden, there comes a crisis in the fortunes of father and son. The latter, by an unlooked-for chance, becomes most in want of money just as the former is least able to furnish it. At the same time, too, the father is made aware of the prodigal courses of the son. He finds that riches have ruined him: he wishes to try if poverty will not restore him. The one was a moral laxative; the other may be a moral tonic—a moral corrective. In fact, by a lucky chance, prudence seems to prescribe what necessity would dictate, and the supplies are stopped. Now, mark! The father loves the son. He sees little serious evil in the boy's being cast upon his own resources. He thinks it will merely cause his son to rough it for a time. He has no idea that his debts amount to the sum they do. Now, then, comes the chance. Down upon the son with all the terrors, all the grinding, crushing powers of the law. But let one arm hold the thunderbolt—it will be grasped more steadily—it will be launched more surely. Will that arm be yours?"

"Again," asked Sir Harrowby; "again—how should I benefit?"

"Short-sighted that you are! The father in that case will pay the son's debts—pay you."

Sir Harrowby clenched his hands—the veins in his forehead dilated—and his eyes gleamed with greed and exultation

"Yes, I see — I see! But, yet — no — stop. You offer me these advantages — why do you do so? How would they benefit you?"

"To pay the son's debt would ruin the father. But the father would pay the son's debts — and the father is my enemy. There! — is the logic good?"

"Then you barter money for revenge?"

"Every one has his whims. I want you to barter honour for money."

"You ask me," said Sir Harrowby, with an uneasy smile —"you ask me to do what no gentleman ought to do!"

"I ask you to do what no gentleman would do!"

"And you expect me to comply?"

Werwold paused for a moment, looked keenly at the baronet, and then said,—

"Yes."

There was a pause, filled up by the gay dancing music of the ballet. Sir Harrowby Trumps squeezed his forehead with his brawny hands, and then said,—

"You have bought up all the young man's debts — why don't you sue yourself?"

"Because it is too dirty a business for me to appear in!"

"By jingo, old man, you're a cool talker! But consider my reputation — Lorimer was my friend."

"It is because I have considered your reputation that I have made this proposition."

Trumps' cheeks coloured, and his eyes flashed. Then he appeared to make a mighty effort over himself, and sat motionless — in thought.

Werwold's eyes glared at him over the bouquet. At length Sir Harrowby spoke.

"We understand each other — give me your hand.'

And he held forth his own.

"No!" replied his companion. "I will pay you your hire; but I will not give you my hand."

"By the Lord!" shouted the baronet, "this is coming it rather too strong. Is the one better than the other? Ain't we both on the same high way?"

"Travellers to the same point are not always friends of the same mettle."

Sir Harrowby Trumps gazed at his companion for a moment and then said, quietly,—

"I am at your orders."

"Good!" replied the other. "You will hear from me by eight o'clock to-morrow morning."

A volley of "bravos" at this moment rung through the house, and the baronet looked towards the stage.

"It's Chateauroux's new *pas*," he said.

Even as he spoke the dancer finished a brilliant series of sparkling *entre-chats*, by suddenly becoming as motionless as a marble statue before the centre footlight. A peal of applause rose from boxes, pit, and gallery.

"We shall often see each other now," said Werwold. "I need not recommend secrecy, of course."

Meantime the *pas* had been encored, and Mademoiselle Chateauroux was again bounding round the stage. Werwold followed her motions with his eyes.

"Yes!" he murmured; "yes — good — very good. She has *à plomb* — grace — brilliance."

Sir Harrowby Trumps eyed this strange connoisseur in wonder. In a few moments the *pas* was concluded, and Werwold, shouting "Brava! brava!" leant over the box and flung his bouquet at the feet of the *danseuse*. It happened to be the only one thrown at that particular moment, and Spiffler's quick eye rapidly followed its line of flight to the point from whence it proceeded.

"By Jove!" he cried, "there's the man who knows the secret of 'Treuchden.'" And without staying to enlighten his astonished comrade further, he made his way through the centre avenue of the pit, up the spacious staircase, and along the corridor of the tier, in which Werwold (or Benosa) and Sir Harrowby Trumps had been placed. The door of their box was open; but the box itself was empty, and the box-keeper, when appealed to, stated that "Both the gents was just gone."

CHAPTER XII.

THE TRAP WORKS.

Two days have elapsèd since Mademoiselle Chateauroux anced her new *pas* at the Opera, and we have to transport the reader to the drawing-room of the house in Cecil Street, .Strand, to which the coachman was directed to proceed when Clement Lorimer was recognised by a young lady, in a fainting condition, in the street.

The room is a large and handsome one. It contains no lack of furniture, both gaudy and comfortable. Mirrors gleam from the walls, and damask and muslin curtains hang in festoons down the sides of the long narrow windows. Still the apartment lacks the more refined comforts of social life. With the exception of an evident circulating-library volume or two, no books are arranged upon the tables ; neither harp nor piano stand in snug corners; no loose music is strewed carelessly about, and the china card-bowl is as devoid of cards as of punch. The whole place has that primly and superciliously neat look which denotes the better class of lodging-house.

Two persons occupy this apartment. One of them the lady saved from the floating spars by Clement Lorimer, the other Clement Lorimer himself. He is stretched upon a sofa. The pallor of his features and their thin shrunken appearance tell of the smart fit of illness just recovered from, and the movements of his limbs as he tosses restlessly on the couch are feeble and languid.

His companion is a fair girl of twenty. She sits by the sofa, stooping over her needlework ; her rich chestnut hair arranged in massive folds upon her cheeks, hiding the face of its wearer except when she looks gaily and frankly up, in conversation with Lorimer. Then you may see that this face is of gentle and winning beauty ; that the eyes are large, and lustrous, and blue, shaded by the long soft lashes ; and that the features, although not perfectly regular, are pretty in themselves, and lighted up with an exquisite expression of

innocent gaiety, blended, sometimes, with a passing shade of
deep thoughtfulness, at others with an arch look of shrewd
naïveté.   Her tall *svelte* — we have no corresponding English
word — figure is shewn to advantage in a high well-fitting
morning-dress, and a single antique brooch fastening a pink
riband round her neck is the only ornament she wears.

"Now, Mr. Lorimer," she said, and the ringing tones of
her voice tinkled gaily, "although, as a true-born American,
I am a stanch Republican, yet now I intend to be a despot.
You must not dream of stirring out to-day.   You are such a
fidget — you will be sure to worry yourself into a fever again."
She paused, and then added in an altered tone, "We are not
old acquaintances, Mr. Lorimer, but circumstances have
caused us not to be ordinary ones."

Lorimer looked intently at her.   "Circumstances, indeed!" he said, in an abstracted tone.   "But I cannot — I
will not remain longer inactive.   I have fallen from a tower,
but I have recovered from the stun.   How shall I ever sufficiently thank you, Miss Eske, for your kindness? — the General and Mrs. Pomeroy, for their kindness towards a poor
homeless fellow like myself?"

The words were words of humility; but as Lorimer uttered them his cheek coloured, and his lip curled proudly.
Then he saw the soft blue eyes of his companion fixed so
meekly, so tenderly reproachfully on his own, that a pulse-
like thrill passed through his soul, and he added, in tones
which were low and slightly faltering,—

"At all events, whatever may be my future fate, can I
ever forget the face which looked its meek brightness into
mine when the cloud was at its gloomiest?"

It was now Miss Eske's turn to colour.

"You know my position," Lorimer continued; "you
know my most singular — I fear people will soon have to
add, most fatal — history.   As soon as I recover my health,
and I have nearly recovered it, I must act — I must make
some effort to penetrate the riddle of my being.   I must do
something — I must turn to something — though I am sure I
hardly know what.   I feel I ought to do everything.   I know
not how to set to work about anything; but this I do know,
that every moment passed without exertion seems to me to be
a moment of crime."

"If we—I mean, if the General and Mrs. Pomeroy could in any way be of service, oh, believe me!—they are odd people, perhaps, not like you polished Londoners—but they have good, kind hearts."

"I know it—I know it; but this is my own battle, and my own arm must fight it."

"And you will win, too!" said the girl, with a sudden glow of enthusiasm; "win what you have lost, and more than what you have lost!" Then suddenly stopping, as if she thought she had expressed herself too warmly, she ccloured deeply, and bent over her work in silence.

Lorimer looked fixedly at her, and made a motion as if to take her hand; then, checking himself, he said, "I don't know—I hope so. When the first shadow of these evils fell upon me, I felt bold and strong, and almost longed for a struggle which would put my mettle to its proof. Then the mood changed. As we approached London—that night——" He paused, and then went on: "that night, which was the first of my illness, I felt my spirits, my energy, ebbing from me."

"You had been over-fatigued—over-excited," interrupted Lorimer's companion.

"Perhaps so," he rejoined. "I would fain hope that it was the failure of the body, which for a time broke down the mind. Yes! it must have been so—now again I begin to feel nerved for the battle; but I shall only know where my enemy is by the quarter from which the next blow will be struck at me!"

"Let them strike—do you ward," exclaimed Miss Eske. "Oh, if I were a man, I should wish nothing better than to bear my cwn brave heart against the odds of fortune!"

Lorimer gazed upon the beautiful girl before him—gazed upon her kindling eye, and her veined and dilated nostrils.

"Miss Eske!" he said, "Marion Eske! will you allow me to call you?"

"You are the preserver of Marion Eske! call her as you will, and you will call her as she likes."

"Then—Marion—good, bold-hearted Marion, why did we not meet before?"

"Have we met too late for me to speak an encouraging

word to one who, even though he be an invalid, scarcely requires it?"

"No, no!" replied Lorimer, in a low and significant tone. "Let fortune go as it may—if we have met while both are young, while both can love—we have not met too late."

He took her hand in his, and was drawing it, in spite of the coy struggles of its possessor, towards him, when a loud knock sounded at the street-door.

"Here come the General and Mrs. Pomeroy!" she exclaimed. "Shall I report that you have been a good patient?"

"I think I can trust you," he replied, "to say nothing very bad of me."

At that moment the door opened, and the General and his lady entered. General Pomeroy was a little, thin, sallow man, of meek and pacific appearance. His warlike title he owed to some nondescript rank—it was not easy in Europe to discover the exact grade—which he held in a regiment of Massachusetts militia. In America, brevet military ranks are of no difficult acquirement, and General Pomeroy found the warlike handle to his name so extremely respected in Europe, that he was by no means in a hurry, by any overt act or statement, to reduce himself as it were to the ranks. We have said, that in person the general was small. He had little twinkling grey eyes, but their keen expression was counteracted by the easy good-humoured smile which played around his thin lips. As for his dress, it was constructed in that happy medium which it has been reserved for American tailors to discover—between the styles of the English sloven and the French swindler.

Mrs. General Pomeroy was a very stout lady, in resplendent satin, and decorated with a very heavy and massive gold chain, supporting a very small Geneva watch, made at New York. She was, she said, of a highly nervous temperament—an assertion which would be perfectly credible were fat one of the symptoms; and furthermore, she was afflicted with a strange disease, which she stated had prevented her from sleeping a single wink for many years: at which assertion, and it was usually made every day at breakfast, the general was accustomed to wink secretly out of that eye furthest from his lady, and immediately to make some observation respecting the unpleasantness of snoring — as regarded listeners — and which he said he could corroborate from personal experience.

"And how do you find yourself, Mr. Lorimer, now?" inquired the General, bustling up to him. Mr. Lorimer was daily, almost hourly, recovering strength; and so he said.

"We've a-been sight seein' till we've almost walked our legs right off — this mornin' — ain't we, Mrs. Jiniral?" observed the Transatlantic man of war.

"Don't talk to me, Jiniral!" replied the lady, stretching herself on an easy chair. "What with not having had a wink of sleep last night, and you lugging me up and down this great smoky, black town, I'm a'most done up, and that's a fact."

"We ve been to see Westminster Abbey," resumed the General. "It's neat, considerable neat — rayther a goodish location; but it ain't up to Deacon Barl's meetin'-house in Applesquash Town — nohow!"

"It ain't to be expected in the Old Country, Jiniral," responded the nervous lady; "but it's not so bad, considerin'. There's no Poet's Corner in Deacon Barl's."

"In course not," responded the General. "Ours is a free country — it is — and as long as a man has dollars to pay his location, he may go to any corner he likes, whether he's a poet or not — exceptin', of course, the niggers, who have a tarnation gallery to themselves, quite handsum, with strict injunctions to the first rank not to go ahead in the way of spittin'."

"And after the Abbey?" prompted Lorimer.

"Oh, then we had a look at the Houses of Lords and Commons!" said the lady. "My lawful heart alive, but this is an aristocracy-ridden country! There was the Jiniral, and not a soul takin' notice of him; while the porters and people about were touchin' their hats like mad to all the old fogies who were goin' in and out."

"Yes, my dear," struck in the General, "but there was the Duke of Gravesend. You know he was pointed out to us goin' into the committee-room — he was; a sort of kinder skeared he'd a-been, if he knew that there was lookin at him a citizen of that free and enlightened country where

I

there's no nobility but dollars and no serfs but niggers. You saw him, Mrs. Jiniral?"

"I guess I took no notice—I despise aristocrats and aristocracy too much to look at 'em; but if you mean the individual with the high-coloured face and black hair, very glossy—and dark surtout with silk buttons—and them light plaid trousers, tightly strapped over his boots—and his gloves very neat and not a wrinkle in them, for you could observe his nails through the kid—and no jewellery about him but a couple of bright little diamond studs in his shirt; if it's him you mean, yes, I saw him. They told me he was a duke; but I calculate I wasn't going to notice him on that account."

Lorimer and Marion Eske exchanged glances.

"We'll go to the theatre to-night," said the General; "to Drury Lane. It must be a poor place compared to the Bowery or the Park. You won't be riled, Mr. Lorimer, when I say it's jinirally admitted to be so. What do you think, Mrs. Jiniral, ayre we a-goin' to the play?"

"Well, I don't know," said the lady, "but I require excitement—my nerves, Mr. Lorimer, are in that unstrung state. Dr. Bodge—that's Bodge of Applesquash Town, Mr. Lorimer; you have heard of him, I guess—says I'm all one nerve. Didn't he, Miss Eske, my dear? But, lawful heart alive, here have we been gallivanting about all day, and havin' no end of luncheons at pastry-cooks'——"

"Rig'lar prime uns," said the General; "loud uns—chicken fixings!"

"While you two have had nothin' all the morning! Ring the bell, Jiniral."

The military man complied, observing, that he would not be the worse himself of something in the drinking line. "But Lord, now, Mr. Lorimer," he continued, "your drinks ain't fit to hold the candle to ours. You don't go ahead in the Old Country. I asked to-day in a pastry-cook's—Farrance was the name—for a 'sling" then for a 'cocktail,' then for a 'yard of dead-wall,' then for a 'gullet-scraper'—Lord! it wasn't of the least use—nohow; the girl looked at me as though I was a coon a-turning hisself outside in on a rail! But you're an inferior people—it's a fact. We are young—we improve—we progress—we go ahead. The Old Country's at the end of its tether; and that's a proposition there's no disputin', or may I be rubbed down with alligators' teeth and knocked into immortal gravy!"

Here the General's eloquence was interrupted by the luncheon tray, the contents of which Mrs. General Pomeroy, in despite of the combined effects of previous lunches and nervousness, attacked with vigour and effect. So also did the General, while Miss Eske presided with infinite grace over the meal.

Lorimer was engaged upon the wing of a chicken, when the postman's rap heralded a letter.

"I guess it's from our minister," said General Pomeroy. "I despise the tarnation vanities of kings and queens; but that's no reason why one of our free and enlightened citizens should not be presented at Court."

But the letter was no favourable response from the American minister. In fact, it was not for General Pomeroy at all; but for Clement Lorimer, who started as he recognised the great sprawling superscription.

"From Trumps!" he muttered. "What can he have to say, or how has he found me out?" Then nervously bowing for permission—a piece of ceremony which neither the General nor his lady appeared to understand—he broke the seal and cast his eye over the contents of the missive. It was an extraordinary one. Lorimer could not believe that he read aright. His colour came and went, and he sank back on the sofa with his eyes mechanically fixed upon the paper.

Miss Eske looked anxious and frightened. The General put down an untasted glass of sherry, and Mrs. Pomeroy entreated him just not to make himself nervous — for she knew what it was — she just did. After a moment, Miss Eske ventured to hope that there was no bad news.

Lorimer made an effort and said, "No—not bad—only surprising—very, very surprising!"

Both General Pomeroy and his wife looked very much as if they would have liked to hear this surprising intelligence; but they had too much natural good feeling to hint their desire, particularly in the agitated condition into which they saw Lorimer had been thrown.

Apologising for the necessity of answering the letter at once, Lorimer rose to withdraw, whispering as he passed Miss Eske,—

" The next blow is struck ! "

" And from an unexpected quarter ? "

" Amazing — overwhelming ! " said Lorimer ; " but I shall know more by sundown."

CHAPTER XIII.

SQUEEZING THE DRY SPONGE.

In one of the gaunt, musty, old-fashioned streets which abound in the neighbourhood of Soho Square, and in a shabbily furnished, slovenly, and not over clean room, sat a wan and worn-looking woman, who had once been beautiful. Her neglected hair—the grey thickly mingling with the black, fell in elf locks down her cheeks and streamed on to her shoulders, over which was tightly strained a dingy old shawl of uncertain pattern. There was a melancholy air of chronic desolation and misery in the woman's whole appearance. She seemed faded, and withered, and shrunk ; and only her large black expressive eyes appeared to possess anything of the pristine fire and energy of their owner. Round her were scattered heaps of engraved and manuscript music ; and in a corner of the room stood an open pianoforte, almost the only handsome article of furniture it contained. Taking up a sheet of blotted manuscript music, the occupant of the chamber placed it upon the piano, and ran her long thin fingers over the keys, evoking a brilliant and elaborate prelude. Then adding her voice to the instrument, she began to sing. A critic, were he present, would have been startled by the mingled richness and clear ringing brilliancy of the soprano possessed by the performer ; and he would soon have known, from the ease and precision with which she warbled a florid and difficult piece of music, that he was listening to a vocalist of the highest order.

She was so engrossed with the music before her, that she did not hear the door open or a heavy step cross the floor, and it was not until a man's hand was laid upon her shoulder that she turned round with a start and a little gasping sigh.

Sir Harrowby Trumps stood at her side. Without evincing any emotion at his appearance, she shrugged her shoulders as though chilly, swathed the shawl closer round her, folded her arms, and said,—

" I did not expect you !"

" Well—there's the more pleasure in seeing me—eh ? " said the baronet.

She shrugged her shoulders again, and a melancholy half-smile stirred her thin white lips.

" Come Polly, old girl, give us a kiss — things are looking up, so try and be jolly."

She submitted to his embrace with perfect passiveness, and then he sat down near the music-stool, on which she remained as motionless as a statue. There was a moment's pause.

" Well," resumed Sir Harrowby, " you ain't looking well, I must say. What will put colour into these cheeks of yours, eh ? "

" Paint I " said the woman.

" Don't get aggravating," replied Trumps. " You're very well here."

" On fifteen shillings for seven days? That was what you left me out of my last week's salary."

" What can I help that? I had only a pound myself —the Jews took the rest."

The vocalist again shrugged her shoulders and was silent.

" Come," resumed Trumps, " I'll soon have lots of cash. Funny things are brewing—and then you may keep the whole of your salary yourself, and welcome."

" Thank you !" she replied, in a tone which was sarcastic from its very meekness.

" 'Thank you!' Yes, I should say so," replied the baronet, losing his good humour fast. " 'Thank you!' Ah, you think you're a persecuted martyr—an injured dove, eh ? Curse it, ma'am, ain't you my wife?"

" Yes."

" And don't all you've got, and all you do get, belong to me, eh ? Who has the law on his side—eh, woman ? Ain't your voice and your talents—not that I ever thought so

much of them myself—but ain't they mine? and the money
they bring, ain't it mine too?"

" All, all yours," replied the vocalist.

" Then don't let us have any more of your whining
'Thank you's!' that's all.   Sing your music, act your parts,
and let your husband draw the money—for the reason that
you can't help it—eh!   Do you hear that? that you can't
help it !—and the best of all reasons going."

" You said," replied the woman, who was Lady Trumps,
but to whom we shall give her stage name of Madame
Lorton—" you said that strange things were brewing."

" What's that to you?" exclaimed her husband.   " I've
an appointment to meet some one here, and the time is almost
up—so clear away some of these piles of music, and make
the place look more habitable."

So saying, he flung himself down in a ricketty arm-chair,
which creaked beneath his weight.   The meek wife proceeded
to perform the task assigned her.

" Do you sing to-night?" said Trumps.

" Yes."

" What?"

" Rosina."

" A sparkling part that—keep up your spirits for it, Polly."

At that moment a low knocking was heard at the street-
door.

" Go into the bed-room and wait there until I call you,"
said Trumps.

She obeyed, and in a few seconds the tall form of Benosa
strode into the room.   Sir Harrowby Trumps, with a great
show of uneasy cordiality, bustled about to place a chair for
his visitor.   The old man repelled his advances with a silent
wave of his hand, and took his seat by the table.

" A fine day," the baronet remarked, hesitatingly.

" The weather is not to the purpose," replied the other.
"You have written to Clement Lorimer, and preserved a
copy of the letter?   Such were my directions — let me
see the document."

Sir Harrowby Trumps produced a draft of the letter,
which he put into Benosa's hands.   The latter read it aloud.
It ran thus,—

" My dear Lorimer,—I feel sorry to stand in the position by you which now I do; but rum things turn up, and
of course no one can blame any one for standing up for his
rights (which the law recognises), you owing me money for
which am much pressed.   In fact, to make a long story
short, you are damnably in debt, and I am your only creditor.
How this is—which will surprise many, and none more than
your humble servant—of course, as you ought to know
something of your own family history—you should be in a.
position to have some idea of.   But that, of course, is your
affair—not mine.   Now I would be the last man in the
world, as you well know, to press hard on any man in the
way of money matters; but as you have probably backers in
the dark—of which I heared hints—it will be all the easier
for you to shell up, them standing the needful.   But, however that may be, there's no use talking.   We were very
good friends and all that; but, of course, being men of the
world, every one knows that the man as is hard pressed himself must press others hard too: it being quite impossible
that I can meet the demands on me without my own debts
are paid up.   You will have a letter from my solicitor in a
day or two, with items which hope will be satisfactory, and
proofs that it's all as I say.   I write these few lines to you
myself in a friendly way, and as preventing any one from
saying as I acted unhandsome by you.
  " Apologising for the intrusion,

" Am yours faithfully,

" Harrowby Trumps."

  " It's the style you like, I hope," said the baronet; " I
took some pains on it."
  " It is the style which I expected," replied Benosa.
" Here," and he produced a packet from an inner breast-
pocket; " here you will find the items and proofs of debt you
spoke of—send them to your solicitor.   I hope he is
grinding one."
  " He's a Jew!" answered Sir Harrowby.
  " That is enough," said Benosa.
  " The epistle will astonish Clem — eh?" inquired Sir
Harrowby, jocosely.

"It will instruct him," replied Benosa, "as to the value of the men in whose faith he had confidence."

Sir Harrowby Trumps flushed up and clenched his hands. At this moment a thundering appeal to the knocker roused the echoes of the silent street.

Sir Harrowby flung open the casement, looked out, and then suddenly drawing in his head, with evident marks of discomfiture, said,—

"It's Lorimer himself—sink him! I never thought he'd have traced me here."

"You fear to meet him!" sneered Benosa.

"Fear!" echoed the other; "no, it's not just come to that yet, I hope;" and he concluded the sentence with a burst of harsh and forced laughter. "But you—do you wish to see him?"

"To see him—yes! To meet him—no! at least not yet. Suppose me away."

Uttering these last words, Benosa glided into one of the window recesses. They were deep; for the walls of the old-fashioned house were thick and massive, and the folds of the dingy moreen curtain entirely concealed him.

The next moment the door was burst open, and Lorimer, pale and excited, rushed into the apartment. Sir Harrowby Trumps tried to assume an easy smile, which sat with ghastly effect upon his twitching, anxious face.

"My—boy, Lorimer," he was beginning, when the other interrupted him.

"Is your name to this scrawl a forgery, or is it not?" And he held the open letter out before the baronet, who took it, and, evidently to gain time, pretended to inspect the hand-writing with great attention.

"Come—yes or no!" exclaimed Lorimer.

"Well, then—no!" said Sir Harrowby. "There!"

"It is your production. Good. What am I to under-stand from it?"

"The letter, I thought, was plain enough."

"So far as it goes it is plain enough; but you know more than you wrote."

"Upon my sacred word of honour——"

"Trumps!" said Lorimer, with such a bitter sneer upon

his features, that even the obtuse and brutal man whom he addressed felt its force.

"Very good," answered the baronet, doggedly. "Find out what you can—I will screw out what I can, and we'll see who'll rise the winner from the game."

"Then," said Lorimer, "you refuse to give me the least inkling of information upon this most extraordinary transaction?"

"Yes. Why should I? I am in my rights. You owe me money; I require it, and I shall have it."

"You know," replied Lorimer, mildly, "that you speak this to a ruined and penniless man."

"That remains to be proved," answered the other. "Some people take a lot of ruining."

"There is a dark complot on foot," said Lorimer. "I am to be its victim, and you—you are its tool. Confess—you were bought for a purpose?"

"Lorimer," said the baronet, with some show of moderation, "circumstances give you license. We were friends, I confess."

"Friends!" exclaimed the other with bitter emphasis. "Why, man, I fed you!"

Trumps started back, and glared upon the speaker.

"Take care," he muttered between his clenched teeth; "take care, or it will be the worse for you! Your day is gone, and your night is coming!"

"Ah, I thought as much!" replied Clement Lorimer, coldly. "This is no ordinary debtor and creditor business: there are springs at work beneath the money. Look to yourself, Sir Harrowby Trumps. You are sailing in deep water. There is conspiracy, foul, hidden conspiracy, beneath me. I do not pay your brains the compliment of saying that you are one of the conspirators, but I pay your meanness the compliment of saying that you are one of the conspirator's engines. Look to yourself! I am roused, and begin to know what is in me. I may not baffle my enemies; but I will fight hard—fight to the last! There is war between us. I will track you—I will dog you. I will follow the wires until I find the hand which pulls them."

"No doubt you will do clever things," sneered Trumps; "but you will not set aside the law—the law which says *that* every debtor shall pay his creditor, or submit to the penalty."

"The law!" rejoined Lorimer. "You invoke the law! It may well be that I shall turn the tables—shall bring the law down on you and your employers. You are frightened now, man! You are blenching!—you begin to fear that even you stand on mined ground! Invoke the law, indeed! There is an awful mystery which the sleuth hounds of the law may trace—a mystery of suspicion, perhaps a mystery of crime—the mystery of my own being! Before long, perhaps, that secret shall be unravelled, and I will know who I am, and the world shall know what you are!"

Breathless with excitement, Lorimer paused. Sir Harrowby made violent efforts to appear calm and unconcerned; but his flushed cheeks and dilated nostrils betrayed his agitation.

"There!" resumed Lorimer. "Tell your employers what I have said. Tell them, that if they burrow I can dig—if they can plot, I can unravel; and tell them, too, that not a peaceable night, not a tranquil day, shall I enjoy, until I have unkennelled them, one and all! until I stand face to face with the deadliest of my enemies—although that enemy should prove my own unknown father!"

At the commencement of the last sentence, Clement Lorimer had clutched the collar of the baronet in his excitement, and gradually drawn Sir Harrowby close up to him, until, as he spoke the final words, he flung him, by a violent, but almost involuntary effort, away; so that, as Trumps staggered heavily against an arm-chair, which he overset, Lorimer passed hastily from the room.

When Sir Harrowby recovered himself, he saw Benosa confronting him. The features of the latter wore their usual cold, impassible look, but Trumps observed that his teeth were closely set.

"He is a bold youth," the old man said, "and bears him with a brave heart. The father ought to be proud of such a son—eh? The father ought to be proud of him, and help him, and pay money to get him out of such clutches as yours, Sir Harrowby—eh? Speak, man, speak! Ought not a father to be proud and fond—ought he not to cherish such a son as Clement Lorimer?"

Any one more accustomed than was Trumps to note the feelings indicated, rather than expressed by words, could not have failed to notice the tone of acute agony in which these words were spoken. But Sir Harrowby was thinking of himself.

"This is an ugly business," he said.

"How easily is a bully bullied!" replied Benosa.

"D'ye take me for a bear to be baited, old man?" shouted Trumps. "I've stood enough of this! I've stood more than ever I suffered yet, and more than I'll suffer again!"

"That is to say, that you will allow many thousands of pounds — a fortune — to slip through your fingers, because your lawful debtor can make fluent speeches?"

Sir Harrowby stood irresolute. Benosa eyed him keenly.

"Choose," he said.

"Between what?" answered the baronet.

"How did you pay your turf debts a day or two ago? I lent you the money — is it not so? Choose, then, between being Lorimer's creditor, and forcing him to pay the money he owes you — between that, and being my debtor, and being forced to pay the money you owe me!"

Sir Harrowby stood aghast.

"Do you think, man!" and Benosa hissed out the words between his clenched teeth, "do you think that the agents I employ slip through my fingers so easily? You will learn better! I can prove my loan. I can prove i was given and accepted to further a conspiracy — an un lawful conspiracy! You hear? This is a free country, Sir Harrowby Trumps; but there, even as you stand, an English man on English soil, you are as much my slave as though you were a Russian peasant and I the Czar!"

"I — I will do your bidding," stammered the baronet.

"You will do wisely," replied Benosa. "You have my instructions — act upon them! In the meantime, I think our business is over. I hope I shall soon have to congratulate you on your accession to fortune. 'It's an ill wind,' Sir Harrowby, 'which blows nobody good.' For the present, adieu! Do not fear but that we shall shortly meet again."

With these words, and with a grave reverence, Benosa

withdrew. As the door closed upon him, that of the bedroom opened, and Madame Lorton appeared. She was paler than before, and trembled excessively.

"Who—who was that man?" she inquired.

"The devil for what I know," vociferated her husband.

"Harrowby! Harrowby! what is all this?" she exclaimed.

"A plan to get money, Poll!" he replied. "Money—thousands on thousands—a fortune, my girl!"

He paced the room for a moment, flung open a cupboard, from which he took a decanter of spirits, half filled a tumbler with brandy, swallowed it, and then shouted, with his hoarse, rough laugh,—

"A new invention, Polly, for squeezing water from a dry sponge!"

CHAPTER XIV.

THE LANDLADY S HUSBAND.

The landlady of the lodging-house in Cecil Street, in which were installed General and Mrs. Pomeroy, U. S., was a pale, pinched-in looking little woman, having a perfect mania for scouring and scrubbing; and a remarkable talent, amounting to genius, for scolding. Her name, as it appeared in fat letters upon the brass door-plate, was Ginnum. Now there was occasionally seen slipping about the house, in a meek and stealthy manner, and with the air of a man who merely existed on suffrance, a dirty little person, with a stubbly chin, no outward appearance of linen, and altogether impregnated with a mouldy flavour. For a long time none of the lodgers could make out who the mouldy little man was, and many guesses were made, and theories constructed, as to his identity At length one ingenious individual hit upon the happy scheme of asking the mouldy man himself. The reply was at once startling and characteristic.

"Sir," said the mouldy man with great meekness, "I am Mrs. Ginnum's husband!"

He was so known ever afterwards. Nobody thought of calling him Mr. Ginnum, or even plain Ginnum: he was always "Mrs. Ginnum's husband."

What the particular duties fulfilled by Mrs. Ginnum's husband were, it would be difficult to specify. He was sometimes absent from the house, as though he were attending to some regular calling. At other times he haunted the lower regions of the establishment. Glimpses were caught of him in the passages, and his dirty face was occasionally seen looking up from the front area. Where he had his meals, and where he slept, were mysteries more deep than the authorship of "Junius," or the identity of the "Man with the Iron Mask." The only piece of legitimate duty he ever appeared to perform was sitting up at night to let the late lodgers in. On these occasions he gave loose to his conversational powers, so far as saying very meekly, "Good night, sir!" as he delivered the flat-candlestick to the retiring guest. The other characteristics of the mouldy little man were, that he was always shabby, and occasionally not sober.

It was upon the evening following the interview described in the last chapter, that Mrs. Ginnum's husband opened the street-door, came out, closed the portal very quickly behind him, and after casting a hurried glance up to the windows, apparently in the fear of Mrs. Ginnum being stationed at one of them, walked quickly up the street, turned westward when he got to the Strand, and then suddenly plunged down a gloomy tunnel, leading beneath the houses to the banks of the Thames. It was a passage black enough, and dismal enough, to have led to a robber's den or a coiner's cave, but it simply conducted those who trod it to a series of coal wharves, stables, and to a waterside public-house. The latter was the destination of Mrs. Ginnum's husband. The premises were apparently familiar to him, for, passing straight through some sanded passages, he ascended one or two flights of stairs, and presently emerged upon the roof of the tavern. The apparent oddness of this proceeding on the part of Mrs. Ginnum's husband will vanish when we state that the roof was flat, that a wooden railing ran round it, and that tables and benches were placed upon the leaden plateau thus formed for the convenience of those customers who liked, in pleasant weather, to enjoy their liquor and the prospect of the river at the same time.

Mrs. Ginnum's husband seated himself at one of the smallest tables, and was presently accommodated by the waiter with a pint of porter and a plate of shrimps, on which dainties he regaled to his evident satisfaction—jerking the savoury marine insect, in a tender and skinless condition, out of its shelly jacket with great skill and success; lazily watching the fast-pulling wherries and heavy barges as they shot past or drifted drowsily up and down the broad river; and occasionally casting a keen glance around, as though he expected some one to join him. At length a coarse, common-looking man, with a snuffy white cravat, made his appearance; being, indeed, no other than our acquaintance Mr. Blane.

"How do you find yourself, sir? A pleasant evening, really—a pleasant evening—for taking one's little refreshment by the river. The cool air here, sir, is quite refreshing!"

. This cordial speech having been duly acknowledged, and its points agreed to by Mrs. Ginnum's husband, the twain sat down amicably together, as though it were not their first time of meeting; and by Blane's directions, spirits and water and tobacco were supplied to them.

"Don't you indulge in a whiff, sir?" said the ex-prime minister of Clement Lorimer, scratching a lucifer-match upon the rough table, and coaxing the blue sputtering flame by placing it in the interior of his hat.

"I'd like to," replied Mrs. Ginnum's husband; "but my missus 'ud feel the smell in my hair."

"Ah, she's particular about smoking! Many ladies are," replied Blane, in a consolatory tone.

"It ain't only smokin'," said the persecuted spouse; "she's a horrid nose for spirits! But I found that she can't smell gin through peppermint, and so I do her that way."

"And very proper, too," said the ex-steward; "but women will be women, sir: that's the nature of things."

"She's very aggrawating though, sir, is Mrs. G.—aggrawating to me and the ser—ants, she is. She has a way, sir, of putting sly little pinches of dust on the cornices and in out-of-the-way corners; and then, if the girl don't sweep 'em away, oh, my! ain't there a row?"

"Cleanliness, sir," responded Mr. Blane, "cleanliness, as was well observed by the poet, is next to godliness; so that the scrubbing-brush may be described as first-cousin to the mitre!"

And Mr. Blane smiled complacently, as though he had said rather a good thing and knew it.

After a short pause, during which Mrs. Ginnum's husband applied himself heartily to the spirituous compound before him, Mr. Blane resumed the conversation by asking,— "Whether business was good up there?" and he indicated Cecil Street with the waxed end of his pipe.

"Well, it's not bad," said his companion. "We're full at present."

"That's satisfactory," replied Blane.

"Very," said Mrs. Ginnum's husband.

"I saw a lady and gentleman, who looked foreign like, go in yesterday when I was passing the top of the street."

"Ah!" said the landlady's helpmate, "they're Yankee Doodles, them is. They're our front drawing-rooms."

"Bless me!" said Mr. Blane. "Good customers, I dare say?"

"Yes," replied the other; "the General—he's a General in his own country—is always making rummy drinks with spirits and things; not bad some of 'em, for I tasted 'em in the kitchen when there wasn't nobody there."

"I shouldn't be surprised," answered Blane. "And do the General and the lady take much of 'em?"

"Oh, they ain't alone!" said Ginnum; "there's a young lady, too—a Miss Eske."

"A relation, I suppose?"

"No—or only a distant one. She's a sort of friend or companion—you know—of the General's lady; so my missus thinks. But, bless you, she ain't treated like ladies as were at our house often treated their companions; they're so fond of her, you can't think!"

"Ah, quite a nice little family!" said Blane, vacantly.

"I suspect," rejoined the other, with what was intended for a sly grin—"I suspect there will be another member of it soon."

"Ah!" said Blane, with affected indifference; "who's that?"

"Oh, a young chap—devilish good lookin', from the little I saw of him; a Mr. Lor—Lor—Lor——"

"Lorimer?" prompted the steward.

"That's the name!" said the other. "He's got the two-pair back bedroom; but he lives in the drawing-rooms with the Yankee Doodles. He's a great friend of theirs. He came one morning in a cab with Miss Eske; but he's been very ill since."

"Ah!" drawled Blane; "and is he better now?"

"Better! oh, yes; quite well. He was out yesterday in the afternoon. The Yankee Doodles went to the play; but he didn't go, and Miss Eske stayed at home with him."

"Oh, Miss Eske stayed at home with him?"

"Yes," replied the gossiping husband of Mrs. Ginnum; "they're uncommon sweet on each other. I wouldn't be surprised if it was a case; and my missus thinks so, too."

"Indeed! your missus thinks so, too?"

"Yes, I heerd her say so this mornin' to cook, and she knows the symptoms."

Mr. Ginnum then proceeded at great and increasing length—for the spirits made him communicative—to impart to Blane the gossip, not only of his own house, but of sundry other lodging-houses in the street: how the front parlour at 37 was three weeks in arrear; and how the two-pair back at 38 had given warning, because he had had his tea made three mornings with water from a cistern in which he himself had secretly deposited the cat, with a clock-weight about her neck.

Blane listened with the same degree of apparent interest as he had paid to the details with which Ginnum had furnished him of the domestic economy of his own household; and the coming night was dark upon the river ere the ex-steward assisted the tottering limbs of the landlady's husband down stairs, making an appointment with him as he did so for another festive meeting.

Having got rid of his companion at the top of Cecil Street, the spy entered a neighbouring coffee-house, deliberately registered the information which he had received in a greasy pocket-book, and then calmly called for and betook himself to the perusal of the evening paper.

CHAPTER XV.

FORMING A CONTINUATION OF CHAPTER II. OF THE PRO-
LOGUE.   THE SEQUEL TO THE SHIP-OWNER AND THE
SHIP-CAPTAIN.

THE scene is the drawing-room in Cecil Street. General
and Mrs. Pomeroy have gone to one of the theatres; Clement Lorimer and Marion Eske sit close to each other upon
a sofa by the window.   Their eyes are mirrored in a long
mutual gaze, and the fair hand of the girl lies in the grasp of
her lover.

"It is a wild tale," she murmured.   "Your life is like a
dream."

"You know its every occurrence, and you do not think
very, very ill of me?"

"Much must be pardoned," she said softly, "in a career
so strange."

"And yet," resumed Lorimer, "there is no life unfla-
voured by a spice of romance."

"Perhaps not," she replied.   "My own family history is
not without its interesting pages."

Lorimer looked all eager attention.

"I do not mean my own life," said Miss Eske.   "I
speak of a maternal ancestor,—a Flemish lady, who emi-
grated from Europe more than a century ago."

"And she had an adventure?"

"A strange one, which caused both her and her husband
to change their names and to leave New York, where they
intended to reside, for another and a distant State.   The
story was long a tradition in our family.   At first it was
preserved a dead and solemn secret.   Gradually the necessity
for guarding it seemed to pass away, and it was more freely
spoken of; and now I cannot see wherein would be the harm
were it trumpeted in the street."

"At all events I have some claim to hear the tale."

Miss Eske rose, left the room, and presently returned,
bearing a carefully-folded packet.   She opened it, and two

K

rolls of paper fell upon the table. Lorimer took up one. It was a manuscript written in a neat but cramped female hand, and in a language perfectly unknown to him.

"If this be the story," he said, "I am not likely to make much of it."

"That is the original Flemish," replied Miss Eske. Here," and she unfolded the companion roll, "is the translation. I am acquainted with the hand; shall I bore you by reading?"

"Bore me!" said Lorimer, playfully. "Try."

"Then listen, and heed."

And with a clear voice she read the following narrative:—

"MY VOYAGE ACROSS THE ATLANTIC.

"At the suggestion of my dear husband, Heinrich Strumfel, now known and to be known as Martin Vanbrugger, I put upon paper the following plain narrative of facts, which we wish to be preserved as a family document (but in no wise to be communicated to strangers); in the hope that it may some day serve as a clue for the discovery of a deep and fatal mystery, which appears to brood over the family of the writer.

"I left Europe on the 10th of May, 1710, in the good ship St. Nicholas, Captain Schlossejib, belonging to the trading-house of Benosa, sailing from Rotterdam, and bound for New York. My sister Treuchden accompanied me on board. She was oppressed with forebodings of coming evil to our family, which prepossessions I strove to combat and to banish. Meinheer Benosa himself recommended me to the care of the captain, a sinister-looking man, who, as I have heard, has since been hanged to the yard-arm of an English ship-of-war in the Spanish Main, the said Captain Schlossejib having become a noted and dangerous pirate. This I mention as shewing the character of the man. We left our moorings below Rotterdam with a fair wind, and passed the bar of the Rhine, called the Brill, in about three hours; after which we stood to the south-west, intending to double the extremity of England, and so into the Atlantic Ocean.

"The weather, though occasionally boisterous, was good upon the whole, and we made fair progress. I suffered at first from sea-sickness, and so kept my cabin. Captain Schlossejib, during this time, frequently inquired how I did, and was attentive in sending such delicacies as he thought might tempt the appetite of an invalid. We had weathered the Land's End, as it is called, of England, and were fairly launched upon the Atlantic ere I appeared upon deck. Captain Schlossejib then congratulated me upon my recovery, and expressed his hope that he would land me safe and well in the New World. This hope he frequently repeated before the crew, and especially before Jin Karl the mate. I took no particular notice of it at first, esteeming the phrase an expression of common courtesy. I have since been led to think that it was dictated by deeper motives.

"We had been three days out of sight of the last portion of Europe we would see, when Jin Karl, the mate, fell ill of a severe fever and ague. He was a kind man, and had been most attentive to me; I therefore did my best for him, and, having some knowledge of simples, as also a stock thereof on board, I was perhaps instrumental in restoring him to health — a service for which he professed much gratitude and devotion to me. By the time of the mate's recovery, we were half-way across the Atlantic, having experienced a fair voyage hitherto, and having every prospect of making a comfortable and successful passage.

"All this time the captain was laboriously polite to me; often talking about the happiness he should feel in welcoming on board my betrothed Heinrich Strumfel, and consigning me to his fond care; but I observed that he was but ill at ease; that, though he spoke to me often, and laughed with me loudly, he was forcing himself to do the one and the other — in short, that his manner was constrained and unnatural.

"On the 3d of June, the weather, which had until then been prosperous, became foul and disagreeable. We were then within one hundred and fifty leagues of the American coast, and expected, unless the wind continued very adverse, to make it within a week. To my surprise the unfavourable change of weather seemed rather to please the captain than otherwise. Squalls, with rain, became frequent; and as these furious gusts blew off the continent which we were approaching, the regular heave of the ocean, which, under long-continued easterly winds, was setting heavily towards the west, became broken and interrupted. What is called a cross sea was thus formed, and the movement of the ship, which had long been regular and easy, became violent, abrupt, and unpleasant; and occasionally, notwithstanding the most skilful steering, the waves would wash our decks.

"During the whole of the voyage it had been my custom about sundown, or soon after, to leave my cabin and take the air in a stern gallery which ran round that part of the ship. On this gallery my cabin opened. A massive, but not very high balustrade of carved work protected those who stood upon it from falling overboard. Above, rose the structure of the poop, which was very high and richly ornamented, according to the fashion of Dutch ships. The wheel by which the vessel was steered was placed upon the main-deck, close to what is called the 'break' of the poop, so that, as the men of the watch were principally in the fore-part of the ship, it often happened that I sat in the stern-gallery alone, and removed from all who were managing the vessel at the time. During the early portion of the voyage Captain Schlossejib would often join me here. Afterwards, however, he seldom appeared in the gallery, although I once or twice observed him looking down upon me in silence from the poop, and wondered why he did not speak.

"About the same hour as that in which I was accustomed to leave my cabin for the stern gallery, it was the practice of the captain to retire to his apartment to write up the log or journal of the day's proceedings; it being after he had performed that duty that he occasionally joined me, when he would inform his passenger how far the ship had run during the previous twenty-four hours, and what appeared to be the prospects of the voyage. In this cabin the captain kept his best telescope, which was only taken on deck on particular occasions.

"Such was the state of matters upon the 12th of June. That day was peculiarly stormy. The west wind blew in strong gusts, each squall being accompanied by thick gloom and heavy rain. The sea raged furiously, the pitching motion of the ship was violent, and, owing to the broken nature of the waves, extremely uncertain. Notwithstanding the unfavourable state of the weather, I had, as usual, repaired about nightfall to my favourite gallery. The captain,

understood, was in his cabin, occupied in writing up his
log—a seaman who entered the gallery for some purpose
told me so—but a few minutes before, I had seen Schlossejib
looking down at me from the poop. I was sitting pen-
sively, leaning upon the balustrade or rail, and watching
the foaming seas which gambolled beneath, when a squall of
unusual fury struck the ship, bending her over until the brine
was on a level with the leeward portion of the deck. The
shock was violent, and when the St. Nicholas recovered from
the first blush of its fury, she moved rapidly on, plunging
and wallowing in the broken water. Amid the noise of
wind and waves, however, I could hear a cry raised that a
strange vessel was close to us; and, sure enough, there passed
presently, almost obscured in the gathering gloom, a dimly-
seen ship careering before the wind. The squall had by
this time abated, but there appeared to be every chance of a
foul night. Still I lingered in the gallery, when the mate,
Jin Karl, suddenly came to me with horror in his face,
'Thank God you are here! I am not yet too late.' These
were his first words. Full of surprise, I asked him what he
meant. Judge of my terror when, in broken sentences, he
told me that the fury of the late squall had caused Captain
Schlossejib to come abruptly on deck from his cabin—that
almost at the same moment the strange sail appearing pretty
near us, the captain had, in a moment of forgetfulness, as it
would seem, sent him below for the best telescope, and that,
as he was reaching it down from the brackets, his eye fell
upon the open log-book, the last item inscribed in which was
a record of my having been unfortunately lost overboard
from the stern-gallery during a violent squall of wind! The
ink in which the words were written was still wet, and the
hour at which the alleged accident had happened was recorded as half-past eight, it being at the moment we spoke
together within about twenty minutes of that time.

"This horrible and extraordinary announcement flung me
into a violent state of agitation, and indeed the honest mate
was almost as much terrified. We could not doubt but that
the captain intended to murder me, and that he had laid
his plans with devilish ingenuity But what could be his
motive? How could he be a gainer by my death? All a
once the forebodings of my sister Treuchden flashed upon

me. I recognised their truth and sank trembling on my knees.

"'Leave me,' I said to the mate,—'leave me to my death. Ours is a doomed race; there is a curse upon us. The Jonah must be flung into the sea.'

"But Jin Karl, though puzzled and terrified, had a warm and honest heart.

"He stood for a moment irresolute, and then a sudden thought illuminated his countenance. Through the open door of my cabin could be seen a trap leading to some of the lower recesses of the ship.

"'If the captain believed you dead — believed that you had really fallen overboard——'

"I saw the honest fellow's eye fixed on the trap as he spoke, and a gleam of hope warmed heart and brain.

"'Yes, yes!' I exclaimed, 'God has sent you that thought. Quick! I trust myself to you. There is not a moment to lose. I may be hidden in some secret corner of this huge ship. You know them all, you will be my protector, my saviour; is it not so?'

"'I will!' exclaimed the sailor. 'You shall not die.'

"Then we hastily passed into my cabin. A cloak with white linings belonging to me lay upon the cot; I pointed to it.

"'Could it not be thrown overboard,' I said, 'and the captain's attention called to it?"

"Jin Karl nodded eagerly.

"'Leave all to me,' he said. 'Meantime there is not a moment to lose;' and he wrenched open the trap-door. It revealed a dismal hole, dark and stifling.

"'The hardware crates cannot be more than four feet below,' said the mate; and taking me gently in his arms he let me carefully down the hatch. I found that, standing upon the packages beneath, I could just raise my head above the cabin floor.

"'Sit, or, better still, lie down,' said the mate: 'I shall find means to come to you.'

"The trapdoor was closed, and I was left in utter darkness. It was a terrible situation. The huge timbers groaned and creaked around me. The noisome bilge-water exhaled its sickening steams. I felt giddy—my brain

whirled, and I fainted. I was roused by loud trampling above
me, and I heard a confused noise of hollaing voices.   The
alarm of my being overboard was evidently being given, and
I could perceive, from the faintly-heard fluttering of canvass,
that some manœuvre was being performed—probably a feint
of attempting to pick up the supposed victim.   These sounds
gradually subsided, and I heard nothing save the ordinary
noises of the vessel, until Karl paid his promised visit.   He
came with a dark lantern, having made his way through the
cargo and stores from a distant part of the vessel.   From him
I learned that my conjectures as to what had taken place
above, were correct.   First making sure that Schlossejib was
still in his cabin, he flung my cloak into the sea, and in a
moment afterwards shouted that Mademoiselle Louise had
fallen overboard in a violent lee-lurch of the ship.   The
captain rushed directly from his cabin, and Karl, with every
sign of horror, pointed to my cloak as it appeared dimly seen
on the ridge of a sea.   As he did so he watched the captain
narrowly, and saw the flush of savage joy which rose into his
face.

" A few ineffectual endeavours were made to rescue the
supposed unfortunate, and then the usual routine of duty was
resumed.   The captain had sealed up my effects, and had
then gone into his cabin to add in the log-book—so he told
his mate—the record of my loss to the other entries of the
day.   Karl had afterwards stealthily peeped through a cranny
in the door.   The captain was rubbing his hands gleefully
and chuckling to himself.   Of course not a soul on board
but fully believed that I had fallen overboard.   The sailors
talked over my fate for a couple of days, and then, in the
excitement of the approaching termination of the voyage,
I was forgotten by all but the staunch-hearted mate.   He
laboured hard to make my prison bearable.   He formed
for me a rude bed of canvass.   He brought me the little
food I required when it was his watch at night, and supplied me with candles and books wherewith to while away
my solitary hours.   Since my disappearance he said that the
captain had been in excellent spirits, and so remarkably
good-humoured that the crew talked of his change of disposi-
tion as something marvellous.

" But there is no need of recapitulating at length the

monotonous round of circumstances which formed what I may call my prison life. Jiu Karl and I, after many anxious consultations, had settled the policy to be adopted upon our arrival, and our plans had hardly been matured when we entered the harbour of New York. In the evening I received a visit from Karl, who exhorted me to be prepared for disembarking at midnight. The hour came, and the trapdoor leading to what had been my cabin was raised. I was assisted up by the muscular arm of Karl, who led me out on the stern-gallery. A rope-ladder formed the means of descent to a boat beneath. The night was dark and gusty. The captain had gone on shore, and the solitary seaman who formed the harbour-watch was dozing on the forecastle. We experienced, therefore, no interruption in our proceedings, and as I clambered down the rope-ladder I was received into the arms of my dear Heinrich Strumfel. Jin Karl followed me into the boat; he and my betrothed constituting, indeed, its entire crew. In half-an-hour I set foot on the soil of America, and was shortly thereafter lodged in an obscure but respectable inn, passing under the assumed name of Madame Wilfreid.

"The rest is soon told. Heinrich concurred in my view of our situation, and thought it expedient to remove from New York. After, therefore, making a suitable show of concern for the alleged loss of his betrothed wife, he wound up his affairs; and I having preceded him here, he shortly joined me, and under a-feigned name we were married. This course was adopted with the view of saving me from any ulterior attempts of my secret enemies, whoever they may be. No doubt they believe me drowned."

Miss Eske threw down the paper.

" Such," she said, " was the adventure of my ancestress."

Lorimer mused deeply.

" A strange story, but told with all the simplicity of truth. Madame Wilfreid, or Vanbrugger, was ——"

" My great-grandmother," said Miss Eske.

" And her real name ?" said Lorimer.

" Was Louise Vandersteiu !"

CHAPTER XVI.

FATHER AND SON.

NEARLY in the centre of the group of comfortable but essentially *bourgeois* squares, which acknowledge that of Russell for their chieftain, there is situated an odd locality, which combines in itself the characteristics of an arcade and a mews. The passenger who seeks a short cut from the stupid respectability of Bernard Street to the respectable stupidity of Guildford Street, and with that view plunges beneath the wide archway which opens near the western extremity of the former thoroughfare, will observe, stretching away upon his left, the curious row of houses to which we refer, and which a painted board will inform him is locally called " The Colonnade."

This finely-titled locality consists of a string of shabby, dingy old houses, whereof the leading peculiarity is that they project over the raised pavement which runs before them, and are, therefore, partially supported by a row of pillars which rise from the outer margin of the pavement to the level of the first floors. Opposite these houses runs a set of stables and coach-houses; and behind them, again, tower the dingy backs of the mansions of Guildford Street.

The Colonnade is inhabited by a community of small tradesmen and mechanics, such as abound in poor neighbourhoods and shabby suburbs; but one wonders how they came to nestle in the cold shade of the grim gentility and gaunt decorum which surrounds them. What, for instance, can the majestic ladies and gentlemen of Russell Square possibly want with marine-store shops, and cheap curds-and-whey shops, and small coal shops, and children's schools at fourpence per pupil per week? None of the fine linen of Guildford Street can, we conceive, be allowed to flutter, drying, between the pillars and the mews. None of the genteel masters and misses of Brunswick Square can possibly sigh for the sticky bull's-eyes and greasy rock which abound in the cracked and broken windows of the confectioners of the

Colonnade. No, the place must, in some mysterious way, be self-supporting. It is a compact, thriving little vulgar colony, stuck by some unknown chance into the very centre of the region of starched, staring, middle-class gentility, just as we hear of mysterious tribes of Welshmen having been found amid the Pawnees and the Sioux, and clusters of people being discovered in remote and almost inaccessible nooks of the Italian Alps still speaking the language of the Forum and the Colosseum.

The Colonnade is not, if the truth must be told, a particularly eligible place of residence. There is a fusty, greasy atmosphere about it—a faint odour of stables and litter. The dust from curry-combs mingles with the sickly vapours of low cook-shops, and the hot whiffs of soap-suds and ironing and mangling, which float from doors and windows. For the locality is a great resort of cheap washerwomen. Clothes-lines stretch from pillar to pillar, and from the pillars to the stables on the opposite side of the way, and on fine drying forenoons the whole place is one flutter of linen, or, at least, of garments which are usually understood to be composed of linen. Children, of course, abound, clustering round the windows of the eatable-displaying shops, pointing out to each other, with their dirty little knobs of fingers, the most luscious lumps of congealed flour and treacle, and speculating upon which tumbler of curds-and-milk they would choose in the remote and improbable contingency of their becoming owners of half-pennies. The adult inhabitants of the Colonnade are also given to the partially *al-fresco* conferences which the nature of their locality invites. Begrimed mechanics lean over the mouldy railing which fences in the paved and covered way and chat listlessly to the grooms, who sit, polishing harness, at the stable-doors opposite. Slatternly women and big girls emerge from the houses with pails and tubs of dirty hot and frothing water, and resting them on the rail, scream and chatter to each other, or occasionally exchange compliments with the coachman, who, after having set down his employers in Russell Square or Guildford Street, drives the sober-looking family equipage to its resting-place in the Mews.

It is on the evening of a hot summer day that we must beg the reader to accompany us to the Colonnade. About the centre of it, by the side of an open door, there is a board, a couple of feet long, and half as wide, with a pictorial representation, in colours of a glowing red, of a hard-working female, industriously turning a mangle; while, in order that there may be no mistake as to the identity of the laundress, an inscription, in thick, pluffy letters, informs us that we may consider the work of art to represent "Mrs. Dumple," by whom, the legend goes on to state, both "washing and mangling are taken in."

It is to the ground-floor room in Mrs. Dumple's establishment that we have first to introduce the reader. It is a dim, dank, close-smelling apartment, reeking of the fumes of linen in the wash-tub, and linen undergoing the process of the flat-iron. By the wall, opposite to the single window, stands a mangle — supposed to be that delineated upon the sign-board, but now in a state of rest. The large table which occupies the centre of the room is covered with many layers of shirts, most of them in various stages of decomposition; while the pile of washing-baskets in a corner appears to prove that Mrs. Dumple enjoys a good business connexion. A set of tables, chairs, stools, presses, cupboards, and cooking-utensils, of the class which generally adorns the common room — used alike for business and domestic purposes — of such establishments as Mrs. Dumple's, lie scattered about; and between the ironing-table and the small morsel of glowing fire — before which stands a small battalion of flat-irons, rearing, as it were, upon their hind legs, in order to catch all the heat going — bustles about the portly form of Mrs. Dumple herself.

She is a matron of sober fifty, with red, fat cheeks, and thin, weevily hands, whitened and pared down by the labours of the washing-tub. But, upon the whole, she seems to have thriven on her business. Her broad, vulgar, healthy face runs over with a fat expression of unctuous, buttery good-humour; and her dimensions appear to have owed their origin to some more substantial sustenance than the washer-woman's proverbial favoured tea.

Besides this estimable matron, two other persons were present in her ground-floor parlour — a youth in his teens and a little boy not yet arrived at that sage epoch in life. The latter, as might be discerned from his square paper cap, formed of the sheets of an unsuccessful almanac, was undergoing the novitiate to the life of a journeyman printer. He was a curly-headed, black-eyed varlet, about ten years old, endowed with a keen, sharp face, from which shone a pair of remarkably bright and intelligent eyes. This young gentleman was apparently the victim of that distressing complaint known as the "fidgets;" in a continued paroxysm of which he was eternally jerking himself about, flinging his limbs into impossible attitudes, and using the chair near which he was stationed for every possible purpose except that of sitting down upon.

The third occupant of the room the reader has already been introduced to, although it is possible that in that thin, pale face, sunken eyes, and dejected and melancholy expression, he would hardly recognise the once healthy and robust features of Richard Flick, the son of the jockey.

"Gill," said Mrs. Dumple, "I wish you had as many pounds weight on your bones as I have, and then you'd sit quieter."

Gill, by way of reply, leaped upon his chair, sat down upon the back, and then tilting his weight rearward, upset the article of furniture, slipping off the back as it fell, and tipping neatly down upon the edge of the sitting portion of the chair, as, in the mids of a loud scream from his mother. it came with a crash to the ground.

"I'm only lively, mother," said Gill; "nothing like being lively."

"I wish you were in your bed," sighed the matron. "You're after some mischief as long as you have your eyes open. I'm sure no poor, lone widow can manage such a imp. —You're a limb, Gill—a limb."

"Don't talk of bed, mother," responded the son, extending his own along the front legs of the chair, and swaying his body downwards, until his head rested on the back of the prostrate article of furniture,—"don't talk of bed—I've slep two hours to-day already."

"Slep!—where, Gill?" asked Mrs. Dumple, in some surprise.

"On the door-mat, second pair back, 13 Little St Peter's Street, Camden Town. That's where Mr. Spiffler lives now, that is——."

" Mr. Spiffler!" rejoined Mrs. Dumple; "who is Mr Spiffler?"

" He's a author, he is; and I go for his copy—that's the writing that's to be printed, mother, you know."

" But why do you sleep on his mat, Gill?" inquired the matron.

" Because he's never done his copy in time; no author ever has—and so I wait."

" Well, I do think Mr. Spiffler—if that's his name—might have let you wait in his room," replied Mrs. Dumple, coming down upon one of the wrist-bands of the shirt then undergoing the ordeal of ironing with a spiteful dig.

' So he wanted me," said Gill. " Bless your soul! he's a very good chap is Spiffler; but I wouldn't, 'case I liked to keep sliding down the banisters—and so I did, till a splinter——"

Here Gill stopped, wriggled himself on his seat, and grinned.

" It's no more nor you deserved, Gill," said Mrs. Dumple.

" And so then I rolled the mat up comfortable, and wen to sleep till Mr. Spiffler had done a comic story that w wanted to make up."

And so saying, Gill Dumple caught up the chair, an placing the back of it upon his chin, proceeded to balance it in the style of the most artistic acrobats.

During this conversation Richard Flick had preserved a moody silence; at length, when Master Gill, fatigued with his juggling feats, put down the chair, and condescended to sit, tailor fashion, upon it, Flick spoke,—

" Do you think, aunt," he said, " that the doctor will let me see him to-day? Oh, I wish—I wish he would!"

" My poor boy," replied Mrs. Dumple, "you know he said yesterday that he thought your father would be well enough to see you to-day. He has had a sore time of it, poor fellow!"

Richard wrung his hands.

" And all through me. Oh, I heard him rave about me, when I crept out of bed at night, and sat crying on the stairs."

" We have all our troubles, Richard," said the matron. " I'm sure the trouble I have about shirt-buttons wouldn't be believed by nobody who don't get up linen. But they will come off, and it's no use talking."

"You'll be sure to ask Dr. Gumbey when he comes, Mrs. Dumple, about my seeing my father. Tell the doctor I know that I can say something to him that will cure him better and faster than all the drugs in the world."

"I hope you can—I hope you can," replied Mrs. Dumple; "but what is it, Richard?—is it about the race, eh?— the race—or the horse that he was raving about when the brain-fever was on him? You may tell me, Richard,—me, that's your father's own sister; and who, I hope, acted as such when he was carried here mad with delirium."

"No—no, aunt; I wish I could: but it is impossible. I can only tell my father. It's a secret—a dreadful secret."

"Oh, very well; if it's a secret, in course I couldn't keep , or be expected to keep it. I'm such a one for blabbing, s is beknown to all the Colonnade,—in course I am." And the offended laundress dashed her iron over a wristband with such fury, that the button was wrenched off and flung nto the lap of Master Gill, who immediately seized it, stuck into one of his eyes, and winked with the other.

At this moment a tap was heard at the door, and the smooth, clean shaven face of Doctor Gumbey was presented.

"How are we?" he said; "how is the old gentleman up-stairs, eh? Going on well?—not a doubt of it; oh, not a doubt of it."

Mrs. Dumple hurriedly smoothed her cap, slipped off a rather dirty apron, diverting the doctor's attention by a series of curtseys, during the performance of these operations, and then prepared to marshal the visitor up-stairs.

Richard had slunk into a dark corner, as if ashamed to face Doctor Gumbey; but, as Mrs. Dumple was leaving the room, he twitched her gown as a mute refresher, in reference to the interview with his father. The matron nodded, and, preceding the doctor up the narrow stairs, the boys were left alone together. Flick then came out of his corner, and dropped down upon the chair which he had formerly occupied near the window, and Gill, approaching him, saw the tears running down his face.

"Come, cousin Dick," said the diminutive printer, "don't

cry so. Your father's getting all right, you know; and I'm
sure mother's very kind to him."

" Yes — yes; you're all very good — very kind; and if
it hadn't been for you here, he must have gone to the hos-
pital, and I must have gone — I don't know where — to the
work-house."

" Yes, but you didn't—and what's the use talking of them
things? Be lively — I'm lively."

Flick shook his head, and making no answer, appeared to
listen attentively for the return of Mrs. Dumple and the doctor. At length their steps were heard upon the creaking
staircase. Richard's pale face grew paler; his breath came
thickly and in sobs; and rising from his chair, he felt, with a
trembling hand, in an inner breast-pocket. As he did so,
Gill heard the crumpling of paper.

The next moment Gumbey and Mrs. Dumple appeared at
the door.

" And so you wish very much to see your father, my
boy, eh?"

Flick bowed; he could find no words to speak.

" You know he has had a very severe and dangerous illness, my boy; and it was necessary to keep him very quiet,
and prevent his being excited, you see."

" Yes — yes, I know; but now ——."

" Well, now, he's convalescent — decidedly convalescent;
and I think you may go up to him."

" God bless you, sir!" said Flick, making for the door.

" Stop — stop one moment, my boy!" said Dr. Gumbey;
' we must do nothing hurriedly — nothing rashly; we must
say nothing that would be likely to bring on agitation."

" What I have to say, sir," cried Richard, " may agitate
him, but it will be with joy."

" I am the best judge of that," rejoined Gumbey, soothingly. " What is it, my good boy, eh? Speak to me as
a friend — as a well-wishing friend."

" I know—I know you are," exclaimed Richard; "but
what I have to say is a secret must be known to none but
my father and myself."

" Humph!" muttered Gumbey, " I thought as much!"
And then he added aloud, " Well, I shall not seek to intrude
on your confidence. Your father waits you."

Richard sprang up the narrow stairs four steps at a time; and Dr. Gumbey, after gravely nodding to Mrs. Dumple, walked up the Colonnade, pondering deeply.

"There has been some deep business brewing," he thought. "Lorimer disappeared—Trumps rich—the ravings of that old man, talking as he did of forgery, drugging horses, and of his lost and ruined son! There's some deep knavery been working underground, and sooner or later will come the explosion."

The doctor's carriage was waiting for him in Guildford Street, and he got in, telling the coachman to drive to Sir Harrowby Trumps.

In the meantime Richard Flick had reached the door of his father's sick room in half-a-dozen bounds, and, after pausing a moment on the threshold to wipe away the gathering perspiration from his forehead, gently raised the latch and entered. It was a small apartment, of which more than one-half was taken up with the bed. Upon the table, placed near the window, lay an ominous collection of empty phials and such-like relics of the doctor's presence. A few common rush chairs completed the scanty furniture. The window was partially open, and, the little muslin curtain being drawn aside, the waning light of the summer evening lingered dimly in the room, falling with mild and subdued radiance on the form which, propped up with pillows, lay upon the bed.

As Richard caught sight of his father, he stopped short, uttered an exclamation of horror, and gazed as though fascinated upon the sick man. And, in truth, the poor jockey presented a dismal figure. Always remarkably thin and hard-featured, the sharp fever had ground him to the bone. His face was not pale, but white; the projecting cheek-bones gave it a ghastly expression, and the eyes, sunken as they were, and alternately flashing and becoming glazed and dim, were encircled with two darkly livid rings. As his son stood gazing on him, the invalid slowly, and as if the effort were painful, raised one of his grisly, wasted hands— a mere cluster of bones, covered with yellow skin — and, pointing to his own face, said in a low, faltering voice,—

"It is you have done this, Richard!"

Uttering a cry of anguish, the youth sprang forward,

and, flinging himself on his knees by the bed, hid his face with his hands.

"When your mother died," said the jockey, in the same solemn tone, "I thought I could never bless God that she was took away. I was wrong, Richard—wrong!"

"Father! father!" exclaimed the son, "I am not so very, very guilty!"

"Guilty!" repeated the jockey—"arn't you a felon, there, where you kneel? I bought you from the gallows—bought you with the honesty I was proud on—the honesty which, when many things went wrong, kept my heart glad and warm. But now I've sold a race. I'll never ride another, and I won't trouble you long, anyhow."

"Father," exclaimed Richard, "listen! I have a wild story to tell you. I did all for the best; I was rash, but not dishonest."

"You're a forger!" said the old man, briefly.

"I was haunted," said his son—"haunted, tempted, ruined by a man who"—and his voice faltered—"who must be a sort of Satan."

"A sort of Satan?" repeated the old man, dreamingly.

"Yes," said the son, "a sort of Satan, with a devil's mind and a devil's tongue—a man, tall, old, with bright eyes and grey hair."

"Ha!" exclaimed the jockey, with a start, "and a low-sounding, hollow voice, which you could not help listening to, and which went into you—into your very brain!"

"Yes, yes—you know him—it must be the same!" cried Richard; and then, in a low, rapid tone, broken by sobs of eagerness, he poured out, with a wild, simple eloquence, the whole story of his connexion with Benosa—how the old man had gradually worked upon him—gradually, as he said, enthralled his very soul, so that he seemed to be acting under a strong spell, until at length the triumph was achieved, and the few strokes of a pen accomplished, which made their writer a felon.

The jockey listened with tremulous earnestness, occasionally lifting his clasped hands in thankfulness, until, as his son paused in his impetuous narrative to catch his breath, the old man burst into a passion of tears, caught Richard's

L

head between his hands, and, drawing it towards him, kissed the throbbing brow.

"You have been rash, Dick," he said,—"rash and foolish, but not wicked; and you were rash and foolish for me."

There was a moment's pause.

Then the old man, starting up, exclaimed,—

"But the cheque, Dick! the cheque!—he has it—that devil has it, and you are still in his hands!"

Richard tore open his waistcoat, and snatched from his breast a carefully-folded packet.

The old man glared at it in breathless suspense.

'When this man—this Satan," continued the son, "left me, he said that the cheque would be in the post-office, addressed to me, by the time the horses started. Oh the agonies I suffered all that long day! I had a holiday, and I wandered from one end of London to the other. I could not rest—could not pause. I think I must have been in a fever, for my mind wandered, and was clouded, and I thought I saw forms and figures in the air, and sometimes I found myself laughing and sometimes crying, I didn't know why. I had determined not to go home till an hour after the last postman would have gone his rounds, so that I might know at once whether the tempter would keep or break his word. The servant who let me in said that there was a letter for me on my table. I rushed up-stairs, locked and bolted the door, and caught up the paper; I almost fainted as I broke the seal, and I was staggering to a chair, when the cheque—the terrible cheque, fell upon the floor."

"And you have it now?"

"Here," resumed Richard, tearing open the packet which he had produced—"here, with the letter in which it was enclosed! I have had them on me night and day."

The jockey took the cheque, glanced rapidly at the signature, and then, with impassioned gestures, tore the paper into fragments, and flung them wildly in the air.

"And now the letter!" he said.

Richard handed it to him, and the old man, with a faltering voice, read aloud the following words:—

"Boy,—I return the cheque: it has done its work. Do you take warning by what will ensue. Be chary of trusting the unknown. Commit not the semblance of a crime, lest the shadow prove a herald to the substance. Shew this letter to your father; he is an honest man. Imitate his example, and bless Heaven that both are free to walk in those paths of truth and fair dealing without which there is no peace."

There was a moment's deep silence after the reading of this extraordinary communication. The jockey lay back in bed, squeezing his forehead with his trembling hands. At length he started up.

"Not a day must be lost!" he exclaimed; "we must find out Mr. Lorimer."

"To tell him ——" asked Richard.

"All — every item!" interrupted the jockey; "there's some devilish work on foot, and—who knows?—we may give the clue. I will keep this writing carefully. In the meantime you must try every means to find Mr. Lorimer. I can't sleep until I know we're on the way to get justice done. It must all come out — all! There will be shame for you and me—that's no matter. You were rash, and I was weak; but, thank God, we may match them yet!"

"Father," said Richard, "I think I can find out Mr. Lorimer's present address."

"Do, do," replied the jockey, "that he may know all, and consider what is best to be done."

The old man rose in bed in a state of high excitement; his hot, dry hands trembled as though with palsy, and his eyes glared fiercely

"We'll match them yet!" he shouted, in a hoarse, broken voice. "We lost the Derby, but there's another race to run—a longer and a fiercer one; we're at the starting-post—ha! ha! ha! Let's see this time who will win the stakes."

And with another burst of mad laughter, which very much alarmed Richard, for he feared a relapse, the over-excited invalid fell back and fainted.

CHAPTER XVII.

THE " FLAIL" SUPPER.

ABOUT ten o'clock on the night following the day when
the scene related in the preceding chapter took place, Mr
Spiffler might be seen proceeding to his lodgings followed
by an emissary from the neighbouring fishmonger's shop
who bore a huge dish on which sprawled a couple of scarlet
lobsters, split and ready for the festive board. Close to the
lobster-bearer marched a shambling youth, with a dirty face
and red hair, the potboy of the "noted stout-house" at the
corner, carrying a huge tin can, which, taking a *primâ-facie*
view of all the circumstances, appeared to contain beer.
Having arrived at the door of 13 Little St. Peter's Street,
Camden Town, Mr. Spiffler opened it with a latch-key,
shouted down the kitchen-stairs for Sarah-Jane, to whom, on
the appearance of that maiden, he intrusted money sufficient
to pay for the dainties waiting at the door; and being informed by her that the cloth was laid and all ready, marched
gravely to the second floor.

Mr. Spiffler's room might be described as a sea of old
newspapers. piles of MS., long printed ribands of "proofs,"
heaps of half-torn magazines, piles of stitched French farces,
and masses of books; this literary ocean being bounded by
the four walls of the apartment, and studded with a desk, a
round table, a musty sofa, and a group of chairs, which rose
like islands above the tumbled masses of daily, weekly, and
monthly literature, which lay littered in some places a couple
of feet deep upon the floor.

Mr. Spiffler, after glancing at the table, and remarking
with satisfaction that the cloth was laid for supper, and
adorned with knives and forks for five, seemed to think that
the room was in a somewhat disorderly condition for the
reception of company, and proceeded to tidy it by kicking
huge masses of paper from the more central portions of the
apartment into the corners, where they lay in wreaths which
would have delighted the eye of a butterman. After having
performed this necessary operation, Mr. Spiffler lighted the

candles by the help of the taper he had carried up-stairs, and after having exchanged his coat for a species of garment which seemed a cross betwixt a shooting-jacket and a dressing-gown, sat down to his desk, wrote a few memoranda on a slip of paper, and then, lounging to the window, flung it open and looked forth as a loud rap sounded on the knocker beneath.

"All right—just a-going to begin, and only waiting for you to say grace!" shouted Mr. Spiffler to the gentleman beneath, who returned the greeting by replying, in a rich Dublin accent, that "that was the toime of day!" and in a moment or two the Irish gentleman entered the room. He was a strapping fellow, well-dressed, good-looking, and abounding both in speech and gesture, with a great deal of superfluous energy.

"Hiere we are, my dear fillow!" he exclaimed, grasping Spiffler's hand in both of his; "I haven't been so deloighted since I left old Trinity College. And where's the rest of the boys? By Jove, won't we work it? The Satirical peaper they had in Dublin, which has never been surpassed in Europe, will foind its match at last!"

"Sit down—sit down, Con!" said Spiffler, "we'll discuss it all to-night. There's Sharpe and Trotter coming, and an old fellow—Jorvey—who is to be our printer, and —hark! in your ear—our capitalist!"

"You don't mean it!" returned Con O'Keene; "a respectable old gentleman who unites enterproise with capital—I shall be quite pleased to be introduced to him! Do you think, as we're to be connected in the way of business, he would enter into a little commercial arrangement with me in the way of a beel?"

"No, no!" said Spiffler, decidedly, "I bar that—none of that with our capitalist! Find a Jorvey for yourself—I can tell you they're not to be picked up every day!"

"Pardon me, my dear boy!" replied the Trinity-College alumnus, "but you speak as if there were some doubt about moy taking up a beel when it falls due."

"No, I don't," said Spiffler—"there's not the least doubt about that matter!"

"Now that's ungenerous, my dear boy!" said O'Keene, "and I won't forgive you till you come over to Dublin and taste me father's claret, and have that cruise we planned in my yacht in the Bay."

The unfolding of this magnanimous plan of revenge by Mr. O'Keene was interrupted by the arrival of Mr. Sharpe, arm-in-arm with the capitalist Jorvey, to whom the three gentlemen paid great deference, and welcomed with many expressions of disinterested attachment. The printer was a fat, good-humoured-looking man, with twinkling little grey eyes, and a habit of assenting to every proposition made to him. Mr. Sharpe was a young man of two or three-and-twenty, stylishly dressed, with glossy hair, on which a great deal of pains and oil had obviously been expended; he had a rather Jewish, but intelligent cast of features, and enunciated his conversation with the rapidity of an accomplished, touch-and-go farce actor.

Shortly after the arrival of these gentlemen, Sarah-Jane appeared with the lobsters, and Mr. Trotter, being still an absentee, the Trinity College man proposed and carried a motion for a small glass of brandy all round, to prevent the possibility of the lobsters disagreeing with them. The ceremony was hardly complete when Mr. Trotter, a somewhat seedy-looking young fellow, with shoes, no straps, an unbrushed coat, and a hat apparently brushed the wrong way, appeared, and the discussion of the shell-fish and porter commenced.

" They're remarkably foine lobsters," observed Mr. O'Keene; " but you should see the fellows that go crawling about the rocks on me father's estate in Oireland."

" I thought that that estate was inland," said Trotter.

" The one you mean is," replied Con; " but the one I speak of is on the coast of Galway. It was given to an ancestor of ours by Malachi—the same who wore the collar of gold—for feudal services performed in the wars with the ancient Picts. It's called Carrig-na-Houlan."

" What's the rental?" asked Sharpe, abruptly.

" Why, sure, it's good round sum in paper; but then, as the tenants always shoot the agent on the noight bifore quarter-day, it's of little practical binifit."

" Never mind, O'Keene, my boy," said Trotter, " if your tenants don't pay you rent, you don't pay your landlord, an so it comes all right in the long run "

"Yes," cried Sharpe, "only that old Briggs will get pressing some day, and we shall have O'Keene waiting for him with a blunderbuss round the corner to commit an agrarian outrage."

"Have another claw, Mr. Jorvey," said Spiffler. "You and I will eat the fish while these fellows talk. Trotter, my boy, the beer is next you—just fill our friend Jorvey's glass."

"And moine too," put in the Irish landlord. "They may say what they loike about us poor Oirishmen, Mr. Jorvey, but we're not a bad set of fellows after all."

The supper went off swimmingly, Mr. Spiffler and his friends vieing with each other in paying the most delicate attentions to the typographic capitalist, never allowing either his plate or his glass to remain empty, and predicting the vast fortunes to be made by the union of mind with matter—that is to say, by a judicious junction of the contents of their own skulls with those of Mr. Jorvey's pockets. Con O'Keene, however, went beyond all the rest in his professions of everlasting friendship for Mr. Jorvey, pressing on the acceptance of the decent tradesman a pair of rifle-barrelled and hair trigger duelling pistols, with which his (Con's) uncle, by the mother's side, the Marquis of Howth, shot his uncle by the father's side, the Duke of Bannagher, owing to a slight family difference, the result of which had however been, to keep the unfortunate Con out of an estate in Derry with a yearly rental of £15,300.

In the midst of this curious romance of the Irish peerage the last relics of the eatables were cleared away, and certain bottles of spirits, flanked by cigars, with pipes and a blue glass jar of Turkish tobacco for those who liked them better, having been produced, and Sarah-Jane having contributed, as her share towards the festivities, copious jugs of steaming hot water, the business of the evening fairly commenced.

"Now, this is what I loike to see—this is really gratifoying to see," exclaimed O'Keene, "men of litters and men of business mingling——"

"Mixing," suggested Sharpe.

"Mingling and mixing," continued the Irish gentleman, "in all good fellowship around the festal boord."

The capitalist assented, and, having mixed his grog, drunk to "the gentlemen all."

"Ah," continued Spiffler, "I hope we shall have many such merry meetings. Never was there such an opening for a good weekly slasher, and never—I say it fearlessly—was there such a combination of literary talent, with commercial enterprise and liberality, as the 'Flail' will shew the world!"

"Mr. Jorvey," shouted O'Keene, "I envy yer feelings as a man and a phoilanthropist! To you I dedicate this bumper —to you, sir, and to the 'Flail,' with which my friend Mr. Spiffler is so good as to promise me a humble connexion. Moy name may not be known to ye, sir, but go to Trin Coll. and ask there. Go to the gay and dazzling ceercles of our poor old Oirish capital, and ask there—there, sir, for your humble servant, Cornelius O'Keene!"

The capitalist, according to his custom, gave a nod of assent, and followed it up by a gulp at the comfortable jorum before him.

"Yes," said Spiffler, "as we intend to come it rather strong—to lash fearlessly the vices of the age, and to dash the caustic of satire relentlessly into the ulcers of society ——"

"Come, come," interrupted Sharpe, "don't give us the prospectus entire."

"I beg your pardon, gentlemen," resumed Mr. Spiffler, "I meant that, as we are going in hard for personalities ——"

"Hear! hear!" said Trotter and Sharpe.

"We have wished that Mr. O'Keene should attend to the department of seeing able-bodied persons, of suspicious appearance, who may ask for the editor ——"

"To seeing them, first at the office," broke in the champion of the "Flail," "and afterwards at any place which may be feexed on as convanient; with noine paces—less if desired —between the muzzles of the pistols."

"A desirable precaution, my very dear sir," said Spiffler. "Great social reformers always encounter opposition. Socrates was poisoned for proclaiming his unbelief in the false gods of the Athenians. Galileo was imprisoned by the Inquisition for asserting that the earth moves. While I myself, when I was doing the 'Weekly Stinger,' was brutally horsewhipped by Major Blazaroon

for complimenting him upon the manual dexterity by means
of which he could make dice turn up whatever number
he wanted. However, that's apart from the question."

"What's to be the politics of the 'Flail?'" inquired
Trotter. "You know, I'm only to do the literature, theatres,
and fine arts."

"We will be guided by a simple rule," replied Spiffler
—"always pitch into the losing side."

"But if both sides are fighting a doubtful battle?"
inquired Sharpe.

"Then take both sides," replied Spiffler. "These views
are in accordance with your sentiments, my very dear sir?"

The capitalist raised his tumbler to his lips, and nodded
over it.

"Having," continued Mr. Spiffler, "the great good fortune to find my own sentiments in complete accordance with
the enlightened political views of our good friend Jorvey, he
has signified his wish—a wish which, since I have known and
appreciated his active and powerful mind, has been my law
—that I should undertake the management of our new
journal ——"

"Hooraw!" shouted O'Keene. "Hooraw for the editor!
Nish! nish! nish! Hooraw! and a touch up with the
crowbar!"

"Con," said Spiffler, "hold your Celtic tongue. Honoured,
gentlemen, as I am with the full—I trust I may say the full
confidence ——"

The capitalist took a fresh mouthful, and nodded.

"—The full confidence of our excellent friend, I have looked
about me for coadjutors. Drodgiman, who is too much
occupied with the necessary preparation to be here to-night,
is to assume the sub-editorial scissors and spread the sub-
editorial paste. Our friend Sharpe, formerly of the 'Stinger,'
afterwards editor of the 'Monthly Blazer,' a magazine which
did honour to our national literature, will assist me with
leaders and the original matter in general. Trotter, there,
will look after books, theatres, and pictures—of course
cutting up the kangaroos."

"Eh?" said the capitalist, "the kangaroos?"

"The kangaroos," rejoined the editor—"the kangaroo,
sir, is an animal not provided by nature with any means of

self-defence, either by teeth, claws, or heels, and is, therefore, a creature which offers great advantages to the bold hunts- man. Of course there are literary, dramatic, and artistic, as well as Australian kangaroos. I alluded to the three first when I talked of cutting up. Well, Trotter does the general literature and art—the fancy biscuit-baking—slicing the kangaroos—while our Dublin friend, here, cannot but be useful from his scholastic acquirements."

"Ask at Trin. Coll.," said Con.

"As well as from that gallant and resolute character, which is ——"

"Not unknown in the Phaynix," interrupted the Milesian.

"Our excellent friend Mr. Jorvey," resumed the editor "being our proprietor, and having opened an account for the carrying on of the 'Flail,'—a transaction which I fervently hope he will never repent of ——"

Here Mr. Spiffler's speech—for speech it was—was drowned in loud acclamations. Mr. Jorvey's health was simultaneously drunk by the editor, the contributor, the cutter-up of kangaroos, and the cutter-up of indignant people who had been libelled,—compliments which the capitalist, whose oratorical powers were limited, returned by drinking "gentlemen all" again, concluding with the brief but emphatic peroration of—"Here's luck!"

The festivities now proceeded apace. The candles soon blinked dimly through clouds of tobacco-smoke, while up from the festive mist uprose the loud clamour of gradually thickening voices—that of Con the loudest and most con- tinuous of all.

"Soilence, jointlemen," he thundered, "for the toast— the toast of the evening! No heeltaps!—no skoy-loights! Here's success to the 'Flail!' may it thrash the straw so many men are made of—may it always go against the grain of humbug,—and, ever merry, ever satiric, may it never stop flinging about the chaff!"

"Bravo, Con!" shouted the party; and O'Keene himself, who, having drunk about four times as much as any other two men present, was fast verging towards uproariousness, flung his glass behind him with a wild convivial shriek, and demanded whether any body then present was prepared to deny title of the "Flail" to be the leading journal of Europe.

" When it appears," added Spiffler.

" Talking of that, I edited a paper called the ' Eye' once," exclaimed Trotter; " and do you know the first leader I wrote in my first number, which was accidentally delayed ? "

" No ! no !" shouted a chorus of voices.

" It was short and sweet :—' Here we are with our Eye out at last.'"

A roar of laughter followed this, in which even the capitalist joined.

" God bless you, sir !" cried Con. " Sure it's you that has the turn for humour. I honour ye, sir—I do. Allow me to have the pleasure of shaking hands with ye, sir. The cold world may understand me not, but there are souls, sir— souls which—but never moind that. They'll laugh at me— let them. Jorvey, I love ye !"

And, amid the screaming laughter of the rest, the overflowing Irishman seized the astounded printer by both hands, and swore that he would never know happiness till Jorvey, the dearest friend of his youthful prime, should have resided a year at Carrig-na-Houlan Castle, and hunted a winter with the Carrig-na-Houlan hounds. Meantime the less impulsive Saxons settled the details of business fast.

" We'll walk into the ' Welter ?'"

" And into the ' Sunday Knout,' double hot and strong."

" Don't forget Choker's work—he cut me up once— squelch him !"

" Nor Dramley's novel—he's an ass !"

" Yes; but he's a good chap, let him down easy."

" Say he's as good as James."

" Do you call that letting him down easy ?"

" A good word for Jones of the Adelphi—mind he's a friend of mine."

" Let's go in for Smith of the Haymarket being a stick —I'm not on the free list."

" I'll notice my own farces, mind."

" Very good—that saves trouble."

" Of course we praise the Opera?"

" I see no objection."

" And Chateauroux ?"

" Yes."

" And Lorton ?"

" We'll see what they say about boxes."

" But—stop—hold hard! what the devil is Con about?"

This question broke up the whispered conference. And, indeed, it seemed one natural to ask, for Mr. O'Keene, having cut his straps with a knife, was standing on a chair, with one foot on the back, and his trousers raised almost to the knee, calling on Jorvey to remark and wonder at the symmetrical proportions of his leg. This exhibition having been duly admired, Mr. Con volunteered a song, dashed off full tilt into the " Shan-von-Voh," modulated the strain into " She is far from the land," diversified it with a verse from a lyric beginning " Whisky, drink divine," wandered into " The bells of Shandon," floundered for a moment in " The night before Larry was stretched," and then burst into tears, because, as he sobbed out, the strain reminded him of the fate of his great-great-great-grandmother, who was one of the fifteen hundred virgins burned by the heretic tyrant, Oliver Cromwell, at the Cross of Limerick.

After this era of the evening the recollections of all the party became somewhat cloudy, it being only Mr. Spiffler who remembered the next day that the festivities had been put an end to by the indignant entrance of the first-floor lodger, seconded by the landlady, while Master Con was in the act of performing a series of terrific howls, which he said were correct imitations of the cry of the Banshee, or tutelary spirit, which watched over the fortunes and misfortunes of the illustrious house of the O'Keenes of Carrig-na-Houlan !

CHAPTER XVIII

HOW MINERS MAY BE UNDERMINED.

" Once more, then—I ask it on my knees—grant what I seek?"

" No !"

" By the best memories of our old love?"

" No !"

" Out of pity to the wretch before you?"

" No !"

Then followed a pause.

Lady Harrowby Trumps, or Madame Lorton, rose from her knees, and Sir Harrowby Trumps walked to the window, put on his hat, and whistled.

"You are going?"

"Yes!"

"When you come back I shall not be here."

Sir Harrowby shrugged his shoulders and walked out. Lady Trumps listened to his footsteps on the stairs. They stopped for a moment, and she started up. She thought that he was returning—no, the latch of the street-door rattled, then the door banged to, and a cab drove noisily away. She drew a long breath, and clenched her hands and her teeth. She was dreadfully pale, and a wild, tortured expression was on her face.

"His blood be on his own head," she said; and then wrung her hands, and swayed herself backwards and forwards, as though writhing in mental misery. This was but for a minute. She became motionless, and then rose calmly up, walked into a neighbouring room, returned with a desk, unlocked it, and from a secret drawer took out a letter and read from it these words,—

"If ever you should hate the husband you now love, seek the writer."

She repeated the words over several times mechanically and rang the bell.

"A coach to the door directly," she said to the servant. Meantime she hurriedly wrapped her shawl about her, and taking up the letter glanced over it again, appeared to make a mental memorandum of the address, and presently drove away, placing the document in the bosom of her dress.

We must precede and anticipate the arrival of the coach which carried Lady Harrowby Trumps from her apartments near Soho Square.

In a dingy lane, in the outskirts of Bermondsey, lying amid mean suburbs, unpaved and unlighted, and spotted here and there with blotches of waste ground, bestrewn with heaps of rubbish, and scooped into holes by swarms of uncared-for, dirt-grubbing children, stood an old-fashioned house which had been a brave hall once. It was placed a little back from the lane, and two or three scrubb-

trees rose above the wall, between that boundary and the mansion, and a mud-incrusted and battered old postern admitted
the visitor from the lane to the hall-door. It did not seem
to be a much-trodden entrance, nevertheless we will pass it
—pass through a dark, narrow lobby, ascend a dark, oaken
stair, and enter a small, wainscoted parlour. It was scantily
and shabbily furnished, and even in the warm summer's time
its atmosphere was dark, and cheerless, and chill. Narrow
windows, made still narrower by heavy damask curtains,
admitted grey wedges of light which fell upon an old oaken
table highly polished, upon some half-dozen high-backed,
tapestry-covered chairs, upon a few hard, old-fashioned portraits in dark wooden frames, and on an antique escritoire,
on which were placed writing materials ready for use.

Into this sullen-looking room, there walked about an
hour after Lady Harrowby had left her house, a woman of
very remarkable appearance. Those of our readers who are
familiar with the female forms produced by the very early
Flemish artists, with those stiff, rude, flat, cast-iron looking
figures, without mellowness, or roundness, or grace, which
were the offspring of the first century or two of oil-painting,
will have an idea of the appearance of the person we wish to
describe. She was a woman not past the middle age, but so
thin and spare, with a face so worn by the rigour of asceti-
cism or solitary suffering, that she seemed much older. She
walked perfectly uprightly, and sat down at the escritoire, the
spinal column still preserving its unflinching rigidity. Indeed, she looked less like a woman than a gaunt statue
worked by machinery, her face was wan and worn, and full
of deep lines and wrinkles, and her hair, perfectly grey, fell
in clusters down her cheeks. She wore the very deepest
widow's weeds, and the material of the dress, which hung
around her in straight, ungraceful lines, could hardly be
discerned, so deeply was it trimmed with festoons of crape.
She seemed a creature joyless and griefless, because she was
passionless; a sort of halo of coldness encompassed her.
She was a living death.

We have said that this woman sat down to the escritoire.
She had written about half a page, in neat, but stiff characters, when the sound of wheels was heard. They seemed to
top at the door, then a deep, hollow-sounding bell was rung,

and in a minute after a withered old woman brought in a card.

"'Tis her at last," muttered the widow. She took the card and added, "I thought so—admit her." The servant departed, and presently a lady having her features hidden by a thick veil entered.

The widow rose and said, very courteously and quite calmly,—

"Lady Harrowby Trumps stands before me."

The person addressed bowed, and replied in an agitated voice, "And I see ——"

"The writer of a certain letter to you, which you have, perhaps, taken the precaution to have about you."

Lady Trumps answered by producing the note, the brief contents of which the reader is already acquainted with.

The lady of the house glanced at it, signed her visitor to a seat, and then stood motionless before her.

"I wrote you," the widow said, "to come hither should you ever hate your husband. You have come!"

Lady Harrowby made a gesture of mingled passion and despair.

"I know not who you are, madam," she exclaimed, "I yielded to the impulse of a moment. Perhaps I did wrong—I will return. My life is one dreary waste of toil, insult, and neglect; but yet—but yet—I do not—cannot hate him ;" and she wrung her hands and groaned aloud.

The widow looked at her with a stony smile and cold glittering eyes.

"He lives upon your earnings?" she said.

Lady Harrowby Trumps bowed her head, weeping.

"And yet," she exclaimed, "if he had only given me that money to-day—I know he has it—I would toil for him, and suffer for him, without a murmur."

"Then you asked money not for yourself?"

"No, no !" exclaimed the other, with vehemence. "Not for me—for my father—my father whom I left when my husband first won me—for a poor, wifeless, heart-broken old man, deserted and lonely in his age, and dying—dying of absolute, literal want !"

And she burst into an agony of tears. The widow stood calmly by until the paroxysm had passed away. Then her

visitor, compressing her forehead with her hands, and
striving, as it appeared, to regain her composure and presence of mind, said vacantly,—

"But to whom—to whom am I telling all this? My
sufferings, my state of mind is such, I hardly know what I
say—what I think. Who are you, madam?"

"Look at me," said the other. "Does your heart
whisper no words of terror and of shame?"

Lady Harrowby Trumps started and looked wildly
around, while her breath came thick and fast.

"I am," said the lady of the house,—"I am Esther
Challis!"

Lady Harrowby Trumps winced as though she had received a blow. Then her face became of an ashen hue,
and her dimmed eyes wandered vacantly; she was as one
stunned.

"Esther Challis!" she murmured at last, apparently
speaking to herself. "Esther Challis! but she is dead—
dead, long years since—dead—dead!"

"Yes!" replied the other, "dead to the world—dead to
joy—dead to affection—dead to hope; but, alas! living
still."

All at once Lady Harrowby Trumps started up.

"What have I heard?" she screamed. "Was it a dream
—a vision—or has the grave given up its dead? Speak!
—say the words I heard again. Who are you?"

"Esther Challis, the first and only wife of Harrowby
Trumps."

The lady we must now call Madame Lorton fell forwards, without making an effort to save herself, and her
forehead smote the ground. The woman who had made the
astounding revelation we have heard struck the floor thrice
with her foot, and almost immediately the withered old
servant appeared. Her mistress signed to her and without
manifesting any surprise at the occurrence, she aided the
former to raise the prostrate form of Madame Lorton and
place her on an old-fashioned couch. She then set a tumbler
of fair water on the table and withdrew. The lady of the
house, whom we shall henceforth designate by the name
which she bore in the neighbourhood, that of Mrs. Challis,
stooped affectionately over the fainting woman, sprinkled

water in her face, and applied the usual pungent remedies to her nostrils. In a short time Madame Lorton stirred, opened her eyes, spoke two or three disjointed phrases, and stared wildly about.

"Where am I?"

"With Esther Challis," was the reply.

A violent shudder ran through the questioner's frame. She screamed faintly, then making a violent effort, was tranquil for a moment, and the next instant burst into silent tears.

"Good!" said Mrs. Challis; "the worst of the shock is over. She will soon be calm."

Mrs. Challis was right.

After a lengthened pause Madame Lorton said faintly, "This has been a terrible day."

"Scales have fallen from your eyes," replied Mrs. Challis,—"you ought to be grateful. There is light and sunshine for you yet."

Madame Lorton shook her head.

"At least," continued the other, "there is deliverance from insult, from tyranny."

"You say true," exclaimed her companion. "Henceforth I am his slave no longer—henceforth he has no power over me—henceforth I am free."

She had started up in a sort of desperate exultation, when her eye suddenly fell upon and remarked the dress worn by Mrs. Challis.

"Widow's weeds!" she murmured, "widow's weeds!"

"And am I not a widow?" replied her companion, in accents of inexpressible mournfulness. "Am I not a widow —a lonesome widow, more terribly, more deeply a widow than she whose husband lies in the churchyard, and whose spirit she can hope to meet again in heaven?"

There was such meekness, such tenderness, and yet such deep despair in the voice, that Madame Lorton bent before it as before the very presence of suffering and resignation.

Neither spoke for several minutes. The silence was broken by Madame Lorton.

"And why—why," she said, "was this awful secret never revealed until now?"

"For your sake," said her companion.

M

" For mine ? "

" Yes ! so long as I believed his conviction would destroy your happiness I forbore all proceedings. You could feel no injury knowing none. So long as he retained your affections he was safe. Often has my very soul cried out within me to smite and humble him ; but while you, an innocent person, loved him, the blow could not fall on one without striking both. I said to myself it is better that the guilty should escape than that the innocent should perish. If she ceases to love him, not as a husband — for he is not hers — but as a man, then I am free to act."

" But," said Madame Lorton eagerly, " does Sir Har—— does he—I mean—know that you still live ? "

" Well," replied the deserted wife.

" And yet he seemed to have no fear of your vengeance —no dread of the law ? "

" He knew me too well. He knew he was safe in your innocence and my compassion for it. Soldiers have ere now placed their women and children in the front rank, and the enemy has not fired."

" 'Tis a coward's device," said Madame Lorton.

" My husband is a coward," was the reply. " Do you still love him ? "

" Can you ask me ? " said Madame Lorton, with a shudder.

" Good ! " replied the wife of Sir Harrowby Trumps,— " the shield is broken, and the steel can reach him."

She paused for a moment, and then said with an expression of the most perfect courtesy, and taking Madame Lorton's hands in both of hers,—

" I offer you hospitality as one sister might to another."

" You are good — very good," murmured the singer , " but my father—I must go to my father," and her voice became choked with sobs.

" So be it," said Mrs. Challis, " but you talked of money." She went to the escritoire and took from it a cheque which she presented to her companion. " Do not scruple to accept it. From the proceeds of your profession, now freely your own, you can reimburse me at your convenience."

Madame Lorton rose with difficulty, her face ghastly pale, and her limbs trembling and bending beneath her.

" What," she murmured,—" what do you mean to do?
Will you yourself——"

" Not until it becomes necessary," answered Mrs. Challis,
anticipating her thought. " Others will be glad to take the
first steps ; besides, I can bring down on him a more awful
catastrophe than a mere prosecution for bigamy. He is
engaged in a dark and dangerous plot."

Madame Lo. on started. " You know aught——" she
was beginning, w. en Mrs. Challis interrupted her again.

" If I am dead to the world, I still see it with the eyes
and hear of it with the tongues of others. I have means
and I have agents. I know much—for those who bide their
time must watch their time. I have waited and I have
watched, and the moment is at hand. My husband had
once a thoughtless, heedless friend. That friend he is now
leagued to ruin. Why, I know not. That is a matter with
which I am unconcerned ; but the friends have become enemies, that is enough for my purpose. Two men fight in
unequal strife—the stronger is my foe ; but I have the means
of placing a deadly weapon in the hands of the weaker ; and
then if the battle be not won by me, it will be, at least, won
for me."

In less than an hour after this conversation, the withered
old servant deposited in the neighbouring post-office a very
long letter, the superscription of which bore the name of
Clement Lorimer.

CHAPTER XIX.

THE COUNTERPLOT BEGINS TO WORK.

THE household in Cecil Street in which we are interested
remained during the progress of these events in a generally
unchanged position. Clement Lorimer was still an inmate
of the lodging-house ; the prompt payment of a few slight
personal debts, owing to him by some of his more honourable friends, permitting him to pass, without trenching on the
kindness of others, the short breathing time which the law
allows its victims between the period of its first marking the

quarry and its final swoop. It had been one of Lorimer's
earliest cares to visit many of his principal creditors, men in
business, with the view, if possible, of gaining some clue to
the person who had bought up their claims, in order, as it
appeared, to concentrate them all in one hand. Everywhere
during these researches he was met with the same story.
Different persons, apparently attorney's clerks, had called
upon the tradesmen, stated to them in a sort of half confidence, that the unknown guardian of their debtor had determined to arrest the course of Lorimer's ruinous extravagance,
and that with this view, while he wished no person in business to suffer in the matter, he still intended to arm himself
with a power over Lorimer which would effectually enable
him to control the conduct of his ward in future.

"What were we to do, sir?" said the tradespeople. "It
seemed not altogether an unlikely story. You were known
to have suffered terribly on the turf; and—and it was said—
beg your pardon, sir—that you were out of the way—and,
in fact, there was the ready money, and we took it."

To this explanation Lorimer could take no exception.
None of those amongst whom he pushed his inquiries had
seen any person who appeared to be a principal in the matter.
Every thing was conducted by means of adroit agents. More
than once during these researches Lorimer thought of Blane.
He was convinced that that worthy could, if he chose, give
him important information, and the more he thought of his
ex-steward's demeanour, of his sly, peering, noiseless, self-
satisfied manner, the more firm became his conviction that
the man had been an adroit and intelligent spy. But he
could obtain no information respecting Mr. Blane's where-
abouts, although that worthy was actually in daily communication with Mrs. Ginnum's husband.

It was when puzzled and almost broken-hearted with the
fruitless result of his endeavours to ascertain who the fisher-
man was in the meshes of whose net he was enveloped that
Lorimer was visited by Flick and his son. The jockey was
very feeble and terribly wasted, and when Lorimer took his
hand, he burst into tears, and, sinking on a chair, cried like
a child. Then, from first to last, without prevarication and
without reservation, father and son told their stories. Lorimer listened with almost affrighted interest. The forged

cheque, as we have seen, had been torn up, but the letter in which it had been enclosed was placed by the Flicks in Lorimer's hands. He had no recollection of the writing. The next question was touching the identity of the man who had begun the work of temptation with the son and crowned his task by the corruption of the father. Lorimer was much struck by the report given by both of his informants of the solemnity, and even tenderness, of manner of the unknown. The jockey could repeat, almost verbatim, the conversation which had occurred in the stable the memorable night before the Derby. The words, "You may be a happier father yet —a happier father than I am," haunted Lorimer strangely. He compared the sentiment with the tone of the note enclosing the cheque and with the general tenor of the conversations held with the son at the eating-house in the City; and the more he ruminated, the more dark and mazy seemed the windings of the labyrinth. Half-formed suggestions — momentary glimpses — fanciful guesses — every species of mental jack-o'-lantern glimmered by turns, each for an instant, across Lorimer's brain, and then left it in darkness more profound than before. It was, however, evident, that the person who had hocussed the horse was one of Lorimer's principal enemies, if not his only foe. Then he suddenly recollected the face he had seen looking in at the window of the grand stand. The jockey at once admitted that he had also, in the same room, and at the same moment as Lorimer, caught a glimpse of a face which had startled him, so that he could not conceal his agitation. It was, as Flick said with a certain awe, the face "of the man." Thus one point was gained—Lorimer had seen his enemy. The next step was clearly to trace out the person in question, to track him and confront him. And now another light flashed upon the path. It will be recollected that Owen Dombler, the fellow-clerk of Richard Flick, was an acquaintance of our literary friend, Mr. Spiffler. On the evening subsequent to Owen's visit to the Opera with the latter, he had called upon Richard at his poor lodgings in the Colonnade—called upon him, indeed, with a note of dismissal from the firm of Shiner and Maggs, for the jockey's son had been obliged for a time to desert his post in Fenchurch Street to attend upon his father during the latter's illness; and as Messrs. Shiner and Maggs were not in the habit of entertaining more cats than caught mice, and, moreover, had no mind to keep on hand any samples of filial affection, they had despatched Dombler with a polite intimation that the services of Mr. Richard Flick would in future be dispensed with. After conveying this message Mr Dombler had naturally adverted to his last night's operatic entertainment, and described the frantic way in which Spiffler had run out of the pit to ascertain, if possible, something about a curious-looking old man who had flung a bouquet to Mademoiselle Chateauroux from one of the boxes near the stage, and whom he (Dombler) remembered to have seen on the course at Epsom. To this narrative Richard Flick had at the time paid little attention, he was far too much occupied with the subjects of his father's illness and his own dismissal. Since the explanation come to with the jockey, however, his mind had reverted to Owen Dombler and the story of the old man in the box. He had, therefore, gone into the City, seen the clerk, and although the description given by the latter of the appearance of the bouquet-thrower was vague in the extreme—he had, in truth, caught but the merest glimpse of the person in question,—he was yet able to inform Richard, upon the authority of Mr. Spiffler, that the old man was in the habit of visiting an obscure and remote churchyard in the vicinity of Hackney, and of gazing fixedly upon a tombstone on which was inscribed a curious name which Richard had quite forgotten. He believed, however, that it was a female name—a Dutch, or German, or Flemish name. Involuntarily Lorimer's thoughts recurred to the manuscript which had been read to him by Miss Eske.

"A Flemish name," he said, with a half smile at his own absurdity, "was it Trenchden?"

"Yes," said Richard Flick, in a tone of perfect decision, —"yes, that is the name."

Again Lorimer sank into an ocean of dubious, darkling dreams. Vague presentiments, misty fragments of floating theories, sailed over the dim firmament of his mind, assuming fantastic shapes, and forming themselves into strange and wild combinations, but it was all cloudland, and these fleet ing shadows soon lost the little coherence and outline they possessed, and united into a deep gloom, through which the inward eyes of the brain strove fruitlessly to penetrate.

At length Lorimer roused himself, and the result of a long conversation with his visitors was, that Richard should ascertain precisely the locality of the churchyard in question, and that his cousin, Gill Dumple, should be despatched there next Sunday — the only day he could be spared owing to his duties in Mr. Jorvey's establishment — with instructions carefully to watch the appearance of "the man," and, if possible, without being suspected, to track him to his home, wherever that might be.

After the departure of Flick and his son, Lorimer descended to the drawing-room occupied by the Pomeroys with a lighter heart than he had known for some time. Miss Eske was there—alone. It is astonishing how often Clement Lorimer found her alone. He went up to her and took her hand.

"Rejoice with me, Marion," he said, "I think I hold one end of the clue. We shall baffle our friends at the other, yet."

Miss Eske started joyfully up. "Oh! can I help—can I do anything?"

"Have you not done wonders? Do I not feel that in fighting for myself I am fighting for you; and then can I lack either heart or courage?"

He led her into the window recess, and they talked in low, sweet whispers. While they are thus pleasantly engaged let us bestow a word upon the general and his lady.

They found London agree marvellously well with them, and liked it better and better every day. The general, like all Transatlantic republicans, entertained a profound reverence for a title, and having brought some good credentials from New York, was not long in making the acquaintance of no less than five City knights, two or three baronets, and an actual live lord — an Irish one — who drank sixteen tumblers of whisky punch in one evening at the general's expense, and then considerately saw the Transatlantic man of war home to Cecil Street. The general, himself, when he entered the drawing-room where his wife was sitting up for him, was by no means steady on his legs,—a phenomenon which he accounted for by observing that the whisky which he had imbibed had been distilled from barley grown in a monarchical country, and which could not, therefore. ʰ²

expected to be so wholesome as true blue republican strong
drinks.   Mrs. Pomeroy did not by any means subscribe to
this view of the matter, but as soon as she understood the
noble company in which the whisky had been consumed,
ner soul was appeased, she gulped down an incipient curtain
lecture, and took advantage of the general's hilarious dispo-
sition to extract from him a promise that he would rent a
house for, at least, six months in London, and job a carriage—
say a nice two-horse phaeton—for park and shopping purposes.   Mrs. Pomeroy having, without much difficulty, obtained the necessary permission, straightway called Mrs.
Ginnum into conference with respect to the house, while the
general himself undertook the providing of the vehicle.   This
last matter was soon arranged, the only difficulty being with
respect to the heraldic insignia to be emblazoned on the
panel.   The republican dignitary enlarged to the astonished
coach-builder upon the contempt in which he and the other
free and enlightened citizens of the United States held all
such relics of an effete and barbarous feudal system.

"Then don't have 'em, sir," said the tradesman; "that's
soon arranged."

But it was not arranged at all so easily.   The general had
a peculiar scheme of his own in view.

"You see," he said, "I don't kinder like that, nyether.
The folks in the old country here-away, who aien't so spry and
right down, slick, go-ahead, as us on t'other side the Herring-
pond, think them gimcracks on a man's carridge a great
thing, and not to be sneezed at nohow.   Ne-ow, I aien't a-
goin' to degrade myself to the level of them aristocratic pre-
judices, and have a whole bilin' of griffins, and hands with
daggers, and lions-rampant, and them sort of things, which
altogether belong to the old country, I calculate.   No; I
aien't a-going to have them, I guess; but then I aien't
a-goin' to let down the dignity of Uncle Sam by havin' nothin'
on the panel, nyether."

"But you must have either armorial bearings, or nothing,
sir," said the coach-builder.

"No, I needn't ne-ow.   I'll have a pictur', I guess.   It
shan't be arms, but it 'ill leuk like them.   I'll have a 'coon
a-sittin' on a rail, with a couple of our free and enlightened
citizens on each side, wollopping their niggers with one

hand and holding out the peerless flag of freedom with the other."

"Any motto, sir?" said the tradesman.

"No; I guess I aien't goin' to have a motto—nothin but a few words written on a scroll at the bottom, 'America expects every man to larrup his own nigger' So, you see, it won't be one of them aristocratic and feudal humbugs of coats-of-arms; but a right-down, straight-up, good, democratic, emblematic pictur', and an ornament beside."

It was on the Saturday afternoon on which Madame Lorton had visited Esther Challis at Bermondsey that the general's phaeton, decorated with his ingenious apology for a coat-of-arms, was reported ready for service. On that same afternoon, at a later hour, Lorimer received the letter which, as we saw, had been addressed to him by the real wife of Sir Harrowby Trumps. It enclosed copies of the two wedding certificates, **with full** memoranda of the dates of the marriages, the names of the witnesses, and an intimation that ample evidence would be forthcoming in the event of a charge of bigamy being brought forward. The writer concluded by stating, that her object in possessing Lorimer with the information which he had just received was partly that of furnishing him with the means of checking a conspiracy being hatched against him, and in which the writer had reason to believe that Sir Harrowby Trumps was deeply and foully implicated. Should Lorimer not wish to come forward as an accuser, the documents enclosed would still be of service in the way mentioned.

Such was the tenor of the extraordinary communication over which Lorimer was deeply pondering when the general, bursting into his room, announced that the phaeton would be ready for a drive in the Park the next day, and trusted that his young friend would occupy a seat. Clement was on the point of politely declining the offer when a thought suddenly struck him.

It was now, of course, an object of primary importance for him to see Trumps, and it occurred to Lorimer that a public appearance in the Park, while it would probably bring about that end, would also be of use in dispelling the persuasion which he found had been so industriously circulated amongst his tradesmen, that he was out of the way, hiding,

in fact, from his creditors. Besides, the temporary depression
of spirits which had followed his illness had rapidly given
way under the influence of the active occupation in which he
had lately been engaged. Friends, too, seemed to be springing up from hitherto undreamt-of quarters; and, above all
there glowed i. his soul, purifying it, chastening it, strength-
ening it, the influence of a deep and holy passion. Let our
readers take it as an axiom, that no man really knows what
he is made of—no man knows the force of the secret springs
of his heart and his brain, until he has been in trouble and in
love.

"So I hope we may count upon you, Mr. Lorimer: the
car is none of your common doings—quite a chicken fixing;
and, in course, Miss Eske will be of the party,—I calculate
there's an inducement for you,—and Mrs. Jiniral guesses so
too."

So Lorimer yielded a ready assent, and the hour was
fixed upon there and then.

CHAPTER XX.

" CHECK TO THE KING."

WE are in Hyde Park. The afternoon is brilliant, the
season is at its height, and the rich blaze of the summer sun
streams gladly upon the broad, trampled greensward, the
stately avenues and picturesque clump of noble trees, and the
shining waters of the Serpentine. Above, all is cloudless and
blue; while towards the horizon, on either hand, a filmy
summer's haze floats over the earth, through which you can
see dimly, and as it were impalpably, the outlines of the long
extended ridges of building, stretching to Bayswater and
Kensington, the bricken ribs which encompass this, the principal of the "Lungs of London."

The time is about four o'clock on a Sunday afternoon;
the hour and the day when the Park is a vast, open-air parliament, to which every class and rank of society pours its
representatives. You can trace the various foot-paths by the
streams of pedestrians which mark their course. The ex

pause of green turf is dotted with loungers. Crowds of shouting and screaming boys fly hither and thither over the sward and among the trees; groups of equestrians speed along the tan-covered avenue of Rotten Row; while, on the great carriage thoroughfares, particularly in the vicinity of the Apsley-House corner, and by the northern bank of the water, two stately ranks of glittering equipages move slowly in a double line, the trampling of the glossy horses and the rattle of the wheels scarce heard amid the loud, continued buzz and the restless stir of the swarms of foot-passengers who occupy either pathway, and between which the double line of vehicles slowly passes in stately and brilliant review.

And herein is one of the true sights of London. No city of the earth beside could furnish such a show. Watch the never-ending stream of carriages pass by. How the eye dazzles and the brain whirls before the rapidly-changing phases of the brilliant pageant! It is a sort of equipage-kaleidoscope. There they roll on, hour after hour, a wondrous procession of high-bred, champing horses, of brilliant panels, of gaudy liveries, and richly-draped hammer-cloths —the stream of vehicles here and there varied by a single horseman, who rides bowingly by the side of a carriage, or dashes along threading his way between the revolving wheels Now passes, perhaps, the perfectly-appointed equipage of some brilliant leader of *ton*—following it comes the old-fashioned, comfortable chariot of a comfortable dowager—here is the gaudy carriage of a foreign ambassador, marked by the chasseur, with his short sword and long feather, perched behind—then comes, perchance the quiet brougham of an actress, or dancer, followed by the flashy, jerking cab of the gentleman who flung her the largest and heaviest bouquet of the shower which last night rained upon the stage. And so the grand review of beauty and fashion goes on: and the people on the footpaths stare, and remark, and criticise; and knowing men of town recognise liveries and point out notabilities, happy when there is a momentary stoppage in the march, and they can remark the lady who reclines in the carriage on the panels of which bloom the ducal strawberry-leaves.

The afternoon wears on, and General Pomeroy's phaeton has made some half-dozen journeys from the Achilles to the bridge across the Serpentine, happily without anybody re-

marking the peculiar substitute for armorial bearings which
the democratic ingenuity of the general had invented. That
worthy gentleman reclined upon the cushions with a gratified
and patronising air, which seemed to say to all beholders,
" Look at me! there's no charge. I'm a free and enlightened citizen. Take a lesson by me. I'm not one of
your aristocrats. I'm one of Nature's nobility, , am."
And, by the way, it is a curious fact, but a true one, that
there is hardly a thorough-paced, democratic leveller going
who does not console himself for the personal insignificance
to which his doctrines would necessarily reduce him, by a
certain inward opinion that he is, at the very least, a duke in
that convenient, but rather indefinite, species of aristocracy
called the " nobility of nature."

Mrs. General Pomeroy was also, of course, in full blow.
She had, for once, forgotten her nerves, and had not alluded,
since they had passed the Apsley Gate, either to the delicate
state of her exceedingly corpulent frame, or to the fact that
she had never enjoyed a wink of sleep since she had been
lulled to rest by Dalby's Carminative and Godfrey's Cordial
about the remote era when she was weaned.

" There's a pretty considerable percentage of carridges
here," Mrs. General Pomeroy remarked; "but it aien't up,
nohow, to New York. It's generally admitted, Mr. Lorimer,
that the old country can't touch us in these fixings."

" It arn't to be expected," replied the general. " We're
young—we're slick—we're spry—we're go-ahead. Oh! we're
as tarnation smart as a 'coon with three legs chasing a 'tarnal
flash of lightning up the rainbow."

" The Marquis of Pimlico," said Lorimer, indicating a
gentleman who drove his own cab. " You wished me," he
continued to the American lady, " to point you out some of
our aristocracy."

" Yes, I convene I did," was the reply; " that I might
not look at 'em, in case they should think there was a female
citizen of a free and enlightened country who could be found
to stare at a man for nothin' except his bein' a lord. Well,
now, but the marquis ain't bad-looking nohow, Mr. Lorimer,
and that's a fact. Don't you think now, jiniral, that he's
like young Hiram Peabody, who keeps the dry-goods store in
Chesnut Street, Applesquash Town, opposite Deacon Barls'?"

" I expect that Hiram's more distinguy about the whiskers," replied the general. But the reported similarity formed a capital excuse for the aristocracy-contemning couple to stare at the aristocrat with all their eyes.

Just at that moment there was a pause in the rolling tide of carriages, and some loungers on the pathway, who had probably espied the curious armorial bearings of General Pomeroy's equipage, honoured its occupants with a lengthened and very critical gaze, which was, perhaps, directed as much to the mild and gentle beauty of Marion Eske as to the robust charms of the Transatlantic matron. Nevertheless, the latter lady thought proper to take the half-heard expressions of admiration to herself, and she nudged the general accordingly; at the same time flinging her drapery around her in what she considered the most becoming folds, and assuming the most graceful air of fashionable languor which she could call up at a moment's notice.

" I expect," whispered the general, " that they are taking you for a Britisher peeress."

" I calculate that's hardly complimentary, jiniral," replied the lady, swelling with delight; " I hope, now, I ain't much like a peeress. These loafers stare so, I guess. I'm quite riled; but the common people of this location can't be expected to have the manners of our free and enlightened citizens."

A movement in the string of carriages soon removed Mrs. Pomeroy from the gaze of Marion Eske's admirers; and she thought, in her inner soul, with what delight she would tell Deacon Barls, when they returned to Applesquash Town, how once, in Hyde Park, the resort of the British aristocracy, she had been humbled and insulted by being taken for a British peeress.

Meantime, of course, Lorimer recognised a few friends and many acquaintances. This was his first appearance in a place of public resort since before the Derby, and he keenly watched the faces which he knew. From most of his old companions he received a surprised but easy nod. A few on horseback rode up to the side of the carriage, greeted him warmly, and Lorimer's heart swelled as they wrung his hand, and told him how happy they were to see that the absurd reports circulated about him were without foundation. More

than once there was whispered in his ear, "Take care of
Trumps, my boy! there's something wrong there—be alive
in that quarter." To each of these friendly warnings Lorimer
nodded gaily: he felt that the ball was somehow rolling to
his foot, and Miss Eske, as she watched the flush of his
cheek, and the brightened sparkle of his eye, thanked God in
her heart that health and energy seemed returning to her
lover.

Only once did Lorimer's cheek partially blanch, and then
flush up crimson. Fortunately, Miss Eske, who was talking
at the time to Mrs. Pomeroy, did not observe these momentary—and they were but momentary—symptoms of confusion, but they were occasioned thus. In the opposite rank
of carriages rolled a brilliant open curricle, the harness of the
sleek and champing horses blazing with silver. This vehicle
contained but one person, a lady, who lay sinking back in a
couch formed of rich shawls and cloaks. As she passed, her
eyes—large, lustrous, black eyes—shone full into those of
Lorimer, but not a muscle of her olive-coloured face moved.
That she saw Lorimer was evident, but not a spark of recognition lighted up the long, fixed stare. For an instant he
thought she was about to make a sign, as she raised her
exquisitely gloved hand, but it was only to place it upon the
head of a King Charles spaniel which occupied the cushion
beside her, and then, as she stooped to caress the dog, the
two carriages separated, and Lorimer saw her no more.

Certainly Mademoiselle Chateauroux excelled in the art
of giving the cut direct. Lorimer's lip curled, and there was
the bitterness of contempt, not of outraged feeling, in his
smile, as a cavalier, who had been proceeding at a hand
canter, suddenly checked his horse by the side of the carriage, and in a coarse, familiar voice, said,—

"Ah, Lorimer, how de do?—smiling, eh? That's right,
take it easy: I always do." And the coarse, sensual face of
Sir Harrowby Trumps appeared, as its owner was on horseback, on a level with the occupants of the phaeton.

"Your American friends, I presume?" continued the
baronet, with insolent familiarity. "Glad to see them: introduce me to the young lady."

Lorimer coldly mentioned the necessary names. The
general and his lady looked delighted at the introduction;

Miss Eske, who alone of her party knew something of the real character of the man before her, shrunk back, and looked inquiringly up into Lorimer's face, as though to ask how she ought to meet his advances.

"Not much of this sort of thing on the wrong side of the Atlantic—eh, general?" said Sir Harrowby, reining in his impatient horse—a fine grey—and pointing to the opposite line of carriages.

The worthy general and his lady were both so much taken by surprise at this audacious apportionment of the right and the wrong sides of the ocean, that ere they could answer Trumps went on, talking at Miss Eske,—

"Ah!—humph!—not a bad sample of Uncle Sam's beauty, eh?" he said, addressing Lorimer; "but I hear they don't last. Never mind, make hay while the sun shines —that's the way."

Lorimer restrained himself by a mighty effort: he felt that he could have hurled the ruffian from his horse, but he answered calmly,—

"I have heard of a rare beauty *here*, I think you knew her once."

"Ah!" replied the other: "name!"

"Presently," answered Lorimer; "I think of going to see her."

"Then you'd better make haste about it—or—that is, if you don't pay up, you know,——she'll have to come and see you."

"Ah, you still intend to go on with that action?"

"*Morbleu!* as somebody says, I should think so"

"You dream you'll get your money?"

"I know I'll try."

"Is there no influence would induce you to spare me?"

Sir Harrowby laughed one of his coarse horse-laughs.

"I did hope that there might be," said Lorimer, with a scarce perceptible smile.

"You did!" said the other. "Ha! you may see another Sunday here, but that will be the last until——"

"Until you relent, eh?"

Sir Harrowby laughed again. The general and Mrs. Pomeroy listened with open-mouthed curiosity, and Marion Eske with fear and awe, to this strange colloquy.

"There are other prisons besides the Fleet and the King's Bench," said Lorimer, musingly.

"Ah, yes!" answered the baronet: "there's Horse-monger Lane and Whitecross Street."

"And Newgate!" exclaimed Lorimer, with vehemence.

Trumps started, and looked wonderingly up in Lorimer's face.

"Some to the Farringdon Hotel, and some to the neighbouring establishment in the Old Bailey,—which party would you rather join, Sir Harrowby?" Clement asked, in his former apparently dreamy mood. "Such good friends as we have been may not be separated so far after all, Sir Harrowby Trumps."

The brow of the baronet grew dark: he muttered to himself, and then abruptly asked Lorimer what he meant.

"Nay, nothing of consequence," said Clement. "I was only wondering where we should be if all had their deserts. Never mind, it is over now."

"Poor devil!" thought the baronet, "I see — it's all up — brain affected — he looks quite vacant."

As he mused in this manner Trumps could not have observed the eyes of Lorimer, which were fixed upon him as are those of a hawk upon its quarry.

"Touching that beauty—that lady I spoke of," resumed Lorimer, "she assures me that I shall have all her interest with you."

"Her interest with me!"

"Yes, and it ought to weigh heavily in my favour."

Sir Harrowby looked moody and puzzled for a moment, and then muttered,—

"He is raving—it has been too much for him. Well, it doesn't much matter, mad or sane it's all one to me—but I'll humour him." Then he continued, in a coaxing tone, as one would speak to a child, "So you say I know this lady?"

"You do: better than any one else."

"And she knows me?"

"She does: better than any one else."

"Come, then," said Trumps, soothingly, yet anxiously, "where have I seen her? Give me the clue, man! tell me a place where I have seen her."

" Before the altar," replied Clement Lorimer.

My wife !" growled the baronet; " what has Madame Lorton to do with it?"

" I talk of your wife," said the other, " and Madame Lorton has nothing to do with it."

The colour on Sir Harrowby's cheeks began to come and go, his lip quivered nervously, and he struck his spurs into the flanks of his gallant grey, and at the same moment severely checked the noble animal with the powerful curb which he used. The keen eye of Clement Lorimer lost not a single symptom of his manifest uneasiness. " It was no hoax," he whispered to himself.

" Who the deuce, and what the deuce, are you talking about?" he roared out at length.

" You wish to know?—you really wish to know?"

" Yes! yes!"

" Nearer, then,—nearer! you will hardly have forgotten her name. It was once—ere it was changed——"

" What?" shouted the excited man, " what?"

" Esther Challis!"

Sir Harrowby Trumps gave a violent start, and all but lost his saddle; when he recovered himself his bloodless lips were quivering and he was ashen pale.

" Some to the Fleet," resumed Lorimer, as if he were still talking to himself, " and some to Newgate."

" It's a lie!" shouted Trumps, furiously; " it's a conspiracy—a lie! she's been dead these fifteen years. Who dares to say otherwise?"

" You know this hand?" said Lorimer, calmly, and he held out to Sir Harrowby a letter stamped with the postmark of the Bermondsey district.

Large drops of perspiration started out upon the forehead of the man he addressed, and a fearful imprecation half burst from, half died away, upon his pale lips.

" Listen!" said Lorimer: " remember what I told you near Soho Square—if you can plot I can unravel: you see it was no idle boast. I have you, man! the trap is down upon you—you are at my mercy."

Sir Harrowby's lips moved, but no sound passed them.

" If by noon to-morrow," said Lorimer, in a deep, stern whisper—"if by noon to-morrow I have not a receipt in full

for the sums you say I owe you,—you need not send it to my
rooms, for I shall be at Bow Street."

"At Bow Street!" repeated the other, mechanically.

"Yes," cried Lorimer, "where you shall be before night;
only I shall be simply in the office, you will, probably, pay a
visit to the cells."

There was a pause, partially filled up by the soft, sleek
tones of a well-remembered voice. It was that of Dr.
Gumbey, who passed in a gentleman's cab which formed one
of the opposite line of vehicles, and who, leaning out, waved
his hand to Lorimer and Trumps, exclaiming, "How do?
—how do? glad to see you together again."

Lorimer slightly returned the salutation, Sir Harrowby
took no notice of it.

"Speak," said Clement, at length—"speak, shall I hear
from you to-morrow?"

Sir Harrowby Trumps clenched his hands, and glared up
in the face of the other with a wild expression of impotent
fury.

"Yes or no?" repeated Lorimer.

"Yes!" shouted Trumps, the foam flying from his lips.
As he spoke he struck his spurs deeply into the side of the
horse, which plunged, lashed out its hind legs, and then bore
away its rider at a perilous pace through the throng of
equipages.

"What is all this?—what is it?—what does it mean, Mr.
Lorimer?" burst simultaneously from the general and his
wife.

"It means," said Clement, sinking back upon the seat,—
"it means that we are playing chess for life and death, and
that I have given check to the king."

CHAPTER XXI.

THE FINAL SCHEME

On the morning of the self-same Sunday on which the
events which we have just chronicled took place in Hyde
Park, Mr. Gill Dumple sallied forth from the Colonnade

upon his north-eastern mission of espionage. In due time he arrived at the churchyard of which he was in search. The church, of poverty-stricken Gothic, was open, and the low, booming sounds of the organ floated with a lazy hum out into the summer's air. The graveyard was empty. Nothing stirred in it except a stray butterfly or so, fluttering from stone to stone, and settling on the twigs of the stunted shrubs which grew here and there. Gill speedily found the very peculiar tombstone of which he was in search. There it stood, in its significant mystery, a block of glittering marble, with its one word graven as deeply as chisel could cut. There was a little clear space around that single grave, whereon some simple but sweet-smelling flowers, evidently carefully tended, grew, forming a border to the green live turf which capped the little hillock beneath the marble stone. All beyond was mere rough earth and gravel. So the little birds which haunted about came to the single green grave, and seemed pleased to rest their feet upon the little spot of melancholy verdure.

The afternoon passed slowly and drowsily away. The heat was intense, and Gill, who was something tired of waiting, at length pitched upon a convenient stone, and stretching himself beneath it in the shade, dropped off to sleep. He wakened with a start and a consciousness of having neglected his duty, and suddenly springing up, his face flushed all over as he saw a tall, stately old man, standing before the marble stone.

There could be no mistake as to that man's identity. There was the gaunt, wasted form, the grey, flowing hair, the face so marked with myriads of slight crossing lines, the stern and finely-cast countenance, and, above all, the black, flashing eyes, which burned with that strange, fitful fire, whereof the fuel is a subtle influence—a mighty but a secret pestilence, which has its dwelling in the material masses of the brain—warping their healthy action, scorching and withering their healthy powers.

Benosa was dressed in his usual long single-breasted surcoat. Gill knew not how long he had been standing in the position in which he appeared when the boy waked. Trembling, he knew not why, the spy crept behind a neighbouring stone, and watched breathlessly. Presently Benosa stooped, and appeared to be engaged in rearing a drooping flower. He also detached a few withered blades of grass, and placed them reverently in his breast. Then he stood again motionless, except that he occasionally bent his head and moved his lips before the sepulchre. This lasted for nearly an hour. Then the first toll of the bell for evening service was heard. Benosa started, inclined himself in a more marked manner than he had yet done towards the tombstone, and then walked slowly away. At a safe distance the spy followed him.

On leaving the churchyard, Benosa directed his steps to the eastward. His eyes were fixed upon the ground, and Gill felt that he could follow him closely without risk of being observed. The twain proceeded accordingly through a labyrinth of obscure streets, all of which Gill carefully observed. At length, after a good half-hour's walk, they emerged from a poor, squalid neighbourhood, into a locality where there were many gardens, bounded by high walls and intersected by narrow lanes. As they proceeded down one of the latter, Gill observed over the wall the higher windows and the roof of an old-fashioned house, built of red brick. There was a gate for carriages, a ponderous mass of wood, studded with nails, in the wall, and beside it a small postern. At the latter the watched man paused, when suddenly the noise of horses' hoofs was heard in the still lane. Benosa and Gill looked instinctively backwards, and saw a gentleman mounted upon a grey horse approaching at a gallop. The rider shot past Gill, who observed that his face was red and excited, and that the horse was in a lather of foam. The horseman waved his hand to Benosa, however, and pulled up his panting grey at the gate with a jerk which threw him on his haunches. The old gentleman immediately disappeared by the postern. Then there was a creaking and jangling as of iron bars shot backwards—the ponderous gate swung open, the horseman rode in, and the portal was closed behind him. Gill Dumple started off westward in high spirits. He had accomplished his original mission, and somewhat more besides.

We follow the man on the grey horse. He rode up to

the door of the old-fashioned house, leaped off his horse (which directly marched on to a green plot of shaded sward), and following the guidance of his conductor, entered a small apartment. The reader is already familiar with that gloomy parlour, its narrow windows and its dusky draperies. It is the same room wherein Benosa, then called Werwold, held conference with Dr. Gumbey, touching the mortal illness of the lady whose grave the old man had that day visited. The master of the house sat down as was his wont with his back to the windows, and carelessly asked to what he was indebted for the pleasure of the company of Sir Harrowby Trumps.

The baronet seemed to have some difficulty in framing his reply. He made several abortive attempts to speak, and at length exclaimed bluntly,—

" The long and the short of it is, that I don't like this business of young Lorimer."

" You find it connected with some unpleasantness, I dare say," said Benosa.

" I do," replied the other; " and so I mean to cut it."

" It is not what you mean to do," answered the old man, " which will be done ; it is what I mean you to do."

Sir Harrowby's face became purple, and the veins on his forehead stuck out. Then he made an effort and said, calmly,—

" You can get some one else ; there's no lack of men to do the work ; and I will assign the claim. Come — that's reasonable."

" Very reasonable ; but I decline the proffer."

" Why ? " shouted Trumps, hoarsely. " Why ? "

" Because partnerships of which I am a member are only dissolved by death."

" Then you think me your slave," exclaimed Trumps, bitterly, and labouring to keep his fury under.

" You live by me," cried the other.

" Well," said Trumps, " but I can cease being your dependant for the future."

" True : but can you cease being my debtor for the past ?

Trumps started and groaned.

" Let us give up this foolish conversation," said Benosa, mildly. " Serve me, and you end your days in luxury —

seek to withdraw from that service, and you end your days in gaol."

Trumps writhed in his seat, and his breast swelled as though he were about to weep.

" Have mercy on me," he said, in a choked voice, " and let me go. I will never come across your path. I swear it !"

" There is no mercy in me, man," said Benosa, in a hollow voice. " Pity me !—pity a man who would spurn you from him like a crawling reptile ! but who cannot, who must work with you—who must wield the hammer until it, or the substance it is employed upon, be crushed by the blows."

This was spoken in tones in which there was so much blended calmness and despair, that the baronet sat staring at his companion in stupid amazement, utterly unable to read the riddle of his strange mind. At length he said,—

" Well, be it so ; I will go to prison. Better the Fleet than the hulks."

" The hulks !" repeated Benosa.

" Ay," said the other, with a species of dogged coolness. " Lorimer—curses on him !—has found out a secret I thought safe for ever. Never mind ! Ha, ha !" and he laughed a ghastly laugh. " You'll come and see me, eh ? You'll come and see your poor debtor, eh ? Won't you ? We'll be jolly together—you and the dupe you've caught in your net. Poor old Sir Harrowby ! Bravo, old angler ! With your keen eyes and your cold, quick brain, you know how to land the fish, eh ? By Jove, Lorimer will be in too. You'll come and see both of us, eh ? I know you will, and then—and then——"

He started from his chair, in a burst of frenzy, and advanced close to Benosa, churning his teeth and clenching his fists, his cheeks pale, his forehead purple, and his bloodshot eyes flashing and dilated. The old man never stirred.

" You'll come and see us," Trumps shouted ; " and then, when the wine is in our brains—when we're mad with drink and despair—we'll roar and sing ! The three—all the three —debtors and creditor ! And we'll keep it up till morning, when, mayhap——"

He sunk his voice to a whisper, which hissed through the room.

" —Till morning, when, mayhap, the turnkeys 'ill find an old gentleman, livid in the face and black about the throat, down on the floor amidst the empty bottles, eh?"

And Sir Harrowby flung his clenched hands upwards, and shouted the laugh of temporary mental aberration.

Still Benosa never stirred. Trumps, exhausted by this burst of half-maudlin passion, sunk down again on his seat, staring at the unmoved face opposite to him, behind which dim and awful thoughts seemed to move, thrilling through that warped and jarring, but awfully gifted brain. There was a deep silence in the darkened room. At length Benosa spoke.

"Lorimer has dug a counter-mine then,—good. He can transport you?"

"Yes!" said Trumps, his passion bursting out into a new channel, and imprecating curses upon his ancient friend.

"Then you would not care to have him silenced for ever?"

"Of course not," said Sir Harrowby, boldly.

They looked at each other in silence for more than a minute. Then four distinct taps were heard at the door, and a very old woman entered.

"The man you know of," she said, "is below."

"Shew him up," replied Benosa. "Sir Harrowby, step this way; I will not detain you long." And he ushered the baronet into the library which, as we know, opened from the parlour.

As the door was closed upon him, Blane entered the room. Benosa nodded to him, and the spy coming close to his master, said, in a low tone,—

"He is still in Cecil Street; he drove out to-day with the Pomeroys in the Park, where he met Sir Harrowby. He is shewing again. He has been making inquiries. He seems determined to die game."

"Does he appear to continue his attentions to Miss Eske?"

"Yes; they love each other."

"She is a companion?"

"Yes; an orphan without friends."

"Are the Americans to stay long here?"

"For some time, and they are looking out for a house."

Benosa was silent for about three minutes. Then his face lighted up with a look of devilish inspiration—his pale lips moved, and his long, thin fingers were clenched convulsively.

Blane eyed him askance. Even he would have shrunk away had he known the awful scheme which was rising up in Benosa's brain—like the pitchy smoke in the "Arabian Nights," which, at length, took the form of a gigantic and cruel genie.

At length Benosa said, abruptly,—

" The Pomeroys are looking for a house. The house in Abingdon Street has been repaired and re-furnished ?"

" Certainly it has, by your directions."

" And the hidden door on the river side, and the secret staircase constructed by my father for his smuggling transactions, are available ?"

" Perfectly."

" Can you manage so that the Pomeroys take that house ?"

" I think I can."

" Good: do so. You may go."

And Blane retired. Benosa then re-introduced Sir Harrowby, motioning him to his old seat.

" I have an interest in the life of Mademoiselle Chateauroux," he said, abruptly.

Sir Harrowby stared.

" You know her well," Benosa continued. " Can you prevail on her to have her life insured ?"

" What will she gain by the transaction ?"

" The most brilliant set of diamonds she can point out in London."

" Of course you pay the premium ?"

" Of course."

" Then it can be done."

" For five thousand pounds,—in three offices at least,— five thousand in each. The policies to be assigned to Clement Lorimer, and the insurances to be effected in the name of Marion Eske."

Sir Harrowby Trumps sat tongue-tied in amazement.

" You will see to this; it is your duty: set about it straight. Your horse has been fed: mount and ride."

CHAPTER XXII.

THE BY-PLAY OF THE DRAMA.

THE exigencies of the story here require the interpolation of a chapter devoted to several of the subsidiary branches of our narrative, it being understood that a portion of the incidents which we are now about to relate took place subsequently to the events in the next chapter, through which the main current of the history will again flow.

Sir Harrowby Trumps obeyed the instructions, and went about the will of Benosa, as a malignant demon might be supposed to execute the behests of a hated but potent enchanter. First, he communicated with Mademoiselle Chateauroux, framing his statements in accordance with a detailed series of instructions which he had received from Benosa on the morning of the Monday following his interview with Clement in Hyde Park.

The *danseuse* was considerably perplexed by the proposal.

"*Ventre St. Gris!*" she exclaimed, "what is my life to any body but myself? Why should a stranger wish to insure it?"

"A whim," Sir Harrowby replied,—"merely the whim of an old fellow who has more money than brains, and who has desired me to ask whether you had any objection to gratify him. Remember the diamonds."

"Yes, I remember," said the other. "The insurances will gratify him, and the diamonds will gratify me. Now, I don't care about his pleasure, but, *mort de ma vie!* I do about my own."

Mademoiselle Chateauroux then plied the baronet with questions and guesses as to who his principal in the business was; but, as may be supposed, she gained little by her quiries. Again and again she was on the point of absolutely declining the proposal, when a timely word from Sir Harrowby altered her mind. In fact, the baronet was astonished at his own powers as a negotiator, forgetting that he had only one argument to urge, and that that was easily

stated, it being indeed comprehended in the single word—
"Diamonds." At length, therefore, the Favoritta yielded,
acquiescing in the propriety of allowing the transaction to
take place in an assumed name, and solemnly pledging herself to the profoundest secrecy. With her assurances to this
effect Sir Harrowby took his leave. Two hours after his
departure Mademoiselle Chateauroux received a card inscribed with a name unknown to her. The owner of the
name and the card having been favoured with an interview,
described himself as a London emissary of the Italian
Opera at St. Petersburg, and declared his commission to offer
to Mademoiselle Chateauroux an engagement on the most
brilliant terms, provided she could leave England within a
fortnight. The Russian agent concluded by handing the
danseuse a cheque upon a London banker as an earnest of the
shower of roubles which would descend around her on the
banks of the Neva. He then withdrew, begging that in
the course of the evening — before foreign post hour — he
might have her decisive reply.

Mademoiselle Chateauroux pondered deeply on the events
of the day, and soon determined upon the course to be taken.
It had struck her more than once, in her interview with Sir
Harrowby, that the fact of her life being insured for several
large sums gave to some unknown person an interest in her
death, and the thought blenched her sallow cheek. Now,
however, she reasoned, as she could and would immediately
start for a distant part of Europe, and without giving notice
to the insurance offices,—thus, in all probability, vitiating the
policies—the interest in her death, the existence of which
she dreaded, would necessarily be extinguished; while, at any
rate, she would be far removed from the influence of any
machinations in London which might be connected with Sir
Harrowby's proposal.

Her engagement with Mr. Grogrum was nearly at an
end. The few days which it had to run would not prevent
her from fulfilling the condition annexed to the St. Petersburg offer,—and that offer she therefore determined to
accept. In the course of the afternoon she accordingly
wrote to the address left by her visitor formally accepting
the Russian engagement, and acknowledging the amount of
the cheque received from him. That same night the tidings

of her engagement were despatched to St. Petersburg; the agent of the Russian management informing his principal, *in* a confidential note, that the London firm to which the theat ♪ was indebted for a certain advance made to secure the services of a celebrated tenor, would quit half its claim on the day on which Mademoiselle Chateauroux appeared as *première danseuse* on the St. Petersburg boards. Under these circumstances, the agent concluded that he had not exceeded his duty in offering an engagement to the lady in question, whose reputation was European, and who would in any case be an acquisition to the theatre.

The sequel will shew Benosa's reasons for wishing Mademoiselle Chateauroux removed from the scene of his operations as soon as she had performed the part allotted to her in the terrible drama which his scorched and fevered brain was piling around the destined victim.

Dr. Gumbey, the bland, was the next personage upon whom, in pursuance of his instructions, Sir Harrowby Trumps called. From what we know of the doctor's connexion, and his peculiar system of practice, which included the pledging of his word that people were ill when they were well, we may conclude that he was not over-particular in placing his signature to a declaration, that a person whose name was left in blank was in a perfectly sound and satisfactory state of health, and quite free from any acute or chronic complaints having a tendency to shorten life.

"Raising money, I suppose, eh?" he said, as he flung down his pen after making the necessary signatures.

Sir Harrowby grinned, and muttered an unintelligible something about "A form—merely a form."

Dr. Gumbey had far too much tact to press an embarrassing question. So he turned the conversation, and said, that he had been really quite delighted yesterday to see Sir Harrowby in the Park, apparently on such a friendly footing with their old chum Lorimer, whom indeed he (the doctor) was most happy to hear would soon appear again in society.

The baronet winced at the remark, bundled up the papers which Dr. Gumbey had signed, and took himself off with short courtesy, leaving, however, a cheque as a plaster for any wounds which 'r doctor might have inflicted by the

certificate which he had just given, upon his sensitive conscience.

When Gumbey was left alone, he flung himself into his
easy chair and pondered deeply.

" There's some one sailing in deep water," he thought.
" But who could have imagined Trumps being intrusted with
a bit of diplomacy which may have its *dénouement* at the Old
Bailey? I should as soon have thought of employing a bull-
dog to do the work of a weasel. Why, the thrice-sodden ass
had not even brains to observe that I altered the form of
each of my signatures, and that not one of the three is precisely that which I ordinarily use.—A man," pursued the
doctor, communing with himself, "must take care of his
interests in this wicked world." Then he looked at the
cheque which he held in his hand, folded it up, and deposited
it in his pocket-book. "If the worst comes to the worst,"
he continued, "it will be quite clear to any judge of hand-
writing that the signatures for which I pocket this cool
hundred are nothing but wicked and indeed clumsy for-
geries."

Exactly that night week, that is to say, on the night of
the following Monday, a Jew attorney, located in a miserable
den of an office in Whitechapel, was making out certain legal
instruments, by which one Marion Eske assigned to Clement
Lorimer three policies of insurance effected upon her life,
each for 5000*l.*, in consideration of value received; while
about a mile from him one of the stately steam-ships of the
General Steam Navigation Company was moving down the
Pool, conveying away the person in whose favour these
policies had been actually, though not nominally, granted,—
Mademoiselle Chateauroux was, in fact, on her way to Ham-
burgh, from whence she intended to push on for the capital
of Russia.

When Blane had informed his master that he could
manage to induce the Pomeroys to take the house in Abingdon Street, he had not over-estimated his powers. He
worked, of course, through the medium of Mrs. Ginnum's
husband, who was instructed to convey to his better half the
fact, that if she could prevail upon Mrs. Pomeroy to take
a certain house in Abingdon Street, which the owner had
peculiar reasons for wishing to see promptly let, not only

would the rent be found moderate, but she herself would receive a suitable amount of remuneration for her services.

Accordingly Mrs. General Pomeroy, attended by Mrs. Ginnum, set off in the phaeton to inspect the mansion in question. It was in a very different condition to that in which we have seen it on a former occasion. Outside and inside had been subjected to a thorough process of revivification. Bright curtains gleamed through the glittering windows, and the once mudded door and rusty knocker looked as brave and fresh as the art of the painter and the ironsmith could make them. Inside the improvement was still greater. There was still something of a grave, antique air in the gilded cornices and the heavy wooden pannellings of the rooms, but rich carpets and a profusion of handsome furniture in the newest taste took away all appearance of gloom from the dwelling. The house stood upon the Thames side of Abingdon Street, and a little plot of grass stretched at the back between the walls and the water's edge. Mrs. Pomeroy was delighted with the appearance of every thing, and not less with the moderate rent at which so desirable a residence could be secured; and a neighbouring house-agent, to whose charge the property had been intrusted, having been summoned, the bargain was concluded, and the keys handed over to the new tenants, who in a couple of days took possession.

Miss Eske was then installed in a little back drawing-room, looking upon the river, which was specially made over to her in the light of a boudoir. It was a little room, brilliantly furnished, but toned down as to effect by the solid masses of cornice which extended round it in ridges of carved wood, and by the massive appearance of the oak pannelling, which when struck gave back a deep, hollow sound. The door of this apartment was of great strength, and crossed and recrossed by bands of iron. It had, however, been so thickly overlaid with paint and varnish, that it was only by the weight of the door, as it was moved, that its solidity could be estimated. Miss Eske was much struck, moreover, with the immense thickness of the walls in the vicinity of the windows of her apartment, which was situated in the left-hand corner of the house, and beneath which a low out-building ran down to the water's edge, the structure in question appearing to belong to the wood wharf which bounded the Pomeroys' mansion on the left,—a similar mercantile establishment lying upon the right.

These were details of which Miss Eske took but very passing notice; but it is fit that the reader should be acquainted with them, for reasons which will shortly appear. The Pomeroys, then, are to be considered as installed in their new house. Lorimer retained his rooms in Cecil Street, but was of course a daily visitor.

The first and second numbers of the "Flail" came out with brilliant success, Mr. Spiffler's schemes having for once fructified into golden produce. In the second number appeared the following paragraph :—

"TRUTH STRANGER THAN FICTION.

"The reappearance upon the town and the turf of a gentleman lately celebrated on both may be confidently looked for. Discoveries of a very remarkable nature connected with a late racing event, upon which immense sums changed hands, are said not only to be in the course of making, but to have given a clue to certain mysterious proceedings, the exact character of which we forbear hinting at, but which will, in all probability,—so it is whispered—give ample employment to the gentlemen of the long robe, and perhaps add another to the catalogue of *causes célèbres*. In an obscure London churchyard is a mysterious tombstone bearing merely a single female name, with which it is not improbable that the world will sooner or later be made acquainted. A baronet of sporting reputation and eminent dramatic and vocal connexion is said to be not unconnected with the train of events to which we allude; although it is not distinctly known whether the late sudden retirement— we trust it may prove but temporary—of Madame Lorton from the scene of her triumphs, is in any way mixed up with the very curious and piquant affair which we have the good fortune to be the first to hint to the wonder-loving portion of the community."

"There !" said Mr. Spiffler, as he struck off the above paragraph, founded, it will be seen, on facts partly discovered by himse'f and partially gleaned through Owen Domblet from the Flicks,—"There ! we shall see if that does not pro duce much the same result as pitching a stone into a hornet's nest."

And, in effect, on the evening of the publication of the paragraph in question Sir Harrowby Trumps called at the "Flail" office, and having inquired for the editor, was ushered into a room in which sat Cornelius O'Keene, of Trinity College, Dublin

CHAPTER XXIII.

BENOSA WEAVES THE CROWNING WEB.

BENOSA, our readers will remember, had been dogged to his East-end house on a Sunday afternoon, and the complicity existing between him and Sir Harrowby Trumps had circumstantially been proved by the fact of the latter having joined the former immediately after the scene with Lorimer in the Park, as if to communicate to his accomplice the check which their scheme had received by the power which Clement possessed of completely turning the tables upon the agent who had been chosen to work his destruction. The discovery made by Gill Dumple was, of course, communicated through Richard Flick to Lorimer, who resolved to allow a couple of days to elapse, so as permit any suspicion which his unknown foe might entertain of having been watched to subside, and then himself to make his way into the old house beyond Spitalfields, and confront the extraordinary personage, who seemed his evil genius, face to face.

The night previous to the day on which the Pomeroys were to remove to Abingdon Street was chosen by Lorimer for the adventure, and he commenced his walk about nine o'clock. The day had been glaring and hot, and the streets were filled with passengers enjoying the cool air of the evening. It was a fairer night than one often enjoys in our smoke-girdled city. The sky was a cloudless expanse of deepest blue, and but a few stars twinkled with a faint and powerless glimmer, for the broad, red moon had risen in the heavens, and dusky, swarming London lay stretched

out supine, bathed up in the coldly mellow light. Lorimer
walked thoughtfully eastwards, avoiding the noise and bustle
of the main thoroughfares, and striving with all his topo-
graphical powers to avail himself of the quietest and most
direct line of progress. Ten had struck from the steeple of
some obscure church ere Clement had extricated himself from
a labyrinth of shabby, dirty, and crowded streets, and entered into the district, if we may so call it, in which Benosa's
house was situated. Here all was quiet and solitary. Long
lanes, formed by high brick walls, some of the former so
narrow as to be obviously intended for foot-passengers only,
intersected each other. Inside these walls were gardens and
orchards; projecting boughs, indeed, sometimes stretched
across and above the pathway; and now and then you could
catch a glimpse of the upper part of the old-fashioned Queen-
Anne style of houses which were built in the midst of these
inclosures, and which were approached generally by massive
gateways, now fast locked, flanked on one side by small
postern doors for foot-passengers.

Gill Dumple, who had a good head for localities, had
given such an exact clue to the house of which he was in
search that Lorimer had no difficulty in finding it. A
clump of peculiarly tall trees grew before it, stretching up
far into the soft moonlit air, and waving with a gentle sway
as the light breaths of summer air wandered by them through
the night. The place seemed sunk in repose. Floating from
the westward came the low, faint hum of the swarming
world which Lorimer had left, but in the tranquil lanes his
own footsteps only broke the silence. He paused at length
before a gateway. It was the same at which, a few months
after his birth, Dr. Gumbey's carriage had waited while its
proprietor was communicating to a husband the puzzling
and hopeless nature of a wife's malady. It was the same
through which, a few days thereafter, that wife had been
carried to the obscure churchyard where Spiffler discovered
the tombstone, the inscription upon which had given the
clue to the investigations which were now about to lead up
to the last grand catastrophe of this history. Many
thoughts, many hopes, many fears, thronged into Lorimer's
mind as he stood before the portal. Was he about to make
some grand discovery in his history? or was he about to be

flung back baffled and bewildered, the air-built castles which he had been rearing toppled over and laid in ruins by one blast of the cold wind of prosaic reality?   He paused a moment and gazed through the little wicket which had been left open in the postern.   An old-fashioned house, similar in taste and structure to the dwellings around, rose greyly and grimly into the air.   From one narrow window, upon the ground-floor—and from one only—there shone a subdued red light, the drawn blinds of the other windows seemed white and pale in the moonshine.   A massive bell-handle projected from the door-post of the gateway; Lorimer stretched forth his hand to pull it, but ere the wire is touched, and the smitten metal echoes, we must put back for an hour the course of time, and ask our readers to be present in the room in which shone the light from the moment at which Lorimer left Cecil Street upon his eastern expedition.

The apartment in question was that into which Benosa went after the visit of Dr. Gumbey, as is recorded in the third chapter of the Prologue.   It was a small library, opening from the ground-floor parlour, and in a corner, bricked into the wall, was a ponderous iron safe,—this safe we have already seen Benosa open.   It was open now, and disclosed, as before, a small inner safe, the door of which swung out between two of the shelves of the outer receptacle.   The heavy, iron-clamped box, already mentioned in this history, lay upon the floor, and a mass of papers, written in neat, but cramped, and antique-looking penmanship, was spread upon the table.   Over these papers bent Michael Benosa.   A lamp, which gave forth a deep and intense flame, burnt beside him, and upon a small, neighbouring table were arranged chemical instruments, such as glass tubes and retorts; a blow-pipe, and papers of drugs lay before the operator.

Benosa was dressed in a long grey wrapper, which added to the apparent height of his gaunt form.   Both of his hands clutched a piece of closely-written parchment, upon which his bright, staring eye-balls were intently fixed.   Once or twice he flung down the document, and grasped his temples with his big, shaking hands.   Then he began to read again, in a mumbling, murmuring voice, which gradually died away, and his eyes were lifted from the manuscript and wandered with a fierce but unmeaning stare round the apartment.

All at once he started up, pushed the arm-chair in which he had been sitting violently back, and paced the little room with heavy and rapid strides.

"I cannot," he exclaimed,—"cannot—cannot—cannot! My mind will not obey my will; my thoughts wander out abroad, and I would fain follow them. Oh, for motion — violent, rapid, desperate motion!—to be on horseback now, and at the speed, although an unknown gulf lay before me— to be on shipboard with the tempest sweeping us like foam over the careering waves — to be anywhere—anything, save where I am and what I am!"

He sunk into the chair again, and hid his face in his hands, then he resumed more calmly,—

"I am very weak when these fits come over me. When my brain does not burn, as it does now, my will is invincible. It rules with a rod of steel, but once let this strange feeling haunt me — this feeling of mysterious restlessness, these intolerable promptings to wandering thoughts and wandering steps, and I become a more weary slave than the meanest man who cowers before his passions and lets them order him to do their, not his, bidding. I would I knew the cause of these periodical attacks of incapacity for work or continuous thought."

Alas! he could have told right well in the case of another than himself. That most mysterious of nature's secrets was working in his person, that most extraordinary, most inexplicable link between our spiritual nature and the system of the universe, was making itself felt in all its terrible symptoms. That subtle disease, which was long thought to be not a disease, but the actual presence of an evil spirit within the very temple of the mind, was gradually, but certainly, overturning the fabric of Benosa's intelligence. Sometimes the morbid influence lay passive and at rest— the devil was chidden by the healthy powers of nature. Anon it roused itself and worked busily; then would it glare out in flame from the victim's eyes, and toss his thoughts wildly about within his mind, and people the empty air about him with shapes representing to his actual vision the

personages of these long, intolerable, waking dreams.   And
ever when the devil was most active and most potent, a
bright, broad moon shone above the roof, and inanimate
nature slept gently in the silvering night beams.

After sitting some time, his face buried in his hands, and
his body swayed backwards and forwards, impelled by that
restless impulse of which he complained, Benosa suddenly
appeared to make a powerful effort to regain that despotic
sway over himself of which he boasted.   He drew his chair
again to the table, trimmed the lamp, took up the parchment,
and curbing his very soul down to the task, resumed his
studies.

In a few moments he murmured triumphantly, "Yes, I
am conquering — my mind obeys me — I understand and
remember what I read."

Then, as if to impress the words still more strongly upon
his memory, he began to speak aloud the sentences he perused.

"These drugs being procured," so ran the document,
"and being compounded in those due proportions, which
have already been specified, produce this effect upon the
human frame, that they cause the exact appearance of death;
the breathing ceases, the pulse stops, and the body becomes
cold and stiff.   Doubtless, in the inner recesses of the body,
there still burns that spark of life which will after a time (if
proper care be used) reanimate the whole corporeal structure — but this is not known to those around; and so a
person having swallowed the drugs whereof I have spoken, it
may well chance that he or she shall be buried, and so in
the end, if they have not relief, perish miserably.   It is
affirmed, too, by many skilful chemists, with I know not
what truth, that during this false or apparent death, the
faculties of the patient do not die, but that he or she shall
be sensible, with varying degrees of exactness depending
upon the nervous system, of all that is done around them,
although utterly unable to express by motion or look that of
which they are conscious.   For the truth of this I vouch
not; it was, however, certified to me by an Eastern man of
Heathenesse very skilful in such matters."

This strange document was signed "René."   The language in which it was written, and in which Benosa read it,
was Italian.

As he concluded the perusal he murmured,—

"So!—an artificial catalepsy. René says not when the drugs will cease in their operation; probably that depends upon the strength and constitution of the patient submitted to their operation. It would be easy to change this life-in-death for death in reality; but, no—blood enough has been spilt; a short period of restraint will suffice my purpose. The day he dies she is free, for I—I—will follow my son."

He paused, and took up a small glass saucer, in which lay a fine powder of a dim, grey colour.

"There, wise and lofty jurisprudence," he continued, "there, supreme and majestic justice of men, there lies a pinch of dust which will baffle you—there lies a grain's weight of pulverised herbs which has yet strength to set in motion all the crushing machinery of the law, which will raise the sword of justice to punish murder, while there is no murder but in the death-blow which that sword will strike!"

His voice waxed louder and louder as he spoke. The glare in his eyes, which the power of the will had for a time subdued, burst forth again from his visage, and the veins started out upon his forehead in red, rigid cords. He grasped the arms of his chair, with fingers which bound the wood like cold, iron clamps, and, bearing himself backwards like a man who confronts something horrible, he sat there, with his teeth clenched, and the hot breath hissing through them, his vision fixed on the vacant gloom which brooded in the corners of the dimly-lighted apartment. The devil which lived in that warped and seethed brain was once more busy, and the maniac saw, as in bodily presence, the shapes which haunted his imagination.

"Yes—yes," he gasped out, "all there—every one, every one—from Stephen Vanderstein who fell first, to Treuchden Vanderstein who fell last. Hush! hark! they are about to speak! Well, I listen—say on—say on—your eyes are more terrible than your voices can be."

His voice failed him and he sat glaring at vacancy. All at once the sonorous peal of a large bell rang through the silent house. In an instant the diseased brain of Benosa identified the sound with the subject of his dreamings. He began to speak

" Yes, hark ! they sound again : the chimes in the Antwerp cathedral which two hundred weary years ago rung the
Vendetta in—Hark ! they are lifting up once more their iron
voices.   Listen—listen all of you—'tis the knell of your race
—of my race.   Yes, rejoice, the Avenger must be swallowed
in the gulf which himself has dug."

Large beads of perspiration began to trickle down Benosa's hollow cheeks, and his damp hair bristled up from the
scalp.   By a species of rigid, involuntary motion he raised
himself from his chair and staggered back,—his eye still fixed
on vacancy—towards the window.   Just as he reached it, the
house-bell rang a loud and startling peal; Benosa started,
clutched at the window curtain, and unconsciously twitching
it aside, a patch of white moonlight fell upon the floor.

In the excited and diseased state of the maniac's mind,
the most trivial external events gave his dreamings a fresh
impulse ; so it was with the sudden stream of moonlight which
illuminated the gloomy apartment.

" Back ! back !" he shouted to his imaginary guests,—
" back ! and trample not in the moonlight !   Leave that fair
spot for him — for him, the best and noblest of you all — for
him in whom our mingled blood runs—for him in whose
person that mingled blood shall be spilt—the ultimate and
most terrible sacrifice of all !"

The paroxysm of insanity had now nearly reached its
height.   Benosa's face was distorted with something scarcely
human, his gaunt frame had ceased to tremble — it shook.
He pointed, with his long, skinny fingers, to the spectres of
his diseased imagination, gibbered and mouthed at them ;
and at length, after one or two convulsive gasps for breath,
uttered one of those hideous bursts of hysterical laughter
which form so terrible a symptom of acute mania.

The echoes of this infernal mirth rang for a moment up
to the very roof of the lonesome house.   There was an
instant of deep silence, broken only by the hard breathing of
the madman, as he stood clutching the tapestry of the window with one hand, and pointing with the other to his
shadowy company, when, suddenly, a loud noise resounded
from the outer room, followed by a momentary trampling of
feet, and then, with a crash of splintering wood and of riven
metal, the door of the library was violently burst open, and

Clement Lorimer leaped into the very centre of the streaming moonlight.

Benosa's form appeared to dilate. He flung his hands above his head, his face glowed as with a white heat, and then uttering a yell — a long loud howl, which made Lorimer's flesh grow cold, and crawl upon his bones — the old man fell like a log of wood upon the floor.

Inexpressibly shocked, Clement stooped over the wretch before him, and lifting him up, placed him carefully in the arm-chair, undoing the cravat from his thin and wasted neck, wiping away the clammy wet from his forehead, and sprinkling the still convulsed and distorted face with fair water. Then he waited in silence for signs of returning animation; these were not long in making themselves visible; gradually the demoniacal expression on Benosa's face passed away, and Lorimer gazed with inexpressible interest upon those worn, but noble and intellectual features, on which he still fancied that he saw stamped a faint impression of his own. At length the old man opened his eyes. He started slightly when Lorimer met his gaze, and passed his hands over his face as if striving to remember how and when his companion had appeared.

Lorimer was the first to speak.

" I fear you have been ill, sir?" he said.

" Ill?" repeated the other, " yes, I have been ill; what then? we are all ill sometimes."

This was said with ill-concealed uneasiness; the keen eyes of the speaker all the time fixed intently upon his companion. The paroxysm over for a time, Benosa's face had regained in a wonderfully short space all its usual expression of astute intellect.

" We are all ill sometimes," he repeated.

" But," replied Lorimer, somewhat at a loss how to continue the conversation, " you seem alone, unattended."

" A wise man," said Benosa, " is his own best attendant. —Sir, I presume you to be a casual passenger, attracted thither by the cries you lately heard, and which form not one of the least painful symptoms of my complaint; I thank you, but will no longer detain you on your way."

" Pardon me for a moment," replied the other; " have we never met before?"

" No!" said Benosa, decidedly.

" Do you not know who I am ?" questioned Lorimer.

" I know not," replied the other.

They eyed each other keenly.

" The Grand Stand at Epsom on the last Derby day ?" suggested Clement Lorimer, speaking with deliberate emphasis.

Benosa shook his head and looked wistfully at his questioner.

" The forged cheque upon Shiner and Maggs, drawn by the jockey's son?" pursued Lorimer, in the same fishing tone.

The man he addressed again made a negative sign and remained impassible as a statue. Lorimer felt the ground melting away. as it were, beneath his feet. He tried again,—

" One Sir Harrowby Trumps sued one Clement Lorimer for a vast sum — the action has been quashed — Sir Harrowby saw you last Sunday ? "

Still no start — not the slightest token of recognition or intelligence. Lorimer determined to play his last card. Drawing near to Benosa, as the latter lay stretched back in his chair, he said slowly and with the most pointed expression,—

" You know nought of these things, or of a tombstone in a lone churchyard not far from hence, on which is engraved the single word ' Treuchden ?'"

With the exception of a slightly perceptible twinkle of the eyelids, and a passing twitch which stirred Benosa's face as a flying gust blackens for a moment the shining surface of a deep still pool, the last question produced no more apparent effect upon the old man than did the others.

There was a long pause. At length Benosa spoke,—

" Having now, sir, signified by my silence that the matters upon which you speak are to me unknown, you will, perhaps, accept my thanks for the services you have rendered a poor old invalid ; you, sir, may have business or pleasure elsewhere — I have need of rest."

And the old man rose and saluted his visitor courteously. Lorimer was strangely puzzled. They looked at each other for a moment in silence. Then Lorimer exclaimed earnestly,

" Listen, listen but for a moment: my history is a wild, a

strange one. I never knew parents—I never knew friends.
My whole being was, and is, a mystery to me. I have had
almost boundless wealth—I knew not whence it came.
In a moment I was smitten down to poverty—I knew not
whence that came. Now, I believe, that I am encircled in
the meshes of a dark plot spun to crush me. Sir, if you be
a gentleman, if you be a father, and you know aught of
what I tell you, speak!"

Benosa's lips moved, but only unintelligible murmurs
proceeded from them. All at once he caught Lorimer's
hands in his, and raising them with a rapid motion to his
lips, repeatedly kissed the fingers of the astonished young
man, pressed them to his cheek and his bosom, and then, fixing a look of unutterable tenderness on his companion, two
big tears rolled forth from his bloodshot eyes, and fell down
his face. The twain stood thus gazing at each other for
more than a minute. Then the grasp in which Benosa
held the young man's hands gradually relaxed, his face
resumed by degrees its usual impassible expression, the tears
dried upon his cheek, and letting go his hold of Clement's
hands, Benosa stood before him with the same icy gleam
in his eyes—the same stamp of cold, ruthless intellect upon
his face, which gave it its usual very remarkable character.

"Enough," he said, "now go."

"Shall we not meet again?" said Lorimer.

"Return to-morrow," replied the old man. He waved
his hand impatiently. Lorimer retired slowly, his eyes still
fixed upon his extraordinary host. Retracing his steps
through the parlour, the door of which he had burst violently open when he heard that terrible peal of laughter,
Lorimer soon found himself again breathing the fresh air
of the summer night.

Benosa watched his departing figure from the window
He stood a moment motionless, plunged in thought, then
a sudden idea seemed to strike him. With an activity
which could hardly have been anticipated in his aged and
weakened form, he swept the scattered papers and chemical
utensils into the iron-bound box, and deposited it in the
inner safe, rapidly turning every lock and shooting every
bolt necessary for its secure custody. Then twitching aside
a piece of dusty tapest   th which one side of the apar-

ment was hung, a recess was disclosed in which hung many
dresses belonging to every degree of society, and evidently
adapted for the purposes of disguise. One of these he
selected; and in two or three minutes thereafter the light
which burned in the apartment was extinguished, and a dark
figure, which could not be recognised to be the owner of the
house, glided rapidly from it into the lane and turned westward.

Meantime, Clement Lorimer sauntered slowly along on
his homeward road, his mind still in a tumult of excitement
from the extraordinary interview which he had just concluded. "What would come of it? Was the old man whom
he had seen really connected with his destiny? Who could
he be? What interest could he have in the part which he
was acting?" The whole thing grew more darkly inexplicable
the more it was pondered on. "At all events," thought
Lorimer, "he bade me come to-morrow, and to-morrow I
will go—but not alone." As these thoughts passed within
his mind, a figure muffled in a dark cloak or great-coat
walked rapidly past him, in the same direction as that in
which he was proceeding. Lorimer called after this person
to know whether he had taken the right path. The individual addressed contented himself with nodding and pointing onwards. In the next moment he was lost in the
obscurity.

"There goes a man who walks well," thought Lorimer;
and then he thought no more about the matter. The
chimes from the same church which he had heard ring ten
as he passed it earlier in the evening were proclaiming half-
past eleven as Lorimer again approached the place. The
streets were pretty well deserted; but it was a poor neighbourhood, and here and there flaring gas-jets still burned in
the open shops, or rather stalls, of cheap butchers. The
public-houses, too, were brilliantly lighted, and the gaily-
painted and gilded casks or vats, seen through the plate-glass
windows, raised wild ideas of the vast oceans of "Cordial
Jamaica" and "Cream of the Valley" which they must
contain, in the weak minds of thirsty wayfarers. One shop
of another kind was still open. Above the door shone the
green light which marks the abode of the dispenser of drugs.
The shutters had been put up, but the door still remained

open, and beside it lurked a man, who as Lorimer was pass
ing exclaimed,—

"Sir, sir, a word with you!"

The individual who spoke was an elderly man, dressed in
worn and tattered clothes. A threadbare old dress-coat was
fastened tightly around him, principally by the friendly aid
of pins; and above it there hung loosely from his shoulders
a tattered great-coat. His hair was long, bushy, and black,
and upon his head he wore an old hat, napless and shining
with many brushings.

Lorimer's first idea was, that the man was imploring
charity, and he put his hand into his pocket.

"No, no, sir," said the stranger, hurriedly; "not that, it
has not come to that yet."

"Well, my man," said Lorimer, "what am I to do for
you?"

"I think you are a gentleman," replied the unknown,
"that is why I spoke to you; I was a gentleman once
myself."

"You did not stop me, I suppose, to tell me that?'
answered Lorimer.

"Pardon me," said the other; "but I stopped you to
ask whether you will render me a slight service?"

"Speak it out then," cried Lorimer; "what is it?"

"You will think me a liar or a fool," returned the other;
"I am neither; what I am about to tell you is true; I am a
friendless, outcast man, there is but one thing which loves
me, and it is dying!"

"What do you mean?" said Lorimer.

"It is a dog, sir," replied the other, his voice faltering;
"the creature is writhing in agony on my bed — it is a
mercy to put it out of its pain; the poor dumb beast has
been my friend for years, I cannot see it in its long, long
agony."

He spoke in a tone of such real feeling that Lorimer
could not help being moved. Following the glance of the
stranger to the druggist's shop, Clement divined what the
other would say.

"You want a poison, then, for the poor creature?"

"A painless poison," said the other.

Lorimer's hand again stole to his pocket.

" No, no," interrupted the other, " I want you not to give it me, but to buy it for me ;" and he held out money.

" Buy it for you ! " exclaimed Lorimer, in great amazement. " Why do you not buy it yourself ? "

" Look at me, sir," said the other, meekly ; " would they not think it was for myself ? "

Lorimer could not help acknowledging in his mind that such a suspicion might well cross the chemist's mind.

" Sir," continued the stranger, " they would not understand my feelings, or believe my word. They would tell me to let my cur die at its leisure. You are a gentleman, you can conceive my motives, can appreciate them : you will do me this service ? they will not refuse one of your appearance."

Lorimer still hesitated.

" You cannot think," said the other, " that I intend to take the poison myself ; God help us, if I wished to lay down the life, which, though often weary, has still its sweets for me, there flows within a mile of us the cold black Thames, which has received many an outcast like myself. But I am not yet hopeless, and, further, I have a whim, a childish whim perhaps—but I wish to bury my poor old faithful dog."

Lorimer hesitated no longer. He entered the shop asked — using the scientific term — for a small portion of the strongest poison known, and received, in a small and well-corked phial, a few drops of colourless fluid.

" Thank you, sir — thank you," said the stranger, as Clement gave him the potion. " My poor old dog will now be soon out of its pain."

With these words he turned suddenly away, and in an instant disappeared in the gloom of a narrow lane. Lorimer, who had been unprepared for this sudden movement, called after him to stay, but his summons was unheeded. Reproaching himself for the rash readiness with which he had complied with what now appeared every moment to be a more and more dangerous request, Lorimer hurried after the unknown. A few minutes, however, convinced him that all pursuit would be utterly in vain.

" Easy, accommodating fool, that I was ! " he thought to himself ; " I may have unwittingly aided the schemes of a murderer. That story about the dog may be a perfect fiction. How could I have been so weak, so rash?"

There was nothing, however, for it but to urge his way homewards. Long ere he arrived at Cecil Street Benosa re-entered his house with the same quick, stealthy step with which he had left it; and, after re-lighting the lamp in the library, tore off a large black wig, threw aside a tattered suit, and placing upon the table a small phial of colourless fluid, muttered,—

"So! one of the links in the chain of circumstantial evidence."

The next day, and the next, and the next, Lorimer revisited the old house in the lane; it was shut up and deserted.

CHAPTER XXIV.

THE EDITORIAL SANCTUM.

WHEN Sir Harrowby Trumps called at the "Flail" office and sent up his card to the editor previous to his introduction to that personage, Mr. Spiffler and Mr. Con O'Keene were in the act of dining in the sanctum, where the leaders, or, as their concoctors loved to call them, "the blows of the Flail," were manufactured. This system of dining, or at all events lunching, in the office, was affected by Mr. Spiffler as one which tended to give the neighbours, who saw the tray carried in from the neighbouring tavern, a great idea of the tremendously onerous and responsible nature of the duties of the functionaries connected with the "Flail," who thus appeared to be unable to leave the scene of their labours even for such an important operation as that of dining. Upon the occasion in question the tray was placed upon a vast chaos of opened and crumpled newspapers, letters, and proofs, which were massed upon a green cloth-covered table, with the most perfect contempt of method and order. The room was a dingy, wainscoted apartment, and the floor was diversified with curious hills and dales, produced by the gradual sinking and settling of portions of the mouldy old house, part of which did duty as the "Flail" office. Behind the editorial chair—a throne of worm-eaten mahogany and greasy leather—were ranged shelves crowded with those books of reference the contents of which frequently enabled the editor of the "Flail" to cause credulous subscribers to wonder greatly at his immense and minute knowledge of names, dates, and amounts of exports and imports. In one corner of the room a smaller table was covered with heaps of book for review, and everywhere, on tables, chairs, the littered chimney-piece, and the floor, were scattered cards of admission to exhibitions, invitations to public dinners, and all the ordinary paraphernalia connected with the "privileges of the press."

Mr. Spittler and Mr. O'Keene, the acting editor and the fighting editor, were severally commencing their third chop, when Gill Dumple, in his paper cap and shirt-sleeves, brought up Sir Harrowby Trumps' card. First ordering the juvenile printer to retire and amuse himself on the staircase for a short period, an interval which he employed in spitting over the bannisters at a gas-jet which burned beneath, the two gentlemen discussed, in rapid whispers, the manner in which the visitor ought to be received.

" He's coome about that leader of yours—there's no doubt of it," exclaimed Mr. O'Keene. " Hooray !—powder and ball, or an action for loibel !—either will do good to the property ! Deedn't I tell ye we would get on and make a noise in the world ?"

" Hush, you fool !" said the editor ; " we're not sure enough of our ground to take a strong position. The article was only a feeler—we must be guided by circumstances. He must come up — you had better see him—I shall be in the closet," indicating an adjoining apartment, " and, in case of need, of course I'm with you in a moment."

" Had Oi not better begin the interview boy horse-whipping him ?" inquired O'Keene ; " it would bring things to a point."

" Horsewhipping !—stuff !" repeated the other. " Listen ! here are your instructions in three words :—Admit nothing — deny nothing — promise nothing. Pretend to know most when you know least ; pretend to wish to say least when you can say most, and, above all, remember a newspaper is like the sovereign ; the 'We' can do no wrong."

In a moment Mr. Spiffler vanished into the closet, and, in the next Sir Harrowby Trumps entered the apartment. Mr. O'Keene received him with suitable editorial dignity, first flinging a number of the *Journal des Débats* over the remains of the feast, because, as he remarked to himself, there was no use in letting the *oi polloi* know that the mystic "We" ate vulgar mutton-chops and drunk vulgar beer, and also with intent to let Sir Harrowby perceive that the "Flail" was no home-made article, but an enlightened organ on foreign as well as domestic politics.

Sir Harrowby looked by no means at his ease as he took the seat indicated by Mr. O'Keene. Had he been acting by himself and for himself, he would doubtless have broken the ice by performing upon the editor the operation which Mr. O'Keene had signified his willingness to undertake with reference to his visitor. But Sir Harrowby Trumps had his instructions from Benosa in his pocket, and it is needless to say, that the bully had been as thoroughly tamed down by his ruthless master as ever was vicious hound by the lash of the whipper-in.

" You're the editor ?" said the baronet, bluntly.

Mr. O'Keene had the honour to be that very humble individual. Sir Harrowby put his hand into his pocket, and produced a crumpled copy of the last week's " Flail."

" You're accountable for all that goes in here then, eh ?"

" *Gérant responsible*," replied Mr. O'Keene, quoting a line from the French journal before him.

" There's a paragraph here," said the other, " about me, and a lot of things : what do you mean by it ?"

Mr. O'Keene took the newspaper which the other handed to him, and affected to search a long time for the article in question.

" It's headed ' Truth stranger than Fiction,' " said Sir Harrowby, impatiently.

" Ah, dear—yes—Oi remember," replied Mr. O'Keene; " well, sir, and what of that paragraph ?"

" What of it ?—I came to ask that ! What do you mean by it ?— what is it all about ?"

" Sir Harrowby Trumps," said the Irishman, " Oi am a gentleman ; as such, I was instructed in the art of reading by a private tutor at me father's castle of Carrig-na-Hoolan ; as an English gentleman Oi venture to presume that ye also are not totally ineducated. If, therefore, ye wish to know what the paragraph manes, Oi would suggest to ye to read it."

Sir Harrowby's cheeks flushed. " I'll stand no nonsense, mind you !" he exclaimed.

" No more will Oi," cried O'Keene, starting up. " If ye want to be taught yer letters, there's a proimer in that box—that's very much at yer service."

So saying, Mr. O'Keene pointed to a long mahogany case bound with brass, which lay in a corner of the room. As he did so, however, his eye encountered the apparition of Mr. Spiffler, who was going through a violent pantomime scene behind the baronet's back, with the evident view of checking the fighting propensities of the fighting editor. Sir Harrowby had involuntarily risen as O'Keene pointed to the pistol-case, but he was also restrained by the positive instructions of Benosa to manage the matter with as little to-do as possible ; and so both the intending belligerents sank into their chairs, and stared fiercely at each other.

" You're very quick with the pistols," said Trumps, with something of a sneer, for of course he was unconscious of the cause which had so promptly subdued the rising passion of the Celt.

" The divil a man quicker between Colraine and Cape Clear," promptly returned the Milesian.

" Well, well," said Sir Harrowby, " we'll talk about fighting when we're done talking about business. And now, again, about that paragraph ?"

" Well, then, about that paragraph. Of coorse it's true, if that's what yer wanting to know "

" But how is it true ' of course ?' " inquired Sir Harrowby.

" Bekase it's printed in the ' Flail,' " replied Mr. O'Keene, conclusively.

" Come, come, this won't do," said Trumps. " You say here, that I'm connected with some d—d mys—— what d'ye call it — mysterious events. What events ? — what do you know about them ? — how am I connected with them ?

What business have you to talk of me, or of my wife, or any thing else in your paper, eh ?"

Mr. O'Keene was about to return a defiant answer, proclaiming the perfect right of the " Flail " to say anything it chose about anybody it chose, when the warning attitude of Mr. Spiffler, as he peeped anxiously from the closet, prevented him ; and so assuming an air of ineffable superiority, he swung himself back easily in his chair, and playing with a scissors which dangled by a steel chain from the desk, he said,—

" Ah — so — yes —very good—very good, Sir Harrowby —quite roight in you to troy to pump, but eet's no go, me dear boy, I assure ye—eet's not the sloightest go."

" So you pretend to know all ?"

" Everoy thing, me boy — everoy thing," replied Mr. O'Keene, acting upon Mr. Spiffler's instructions, and giving force to his assertion by playfully laying his forefinger along his nose.

" There is a secret in the wind," thought Spiffler ; " he would not be so calm if there were not. He's afraid of us— the ' Flail ' is made !"

Sir Harrowby shifted uneasily in his chair. Benosa had for once made a terrible blunder when he despatched such an emissary. O'Keene continued,—

" The last Derby—curious doings, eh, Sir Harrowby ? Queer place the turf—and yet there's queerer places than that. Secrets there, and secrets in the churchyard — the churchyard, eh ?" He looked to Spiffler, and seeing that he nodded, went on with deliberation and emphasis,—" Secrets between jockeys and owners — secrets between fathers and sons — secrets between husbands and wives."

Sir Harrowby started up, uttered a loud execration, and shook his clenched fist in the Irishman s face. But the latter was not a bit backward in replying to the hostile demonstration, and Spiffler rubbed his hands as he whispered to himself that the plot grew thicker — that there was great game on foot, and that the " Flail " would assuredly be in at the death.

An instant's reflection, however, seemed to cause Trumps to feel that if he lost his coolness he lost everything. So he motioned O'Keene to resume his chair, and set him the example.

" After all," said Sir Harrowby, in a hoarse, oppressed voice, " we're men of the world, and men of the world can understand each other ; it's no use bullying—let's come to terms. Suppose you admit that the paragraph was a hoax ? "

" Oi admect nothing," was the discouraging reply.

" But anybody may be wrong, d—n it !" urged Trumps.

" We're not wrong," said O'Keene.

" Then what use do you intend to make of the—the confounded gossip, that you've been printing?"

Mr. O'Keene smiled a bland and elaborate smile which was worthy of Dr. Gumbey. There were libraries of meaning in that smile. It spoke of the extraordinary stores of information patent to the smiler, the wonderful results which that information properly made use of would effect, and it hinted, in the gentlest manner, at the power—the absolute power, of the editor of the " Flail " either to convulse the world with the tidings, and thus ruin and annihilate poor Sir Harrowby Trumps, or to consign them to eternal oblivion, and thus relieve all parties from the doom which hung above them. Although Sir Harrowby was not very good at reading unwritten and unspoken language, he seemed, in part at least, to comprehend Mr. O'Keene's silent budget of hints, for he drew close to him, and said in a loud whisper,—

" Of course, in these matters, the best way is the shortest : —how much ?"

This question appeared to take the responsible editor by surprise, for he made no reply and glanced uneasily at Spiffler, upon whose countenance there fell a deep shade of perplexity and embarrassment. Meantime Sir Harrowby Trumps produced a pocket-book, which he opened, and from which he took several cheques.

" Put in a paragraph in your next number, saying you've been mistaken ; three words will do, and take this cheque for ——" he whispered the amount.

Mr. Spiffler made an eager motion, implying that he wished for information upon the whispered point; and O'Keene, having managed for a moment to elude Trumps' attention, held up five fingers, and then formed two circles in the air with the feather end of a pen.

" Well," said Sir Harrowby, " come—what d'ye say ?"

O'Keene threw a doubtful glance over his visitor's

shoulder towards his principal; but there was no guiding
nformation in the puzzled and downcast looks of Mr. Spiffler.
He, therefore, glanced first at the cheque and then at Trumps,
and muttered some unintelligible words to himself. The
baronet appeared to be fully prepared for this hesitation, and
to have a prompt remedy at hand. Without more ado he
drew back the precious slip of coloured paper which lay upon
the desk, and quietly substituted another in its place. When
O'Keene looked upon it he slightly elevated his eyebrows,
and immediately replied to the eager pantomime question of
Spiffler, by raising one finger and then drawing three airy
circles with the pen. This information appeared at once to
decide Mr. Spiffler, though not in the way in which O'Keene
fully expected it would operate. The editor shook his head
decidedly, and significantly pointed to Trumps and then to
the door, accompanying the motion with those violent contortions of the mouth by which a man tries to speak visibly
instead of audibly, so that O'Keene guessed rightly that his
principal had decided against taking any bribe whatever, and
wished the conference to be put an end to as soon as possible. All this time Trumps had looked discreetly in the
direction of the window, so as to allow his companion to
debate the matter in his own mind without let or hindrance.
Con, while telegraphing to Spiffler, held the cheque in his
hand, gazed with sparkling eyes upon every one of its golden
letters, and rubbed it fondly between his fingers, as though
the thin paper were a luscious velvet, pleasant and grateful
to the touch. And this continued after he had fully comprehended Spiffler's instructions. Poor Con's fingers seemed
unable to unclasp themselves from the magic paper. What
enjoyment was there not comprehended in that little scrap of
transmuted rag!—what days of pleasure and nights of re-
velry! How the very soul of the poor fellow yearned and
longed to grasp that morsel of paper, and hug it to his heart!
But Fate and Mr. Spiffler had decreed otherwise. O'Keene
made a violent effort, and flung the cheque into Sir Harrowby's lap.

" There !" he shouted, "take back yer dross, and don't
think to bribe me, or any honest man, from the discharge of
his duty to his employers and to society."

Sir Harrowby stared with all his eyes. He could comprehend a bribe being rejected because it was too small, but the idea that it could be refused because it was a bribe, as Mr. O'Keene's language would seem to imply, was a phenomenon which even the romance of his nature could hardly conceive. He had trusted this *dernier ressort* from the beginning, and the spring being now fairly broken, nothing remained for him to say. So he stared a moment at O'Keene, took up the cheque, and replaced it in his pocket-book, and then muttering something about informing the gentleman on whose part he acted, rose to go. Mr. O'Keene marshalled him ceremoniously to the door.

"And so you intend to go on printing these things?" said the disappointed emissary, gruffly.

Mr. O'Keene replied by performing another of his Lord Burleigh smiles, and Sir Harrowby Trumps descended the staircase as ill at ease as people generally are who have come off without flying colours in a delicate and dangerous mission.

"Perhaps you'll hear more of this," he said, as he descended the creaking old stair.

"Oi shall be always happy to meet a gentleman of Sir Harrowby Trumps' consideration," replied the Milesian, "or any of hees friends."

And so they parted. When O'Keene returned to the editorial sanctum, he found Spiffler writing with vast rapidity.

"Me dear boy," he exclaimed, bursting into the room, "are ye sure ye understood me? 'Twas a thousand—a cool thousand, begar! Oi niver saw so much thrown away so cool before—niver!"

"Hush!" said Spiffler, earnestly "let no one know of this; nothing venture, nothing have. A secret that's worth a thousand to them may be worth five thousand to us, if we only play our cards well."

"Yes, but we don't know the secret," replied O'Keene.

"We have the clue, man — we have the clue," said Spiffler, who was flushed and excited: "it is a thing of this sort which tries the *nous* in a man. Here is a great opportunity. It will be our own fault if the 'Flail' do not now become a property to all of us."

His pen never stopped as he spoke, and Con, looking over his shoulder, read as follows :—

" TRUTH STRANGER THAN FICTION.

" Under this head we last week hinted at some secret proceedings of a nature which is likely to render them of European celebrity. These transactions are more extraordinary than even we, knowing what we did, dared then to hint. Nor as yet can we speak out. We only assure the public that 'extraordinary' is not the only, though it is the most favourable, epithet, which the transactions in question will probably receive. As for ourselves, the most enormous bribes have been freely offered to purchase our silence. We deem it our duty to proclaim this fact; and that all may know it to be a fact, and not a fiction, we hereby state that the individual who, in our own office, offered us money to betray our public duty was Sir Harrowby Trumps, Baronet.

" In a week or two we expect to have laid bare a tissue of iniquity which will appal society."

" Are — are you not going a little too far?" hinted O'Keene, whose courage was rather physical than moral.

" Not a whit — we have thrown aside the scabbard, and we must not look back. In a month the 'Flail' will either be famous or floored."

And in effect, ere the paragraph saw the light, the rapid march of events had brought about an incident which, coupled with the mysterious announcement of the journalist, produced for the "Flail" a notoriety and an instantaneous circulation which electrified its proprietors. The office was crowded with eager purchasers. Huge placards were surrounded by pushing, staring crowds. Mr. Jorvey sat at the receipt of custom, and was happy; while the editor and his coadjutors, flushed with triumph, revelled luxuriously in a West-end hotel.

The event in question must, however, be reserved for the next chapter.

CHAPTER XXV

THE FLY IN THE WEB.

WE have to change the scene to the little heavily-wain-scoted room in the house in Abingdon Street, which we have described as being apportioned to the peculiar use of Miss Eske. Its present occupants are the General, his majestic lady, and her fair companion. The evening is rapidly closing in, while, from the fragments of dessert upon the table, it is to be safely inferred that so popular is " Miss Eske's room" in the household, that the potentates of the neighbouring apartments do not scruple to invade her realms, even to the extent of dining in her little kingdom.

On the present occasion both the General and Mrs. Pomeroy were magnificent in full evening costume. Although the American warrior had long maintained — and that with incredible gallantry, even to the very teeth of West-end tailors — that New York set the fashion in dress to Paris and London, he had at length been persuaded to lay aside his Transatlantic vestments for garments of a more Christian cut, and perfectly undistinguished by that air of slangy, *estaminet* gentility which characterises the creations of Broadway artists. As for Mrs. General, she was gorgeous in black velvet and bugles. Indeed to look at her majestic form arrayed in those flowing robes, an imaginative spectator would have been apt to pronounce the lady a species of cross between an ordinary fat female of fifty and the Tragic Muse. Miss Eske alone was dressed in plain, stay-at-home fashion; the General and his wife being evidently bound on some grand expedition.

" Ten minutes to eight, and no word of Mr. Lorimer, he promised to be here by half-past seven at latest," said Mrs. Pomeroy, consulting her New York Geneva.

" Something particular must have occurred to detain him," said Miss Eske, bending over her work.

The General slowly sipped the last drops of champagne from a long glass, and pushed it away with a sigh. It is astonishing how Americans, at all hours and at all seasons, will swill champagne. The favourite dinner of a certain gentleman, lately deceased, who was held in high estimation in that particular circle of society which is bounded by the ropes of the prize-ring, was bread-and-cheese and champagne. Transatlantic epicures manifest a kindred taste—at all events so far as liquids go.

"Ah," said General Pomeroy, "I guess he'd a kept better time if you were going to the Opera with us, Miss Eske."

Marion hastened to say that Mr. Lorimer could not have been aware of the slight indisposition which would prevent her to-night from hearing her favourite *Matrimonio Segreto*.

There was a pause. The General fidgeted to the window, watched the lights beginning to twinkle in Lambeth Palace through the gloom, and observed that he thought Deacon Barl as good as any archbishop of them all. The Yankee Tragic Muse put a finishing touch to her array of bugles, and then opined that they must go — Mr. Lorimer must follow. And as Mrs. General Pomeroy had said, so it was done.

"Remember, now, when he comes, Marion, tell him No. 25, on the first tier. We'll leave his name." And with these parting instructions, the General and the Tragic Muse stepped into the carriage which was in waiting to convey them, and departed.

Miss Eske was left alone. The evening was deepening fast, and a servant lighted the lamp. Despite of its gay furniture, the room looked gloomy and sad in the night-time; and Miss Eske had more than once fancied, when she was alone, and all was still that low creaking noises proceeded from the walls, and that heavy footsteps sounded from behind the pannels. On the present occasion, she felt ill and depressed. Every moment she caught herself listening, with suspended breath, for the smothered noises from the walls; and then, with an emotion of impatience at her own childishness, she would rise, shake off the gathering feeling of lonesome awe which she knew would fast deepen into fear, and smiling at her own weakness, would go stoutly on with her work. Still she could not disguise from herself that she was more than usually timid and nervous. Sometimes she almost regretted that she had not accompanied the Pomeroys to the Opera, despite of the sickly languor which had depressed her all the afternoon. She thought of the gay house, the glitter of the lights, the peal of the music, and wished she was submitted to their inspiring influence. Every thing round her appeared to be more dark and louring than usual. The lamp burned dimly,—shadows were piled within the corners of the room; and as the curtains were waved by an occasional breath of wind from the half-opened window, she would shrink within herself, aghast and trembling, at the light rustle of the damask.

At length these nervous feelings were dissipated by the arrival of Lorimer. He had been detained by some trivial accident, and used all his eloquence to persuade Miss Eske to accompany him to join the Pomeroys. At one time she felt inclined to yield, but then, remembering the ordeal of quizzing which she would assuredly undergo from the General upon her headache having so miraculously disappeared before Clement's persuasions, she absolutely refused either to go herself to No. 25, in the first tier, or to allow Lorimer to stay with her—a plan which he supported by a great many arguments of much cogency. We need not linger over such questions as they are generally argued between two lovers; the result was, that Lorimer, having promised to accompany the General and his lady home to supper, tore himself away from Abingdon Street, and Miss Eske was again left alone.

An hour or more went slowly by. Now and again the low rumble of a passing vehicle struck with a dull force upon the ear. Anon the slight noises of the night floated into the room from the river. There was the occasional heavy splash of the one huge oar by which floating barges are steered, or a loud, shrill hail from boat to bank, or from bank to boat; and then again silence within the chamber and without.

Long and stoutly did Marion Eske struggle against the absorbing sensation of mingled fear and melancholy which seemed to encompass her as with a dim, dark halo. She had never before experienced so crushing, so overmastering a sensation, as that which now laid, as it were, a strong, cold hand upon her spirit. Dim forebodings—a restless, aching, indefinite sensation of dread, took possession of her. Every moment she expected something awful or startling to happen, and yet what that something was to be she could not imagine or define. In vain she racked her memory with vain efforts to recollect any similar attack of low spirits. She could neither call to mind having ever before experienced her present sensations, or trace them to any reasonable cause. She had frequently sat alone by night where she sat now. She had sometimes felt nervous and flustered, but on this particular occasion everything like mental and physical energy seemed to have left her. After a fruitless struggle, she surrendered to the overmastering spell which bound her. The work upon which she had been engaged fell from her hands upon her lap. Her eyes became dilated and fixed upon the wainscoting opposite to where she sat, rigid and motionless, as the lady in Comus, in her chair. The evil spell which bound her seemed to have attained the height of its power.

There was deep silence in the room. The lamp appeared to burn yet dimmer and dimmer. The shadows seemed to leave their nooks and to brood all through the air. Marion Eske felt as though she sat in the darkness of the Valley of the Shadow of Death!

All at once a low rumbling noise — faint, yet distinct — rolled through the room. The lady heard it—for a slight start shot through her frame. Her hands were clasped together with a convulsive energy. Her eyes were glazed and dilated — her forehead damp, and her cheeks ashen pale.

A minute passed away and the noise was heard again, a well-oiled but heavy bolt was apparently shot back, and then Marion Eske saw, without any outward manifestation of terror, a slight longitudinal opening appear in the wainscot. It gradually seemed to enlarge, and then the pannel slid quickly aside, shewing a dark space behind in which could be faintly discerned the forms of two men; the foremost was tall and thin, his face was partially concealed by a black handkerchief twisted round his neck; his companion carried a dark lantern which flung a bright spot of light upon the opposite wall.

Miss Eske tried to scream, but her voice died in her throat. The progress of fascination was completed by the intensity of the gaze which the foremost intruder flung on her from out his large glittering eyes. Step by step he advanced into the room.

" The preparatory potion has worked well," he muttered. " The system is in the state recommended for the success of the drug."

Meanwhile the man with the lantern remained motionless in the recess disclosed by the sliding pannel.

Marion Eske followed the intruder with her eyes. At length he stood opposite to her, then she essayed to speak; her white lips moved, and her bosom heaved, and her nostrils dilated, as she struggled madly against the torpor of fascination which was on her. The effort was fruitless—the muscles relaxed, and she sank back staring at the man before her. Without removing his eyes from hers, he slowly produced a phial from an inner breast-coat pocket, and removing the ground-glass stopper, poured the colourless contents into the champagne glass which the General had used, and taking it up, said, in those low, musical tones which we have so often referred to,—

" You must drink this."

Then, for the first time, the intensity of fear combating successfully for a moment the effects of the potion which Miss Eske now knew had been administered to her—though how or when she was not aware—she gasped,—

" It is poison—it is death !"

" No," said Benosa; " it is but sleep—a wondrous sleep —which is both life and death."

Miss Eske, by the effort of speaking, had partially broken the spell which clung around her. She waved her hand impatiently and murmured,—

" No ; I will not—I can not ! Begone !"

Benosa crossed his arms upon his bosom, still holding the glass in his left hand, and then, drawing himself up to his full height, he flashed his glaring eyes down into those of his victim, while, at the same moment, following a slight movement of his right hand, Marion Eske saw the glitter of a blade of steel shine out against his dark clothing. It was either the tacit threat of violence, or the influence of the man's baneful presence acting upon a nervous system artificially wrought into a state of conjoined excitement and weakness, which again crushed the rallying energies of the hapless girl. She shrunk back, at the same time extending her hand for the glass by a mechanical motion ; slowly, but with perfect steadiness, she conveyed it to her lips, her eyes fixed upon those of Benosa. His livid visage never stirred as she raised the draught to her lips, it shewed not a trace of emotion or passion as she slowly drained the glass; but all the while the dreadful stare of his fierce eyes was never remitted, until, in about a minute after Marion had swallowed the last drops of the potion, her face began to grow livid and to change its expression, and the muscles of the fingers gradually relaxed, so that the glass first slipped into a horizontal position, and then fell, and was shivered upon the floor. At the same moment the head of the sufferer dropped upon her chest, and her limbs fell by their own gravity into positions in which they either rested upon other portions of her body or upon the chair.

Then Benosa uttered a low, groaning sigh, and gazed with a look of passionate grief upon his victim. All this time the accomplice within the recess stood motionless. Suddenly Benosa signed to him, and he flashed the lantern over Miss Eske's face. Benosa raised her head, and placed it so as to be supported by the back of the chair. He felt her pulse, it had ceased to beat—he placed a particle of down upon her lips, not a feathery atom moved—he passed his hand over her forehead, it was cold and damp. Then he carefully replaced the phial, the contents of which Miss Eske had swallowed, and produced another and a smaller one—it was the same which Lorimer had purchased at the chemist's in Spitalfields. Glancing over the table, he selected a wine-glass and half filled it with sherry; into the wine he poured about half-a-dozen drops of the colourless fluid contained in the phial; presently an acrid flavour, as of bitter almonds, rose into the room. Benosa again looked round, until his eye caught an inkstand with paper and pens. He took one of the latter, and dipping the feathered end in the medicated wine, touched the lips of the lifeless woman with the fluid.

"In such a complete state of trance," he muttered, "there is no danger; ere the absorbents can act evaporation will have done their office."

Then he again glanced round the room, and his eyes flashed as he saw, flung carelessly upon a chair, a light summer overcoat which Lorimer had left when he departed for the Opera. Catching it up, he deposited the half-empty phial in one of the pockets, and then carefully replaced the garment in its former position.

"More circumstantial evidence," he muttered. "The chain grows longer, and thicker, and firmer."

Then he turned to the entranced woman; she was still, motionless, still to all appearance, and by all ordinary tests dead, and before her stood a glass, half full of wine, mingled with the most quick and fatal poison known to exist

Benosa turned to his accomplice.

"Now, Blane," he said, "now commences your part. To the police-office!"

The ex-steward bowed. Benosa threw one last, long glance at his victim, and then stepped into the recess in the wall. Immediately the pannel rolled into its place, and the heavy bolt was again shot.

* * * * * *

The sparkling finale of the *Matrimonio*, with its rapid intermingling choruses of female voices and its brilliant showers of orchestral harmony, was at its quickest and its most fascinating point when a loud, impatient knock shook the door of the box No. 25, on the first tier, while a gruff voice without loudly summoned the attendant. The occupants of the box started up from their chairs in some surprise, and Lorimer rose and undid the fastenings of the door.

A common-looking man, whom none of the party knew, walked into the box, leaving the door open, so that two or three flustered-looking boxkeepers could be discerned flitting about in the corridor in an evident state of uncertainty as to the proceedings of the new-comer. And, in truth, this man was not quite in Opera trim—he was unwashed and unshaven. A coarse, old, frayed great-coat was buttoned tightly up to his chin, and his large, red, ungloved hands were marvels of dirty muscularity. Doffing a somewhat battered old hat, the new-comer said gruffly, but civilly enough,—

"Sorry to disturb you, mum—and you, gents—but there's a bad job been and took place."

The poor Tragic Muse grew flushed and pale in a moment. At first she thought that war might have suddenly been declared between England and America, and that a sanguinary and unscrupulous enemy might be now taking the first hostile step by consigning two distinguished citizens of the States to a dungeon in the Tower, probably with the view of putting them ultimately upon the rack.

The General, although he might not have the same forebodings, was just as pale and frightened as his wife. They sat staring in stupid silence at the intruder, while Lorimer hurriedly asked what was wrong.

"The young lady," replied the man — "the young lady as you left well and hearty in Abingdon Street three hours ago ——"

Clement Lorimer almost bounded from the floor. The man with the great-coat eyed him coolly and keenly.

"Great God!" he exclaimed, "Miss Eske — Marion Eske — my Marion! What of her? — is she ill — is she —— What of her? What of her? — for God's sake ——"

"Dead," replied the man.

"Dead!" Mrs. Pomeroy sunk backwards, and was only preserved by the ledge of the box from falling to the floor. The poor little General shook like an aspen leaf. Lorimer stood, pale as marble, confronting the messenger of heavy tidings.

"Dead!" he repeated — "dead! When? — how? — how?"

"Murdered," replied the other, with the same laconic but not intentionally uncivil gruffness.

Clement Lorimer stood rooted to the ground, his face working and his hands clasped.

"Merciful God!" he at length burst out, "murdered! And when? — how? — by whom? Is no one taken — no one suspected?"

"There is one suspected," said the man in the great-coat, measuring Lorimer from head to foot with his eyes, and apparently preparing himself for the event of a struggle — "there is one suspected. Information was given at our office not half-an-hour ago."

"And who — who? — for God sake!"

The police agent cast a look to the door of the box, and placed himself between Lorimer and the corridor. Then, lowering his voice, he said, in cool but respectful tones, —

"I am sorry to say, sir, that you are the party implicated. You must consider yourself my prisoner."

"Me!—me!—murder my—Marion—my love—my ——" He stammered out these words, and then sunk back against the wall.

"It's my duty, sir, to caution you," said the officer, "that any thing you say may be taken down and used against you. I don't mean to say you're in the job, sir, but information has been laid, and we must do our duty. I have a warrant about me, if you wish to see it."

But Lorimer replied not; he continued to lean against the wall, his lips still moving — still repeating the ejaculation, "Murdered her — my Marion!"

"Now, sir," said the agent of police, "perhaps we had better slip away quietly."

But at this moment Mrs. Pomcroy rose all trembling,—

"Take me — home — let us go home," she whispered to her husband hysterically.

A mist came over Lorimer's eyes, and he remembered nothing distinctly of what passed for the next few moments. He had an indistinct vision of people moving rapidly about him — of one grim face which was always close to his — of long lighted corridors — of whisperings and rushings of groups round him — of the cool air of the great staircase — of staggering, and being supported as he descended the steps, then of a bustling and pulling up of carriages in the street — of horses plunging hither and thither — of faces which stared into his and then disappeared — of shouts, and loud calls, and the hustling of a crowd upon the pavement — of being lifted into a vehicle, and of hearing two voices which rose up above the tumult, although they did not appear to speak so loud as did many around. The first said,—

"Coachman, to Abingdon Street!"

The second, and at almost the same moment, said,—

"Coachman, to Bow Street!"

CHAPTER XXVI.

LIFE-IN-DEATH.

To be dead in body—to be dead to all the usual tests of life—to be powerless, passive, cold, and yet to be alive to oneself—dimly and faintly to be sure—but to be conscious of a torpid, yet still existing life, of a single spark of animating spirit, still glimmering, but unseen, unrecognised from without, glowing silently in the very depths of the physical nature,—such were the horrible symptoms of the artificial state of catalepsy into which the potion swallowed at Benosa's bidding had flung Marion Eske.

Outwardly, and to others, she presented all the phenomena of death. Of all in the chamber only she herself knew that death was not yet there. The nerves of sensation still acted feebly and wearily, conveying dim, and as it were distant, impressions to the as feebly and wearily acting brain; but the nerves of motion were utterly paralysed and dead. One of the tearful attendants by chance lost her hold of the dead arm she was lifting. It fell as so much wood upon the table, and only the seeming corpse knew that that arm fell against a will which still feebly existed in the inner tissues of the brain. But that living spark of soul was like a wounded general without an army. It could think and feel feebly and languidly, out it could not act. It could not by its operation signify its presence. There were none to obey it. It could only recognise itself—know itself—feel itself. Outwardly all was blank, cold, dead; and those who stood terrified and weeping around could see before them but the moveless thing from which the breath of life had gone out!

And yet, by the wise rule of a good and consistent Providence, awful as were the phenomena of this life-in-death, it was mentally almost painless to the sufferer. To feel acutely one must feel strongly; to realise in all their forbidding horror the probable consequences of such a situation, the mind must be thoroughly able to perform its ordinary functions. It was not so in the case before us. The very influences which put a temporary stop to the physical manifestations of mind, acted so as to weaken, to dim, and to confuse the perceptions of that mind. Thus, the perfect and complete bodily torpor produced partial mental torpor. The blow which annihilated the power of matter, weakened and disordered the power of mind. It discerned dimly and judged feebly. No impression lasted long — no impression left a trace which could be recalled — no impression gave rise to a distinct idea of what would in necessary sequence follow. The mind had no force to fling itself backwards or forwards. It only took cognisance of the actual present, and that dimly, painfully, and partially; its stubborn inertness blunting the keen edge of every sharp emotion, and remaining alive, as it were, only to the stun, never to the smart, of deadly, stabbing thoughts.

All outward sounds, all outward physical things, were presented colourless and phantom-like in the same cloudy mirror; words were partially heard, and when heard only partially understood. A thick but not impervious veil hung in drear folds between the palsied brain and outer things. Through that veil distinct shapes appeared shadows—through that veil sounds of grief and sympathy came fitfully, like low, boding, indefinite voices — through that veil those things which cause emotions and ideas floated in, diminished and misshapen, at once uncouth and indefinite. That veil was like the crape on muffled drums, through which only steals one long, low, melancholy roll!

For some time after the administration of the drug Marion was utterly insensible — dead to the world — dead to herself. A faint sound, like a distant scream, was the first sensation to cleave and stir the depths of her trance. The cry appeared low, indistinct, raised by some one far, far away. And yet it was loud, startling, piercing, uttered at her elbow — in her ear. Then she was conscious of dark shapes rapidly moving around her, raising her from her chair, and placing her in a recumbent position. Soon the dimly seen shapes became more distinct, for her eyes were yet open and staring. They appeared men — strangers. They hurried to and fro. They mingled with female forms who thronged around. There was a confused sound of whispering, and ejaculations, and sobs. Hands were placed upon her forehead and her mouth. A dim form bent long over her. It seemed to place its head to hers. It raised her hands, and then replaced them reverently by her side. Meantime the other shapes stood around. Then they turned to the table and looked and lifted up glasses, which glimmered faintly, and the whispering arose again. Presently the patient began to discern words and broken sentences. At first they were but sounds distinctly heard. Then a black shadow of meaning began to diffuse itself over her brain. She began to comprehend that she was dead—gone away out of the world—that there was a gulf between her and the whispering and the shapes. These ideas rose up, all shadowy, all incoherently, all dimly looming in spectral wreaths of thought. But soon they began to take a certain order, a certain consistency, and she felt—she knew not how—that she was dead, yet alive. It was a dark, indefinite, mysterious idea. She could not understand it—she could could not reconcile it; but there it was, overshadowing her as with a rent and disordered pall, through the holes in which she saw the world.

Then there was suddenly a movement in the now crowded chamber, and a shape she knew and a face she knew were over her. She felt hot tears upon her face—she heard loud, mournful sounds—she saw a circle of pale, woe-worn faces. Then the hand of the shape she knew gently closed her eyes, and all was darkness. After this the sounds and the whispering died away for a space, and there was silence.

It was during this silence that the idea of her being dead and yet alive began to fade away, and at last to let in a dim image of the truth—that she was alive, but that she was deemed dead. For awhile the weakened mind could not comprehend the one idea more than the other. But gradually the true and coherent notion was recognised and faintly understood. Yet no emotion was excited by the attainment of this degree of mental consciousness. No recollections were excited of the past—no fears evoked for the future; only a black, boding sentiment of evil came down and encompassed the soul, like the darkness which was upon the face of the deep.

Then came a half-understood consciousness that people were again around her. She felt herself again raised and moved. Busy hands lifted her limbs, and low voices sounded in her ears. She could feel that some unaccustomed covering was being folded around her.   Then something soft and yielding rose on each side of her head.   After a long interval of darkness and silence the jaded and slumbering mind was aware that the passive form in which it dwelt was laid upon its bed.

Then came a space — it might have been long, it might have been short — of undisturbed calm; for it was one of the inexplicable features of Marion's fearful state that the sense of time was utterly gone.   She felt no tedium — she had no idea of living slowly and continuously on.   The out-ward events, which were conveyed by the half-torpid nerves to the more than half-torpid brain, might have happened closely after each other or at long intervals.   The mind took no cognisance of the pauses between.   They were utterly blank; only during them the dreaming soul would feebly commune with itself.   It would be sensible that it existed — it would think wanderingly and dimly.   Thoughts would form, and rise, and pass away; and all these thoughts were distorted, dislocated visions of things past — they were empty, indefinite, dreamy shadows; but all were darkened, all made black, and boding, and bitter, by one unrealised yet ever-present consciousness of evil, and desolation, and death!

Outward sounds, as we have said, soon attracted a feeble and disturbed attention; and at intervals the overthrown mind struggled faintly to hear them, and then to comprehend their meaning.   Sometimes it was low voices which would chime around the bed, and there would be a soft rustling, as though the curtains were gently drawn aside, and then the voices would sound more mournfully and more near.   Marion often distinguished particular words as sounds familiar to her ears; but the more subtle meaning eluded the feebly grasping brain.   It was only occasionally that the mind was conscious of a general understanding produced by these voices after they had long beaten, as it were, with a faint, muffled noise at the portals of hearing.   Then she was conscious that those who spoke, spoke pitifully, sorrowfully, tearfully.   But some-times they would change their tone, and the idea would arise in the patient's mind that then they spoke of some other object — spoke of it with anger, and indignation, and strong abhorrence.

Q

And when the voices spoke thus, there was often something suggested by a word they pronounced which made the sick mind thrill feebly—which lighted up, as it were, for a moment into a more intense glow the hidden spark of life—which seemed as if it would evoke sensations, indefinite and incoherent, yet sad, and dear, and sweet; but which in a moment faded away and were gone. That word was— Lorimer!

And after these periods of comparative activity, would come the intervals of drear blankness—darkness within and darkness without. Once that dim interval was interrupted by a muttered sound of deep, low voices. Heavy footsteps sounded about. Then Marion felt herself gently lifted and again laid down, the low, deep voices still sounding over her, and this time without the rustle of drawn curtains. Why, she knew not—how, she knew not, but there was a sensation of tightness round her which had not formerly been. She thought she was in some narrow place. Presently came a soft sobbing voice, which she knew; presently tears fell again over her face, and she thought that hot lips touched her forehead. Then there was a brief silence. It was broken by a grating sound, which seemed to be renewed at short intervals all round her. Then suddenly the sense of tightness, of restriction, and of darkness, at once increased tenfold. The air got thick and heavy. No puffs of summer wind passed by— no sound of the world stole into the soul. The chain which bound its faculties seemed all at once stronger—heavier— firmer. The sufferer's limbs could almost feel the thick darkness. The veil which had hung between her and outer things grew impervious, and thick, and hopeless, in its grim intensity!

Time passed on. She began to feel that it did, by an overmastering impression of evil, in which for the first time there was blended a shade of dim, indefinite horror, which remained ever present to her, and thus served, as it were, for a mark past which the leaden hours crawled one by one. This shadow of horror grew gradually greater, and blacker, and more defined, until at last, and by slow degrees, it resolved itself into a ghastly, spectral consciousness, which scared away all other thoughts, and ruled, horrible and supreme, like the awful shape called Demi-Gorgon!

Then Marion Eske knew that she was thought to be dead, and that she lay supine in her coffin.

CHAPTER XXVII.

THE NIGHT VOYAGE ON THE RIVER.

THE day had been close and sultry. Great dusky masses of cloud had since morning overshadowed London. Sometimes a violent gust of wind, bearing a pattering shower of rain, whistled fast through the streets, lashing the sloping roofs, and rattling the streaming windows. Then the deep, torpid calm would resume its sway; the clouds which had been partially rent and scattered, would rebuild their vaporous masses, and that close, choky sensation, which proclaims the brewing of a summer's storm, would again descend with all its louring influence, to weaken and depress the energies of every living and breathing thing.

Evening came, and the storm had not yet burst. Evening darkened into pitchy night. From time to time a hollow, moaning gust would sigh through the air, and the dampened flag-stones would be spotted with the great splashes of huge rain-drops; but the tempest still hung aloof and above. People looked up into the thick night, and wished for the lightning, the rain, and the wind, which were soon to clear and wash the air, and make it cool, and fresh, and pleasant to all who breathed it.

As the night approached its zenith, the flood-tide, which was running fast up the river, began to slacken its speed and to slip by anchored barges and wharves, and the slimy piers of bridges, with a stealthy, gliding motion. Although the night was murkily dark, there was no fog upon the river; and the twinkling lights upon either hand, and the double line of red sparks which marked the span of the bridges, shone out all the clearer for the depth of the surrounding blackness.

The tide was at its full, and the dark river brimming, when a wherry slowly approached the Middlesex bank, making for the gravelly beach which sloped into the water in the rear of Benosa's house in Abingdon Street. The boat was one built for great speed, but yet not without regard to the comfortable accommodation of those who might be conveyed on board. A low, broad seat stretched across the stern-sheets, railed at the back and sides; and on the seat and on the bottom of the boat, before it, was piled a mass of soft, dark cushions. The boat was pulled by two men, who worked noiselessly and talked in whispers. As the wherry approached the beach, they lay upon their oars, and one of them took a small lantern from beneath the thaft on which he sat, and, turning round, held it up towards the shore. Instantly a round star of light danced upon the ripples which stirred the gravel, upon half-a-dozen slimy old piles which formed part of an embankment, the greater part of which had been long washed away; and then upon the river end of that long, low out-building which, as we have seen, extended at right angles from the house down to the Thames. Having by means of the dark lantern ascertained their exact position, the boatmen turned the stern of the skiff towards the shore, and backed her almost to the beach. Before landing, however, he who pulled the stroke-oar — a tall, gaunt man — stood up, and gazed eagerly upon the dwelling before them. Notwithstanding the darkness, he was near enough to perceive the white squares formed by the drawn window-blinds.

"There—that is the room," he said, in a hoarse whisper; "in the left-hand corner—just above the out-house."

Then the oars were resumed, and in a moment the boat's stern touched the wall of the building alluded to, which, when the tide was at its full, rose from the water. He who pulled the bow oar dexterously shipped it, and catching up a short boat-hook, struck it into the bottom, so as to anchor the wherry in the position which it occupied. At the same moment the tall man flashed the lantern upon the wall, and the glare shewed a small door, apparently long disused, and green and slimy from the action of the water, which in very high tides rose a foot or more above the threshold, which in its turn was several feet above the level of the beach. While the bowman held his boat-hook so as to steady the skiff, his companion, without a moment's pause, applied a small key to the door, which at once yielded, shewing a space of pitchiest darkness beyond. Making a sign, which was promptly acknowledged by the other, he who had opened the door stepped from the skiff upon the threshold. The gleam of his lantern shot before him and shewed a cellar-like passage, the walls and roof formed of unplastered brick. Then the door closed behind him. The man left in the boat gazed eagerly up to the window which had been pointed out by his companion.

"This is the most ticklish job of all," he muttered, "but it is to be the last; and then ho for America, with none alive to tell tales about my riches!"

As he spoke, a light gleamed from the window on which his eyes were fixed, "He's about it," he murmured.

Meantime the air appeared to become more and more stifling. Not a breath of wind stirred, and the ripples which the surging of the boat had produced died away upon the dark waters.

Thus ten minutes passed. Suddenly the light from the window was partially obscured, as if the lamp or candle had been moved to a corner of the room.

"He's done it—he's coming!" said the boatman. Another minute elapsed, the door opened, and the tall, gaunt man appeared on the threshold, bearing a burden—something large, heavy, and dark.

"You have got it," whispered the man with the boat-hook.

"I have got *her*," was the reply.

And he who spoke deposited his burthen reverently upon the piled-up cushions. His companion eagerly gazed at it; he could distinguish but a mass of dark drapery. Only once, for a moment, he saw something oval and white, and knew that it was the dead-like face of the entranced woman.

Meantime, Benosa—our readers have doubtless recognised him—piled round the unmoving form of his victim thick wreaths of shawls and cloaks, caught up, as it seemed, in the room from whence he had borne her. Then he lifted from the bottom of the boat, what appeared to be a long bar of a heavy substance, enveloped in some fleecy material, so as to be nearly a foot in diameter.

" 'Tis about the same weight," he muttered. " At any rate there can be no perceptible difference."

Then he disappeared again by the little door.

Blane — for he it was who held the boat-hook — gazed with a sort of gloomy fascination upon the dark mass in the stern sheets. It lay as still as the metal bar which was to supply its place beneath the coffin-lid. In a moment the light again streamed from the window.

" He is using the screwdriver, and shutting down all close again," said the ex-steward. A long, long quarter of an hour elapsed; then the light was extinguished. " Thank the stars," said the watcher, " he has done it."

As he spoke, Benosa stepped into the boat. In a moment the door was swung to, and locked; in the next, the wherry shot down the stream as fast as the muscles of those who plied the oars could urge her. The tide had turned, and as the boat flew beneath Westminster Bridge, Benosa marked the white frothy ripple gliding downwards along the roughened masonry.

Meantime the storm so long brewing gave indications that at length it was about to descend in its fury. The air became absolutely thick and sulphurous. Tiny particles of smut and soot, unable to arise in the loaded atmosphere, settled in showers upon the water and the earth. A dim foreboding of impending danger took possession of those who watched the approaching conflict of the elements. The silence was as profound as the darkness was intense. All at once there fell a few scattered drops of rain, great plashing globules of water, such as seldom descend upon the earth. Then there was a momentary pause.

Suddenly a stream of blue lightning tore across the darkness, and in an instant — and for an instant — the gleaming river, the piles of confused buildings rising upon its banks, the stately bridges, stretching their granite bulwarks from shore to shore, the pale, spectral steeples, shooting up into the darkness — all appeared and all vanished.

" Pull—pull hard and fast !" shouted Benosa. His voice was drowned in the thunder-peal which accompanied, rather than followed, the flash. It was not the usual hoarse roar of thunder; it was rather a sharp, ringing, crackling uproar, like the discharge of a volley of brass artillery. In the midst of the tumult the ashen staves bent, and the wherry flew fast and faster through the buzzing, foaming water. Another flash, as bright—as blue as the first. Two great portions of the sky appeared masses of lurid flame, and between them leaped a forked, jagged stream. Again the river, with its black waters, shone and glared—again the thousand buildings of the great city stood out, more clear than by brightest sunlight in that universal blaze, and again the thunder seemed to smite into the very brains of the listeners.

"Pull harder and faster — harder and faster!" shouted Benosa. "We shall have it in a moment."

And as the last rattle of the thunder died away, a loud, rushing sound came hurtling through the air.

"The squall!" said Benosa. "Keep her right before it, or we shall be over in a moment."

And as he spoke the rushing sound waxed louder. They heard the scream of the wind through the arches of Black-friars Bridge which they had just passed. A moment more, and spots of white foam, gleaming all across the river, shewed where the piers of the bridge stood stoutly out against the angry waters, as they flew headlong before the wind. Then at last—driving before it a thick, sharp, whistling shower of mingled rain and spray, the gust caught the boat. But it was ably manned. Shouting to Blane to sit steadily and keep his oar in the stream, Benosa partially rose as the wherry was borne on in the centre of a rushing ridge of foaming water. The fury of the squall momentarily increased. The fierce wind tore up the troubled river, and scattered it in blinding showers through the air. The whole tideway was a mass of foam, glistening as though the stream had been beaten with rods—while, howling above the water—shrieking through the vast arches of bridges—grasping and shaking piles of chimneys and high gavels upon the banks, and bearing on in horizontal lines the pour of fast falling rain, the tempest swept the weak wherry before it—its crew deafened with the din, and blinded with the drift of flying water.

The black mass of Southwark Bridge, with its crowning tiara of lights, loomed a moment ahead, and then appeared in the gloom behind. Almost at the same time instant, as if

appeared to Benosa, the granite arches of London Bridge
stood out in their colossal dimensions over the foaming
flood.

The squall had reached its height; and almost at the
culminating moment, as the wherry was shooting towards the
centre arch, a wild flaw of wind took her on the broadside.
What followed seemed the catastrophe of a wild dream. There
was a moment's violent tossing amid the white, sparkling
ridges of water—a moment when every sound was lost in the
shriek of the hurtling wind; then a vision of a vast pile of
massive masonry—an uncontrollable lurch of the tempest-
beaten boat—a crash—a collision—a wild attempt to fend off
from the slimy, slippery piers; and almost at the same
instant the wherry, leaking and half stove in, was swept
downwards from the bridge between the crowded tiers of
shipping in the Pool.

The storm was at its wildest as they shot the bridge.
Minute by minute it lulled from the full burst of its fury,
settling into a blustering gale, which drove volleys of
drenching rain before it, and urged to furious speed the
race of the ebbing tide. Not more than three quarters of an
hour had elapsed from the time when the wherry quitted
Bankside until it had swept up to a green and slimy stairs,
which descended to the margin of a little creek in Lime-
house Reach.

In the adjoining street stood a close cabriolet. Thanks
to the weather and the hour, the place was perfectly deserted.
Not a being but his accomplice witnessed Benosa as he
carefully placed the lifeless form of Marion Eske within
the vehicle. Not a being but that accomplice—who belonged to Benosa body and soul—witnessed his master as,
with a strange reverence, he laid the unmoving, unbreathing,
yet still existing form upon the bed on which died the
mother of Clement Lorimer.

CHAPTER XXVIII

"THOU SHALT NOT BEAR FALSE WITNESS AGAINST THY NEIGHBOUR."

SIR HARROWBY TRUMPS sat in a gaudily-furnished chamber looking out upon a bustling West-end street. The walls were hung with flashy pictures in brilliant frames; and a variety of couches and easy chairs, some of them stained and mudded, as though their occupants had been in the habit of lolling about with little thought of dirty boots, were dispersed over the rich Brussels carpets. On the table was a brilliant breakfast-service of silver and china, and beside the chased and massive urn was placed a stand of crystal liqueur decanters, with a couple of curious old Dutch dram-glasses, having long stalks, quaintly cut into sparkling squares and cubes, and ornamented in the cup part with rude emblazonries of gold.

Plunged deeply in an easy chair Sir Harrowby sat musing, while the untouched meal smoked beside him. At length he grasped a decanter and poured a bumper of golden liquor out into one of the old-fashioned glasses, swallowed the drain at a gulp, and then lay back and pondered. Sir Harrowby looked like a man stricken with a ghastly distemper. His face was not pale; the discoloration of the coarse, pimply skin prevented such a change; but its hue was a sort of faded, ghastly green. The baronet's eyes were sunk and terribly bloodshot, and on a close inspection the beat of the pulse in the temples could be seen. He had fallen off in flesh, too; his clothes hung loosely about him, and his brown fingers were emaciated and skinny.

"It is the devil himself," he muttered, "that has me in his clutches! No man could make me do what he has done. O God! how I hate him! But he has me—he has me—every way! He's dragging me to the edge of the rock—I'm coming nearer and nearer to the gulf! God! if I could push him over without going down myself! Oh, would I not? —Over—over—down—down—down!"

His hair bristled up, his eyes flashed, and his fingers

closing, like iron bars, upon the glass which he had in his
hand, the crystal smashed, and broken fragments fell upon
the carpet, while streaks of blood oozed from between the
strained fingers of the excited man He paused and went on,—

"I know I shall break down in that cursed trial,—I can't
meet *his* eye! I've got the story glib enough now, but I'll
fail when it comes to the push. I would cut and run for it
now, but I know that devil has his spies around me—I know
I'm followed, dogged everywhere; I can't move but there's
eyes on me. God! I'm as much a prisoner as him in
Newgate."

He was gradually working himself up into a fury of
passion. "I did what I liked till I took his money: I led
that boy by the nose—I had all I wanted. There wasn't a
luxury or a pleasure in Europe I didn't have my swing of,
and now ——" He paused and drew a long breath.
"What if I was to end it all?—to peach, to save Lorimer,
and damn myself and him? Lord! to see that devil face,
those devil eyes, all quivering, all flashing, when the plant
was blown on! By ——!" and he swore an oath too terrible
to be set on paper,—"by ——! the baffled spite in the old
man's throat would choke him then and there, and save the
hangman's labour."

He spoke these last words in a loud, excited tone. As
they died away the door partially opened, and the dark visage
of Benosa appeared. Sir Harrowby sunk backwards in his
chair.

"Finish your soliloquy, never mind me," said the new-
comer.

Sir Harrowby glared at him and breathed hard and loud
through his clenched teeth.

"You are not disconcerted," said Benosa, calmly ad-
vancing into the room. "As I know what you must think,
it matters little what you may say. Go on!"

He seated himself opposite to Sir Harrowby. Benosa
was dressed in his usual fashion, and bore himself with his
usual sarcastic imperturbability. Sir Harrowby was the first
to break the silence.

"I suppose most men grumble that have much to do with
you," he said sulkily.

"On the contrary," replied Benosa, "when men serve me

well I pay them well; we are, therefore, mutually content. As for you, Sir Harrowby, you really do not know when you are well off; but the period of our connexion draws to an end."

"It had need," replied the other; "I want to leave this country."

"I shall leave it too," answered Benosa, in his deep diapason tones.

"For where?" asked Trumps.

"I shall leave this land," murmured the old man, "and I shall go to no other."

The baronet stared, shrugged his shoulders, and drummed with his shaking fingers uneasily upon the table. At last he spoke.

"Hark ye," he said, "you know you have me in your meshes. I could hang you, but then I would transport myself. You will pay me the final sum the moment sentence is pronounced, and that in gold—no bills or bonds?"

"In gold," repeated Benosa,—"in ingots of virgin gold."

"And the trial comes on the third day of the session?"

"The third."

Sir Harrowby Trumps began, *sotto voce*, to calculate to himself,—"Say, start at three, or make it five, twelve miles an hour, including changes, that makes—let me see—Gravesend, twenty; Rochester—say seven; Canterbury, about eighteen; Dover, say a dozen more; then a quick-going lugger, or steam, as may be handiest, say three hours: that's five for road, three, or perhaps four for water, makes nine. So, in ten hours at farthest I'll be in Calais, and I don't care if I never see the white cliffs again."

Benosa waited patiently until his companion had made these rapid calculations for his sudden flight, and then said,—

"You forget what must come before you start."

Sir Harrowby looked grimly at him,—"No," he said, "I have it perfect now; I'm only afraid of breaking down before these cursed counsel."

Benosa flashed his bright eyes keenly upon the false witness.

"A slip or a falter of that craven tongue, and it had better been plucked from you by the roots!"

" My safety is as much risked as yours," returned Sir Harrowby, sulkily.

" Think that chair the witness-box, this room the court, and me the examining counsel," said Benosa, keenly. " You say you have the tale correctly—we shall see."

The old man rose, imitated, with a species of bitter, mocking irony, the bustling manner of a counsel preparing to examine an important witness, and then said,—

" Your name, I believe, is Trumps—Sir Harrowby Trumps ?"

The baronet stared and hesitated. He hardly knew how to treat this species of rehearsal. The old man repeated his question, and Trumps muttering, " Well, have it your own way," replied in the affirmative to the question.

" You have been for some time acquainted with the prisoner at the bar ?"

" I have."

" Intimately ?"

" Yes, we were great friends."

" And tolerably well acquainted with each other's secrets —on a very confidential footing, I believe ?"

" Yes, we both pu.   together."

" The prisoner was a man of property, eh ?"

" He was and he was not. He never knew who his parents were, or from whence he got his money."

" But he did get it —that's the point, eh ?"

" As regularly as quarter-day came round."

" And, lightly come, lightly go, I suppose — the prisoner was a man of pleasure—spent freely and lived merrily, eh?"

" Very merrily."

" He kept hunters, racers, gambled, and so forth ?"

" Yes, more or less."

" And was altogether what is called a man about town, eh?"

" Precisely."

" Well, he was generally lucky, but all at once the luck appeared to turn ?"

" Yes, at the time of the last Derby."

" The prisoner had a horse entered for that race ?"

" Yes, Snapdragon, he was the Favourite."

" The prisoner backed this horse largely ?"

"Yes; so did everybody connected with his trainer's stable."

"And you all lost heavily?"

"Very heavily."

"Well, what followed?"

"I was unable to meet my engagements on the turf."

"And the prisoner?"

"He went to sea in his yacht."

"And when he returned?"

"He found that he was a ruined man. Whoever had sent him his income got tired of the game and stopped it."

"It was he himself who told you all this when he called upon you?"

"Yes."

"Did he tell you any thing else?"

"Yes; that he had a scheme in view,—to raise money by means of life insurance."

"Did he explain himself more fully?"

"Not then."

"Where did this interview take place?"

"At apartments occupied by my wife in Dean Street, Soho Square."

"You saw the prisoner again?"

"Yes; by appointment."

"And he recurred to the subject of raising money by life insurance?"

"Yes. He told me that he had made the acquaintance of a young lady, over whom he possessed great influence; that he could make her do any thing; and that he had persuaded her to insure in three different offices. He said he wished to introduce me to her."

"And did he?"

"Yes; the following Sunday, in the Park."

"When did you meet again?"

"The following day."

"You then agreed to accompany the young lady, Miss Eske, to certain City insurance companies and to procure the necessary medical certificates?"

"Yes."

"And you did so?"

"Yes."

"The family with whom Miss Eske lived were not aware of the step she had taken?"

"They were not. The day on which she accompanied me to the City they were in the West End in search of a house."

"The policies were afterwards assigned to the prisoner?"

"I believe so; but I do not know of my own knowledge."

"You did not, I presume, anticipate what would appear to have been the real object of the prisoner in obtaining these policies?"

"No. I thought he merely meant to raise money on them."

"Did he ever talk to you of his intentions?"

"Never, broadly out."

"But he dropped hints?"

"I did not take them in that light until subsequent events made me think of them."

"Well, what was it he said?"

"He said that Miss Eske was an orphan; that any relations she might have were in America; and that, even in the event of her death, no person would have any interest in making particular inquiry."

Benosa suddenly divested himself of his assumed forensic air.

"You are apter than I thought you," he said, with one of his bitter smiles. "Perjury never had a readier pupil."

Sir Harrowby started up, clenched his hand, and stamped his foot. Benosa stood calm and impassible, and the baronet, swinging himself violently round, walked to the window, and glared into the street beneath, impatiently drumming on the glass with his fingers. Then he returned, with a scowling visage, to the table, filled out another glass of spirit, stared Benosa steadily in the face, and muttering between his clenched teeth, "To your destruction, here and hereafter!" tossed off the bumper. Benosa stood looking at him, and the cold, hard smile never flitted from his face.

* * * * *

At the moment that Sir Harrowby Trumps shewed himself at the window, two shabby-looking men were standing on the opposite pavement. One of them was the person who had arrested Lorimer at the Opera.

"See there," he said to his companion, "in the first-floor window."

The person addressed looked up. "I see," he said. Trumps was beating a tattoo upon the glass.

"I expect I'll ferret out a charge of bigamy against that man before many days are over," answered the other. "He's not to be lost sight of night or day until he's laid up in lavender. Who are disengaged in the staff?"

"Medlock, Wilson, Portman, and myself."

"Then set them on the track. You must answer for it that he does not get out of the country."

Sir Harrowby left the window.

"He's as safe as if he was double-ironed in Newgate," said the myrmidon of police.

And from that day two sets of spies encompassed Sir Harrowby Trumps.

CHAPTER XXIX.

QUIET AND COUNTRY AIR.

ON the morning of the day on which Lorimer was arrested Dr. Gumbey cut himself shaving. While the blood crimsoned the lather, the doctor held out the razor close to the mirror. The steel rattled against the plate-glass with a low, continuous chime.

"So," said the careful doctor, "getting shaky in the hand. Must be stopped. The season's almost over. I'll be off to the country at once."

And then, very slowly and carefully, as was his wont, the doctor proceeded with his very elaborate toilet. He had divers invitations to dinners, seats, and mansions. A few days, and he might either dwell in a marine cottage at Broadstairs; or aboard a yacht, cruising in the Solent; or in a Highland farmstead amid the Grampians, with miles and miles of grouse-swarming mountains around; or in a noble mansion-house in the centre of a fair English county, with partridges in the yellow stubble, and pheasants in the green coppice woods. But all these pleasant modes of life—so thought the prudent Gumbey—are only changes of th species of dissipation. There will be pic-nics at Broadstairs, club-balls at Cowes, no end of whisky-toddy consumed upon the heather, and stately dinner-parties at the English manor-house. "No," he thought, "I will have a month's perfect quiet; I will go to bed every night at ten, and rise every morning at seven; I will forswear every stimulant stronger than a draught of home-brewed; I will pass every day in the open air; I will not so much as open a letter or a newspaper; and so in a month I shall go to the shores of Kent, or to the Isle of Wight, or to Glen Brouachan, or to Grangely Park, with a complexion as fresh as a ploughboy's, and nerves as steady as steel wires." And as the doctor said, so did he.

Whoever knows aught of the environs of London, knows that within twenty miles of St. Paul's there are not only rural spots, tracts of fields, and wood, and meadow, but even little hamlets and villages, as perfectly sequestered, and iso-lated, and lonely, as though they lay amid the hills of De-vonshire or in the valleys of Westmoreland. One of these quiet little nooks we have now to sketch. It is an old-fashioned, sleepy village. The one street follows a bend or elbow in the road. The houses have a quaint irregularity. Prim three-story dwellings, with trees in front, jostle with old-fashioned cottages, all garrets and chimneys, supported by irregular clusters of out-houses. The summer sun shines hot into that lonely street, and the shopkeepers lounge idly and lean upon their half-doors. As you pass on, you every-where catch glimpses, through lanes and openings in the red brick houses, of the fields behind, and of hedge-rows, and orchards, and gardens. Just in the centre of the vil-lage is the principal inn. A great white beam stretches across the street, and upon it, over the passengers' heads, swings the sign. Not far off is the church, grey and time worn, with buttresses and arched windows carved by Norman chisels. And all around, for miles and miles, lies a great range of fair landscape, woodland, and cornfield, and mea-dow. You can climb hills and sit amongst the fern under the shade of dark, rough firs, and look for leagues on that great panorama, tracing by the mile the wanderings of the broad shining river beneath, which flows ripplingly on through alder-skirted meadows, and up which long teams of horses labour to drag heavy-laden barges. A bridge of peculiar construction, or rather two bridges, as if one had been found too short and another was tacked on to it, span the stream. The village is upon the southern bank—to the left as you cross the bridge from Middlesex—while to the right lies a fair domain of park and greenwood. It once belonged to a duke of the blood, and during one of the revels of our Regency was staked, lost, and won, on the colour of a card.

The autumn day was waning, and a pleasant west breeze was cooling the street, heated by the afternoon sun. Dr. Gumbey sat at the open window of a little parlour in the quiet inn we have mentioned, and looked listlessly down the street. There was a cat sleeping on one door-step and a dog basking on another, and the butcher's pony whisking its tail opposite the butcher's shop. All else was still life, and you could hear the breeze rustling the apple-trees in the orchard behind. Suddenly the doctor heard shouts in the distance. They approached rapidly. Then came the rattle of wheels and the quick trampling of horses at the speed. In a moment, people appeared running to the windows and to the doors of shops. There was a minute of suspense—the shouts, and the rattle of wheels, and the tramp of horses, getting nearer and nearer, and then there shot down the street, amid a whirlwind of dust, a run-away tandem, both the horses at a mad gallop, and the gig, with its two occupants, swaying wildly from side to side.

"Steady!—easy round the corner!" shouted a dozen voices; but the advice was flung away upon the horses, who had the bits between their teeth. They dashed round the corner, the gig rose upon one wheel, and the centrifugal force prevailing, it crashed over, and its two occupants were shot out upon the pavestones. One of the horses fell with the vehicle, lashing out desperately with its hind-legs and driving the unfortunate machine into splinters with every kick. The leader reared and struggled desperately in the traces, but his career was sufficiently checked for a hardy ostler to be able to seize him by the head, and after a short

R

struggle to master him. Meantime, the two gentlemen had been carried into the hotel, and Dr. Gumbey, moved by a natural impulse, hastened to their assistance. He found one lying upon the table, the other on an old-fashioned sofa in the public-room. They were both young men, one dressed with a species of slangy neatness, the other with an odd mixture of negligence and finery. They had been stunned by the fall, which was really a severe one; but a little cold water was all which the doctor deemed necessary to restore sensibility. The gentleman on the sofa recovered first. He opened his eyes, rubbed his head, and finally sat up, gazing round with a half-stupified, half-laughing expression on his really handsome features.

"It's nothing," he stammered, "a thrifle — the merest thrifle—the stones heere are soft compared to them in Oirland."

Dr. Gumbey expressed his satisfaction at hearing this mineralogical fact, and proceeded to chafe the temples and feel the limbs of the young man who lay upon the table. Meanwhile his companion, with many contortions of countenance, was stretching out his arms and legs, so as to ascertain that the bones were all right. A moment sufficed to set his mind at rest on this important point, after which he turned his attention to his fellow-sufferer, and observing that he had studied medicine as an amateur at Trin. Coll. Dublin, took it upon himself to prescribe a dose of Kinnahan's L.L. whisky, in the absence of which he thought brandy might be used with advantage. Before either of these remedies could be applied, however, the patient came to himself, went through much the same process as to his arms and legs as his companion, and with the same satisfactory results. Both were much bruised and shaken, but the only thing broken by the accident was the gig.

"Deedn't I droive beautifully till the mare bolted, Spiffler?" inquired Mr. O'Keene, (of course he has been recognised). "I niver made a neater speel now — niver — except that once, when I weent foive moiles out of the way with the Leemerick mail to run her against Tim Blake's curricle, and upset the whole affair in the dyke under Castle Geheogan."

Mr. Spiffler did not, however, appear to view the catastrophe with a similar admiration of its neatness, for he replied somewhat gruffly, that Mr. O'Keene was a fool for suggesting a tandem, and that he, Mr. Spiffler, was a greater fool for riding in it. "Besides," he continued, "what will old Jorvey say about his gig?"

"Is it the d—d shandrydan ye'r thinking of?" replied Mr. O'Keene, contemptuously. "Me father had eighteen like it at Carrig-na-houlan; he had them built in Dublin for the hens to lay in."

Dr. Gumbey listened to the conversation with the accustomed oily smile upon his face. Presently both gentlemen acknowledged his prompt attention to their cases; the doctor disclaimed all title to praise.

"Oi don't know, Spiff, though," observed Mr. O'Keene; "you were on the outsoide, and you got a tolerable whack on the skull; I thought at one time ye would not get to the Old Bailey on Wednesday."

"The Old Bailey?" said Dr. Gumbey. "Anything particular going on there that day?"

Mr. Spiffler looked at Mr. O'Keene, and Mr. O'Keene gave a very loud whistle.

"Take compassion on my ignorance, young gentlemen," said Dr. Gumbey; "I came down here for quiet, and I have not opened a newspaper or a letter since my arrival—a fortnight ago."

"Why," said Spiffler, "all London is ringing with the case."

"All London," put in Mr. O'Keene,—"all England—all Europe—all the world—wherever the 'Flail' goes, in fact, there's nothing talked of but the trial of Clement Lorimer for murdering Marion Eske."

Dr. Gumbey started from his chair; his plump cheeks grew pale, and his very whiskers seemed to get limp and come out of curl, with horror at the tidings.

"Clement Lorimer!" he stammered; "what—the—the Lorimer who lived in Park Lane—who—who was turf man?"

"And lost the last Derby," said O'Keene,—"the same.

Dr. Gumbey paced the room in such evident agitation that Spiffler and O'Keene interchanged glances. Never before in his long life had the smooth-faced doctor been so perfectly shocked out of his usual impassibility. At last he spoke,—

"Gentlemen, you are not joking with me?"

"Gentlemen," replied Spiffler, "do not joke about such subjects. Mr. Lorimer is now in Newgate waiting his trial on the charge of administering poison to a young lady."

"Poison!—and why—what was she?—what is said to have been the inducement?" asked Gumbey, his face getting more and more blank as his mind realised the full force of the catastrophe.

"The lady was a young American, named Eske, whom he had saved at sea," replied Spiffler. "Nothing was said before the magistrate as to motive, but it is whispered about town, that her life was heavily insured, and the policies—for there were several—made over to Mr. Lorimer."

"Insurance—insurance!" repeated Gumbey, vacantly his thoughts obviously wandering back and catching at some half-remembered clue.

"Oi don't believe one woord of eet," exclaimed Con O'Keene; "Eet's a got-up case—eet's a loy—eet's a conspiracy; and that fellow, Sir Harrowboy Trumps, and the old villain, whose familiar he is, they're at the bottom of it all."

"Sir Harrowby Trumps!" repeated Dr. Gumbey. He paused a moment, and his mind caught the clue. He remembered how he had signed the blank certificates of health which had been brought to him by the baronet. Then the doctor's breath came fast and by gasps, his cheeks got absolutely white, and the perspiration rolled in big beads from under his jet-black wig. For a minute or two Dr. Gumbey stood irresolute. The good and the generous, and the bad and the selfish, in his nature fought a hard battle. He was a cold-hearted, worldly, wicked man; but he recoiled from the idea of a great crime. Perhaps he did so as much from fear of punishment as hate of sin—but that we will not stay to speculate upon. The inward debate terminated, he said in his usual courteous manner,—

"Gentlemen, Mr. Lorimer is an old friend of mine; you will oblige me by coming up to my room, for I am staying here, and telling me the particulars of this horrible affair."

To this the twain readily assented.   Dr. Gumbey led the way up-stairs, placed wine before his guests, and then Spiffler, who told a story clearly and well, related what the public knew of the supposed death of Miss Eske, and of the apprehension, examination, and committal of Lorimer, to stand his trial for the murder.

"The evidence," he concluded, "is entirely circumstantial; but the chain seems strong,—the ruined circumstances of Lorimer, the friendless circumstances of the girl, the insurances on her life, the assignation of them to the accused, the purchase by him of poison in a remote quarter of the town, the fact of his being the last person in her company before she was discovered dead, the certainty that she died by the poison which the accused had purchased, and the damning fact that the vial was found in a pocket of his over-coat; all these circumstances," said Spiffler, "certainly go to make up a strong case against Lorimer."

"Eet's a loy—a plot—a conspiracy, from beginning to end," cried O'Keene, who was more given to impulse than logic.   Dr. Gumbey inquired the reasons for this opinion. Such as they were Spiffler stated them.   There were grounds for believing that Lorimer had some secret, ruthless, and powerful enemies.   The jockey who was to ride his horse had been tampered with in such a manner as to forbid the idea that it was an ordinary piece of turf-swindling; then the income of the accused had been suddenly withdrawn; his debts bought up and concentrated in one hand, so as to be more effectually used as a crushing weapon against his liberty.   To this scheme it was known that Sir Harrowby Trumps was privy; and it had also been discovered that he was in communication with a person who, there was reason to believe, had been the principal actor in the scheme, the success of which was the cause of the Favourite's losing the Derby.   Concerning this man little was known, except that he lived occasionally in an old-fashioned house in the east of London, the locality and appearance of which Mr. Spiffler was describing when Dr. Gumbey suddenly stopped him:—

"I think—I—yes—yes—I am certain of it; I know that house, and I once knew its owner; a lady died there once—it's an old story now—twenty-three years ago—but it was—it certainly was," said Dr. Gumbey, emphatically, "the most unaccountable case I ever came across."

"A lady died—unaccountably, you say?" exclaimed Spiffler. "Can you tell her Christian name?"

Dr. Gumbey paused and pondered: his companions held their breath for his reply. It came at last.

"Yes, I can, I do remember her name, it was an uncommon one—a foreign name, it was Treuchden."

Con O'Keene started from his chair in uproarious delight. "The tombstone—the tombstone!" he shouted, "Murder will out."

Hurriedly, and with a trembling voice, Spiffler then detailed the accidental discovery which he had made of the regular visitor to the curious monument in the East-end churchyard.

"Describe the man," said Gumbey.

"Tall and very pale, with a keen, glittering black eye, an aquiline nose, and a face marked with innumerable minute wrinkles——"

"Enough," replied Dr. Gumbey; "that is the man—that is Werwold! He was of foreign extraction; so was his wife. She died soon after her confinement."

"And the child?" said Spiffler.

"I know nothing of," replied the doctor.

There was a long pause. Mr. O'Keene interrupted it by recounting how the "Flail" had originally broken ground upon the subject. But this had been in the days of the "Flail's" obscurity, and Dr. Gumbey had heard nothing of it. Then the Irishman narrated the visit of Sir Harrowby Trumps to the office, and the great bribes he had offered to purchase silence upon several points, one of which was the tombstone story.

When O'Keene had concluded his information, there was another pause. Then Spiffler spoke:—

"At the time of Madame Werwold's death, had you any suspicion of foul play?"

"I had not then," said Dr. Gumbey; "I have now."

There was another lengthened interval of silence.

"Do you return to town to-night?" asked the doctor. Spiffler replied in the affirmative. "Then," said Gumbey, "I will go with you. I am not much given to putting myself out of the way for other people's concerns, but there are circumstances which break through all rules and overturn all habits."

O'Keene was then despatched to look after a post-chaise. During his absence Dr. Gumbey appeared lost in thought. At last he took Spiffler's arm, and drew him into one of the window recesses.

" Are you personally acquainted with Lorimer?" he asked.

Spiffler said he had seen him casually.

" You have also seen the old man, — the person called Werwold?"

" Certainly," Spiffler replied.

" I said," continued Gumbey, " that it is about twenty-three years ago since Madame Werwold died leaving an infant. Lorimer cannot be much younger or much older. You have seen him, do you trace any resemblance in his features to those of——"

Spiffler grasped the doctor's arm, and a flush rose in his cheek.

" No, no," he murmured ; " it is too horrible to be true."

" Young gentleman," said Gumbey, solemnly, " there are some things in this world too horrible to be false."

As they proceeded towards town in the cool of the evening, they arranged a plan of proceedings. Dr. Gumbey reminded them that whatever might be the suspicions they entertained that the whole accusation was the result of conspiracy, still the avowal of these suspicions would avail nothing without legal proofs to rest them on. For a careful and rigid system of inquiry to be set on foot there was no time. It was determined, therefore, that Werwold himself should be personally encountered. Gumbey had great hopes of what might be the result of directly charging the old man with the murder of his wife twenty years before, and with an attempt to accomplish the legal murder of his son now. If the case were as they believed it to be, it was more than probable that the shock of the double accusation would produce some effect of which advantage might be taken. At ill events the plan seemed a feasible one. Spiffler had not neglected to keep himself informed as to Werwold's doings, and it appeared that he had been lately in the habit of passing every evening and part of every night at his East-end house, only leaving it at an advanced hour. It was settled, then, that he should be encountered late on the night before the trial.

" By the way," said Gumbey, " there is an old fellow whom I know something of who lives just behind Werwold's house. Indeed, I know him through Lorimer. He was the captain of poor Clement's yacht, Blockey,—a chip of sea-soned oak. I know he will be only too happy to do any thing for his old master. Suppose we have a rendezvous at his house. He calls it 'The Clipper.' It is a queer little place enough, built of old ships, and boats, and so forth ; and there is a high flag-staff in the garden, which he calls the clipper's mainmast."

Spiffler and O'Keene readily acceded. They travelled for some time in silence, and as the evening closed darkly in, the far-extending lights of London's suburbs gleamed around them.

CHAPTER XXX.

THE BOOK WITH THE IRON CLASPS.

THE solemn procession of the days went slowly by, and Marion Eske still lay in that wondrous trance. There, upon the bed where Benosa had placed her, her living but move-less limbs were helplessly extended, her face turned upwards and as white as the pillow upon which it lay. The merry sunlight streamed into the room through the garden trees—the sober moonlight came in its turn—the breeze rattled at the lattice—the rain chimed and tinkled on the glass—all the thousand phenomena of the world's life played round that moveless thing in which, by the operation of one of Life's great laws, the appearance of existence was, for a time, sus-pended.

Yet, nevertheless, the sleeping soul began, as it were, to sleep less sound. It stirred in the depths of existence. Marion began to find the sensations produced by conscious-ness sharper and better defined. The day seemed brighter through her closed eyelids and the night darker. Sharp mental pains also ran through her spiritual being. The feeling of a terrible evil which was upon her became more pressing and more intolerable. She began to experience a sensation of unutterable horror, mingled with the idea that there were grief and misfortune to those she loved coupled with her own woe. The consciousness of outward things also grew more and more vivid. At intervals she knew that there was some one in the chamber. Very soon she began to calculate those intervals, and compare them with the times of night and day. Thus she ascertained that once in the twenty-four hours, some time after dark, she was visited by a man who appeared to draw the curtain of the bed and gaze upon her. Then, after a short space, he would withdraw, and a long period of uninterrupted quiet would ensue.

The time of brightness had been, so thought the entranced woman, particularly vivid, and the darkness which had followed was proportionally dense. All day long she had felt something like inward shudderings, which went palpitating from her heart to her brain. After each of these, the power of the will appeared to get stronger, and at length, after a fit of what seemed convulsive inward movements, the Will said to the muscles of the eyelids, "Move!" and, lo! the muscles obeyed. A strange thrill of joy and a gush of loosened thought overflowed the waking brain. Marion Eske felt that the demon in whose thrall she had so long lain was relaxing his grip. Her eyelids obeyed her will. She could open and shut them. Then the lingual nerves stirred, and she began to form words silently to herself. As minute after minute passed, the brain worked more clearly and rapidly. But this awakened faculty only threw light upon the present and upon that portion of the past which lay before the beginning of the trance. That interval was a black blot upon the transparent mind. The dim ideas which Marion had realised during its continuance faded away as she gradually came to the full recollection of what had happened before the fatal evening of the *Matrimonio S'greto*, and at the same time to the full consciousness of what was happening at the passing moment. Between these two periods there was a gulf fixed.

The time for the nightly visit came. Marion Eske wisely resolved to shew no sign of approaching convalescence.

There were footsteps heard in the passage without, the door opened, a light gleamed, the footsteps sounded in the room, the curtains rustled as they were drawn, a deep, low sound of breathing was heard, and then there was a cracking of finger-joints as if a person were violently wringing his hands. Then the curtains were allowed to drop. The footsteps sounded again, the door closed, and presently there was silence and darkness once more.

An hour passed and nothing happened. Then Marion Eske began to be sensible of a burning heat shooting from the head and body towards the extremities. It was the return of the vital warmth. The pain was intense. Muscle and nerve tingled as though exposed to glowing fire. An analogous species of suffering consequent upon the re-entrance of air into the lungs has been often described as being endured by persons who are resuscitated after having been apparently drowned. But with the anguish came the unchecked exercise of muscular power. It seemed as if fire were scathing the limbs and devouring the cramping bonds which held them down. Gradually the sensation of heat—hard, dry, fever heat—reached its height, and enveloped the whole frame. Then the patient feebly moved her limbs, writhing under the torment. The great channel of nervous power, the spine, seemed as yet unaffected. Suddenly what appeared a column of fire shot from the brain downwards. With every nerve, every muscle, tingling and scorching, the sufferer, at one bound, and uttering a low, husky cry, sprung erect in the bed, her arms stretched out and her eyes dilated. The natural weakness, however, produced by the long confinement to a lying posture, triumphed over the excitement of the moment, and the patient sunk down again upon the pillow.

The moment of the involuntary movement of the whole frame had, however, been the turning-point of the crisis. The momentary pang which was as severe as the application of the actual cautery, passed away almost as soon as it had been felt. The general sensation of heat gradually grew less and less intense, subsiding into a rich, genial warmth, which mantled over the whole person. Then a feeling of enjoyable lassitude stole over the wracked muscles. The perspiration broke forth at every pore, and in a quarter

of an hour Miss Eske arose from her bed of suffering, faint
and giddy, but in possession of both mental and physical
faculties.

At first she strove in vain to stand. The room reeled
round her, and she fell upon a chair beside the window.
The curtain was partially drawn, and she looked forth upon
the night. It was dreamy and calm, and flooded with bright
moonshine. Without, rose dusky trees, their higher branches
silvered in the cold light, and through what appeared to be
an avenue in the grounds, she saw a tall, white mast, as of a
ship, stretching upwards into the air. Marion Eske remained
for nearly half-an-hour motionless, her eye fixed on the
bright sky, and breathing with delight the cool, dewy air,
which floated in at the partially-opened lattice. Then she
turned suddenly, as if struck by a sudden thought. Under
the shawl which was flung across her shoulders streamed
ghastly habiliments of white. She looked hurriedly round.
The moon was shining full into the chamber, and she saw
a pile of her own dresses, which the reader will remember
were snatched up by Benosa from the room in Abingdon
Street, lying heaped up on the floor. With trembling hands
she hastily put on and adjusted the simplest and warmest,
and then wrapping a shawl round her head and shoulders,
she stood in the centre of the room, trying to take counsel
with her thoughts.

"Where was she?—in whose power?—with what design had she been carried away?—how long had she lain
senseless?—where were her friends?—where was Lorimer?"
All these mental questions flashed in a confused stream
through her aching and bewildered brain. As yet, however, she could not reason—she could only feel. Her mind
was a chaos of tumultuous motion. None of the sensations
of which she had been more or less conscious in her trance,
it will be remembered, remained to her. The period of that
mysterious sleep had now become a dreamless blank. She
only remembered what had passed before, and was conscious
only of what was passing now. Gradually as she pondered,
the sensation of fear began to gain the mastery over her.
What horrors might she not still expect at the hands of those
in whose power she was? Flight—flight, instant, and swift,
and hidden flight, was her only resource. Flight anywhere

—flight far away. There was no safety for her until miles
lay between her and her prison. Then she paced the room
eagerly, but with cautious footsteps. She looked from the
window There was a black gulf of unknown depth beneath. Then she listened. There was silence alike in the
nouse and through the night. Stepping with noiseless footsteps to the door, she examined its fastenings. They were
undone. She swung the door open. A dark corridor
stretched away from it, ending in a flight of stairs, upon
which shone the moonlight through a small passage window.
Groping her way along the wall, Miss Eske cautiously advanced in the darkness. There was thick carpeting upon
the floor, and she moved as noiselessly as a thing of painted
air. She had almost reached the head of the staircase, when
a low, muttering sound became faintly audible. With suppressed breath and a heart which beat until she sickened
with the violence of her emotions, Miss Eske paused and
listened. The noise was that of the deep bass voice of a
man reading in a muttering and monotonous tone. The
peculiar sound of that voice Miss Eske felt that she had
heard before. She paused for a moment or two, and the
reading still continuing, she stole gently onwards, until she
could lean over the balustrade of the staircase and look
below. There, on the story beneath, she saw a faint gleam
of light, evidently proceeding from a room opening on the
stairs. Partially supporting herself by the railing, she descended step by step. The staircase was old-fashioned, but
massive, and not a particle of wood either warped or creaked
beneath her feet. As she descended the monotonous tones
of the reader became more and more distinct, but as yet she
could catch no word he uttered. At length she stood upon
the landing-place at the foot of the stairs, and saw from
whence the light proceeded. It streamed from a small inner
room through an outer parlour or antechamber, and along a
small passage, until it fell upon the massive and carved bal-
ustrades of the staircase. The door of this outer parlour
stood wide open ; that of the inner room was about three
parts closed, and through the small aperture thus formed
Miss Eske saw ranges of books upon shelves, and part of a
dark opening — a safe it seemed — with massive doors, in the
further wall. From this room came the light, and from this

room sounded the voice of the reader. Impelled by a species of absorbing curiosity, which had fascination in it, the lady stole towards the inner room. The low musical tones proceeded in what appeared to her unstrung nerves to be a terrible, dirge-like chaunt. And she remembered the voice. It was that which in the house in Abingdon Street had bid her drink the potion which had flung her into that terrible death sleep. In another moment she had sunk upon her knees, close to the partially-opened door. She was within half-a-dozen feet of her enemy, and with strained brain and clenched hands she listened to his voice: she listened and understood. Although Miss Eske's knowledge of Italian was imperfect, she was not sensible, until she afterwards recalled every circumstance of the scene, that it was the Italian language to which she was hearkening. Not a word escaped her. The highly-wrought brain caused the memory to do its bidding, and triumphed over difficulties which would have been otherwise insurmountable. Cowering and trembling, but fascinated to the spot, Miss Eske heard pronounced the following words:—

"The Vendetta has been declared by Raphael Benosa between the families of the said Raphael Benosa and Stephen Vanderstein, and between their latest descendants, in whatsoever age they may live, and in whatsoever land they may be,—the Supreme Vendetta, which seeks not only to kill the body, but the soul; and which shall exist until the last man or woman who bear within their veins a drop of the blood of the Vandersteins shall have ceased to exist upon the earth."

Miss Eske leaned half fainting against the wall. As she sought to realise the full meaning of the terrible words which she had heard, the voice of the reader went on unheeded. "The Vendetta!" she thought,—"that awful, and deadly, and secret feud, pursued by southern natures with a resolute enthusiasm to which the blood of the Saxon is a stranger. The Vendetta!—and the name of the family destined to be its victims the name of my maternal ancestors! What am I about to hear?"

The thoughts expressed in the foregoing paragraph passed through Miss Eske's mind, not in the words or the order in which we have set them down, but in a confused, hurrying crowd of half-formed phantom images. Then she roused herself, and listened again. At the moment of her catching the sense of the words uttered by the reader, he had begun the following sentence :—

"The first of May, in the year one thousand six hundred and ten, in the first hour of the day, expired Stephen Vanderstein, the first victim of the VENDETTA. He died in the vigour of manhood ; and the hour of his death was fixed at a crisis in his fortunes, when his loss will most probably impoverish the family. He was killed through the agency of Raphael Benosa, the first executant of the VENDETTA."

A sudden flash of mental light gleamed across the listener's brain, dazzling and bewildering her understanding. She felt that she was beginning to comprehend the secret history of her own race—that a clue was about to be given to a dark riddle which had been handed down unsolved from generation to generation of her own blood. In her agitation she could not repress a slight movement, and her dress rustled. The voice of the reader immediately stopped,—there was a short pause, and she heard a movement as of a person turning round in a chair. Presently the reading was resumed, but in so low a tone that, although she strained every nerve, the listener could catch only unconnected words and fragments of broken sentences. But these always told one black, funereal tale. The volume, the contents of which were in the act of being recited, seemed a huge collection of sentences of death, and records of how these sentences had been carried into effect. In every instance a Benosa had been the avenger, and a Vanderstein the victim.

As the black catalogue was read, Miss Eske leaned, pale and trembling, against the wall, exerting her weakened powers to catch the sense of the dissevered sentences she heard, and at the same time to control an hysterical feeling of excitement which was gaining upon her. At length Benosa's voice died away. There was a rustling of paper, and the listener heard him say,—

"A century of evil and guilt — a hundred long years of vengeance and crime ! How does the next cycle begin ?"

Then the reading recommenced as follows :—

" The twentieth day of September, in the year one thousand seven hundred and ten, sure intelligence has arrived of the death of Louise Vanderstein, a passenger on board the ship St. Nicholas to New York. The following is the extract relative to the affair as made in the log-book of the St. Nicholas, in the handwriting of Captain Schlossejib :—

"'June 12th, one o'clock, P.M., steering west. Blowing hard from W.N.W., with squalls and rain; heavy head sea. Lost overboard Mademoiselle Louise Vanderstein, cabin passenger, who in a sudden lee lurch of the ship fell accidentally from the quarter gallery into the sea.'

"Louise Vanderstein was killed through the agency of Hugo Benosa, the fourth executant of the Vendetta."

A strange, ghastly horror took possession of the listener's mind, and she trembled violently. Thus then, after the lapse of more than one hundred and twenty years, was the cause of the extraordinary attempt upon the life of Louise Vanderstein, or Strumfel, explained to one of her remote descendants. What a terrible thing was that vengeance, which from generation to generation had never slept, which had always swooped in security and in silence upon its victim — and which, if it was once cheated out of its prey, appeared to be now at all events upon the eve of wreaking its undying fury upon the last representative of the Louise Vanderstein who had fled across the Atlantic a century ago! It was but natural that Marion Eske's thoughts should run in this channel—that she should, under the circumstances, deem that she herself was destined to be the present victim, and that the outrage which she had endured was but the prelude to more terrible misfortunes still impending over her head. The idea that her abduction was but the means to an end unconnected with her personal security, could not in her then state of knowledge arise in her mind. She believed herself to be the object of a mystic and a fatal hate, which pursued its victims down the stream of centuries, and which, though once baffled, continued slowly, but surely, to track the footsteps of the unconscious flying, until, in the fulness of time, the moment of fruition arrived. The idea was too terrible to be endured. Her heart sickened; a species of despairing resignation took possession of her. She bade a silent farewell to life. Her head fell heavily upon her shoulder, and she sunk into a species of torpor, supported in a half-sitting, half-leaning posture by the corners of the wall,--that terrible, dirge-like chaunt still sounding in her ear.

The moment that the monotonous accents paused, she was roused by the silence. After a short pause the voice resumed, and Marion listened mechanically. The person who spoke was communing with himself.

" Twenty-three years ago," he murmured in English, " when I made an entry in this book, I said, ' The last but one.' The time has now come for the beginning of the last entry of all."

Then he wrote, speaking the words aloud in Italian, the following sentences :—

" The third day of September, in the year one thousand eight hundred and thirty-three. This day there exists in the world only one person in whose veins flows a drop of the blood of the Vandersteins. Mingling with that blood there runs the blood of the Benosas. He is, therefore, the last and greatest sacrifice. This day he lies in prison, and to-morrow will be tried upon the accusation of having murdered a woman named Marion Eske. The name by which he has been known is that of Clement Lorimer."

The voice paused, and deep silence swallowed up its echoes. Rising from the earth, as though endowed with supernatural force, Marion stood erect, her nostrils dilated, her eyes flashing, and her hair bristling on her head. The feeble light shone upon her, and she was as a woman inspired. Without pause or hesitation, and as though acting under the dictates of a species of instinct, rather than of reason, she walked towards the staircase. There was a degree of noise-less dignity in her motions. She ascended the steps slowly, and, with a mechanical certainty of footing as persons walk in their sleep, she passed along the corridor, re-entered the room where she had been confined, flung open the lattice, and stood as if about to leap out into the darkness.

At this moment a sound of whispered voices rose from beneath. Marion paused; all her senses were strung to the highest pitch, and she heard a voice say,—

" There !—there she is again ! Now, Captain Blockey, the ladder."

There was a tree grew beneath the window, and its topmost branches, swayed by the soft night breeze, rattled against the lower panes of the lattice. Through these branches the upper part of a ladder suddenly appeared, and was laid carefully against the window-sill. Miss Eske paused to see the issue. In a moment the head of a man emerged from the leaves.

" Who are you?" he said, in a low whisper.

" One who needs help," was the rejoinder, spoken in the same tone. The man climbed up the ladder nimbly and stepped into the room. He was a broad-shouldered, muscular person, dressed like a sailor. The moonlight fell upon his face,—it was brown and weather-worn, and bore an eager, startled expression.

" Save him !" said Miss Eske.

" Who ?" replied the sailor.

" Clement Lorimer," answered the lady.

" How can I do so ?"

" By saving me."

Without another word he took the lady's hand and she trod upon the ladder. The branches swayed around them as they descended amongst the leaves. Upon the ground played chequered patches of moonlight, as the rays streamed down between the boughs. Round the ladder stood a group of three persons ; they were Spiffler, Dr. Gumbey, and O'Keene.

" Who — who is this ? " they all whispered.

Captain Blockey flashed his lantern upon Miss Eske's face. None there knew her. She stood silent, impassible, as a sleep-walker.

" Stay !" exclaimed Blockey, " I once saw that face before."

As he spoke the brown visage of the sailor blenched.

" Powers of heaven !" he said, " has the grave given up its dead ? "

" Who — who is she ? " exclaimed three eager, yet whispering, voices.

She replied, " My name is Marion Eske. I stand here living, and Clement Lorimer is innocent."

For a moment you could hear only the deep-drawn inspirations of the actors in this extraordinary scene as they stood, dumb with amazement, round the lady. Suddenly she dropped down amongst them. Over-wrought nature could endure no more — she had fainted. Carefully and reverently they took her up, and bore her away, keeping under the shadow of the trees, and avoiding the sweet moonlight which slept upon the earth.

CHAPTER XXXI.

" HOW SAY YE, GENTLEMEN — GUILTY OR NOT GUILTY ? "

THE morning of the trial came. All around the sombre prison was life, and eager anxiety, and expectation. Crowds thronged the adjacent thoroughfare. All the taverns were roaring full. Hawkers cried spurious confessions and broadsheets of exclusive particulars, invented in printing garrets in St. Giles' But all were eagerly bought, and read, and commented upon. The court opened at nine. Legions of police with difficulty made way for the equipages of the functionaries who came to preside over the issue. As they passed the crowd waved and fluctuated backwards and forwards, round the stern bulwarks of Newgate, which rose, in Titanic masses, over these agitated human billows. The case was one which had roused the attention of all London. Wild rumours flew from mouth to mouth. Bets were offered and accepted upon the verdict. Lorimer had his enthusiastic partisans and his determined enemies. They discussed the bearing of every point of the evidence, so far as it was known, argued them loudly — clamorously — angrily. Men leaned from open windows, and shouted their opinions to friends in the street. Sometimes loud, roaring laughs arose at rude practical jokes. Sometimes a cheer was got up as the gaudy state carriage of some City potentate rolled slowly by. It was a scene of wild excitement and anxiety. Nine o'clock had just pealed from St. Sepulchre's, when there was heard a great shout from either end of the narrow street. Certain huge placards appeared shining over the dusky masses of the crowd, and gradually making their way so as to meet each other and form a line along the street. Around each of these placards was a shouting circle of astonished disputants, for upon each were traced in huge letters the following words :—

"THE FLAIL!

"THE VERDICT WILL BE 'NOT GUILTY!'

"A MOST EXTRAORDINARY DISCLOSURE IS AT HAND!

"As soon as the verdict is pronounced a special and extraordi nary edition of the 'Flail' will be published, containing full and exclusive particulars of the most unheard-of, elaborate, and diabolical scheme of vengeance ever planned !"

Again and again the bearers of these announcements were attacked by the police, but they persisted in their right to exhibit them. The crowd around cheered and rallied the *employés* of the "Flail" by turns. The placards were alternately pronounced hoaxes, disgraceful pieces of trickery, and true announcements in which perfect confidence was to be placed. At all events one great end was gained by the concoctors of the scheme. The "Flail" was in every mouth, and, therefore, would soon be in every hand.

Round the doors of access to the court, the struggling mob fought, and tore, and raved for admission. People fainted in the narrow stone staircases, and were trampled on; others, after hours of struggling, forced their way in. The sombre hall was, of course, one mass of eager spectators, the only vacant places on which the eye could rest were the crimson-covered seats of the judges on the bench, and the enclosure of the dock. A restless hum of eager anticipation rolled through the court. The extremities of the bench were crowded with eager spectators, potentates of the City and the West-end. The wives of aldermen and peeresses of the realm jostled each other. In the square space allotted for the bar were squeezed together a greater number of gowns and wigs than had probably ever before occupied it at one time. The reporters' desk was crammed, so that the spectators wondered how pencils were to be used in it. Not even the authoritative commands of the sheriffs sufficed to keep the lobbies and passages clear, while overhead the gallery was one mass of clustered, squeezed, weltering, human beings.

And amongst the crowd there was one man upon whom many eyes were from time to time directed. They looked

at him because of the ghastly pallor of his face, and the un-
earthly glitter of his great, dark eyes. A long surcoat
muffled him, and his loose neckcloth was tied in a large
knot which partially hid his face. But the great peculiarity
attaching to this man was the extraordinary power which he
seemed to have of wandering, as it appeared, at will, through
the crowded court. Now he was seen in front of the bench
staring vacantly at the empty places; again he was beside
the jury-box, looking wistfully into the faces of the twelve;
anon his bright eyes glittered from a dark corner of the
court, where he seemed crouching in the gloom.

Presently there was a great bustle, and a cry of "Silence!"—the judges were coming into court. The audience
rose as two grave, scarlet-robed men walked solemnly along
the bench, and returned the silent salutations of the bar.
Then some ordinary formalities were gone through, during
which the murmur of anticipation rolled unchecked through
the court. It was hushed to the deepest stillness, when
there was a movement behind the dock, and the accused
stood before his judges.

Pale, very pale, but with a bright eye and a firm step,
and a hand which shook no more than the woodwork which
it grasped, Clement Lorimer stood forth. Before—beneath
—around—glittered that terrible constellation of eyes, fixed
upon his; but his bearing was bold and his spirit high, and,
turning deliberately and slowly round, he gave them back
look for look. A murmur of sympathy ran through the
court. When it was hushed the trial began. Then the
silence amongst that crowded auditory was something ominous. The low voices of the functionaries of the court
going through the usual preliminaries, the rustle of paper,
as depositions and briefs were turned over, sounded with
unnatural distinctness. Then the accused spoke the two
words which many within and without that court, in spite
of the array of evidence, firmly and fully believed. His
voice was low, yet firm and distinct, when he uttered the
plea, and another low murmur of sympathy arose, as with
his eyes fixed on those of his judges Lorimer said, "Not
Guilty!"

Then the counsel for the prosecution commenced his
opening statement. Without being long it was full, elabo-

rate, and to many minds convincing. The chain of evidence was unrolled and displayed link by link. It was a clear statement of consecutive facts, bound closely together by ties of the most rigidly logical inference. Every single circumstance appeared naturally to grow out of another circumstance, and as naturally to give birth to that which followed. As each sentence of the speaker passed his lips, his auditors saw a great design growing up, saw the clouds rising, as it were, from a great fabric of crime, and gradually, and step by step, recognised the consistence and unity of the whole.

The opening statement concluded, the witnesses who were to confirm it appeared one by one. The growing impression in the court was unfavourable to the prisoner. Many who had gazed on him with sympathy looked askance with blank and lowering faces. Every path to the possibility of innocence seemed one by one to be closed impassably up. There was a moral gloom hung brooding over bench and bar. One man only seemed undaunted — one eye only lost none of its bold confidence — one hand lost none of its firmness — Lorimer was brave, for he was innocent.

First, the court was told of the death of the lady. She had been in her usual health on the fatal day — the slight headach of which she complained being regarded as of no consequence. She had been on that evening left alone. On the accidental entry of a servant into the room she was found in a lifeless condition; medical assistance was summoned. It was useless — she was dead. What, then, had killed her? The mechanical agent of destruction was evident. A diluted acid of the most potent description was hardly dry upon her lips. The odour which filled the room — an odour as of bitter almonds, told its own story. Before the victim stood a half-emptied glass of wine. Its contents were analysed, and found to agree perfectly with the moisture upon the lips. In that glass there was a liquid sufficient to kill many strong men. The lady had died by poison. Who, then, had last seen her in life? The two members of the family in which she lived had left her in health. Only one person had subsequently seen her alive—that person was the prisoner. He had been alone with her, and after his departure she was found dead. No other individual could have had access to the room — no other had access to it.

Upon the prisoner devolved the onus of proving himself
innocent.   But he asserted that he had also left her in good
health.   Who, then, could have administered the fatal
potion ?

A vial of acid similar to that found in the glass had
been sold to an unknown customer, late at night, in a remote
and obscure part of London.   That vial had been discovered and identified.   It was found heedlessly left in the
pocket of an overcoat in the room in which the tragedy had
taken place.   That overcoat belonged to Lorimer; — he
admitted it.   But could the vial have been placed there
by another?   The vendor of the drug recognised from
amongst a score of men the accused as his unknown
customer.

Thus was settled what was the poison and partly who
was the poisoner.   A motive was now to be sought for on
the part of the latter—that, too, was found.   He had been
a dissipated man—a gambler, of no fixed or high principles.
His finances had been crippled by losses on the turf.   His
ruin had been completed by the sudden stoppage of an
income which he had from boyhood enjoyed.   He cast
about for means to repair his shattered fortunes.   Chance
threw in his way the deceased.   She was an American and
an orphan.   He gradually obtained unbounded influence
over her.   He persuaded her to insure her life — keeping the
transaction a profound secret from her employers—in three
different offices.   A certain quondam associate of the prisoner, a man of questionable or disreputable character, was
the agent in the affair, and to him the accused had thrown
out hints, which, when they came to be afterwards considered, implied the commission of the crime with which he
was charged.   The policies thus obtained had been assigned
to Lorimer.   In a few days thereafter, they became payable
by the death of the insured.

A great portion of the day had rolled by ere the case
had been brought to this stage.   Step by step the investiga-
tion had been followed with the most breathless interest;
and every now and then, as some dark point had been made
out against the prisoner, a low moan and a shudder had
run through the court; there was despondency and gloom
on every face.   The few who spoke did so in hoarse, bod-

ing whispers. The calm faces of the judges were stern, yet sorrowful. The jurymen turned to each other, and whispered and shook their heads — only one man stood there undaunted. The prisoner alone faced the threatening tribunal with firmness in his bearing and his eye. Innocence makes us very brave.

There was a momentary pause in the proceedings — a pause such as precedes thunder. Suddenly was heard from without a murmur, which swelled and echoed through the court, and then rose into a loud, hoarse shout, caught up by thousands of voices, and reverberating, nearer and nearer, till it rolled and pealed through the air like a great organ-swell. It was that sublimest sound of all in nature — the lifting up of the voices of a great multitude.

Involuntarily every movement in the court was paralysed and every whisper died away. The cheer from without seemed rolling through the passages to the very doors. Then loud exclamations and sharp shouts, and the sway of a tumult and the tramp of clattering feet, rang through the corridors. Every eye was turned to the doors of the court. There was a sudden scuffle at one of them, and loud blows struck against the echoing panel. The presiding judge rose ; but, even as he spoke, the door was dashed wide open, and a group of struggling figures for a moment blocked the entry. There was a confused vision of extended arms and eager eyes, and an outburst of frantic exclamations ; and then, in an instant, disengaging herself from the arms which had partly led her — partly borne her in — a woman, bare-headed, with streaming hair, and her drapery torn by the pressure through which she had been conveyed, burst full into the centre of the floor ; and, in a voice which rose high above the tumult, which still rang and roared without, exclaimed,—

" Justice ! — my Lords, justice ! I am Marion Eske ! "

Of all that assemblage one man alone stood firm and flinched not. Amid all the loud clamour of tongues, the sobbing, the wild exclamations, the shouts of uncontrollable surprise, which filled the air, one man alone stood mute. Clement Lorimer remained rooted to the ground, like a thing of marble. All through the court the bonds of the usual decorum were broken up. The ushers mechanically cried

"Silence!" and "Order!" but no one regarded them. The auditory had risen as one man, and there was a partial rush made to obtain a sight of the woman, thus suddenly, and as it seemed miraculously, appearing in life. But the group of conductors who had led her into court fought round and kept a clear space about her. Only one person burst into it. She was a lady who had made her way,—she never remembered how,—from the bench, on a distant corner of which she sat, to the side of the person whose sudden appearance had caused the extraordinary scene.

"My Marion!—my own poor dear! look — look at me; let me see you. Is it — can it — really be?"

And Marion Eske, with a cry of joy, fell upon the portly form of the worthy Mrs. Pomeroy. As for the little general, he was vainly endeavouring to fight his way through the crowd, which his wife had cleft as though a charge of horse had gone through it.

The remaining portion of the story of the trial need occupy but a few sentences — not the shadow of a doubt existed as to the identity of the Marion Eske now in court with the Marion Eske who was alleged to have been murdered by the prisoner at the bar. The voice of the counsel for the prosecution, as he indignantly flung down his brief, was drowned in that of the foreman of the jury shouting forth a triumphant "Not guilty!" and both were lost in that mighty, crowning huzzah, which hailed the acquittal of the accused, and which seemed as if it had power to lift the very roof into the air.

The tidings had flown like wild-fire to the crowd without, and in ten minutes three-fourths of those who had weltered in front of Newgate were fighting for admission to the front office of the "Flail." Mr. Jorvey, with numerous subordinates, amongst others Richard Flick, who had obtained employment in the publishing department, were flinging wet masses of the journal, steaming from the press, to their struggling customers. Mr. Spiffler and Messrs. Trotter and Sharpe were hard at work preparing a new edition, with the whole of the particulars of the scene in court. Mr. Gill Dumpling was flying with the copy, wet from their pens, to the compositors up-stairs; and Mr. Cornelius O'Keene, purple in the face with delight and excitement, was haranguing the mob from a first-floor window, and quoting the most pathetic of Moore's Irish melodies.

CHAPTER XXXII.

THE END OF THE BOOK WITH THE IRON CLASPS.

IN the midst of the confusion which the extraordinary apparition of Miss Eske had produced in court, Benosa disappeared. People afterwards spoke of the tall man, so ghastly in his pallor, who fixed his great eyes upon theirs for a moment with a vacant stare, and then glided past them. Many turned round in the crowd to watch that strange figure, but none could follow him with their eyes. To each he appeared as a flitting vision. It was gone as soon as seen. There was for an instant the terrible face, and then other countenances swept, as it were, over the spot where it had been, and the gazer turned disappointedly away.

Thus Benosa passed from the court and into the crowded street. Through both he seemed to glide as a dark shadow would shoot athwart the bustling thoroughfare. People bore back from him, a lane was opened as he approached. No one knew him, but he flashed his hollow eyes into theirs, and they shrunk aside and gazed after him as he went on his way.

Benosa heard exclamations of wonder and eager conjectures as he passed. Sometimes he would turn round and look broadly and boldly at those who were struck by his appearance. Anon he would shrink and cower, and quicken the long regular strides which bore him towards the east. Thus he traversed the swarming city, taking no heed of what passed around him, but staring when he did look with the unintelligent fury of a wild beast. Those who met his eye afterwards said that its mixture of bloodshot and glitter was appalling. And all the way he kept up the same hurrying stride; passing through groups who were conversing on the pavement as though they did not stand there, and gliding, like a black spectre, past the crossings, amid the plunging of sharply-checked horses and the holloaing of drivers and passengers. A dozen times the cry was raised, " A man run over !" and there were sudden rushes to the spot, but no accident had occurred. Swearing cab-drivers explained that the man had glided away—as it appeared from under the horses' feet.

Thus he crossed the City,—thus he threaded the great thoroughfare of Whitechapel, with its bearded and Eastern-looking population, dwelling in booths and open shops by the way,—thus he paced the labyrinth of obscure streets where the descendants of the Huguenot silk-weavers dwell, —thus he hurried along, never stopping, never pausing, but holding on—on—on—in a swift and certain course, until his footsteps echoed in a narrow lane across which hung the boughs of orchard-trees. Here was his home, and he locked and bolted the ponderous gate which led towards it behind him. Then he passed into his inner library.

The afternoon was calm and bright. Benosa looked out upon it. There were singing-birds, which fluttered amid the branches of the trees ; and lively sparrows which hopped and gambolled where the rich, hot sunlight fell upon the green. It was, in truth, a bright, balmy, autumn day. Benosa sat in a great old-fashioned chair, and glared grimly at it from the window. He appeared paralysed and smitten down. He only made mechanical motions. Sometimes his lips would quiver, and muttering words would come forth, but they were quite unintelligible. A change, too, was coming over the appearance of the face ; the fierceness of expression was leaving it ; but with it the look of intelligence was also thawing away. The facial angle was changing too. All these symptoms portended that the fibres of the brain—so long tortured and unstrung—were relaxing and softening ; and that the mysterious home of the thinking faculties was being deserted for ever. The eyes grew glassy and the light in them paled. As the hours flew by the Maniac was changing to the Idiot.

He sat at the window until the going down of the sun The darkening of the night appeared to be a counterpart of the darkening of his mind—the wretch seemed to feel this, for he shook his head slowly and mournfully, then letting it droop upon his chest, folded his hands and sat motionless, resigned, as it would seem, to the departure of intellect from its shrine.

And so the darkness came silently around and encompassed him. But Mind, like Life, leaves not its possessor without a struggle. Suddenly Benosa started up and groped about in the gloom. He was searching for the lamp, and in a few moments its kindling glow revealed the face of him who lighted it. There was a wild eagerness of design in it, and intelligence yet flickered in the eyes. He set himself hastily to work, as though he feared to lose a moment. Flinging open the swinging doors of the walled-in safe, he tore out of it the old box with the great clamps and dashed it on the floor. Then he heaved out great heaps of papers and empty vials, which smashed upon the ground unheeded. In the bottom lay the Book. He took it up and uttered the only words he had spoken that day,—

" At least I will know the Cause ! "

There were two sets of clasps which bound the work — the large outer ones and a couple of smaller filaments of iron, which kept closely together some dozen of the opening pages. There were broad seals connecting these clasps with the paper. They bound the leaves on which was written the secret cause of the Vendetta.

With glaring eyes, and hands which shook convulsively, Benosa wrenched open the volume at the part wherein lay hidden the mystery. As he did so, a subtle vapour rose from the pages. It could hardly be seen ; but its influence, in a moment, pervaded the room ; for a moth, which was fluttering round the lamp, fell dead upon the table.

The Book with the Iron Clasps lay open before Benosa, and there the secret Cause was written. What ailed him to read it ? The lines of the writing stretched before his eyes. But they filled with water, and the sight waned, and became uncertain. The lines appeared to run into each other. He saw dimly, portions of well-known words and letters, but he could make sense of none. Suddenly he gasped for breath and staggered. Then he appeared to rally for a moment — pressing his hands against his eyes, and dashing from them the water which welled over these bloodshot orbs. But the vapour rose hot and choking from the open pages. He made a violent effort, and dashed his head down as though to bring his eyes almost in contact with the page. It lay there open, but unreadable. The subtle poison, which exhaled forth in the air, had done its work. Benosa caught up the book, let it drop, and tumbled heavily upon it. In his fall he upset the lamp. The flame of the wick caught the old pages, and their flame caught the window-curtains !

* * * * * *

" Fire ! " The sky is red, and people are rushing, pell-mell, in the direction of the burning object. " Fire ! " the lurid reflexion is quivering over all the firmament. " Where is it ? " cry hundreds. " In Fleet Street ? " " No, in the City." " Beyond that,—in Whitechapel." " Ay, even beyond that ! " And the tramp of hurrying feet flows eastward fast. " Fire ! " There go the engines ! The horses at a mad gallop, — the roar and the clatter, as if heavy guns were being dragged to battle, — lights gleaming from the hurrying machine, — firemen with glancing helmets and belts, clustering to it as it rushes headlong through the street !

" Fire ! " There is the house !—see, the old house in the lane ! There rise the columns of red-hot sparks, and the black smoke tinged and reddened by the flame. The roar of the blaze is answered by the shouts of the spectators. Down through them, cleaving their way like old battle chariots, come the engines. But too late ! — too late ! Red flame comes forth from all the windows. Tongues of fire flicker out at chimney-tops. From top to bottom the house is a glowing furnace.

All at once there is a crash and a roaring blaze, which makes the sky lurid, and an upward driven explosion of sparks and red-hot fragments, as though from a crater.

The roof has fallen in !

* * * * * *

Amid the ruins, when they got cold enough to be stirred, the firemen found the charred remains of human bones, and amongst them certain pieces of iron, which seemed to have been the clasps of a book which had been burned away from between them.

THE EPILOGUE.

THE scene of the Epilogue reverts to that of the first chapter of the Prologue—to Flanders. Our story opened with the first hour of the first day of May, 1610; it closes with the first day of the same month 224 years afterwards—the first day of May, in the year 1834.

That morning was calm and bright. The mists of the early dawn were yet sailing over a broad, smooth river, and rolling away upon its rich, level banks. On either hand lay a great panorama of green cornfields, and pasture-grounds, and long rows of pollards and clumps of tall poplars. Here and there a white sail gleamed above the waters, towering from the clumsy hull of a Dutch-built boat, but there was not a breath of wind to swell the canvass on the river, or to turn the vane which surmounted every trim farm-house along the shore.

One vessel alone made rapid way. She was a noble steamship, the same which had encountered the gale in the Channel when the American liner was lost upon the Goodwin Sands. You could have heard the steady beat of her paddles for miles inland—so still was the air—as she ploughed her way steadily up the smooth, shining stream.

As the morning brightened, two persons ascended from below, a lady and a gentleman. The former uttered an exclamation of delight upon exchanging the close atmosphere of the cabin for the bright and balmy air of the May morning. Then placing her arm within that of her companion, they began to pace the deck together, absorbed in earnest and whispered conversation. The helmsman eyed them sharply and curiously. They were both young, and one was very beautiful. She leaned confidingly on her husband's arm, and now and then, resting her head upon his shoulder, looked lovingly up into his face.

At length they ceased their walk, and the gentleman appeared to be pointing out to his companion the characteristics of the landscape around them. The helmsman caught slight fragments of their discourse.

"And this, then, is Flanders—the famous Low Countries?" the lady murmured.

"The country of your ancestors and of mine," rejoined her companion.

"And looking, perhaps, in all its material points, as it did two centuries and a half ago, when that wonderful chain of events began to run its course, which resulted in the loss of the Derby, in the shipwreck off the Goodwins, in the trial at the Old Bailey, and ——"

"And, finally, in the ceremony performed a few days ago before the altar of a certain West-end church."

"Antwerp, sir!" said the steersman, abruptly. "You told me to tell you when we came in sight of it."

The lady and gentleman looked ahead. Over the flat country, into the clear air, rose several towers, but one glorious steeple shot higher far than all the rest. The bride and bridegroom gazed on it in silence. At length the latter spoke,—

"And it was beneath *its* shade that, two hundred and twenty years ago, the VENDETTA was begun."

*　　　*　　　*　　　*　　　*

A gentleman lounged, reading an English newspaper, beneath the *porte-cochère* of the Hôtel St. Antoine in Antwerp. The sun was hot in the *Place*, but there was a cool breeze blowing through the vaulted archway, and now and then a fragrant smell, as of a preparing dinner, was wafted by. The gentleman wore a very shiny hat, very large and shiny whiskers and moustachios elaborately curled and greased. His clothes had a *semi-militaire* look, and were exaggerations of the prevailing Parisian fashions. We will read with him the paragraph in which he is interested. It ran thus :—

"We have now, in compliance with a very generally expressed wish, given a close and connected view of all the known events of the late Benosa tragedy. We have only, in order to render the sketch complete, to hint at the present fortunes or misfortunes of a few of the principal actors in that strange drama.

"Clement Lorimer, immediately after his marriage with Miss Eske, started upon a Continental trip of some duration.

Mr. and Mrs. General Pomeroy have left England for their American home, whither, we believe, Mr. and Mrs. Lorimer will repair for a season on their return from their Continental tour. Flick, the jockey, as may be seen by our sporting intelligence, rides the Favourite for the Derby of this year. Mr. Grogrum, the manager, as our readers are aware, is in the full swing of an excellent season ; and we are happy to say, that, so perfect is the understanding in the theatre, that Dr. Gumbey has not been called upon to give one sick certificate since the opening night. Mr. John Blockey has, we hear, been appointed to a lucrative post in the Customs ; and Mr. O'Keene, a gentleman once connected with this establishment, shortly leaves London to undertake the duties of consul at a pleasant and healthy settlement on the African coast. Sir Harrowby Trumps was, our readers are aware, sentenced to a lengthened period of transportation. His accomplice, Blane, managed to abscond. A letter has been received from Mademoiselle Chateauroux, who is winning golden opinions at St. Petersburg, stating that it was upon *her* life that the assurances were effected, and that she had agreed to the scheme under the impression that it arose from a mere whim of a rich admirer of her professional powers. Madame Lorton, we have reason to believe, will revisit the scene of her former triumphs ; while Lady Trumps will continue to live in strict retirement in a distant county.

" It is, we believe, tolerably well known, that the fortune left by Benosa was inherited by Lorimer as his heir-at-law."

The reader of this paragraph paused, mused for a moment, and then turned the paper to look at its name. It was called the " Flail," and a note beneath the title shewed that its weekly consumption of stamps was 60,000. Then the reader fell into a musing fit. Some one touched his shoulder ; he started round, and saw a gentleman with a lady on his arm.

" Heavens ! — Lorimer ! " he exclaimed.

" Marion," said the other to his companion, " allow me to introduce an old acquaintance of mine — Captain De Witz."

*　　　*　　　*　　　*　　　*

Night sunk slowly down on Antwerp, but Clement Lorimer and his wife sauntered round the great cathedral for long hours after all was gloom and silence. The moon shone upon the sleeping city, as it shone when the two lights gleamed from two old houses which still stood there, gaunt, and solemn, and grim. The fretted and sculptured spire rose white into the moonshine, and the Belgian sentinel stood before the stadthouse as the Flemish hagbuteer had done, so many generations before.

Hour after hour pealed from the spire of Antwerp Cathedral, and still Clement and Marion Lorimer kept a loving vigil near. Their talk was of the terrible VENDETTA which had at length run its course,—of the mysterious links, in nine hundred cases out of a thousand unknown to the world, which bind century to century, age to age, and make the events of one cycle closely and immediately dependent upon those of another.

As they talked, an atmospheric phenomenon of rare occurrence took place. A lunar rainbow spanned the sky: one of its extremities seemed to rise from the roof of a high old house on one side of the *Place;* the other appeared to rest upon a building of similar appearance opposite to it.

Thus the rainbow bound together the two houses, from which on the night between the 30th of April and the 1st o May, 1610, gleamed the two lights.

The young pair knew this, for the threads of the clue to their mutual histories, which had been so far caught up by Marion in the old east-end house in London, had been traced with sufficient success to prove that Antwerp had been the scene of the opening of the VENDETTA, and some old registers that day examined shewed them the very houses in which the Benosas and the Vandersteins had lived.

"A happy omen," said Lorimer, as the lustre of the Bow grew more and more brilliant ; "the time when Hate and Revenge linked these two Houses to each other is over and gone ; and lo ! now they are bound in a glorious chain —a chain so long the emblem of forgiveness and love — a chain woven by Heaven itself!"

THE END.

www.ingramcontent.com/pod-product-compliance
Lightning Source LLC
Chambersburg PA
CBHW030619030726
47497CB00006B/1562